Dambuster

Dambuster

ROBERT RADCLIFFE

Little, Brown

LITTLE, BROWN

First published in Great Britain in 2011 by Little, Brown

Copyright © 2011 Standing Bear Ltd

The right of Robert Radcliffe to be identified
as author of this work has been asserted by him in accordance
with the Copyright, Designs and Patents Act 1988.

A CIP catalogue record for this book
is available from the British Library.

ISBN 978-1-4087-0268-0

Typeset in Perpetua by M Rules
Printed and bound in Great Britain by
Clays Ltd, St Ives plc

Papers used by Little, Brown are natural, renewable and
recyclable products sourced from well-managed forests and certified
in accordance with the rules of the Forest Stewardship Council.

 Mixed Sources
Product group from well-managed
forests and other controlled sources
www.fsc.org Cert no. SGS-COC-004081
© 1996 Forest Stewardship Council

Little, Brown
An imprint of
Little, Brown Book Group
100 Victoria Embankment
London EC4Y 0DY

An Hachette UK Company
www.hachette.co.uk

www.littlebrown.co.uk

For Eva

Author's Note

This is a work of fiction. Fiction-writers need freedom of movement. However as always I have tried to recount actual operational events with due reference to known facts. Much has been written about the Dam Busters raid of May 1943, some with meticulous attention to accuracy, some less so, some like Paul Brickhill's seminal masterwork *The Dam Busters* (Pan Books 1954) hampered by the unavailability of secret information. Unsurprisingly, factual contradictions arise among sources, such that treading the right line can become a matter of guesswork tempered by instinct. For serious Operation *Chastise* students I recommend the following excellent works: *The Men Who Breached the Dams* by Alan W. Cooper (William Kimber 1982), *Dambusters – The Definitive History of 617 Squadron at War 1943–1945* by Chris Ward, Andy Lee and Andreas Wachtel (Red Kite 2003), and the superb *The Dambusters Raid* by John Sweetman (Jane's Publishing 1982).

R.R., Suffolk, England

Foreword

Memorandum to: Sir Charles Portal, Marshal of the Royal Air Force. From: Air Marshal Arthur Harris, Air Officer Commander-in-Chief, RAF Bomber Command. Date: 18/2/43. Subject: Air Attack on Dams Proposal – 28/1/43.

Charles. This is tripe of the wildest description. There are so many ifs and buts there is not the smallest chance of its working. Unless the thing were perfectly balanced about its axis, the vibration caused by rotating some 12,000 lbs of material at 500 rpm will either wreck the aircraft, tear the bomb loose or both. Nor do I believe a word of its supposed ballistics on the surface. Please, at all costs, stop them from putting aside Lancasters on this wild goose chase. The war will be over before it works – and it never will.

PS. I need hardly add that we have made attempt after attempt to pull off successful low-level attacks using heavy bombers. They have been almost without exception costly failures.

PART 1

'X' SQUADRON

Chapter 1

Sometimes, Quentin Credo mused, leafing through the file, sometimes it wasn't murderous rivers of machine-gun bullets that destroyed a bomber and its crew, or exploding anti-aircraft shells fired from below, or collisions with other bombers in the darkness, or even being hit by bombs dropped from aircraft above. Sometimes it had nothing to do with bullets and bombs at all. Sometimes it was just bad luck . . .

'Rear gunner to Pilot.'

Peter flicked the intercom switch in his oxygen mask. 'Hello Rear, go ahead.'

'Just checking in.'

'Okay, I hear you loud and clear.'

'You too. Thanks.'

'Navigator to Pilot.'

'Go ahead Navigator.'

'Our estimated position is sixty miles northeast of Lyon.

We've about an hour to go to the target. We should probably start the climb to twenty thousand feet.'

'Understood Navigator, thanks.' Probably? Peter glanced up from the blind-flying panel to the windscreen. Probably was not a word his navigator used routinely. But then little about this mission was going routinely, despite the squadron commander's assurances. He peered through the windscreen. Beyond it lay an impenetrable black fog, the same fog that had enveloped them within minutes of leaving Nottinghamshire. In the three hours since, he and his crew had seen nothing – no ground, no moon, no stars, nothing. And nothing, disconcertingly, of the fifty other bombers growling through the turbulent night sky around them. All they'd seen was cloud and darkness. And now ice, Peter noted. A lacy frosting fringed the windscreen, and out on the wings a layer was building. Rime-ice, like sugar icing, not seri-ous, not yet, but one more cause for concern. One among several. He turned his gaze back to the artificial horizon, only to find another: the Lancaster was flying left wing low again. He hauled it level, reaching once more for the aileron trim wheel, yet despite patient adjustment the bomber doggedly refused to fly on an even keel, as if the whole airframe was twisted out of kilter somehow. He gave up trimming, and resigned himself to flying an out-of-kilter aeroplane. Unaided. Beside him the auto-matic pilot panel glowed uselessly, an 'unserviceable' label hanging from it like a taunt. No autopilot meant hand-flying the thirty-ton aeroplane all the way to Turin and back. Eight hours or more without a break, all of it on instruments, bumped and buffeted by cloud and turbulence, and one wing drooping. He flexed his aching fingers, and through his gloves felt the control-wheel start its strange cyclical fluttering, vibrating strongly for a few seconds before slowly returning to smooth flight. As the cycle climaxed, the whole bomber seemed to shudder, like a nervous dog. Something else to worry about. He reached for the intercom switch. 'Pilot to Navigator, just how estimated is that position, Jamie?'

'Very,' replied his navigator. 'I got a reasonable Gee fix about an hour ago, but Chalkie thinks the set's on the blink. Anyway we're out of range of the signal now, and there's no chance of a star-sight in all this clag, so it's strictly dead reckoning. We should probably start that climb to twenty thousand, don't you think?'

Yes, we should, Peter acknowledged privately. But up there at twenty thousand lurked some very unpleasant weather indeed, the Met officer had cautioned: embedded cumulo-nimbus with the possibility of severe turbulence, icing, and associated thunderstorm activity, and Peter was in no hurry to fly into it. On the other hand, the Met officer had added cheerily, the weather on the other side would be much better. So that was all right then. As though as a foretaste, the creaking Lancaster lurched suddenly, bucking in turbulence like a bus hitting a pothole, and Peter was jerked hard up against his straps as he wrestled for control. Comments followed:

'Ouch, that was a big one.'

'Now I've spilt my soup, damn it!'

'Did you feel the wings flexing? God this aeroplane's a wreck.'

'Are you sure we haven't been recalled?'

'Navigator to Pilot, ah, about that climb . . .'

'It's all right, Jamie,' Peter cut in. 'Any minute now.'

He steadied the bomber. Jamie sounded anxious, he thought, but then Jamie always sounded anxious. His navigator sat in a tiny cubicle behind the Lancaster's flight deck, a curtain drawn around him so he could use his map-light without disturbing the pilot's night vision. In all the missions they'd flown together Peter had never known Jamie voluntarily open his curtain. Except to check a ground reference point perhaps, or shoot a star from the astrodome with his bubble sextant. No, Jamie preferred to stay behind his curtain and get on with his navigating in private, no matter how bloody the action, how awesome the bombing, how intense the anti-aircraft fire, or how violent the escape manoeuvres Peter subjected the aeroplane to. Yet the twenty-two-year-old clerk from Croydon never allowed his fear to affect his navigation, which at times bordered on the miraculous. So if Jamie thought it was probably time to climb to twenty thousand feet, then it probably was. Because despite the horrible weather up there, and despite the aeroplane handling like a whipped mongrel, and the Gee navigation set not working, and Chalkie at the radio missing two command broadcasts because of static, and the ice building up on the wings, and the starboard outer engine which for some reason ran hotter than the other three, and would run hotter yet when he increased power to make the climb, and all the other little snags and niggles – despite all these, to complete the mission and bomb the Fiat aero-engine works in Turin, they *had* to make the climb to twenty thousand feet. To get over the Alps.

Turin, the Alps, they'd done it once before, but in the autumn, beneath clear skies and in good weather, when in the moonlight the mountains were magnificent to behold. But attempting it in February, at night, in thick weather and zero visibility, was little short of lunacy. Peter was amazed they hadn't been recalled, mission aborted due to bad weather, as on so many other occasions. But no abort signal had been received, so there was little choice but to press on, and somewhere out there fifty other bombers were also pressing on, preparing to climb over the mountains, drop down the other side, unload their bombs on the marker flares and turn gratefully for home. The only positive note amid all the negatives was an uncanny absence of the enemy. Not a peep, all the way across the Channel and down through France, no night fighters, no searchlights, no flak, nothing. All sitting by the fire warming their feet, Peter supposed, and who could blame them? Instinctively he rolled the Lancaster left and right, making a gentle S-turn, a reflex action he performed fifty times a mission, to clear the rear gunner's view in case of a shadowing night fighter. Moments later came the expected click over the intercom.

'Rear here. All clear below and behind.'

Peter grunted an acknowledgement and reached for the throttle levers. Time to start that climb. As he did so his flight engineer, MacDowell, sitting on his fold-down dickie seat beside him, turned and looked at Peter, eyes questioning. Though they sat inches apart, normal conversation was impossible, because the mind-numbing thunder of four Rolls-Royce Merlin engines just feet away out on the wings drowned all but the loudest shout. They could use the intercom, which meant fiddling with the switches in their masks, but after many missions together Peter had learned to read MacDowell's expression. Currently it spoke of resigned exasperation. Peter held up four fingers, then a wavering thumbs-up, which meant how is the number-four engine behaving. MacDowell gestured at the engine's temperature gauge, which was near the red line, then rolled his eyes and shrugged, which meant your guess is as good as mine, this aeroplane is a piece of junk.

'I say up there!' The rear gunner's voice again. 'Can anyone hear me?'

Peter flicked on his intercom. 'Yes, Rear, Pilot here.'

'Oh, good.'

'What is it?'

'Nothing. You didn't acknowledge my last message that's all. About it being clear below and behind.'

'Sorry Herb, must have forgotten. Won't happen again.'

'Well, okay. Just making sure. These things are important you know.'

'Yes they are. Sorry again, Rear.'

'Navigator to Pilot.'

'Yes, hello Navigator.'

'I really think we ought to be starting that climb if we're going to. Those mountains must be getting awfully close.'

'Yes you're right, Navigator, we're just about to. Hello Pilot to crew, we're going to make the climb now, be sure your oxygen is fully on, and you might want to strap in tight, it's likely to get rough up there.'

'Oh, joy.'

'There goes the soup again.'

'Is that ice I see on the wings?'

'That can be very dangerous.'

'Are you sure we haven't been recalled?'

'Pilot to Radio. Anything, Chalkie?'

'Not a thing, Pilot. But we're a long way from home and the static's awful.'

'Right, well, we'd better get it over with. Everyone check in, please.'

One by one they checked in: flight engineer, navigator, radio operator, mid-upper gunner, rear gunner, everyone but the bomb aimer. Then:

'Bomb Aimer to Pilot.'

'Yes, hello Bomb Aimer, what is it?'

'That God-awful smell down here in the nose. The one I told you about earlier?'

'What about it?'

'It's a dead rat. I just found the bloody thing under my seat. It's totally putrid.'

'Did Kiwi say a dead rat? That's supposed to be really unlucky, isn't it?'

'Unlucky for the rat, that's for sure.'

'God I hate this aeroplane.'

'Jesus what a stink! What should I do with the bloody thing?'

'Tie your hanky on it for a parachute then chuck it out over the target.'

'The Eyeties will think it's a spy in disguise and shoot it!'

'Eat it more like, knowing Italians.'

'Rat-a-touille.'

Peter reached for the four throttle levers once more. As he did so MacDowell, head shaking, slid his gloved fingers, palm up, under Peter's to assist. Together the two men eased the throttles forward, the thunder of labouring engines turned to a roar and the Lancaster began the long climb to twenty thousand feet.

'Rear gun to Pilot.'

'Hello Rear, what is it?'

'Nothing. Just making sure you received my check-in message.'

Herb Guttenberg had a fixation about intercom messages being received and acknowledged. Peter had become aware of this soon after he and his new crew began flying together. 'The rear gunner,' he murmured to MacDowell one day. 'Guttenberg. Why do you think he keeps asking for intercom checks?'

'Perhaps he's a wee bit deaf or something.' MacDowell suggested.

'I'll have a word with the upper gunner, Bimson, they seem to be mates.'

They had first formed as a crew six months before the Turin raid, in the summer of 1942, while training to operate Lancasters at a Heavy Conversion Unit in Yorkshire. Halfway through the training and in time-honoured RAF fashion, the hundreds of trainees were gathered together in a hangar and told to 'get on with it'. Much nervous milling about ensued, as airmen circled each other warily like strangers at a dance, but gradually, as if by magic, one or two began talking, then forming into small groups, which eventually coalesced into complete crews of seven: one pilot, one flight engineer, one navigator, one radio operator, one bomb aimer and two gunners. Inevitably there were a forlorn few 'wallflowers' who failed to find themselves a crew. These joined a pool of 'spare bods' to stand in for crewmen on leave or sick. Peter's crew came together as if by magnet, recognising themselves in each other perhaps, and they quickly gelled, despite a variety of nationalities and backgrounds. Binding them were two crucial traits. Firstly they were all sergeants, proudly equal under the eyes of God, and not an officer among them. And secondly they had all, against intractable odds and at some personal cost, already survived one tour of thirty operations, thus they understood the vital importance of good teamwork. Apart from MacDowell, who was oldest by a decade and thus instantly nicknamed 'Uncle', none was over twenty-four. Comprised of English pilot, navigator and radio operator, two Canadian gunners, a bomb aimer from New Zealand and a Scots flight engineer, all were highly experienced, highly attuned to the job, and unsurprisingly, given all they'd endured, not a little highly strung.

Herb Guttenberg no more so than any. He and Billy Bimson were indeed best friends, MacDowell reported, following

Peter's query about intercom checks. The pair had joined the Royal Canadian Air Force together straight from school, trained together as gunners, and transferred to Bomber Command together when they reached England. There they had parted, Bimson going to 50 Squadron flying in Hampden bombers, and Herb joining 102 Squadron as a rear gunner in Whitleys. One autumn morning in 1941 Herb's Whitley returned from a long mission over enemy territory to find England blanketed by fog. Tired, anxious, and low on fuel, the pilot flew in hopeless circles trying to locate his position and find a way down. But it was no use and eventually, rather than risk running out of fuel and crashing, he set the controls on autopilot and gave the order to bale out. But Herb, dozing in his rear turret, never heard the order, for his intercom hadn't been working properly all night. So while the rest of his crew floated to safety, Herb flew on alone, idly watching the fog-bound earth drift by below. Twenty minutes later the Whitley crash-landed itself into a sheep field outside Kettering. Herb clung grimly on as the machine careered across the field before slewing to an undignified halt. 'Bit of a rough landing, pilot,' he scolded over his dead intercom, then clambered from the wreckage to find himself alone.

Only luck had saved Herb's life and everyone knew it. Afterwards he flatly refused to fly with that crew again, saying someone should have checked on him, particularly as he'd reported intercom problems. Instead he had himself remustered as a spare bod, finishing his tour with several different crews. As did Billy Bimson, MacDowell reported. His Hampden suffered a burst tyre on take-off one day, skidded off the runway, cartwheeled and burst into flames. Only Billy escaped, catapulted clear as the aircraft broke up. The others in his crew burned to death in the wreckage. Billy had that day received a parcel from his young sister back in Ontario, a small teddy bear wearing a fireman's hat. He was carrying it in his jacket when the crash happened. From that day on he never flew without it. He and Herb met up again while on leave following their tours. They vowed then that if it came to a second tour, they would be on the same crew.

So Herb made frequent intercom checks, and Billy flew with a teddy bear stuffed down his jacket, and Jamie Johnson kept his curtain tightly drawn, and all of it was fine with Peter because after forty or fifty missions everyone had foibles, and 'doing a little voodoo', as Kiwi Garvey put it, was perfectly natural. All that mattered was being good at your job, and Peter's crew quickly became superb at it, for Herb's hawk eyes could spot a Focke-Wulf three miles off, and Billy had downed two Messerschmitts in his Hampden, and Kiwi, who was a ship worker from Auckland and always said he joined the air force by mistake, could drop a bomb into a barrel from ten thousand feet. And even Uncle MacDowell, who understood the Lancaster better than anyone and was utterly unflappable, even he had foibles, wearing a clean uniform for every operation, and shining his shoes, and keeping a spotless flight deck, and woe betide anyone who tramped mud aboard. And during the run-in to the target when the aircraft flew straight and level for endless minutes, and bucked and reared in the flak that crashed against the hull like hammers from hell, Chalkie White, who could strip down and rebuild a radio blindfold, his foible was to hold a photo of his wife Vicky inches from his face and stare into her eyes.

The mission had been recalled. From Turin. Everyone had. They just didn't know it, for along with many other defects in the replacement aeroplane they were flying, the long-range radio was faulty. It worked, but not to full power, which together with the extreme distance and poor atmospheric conditions meant that Chalkie had not received all the half-hourly command broadcasts, the last two of which had signalled cancellation of the mission. So everyone had long since turned round and gone home, except for Peter and his crew, who were struggling up to twenty thousand to get across the Alps.

Buffeted by increasingly fierce turbulence, his eyes fixed on the wildly swaying artificial horizon, Peter fought to keep the bomber upright and climbing. Twelve thousand feet, thirteen, slowly the altimeter crept round, but with each passing milestone the machine felt heavier and more lethargic in his hands. Glancing outboard he saw ice was now accumulating rapidly on the wings and around the engine air intakes, while a look up through the Lancaster's huge 'greenhouse' canopy showed no hoped-for clearing of the sky above, only the churning black, now lit occasionally by flickers of lightning. Then hailstones the size of grapes began hitting the windscreen – just a few at first, with a crack like a rifle shot, then came a storm, like flung gravel, deafening even above the roar of the engines. Peter, sweating with effort despite the sub-zero temperatures, shut his mind to the din and urged the bomber upward, while the others, sensing his labours and with no means of helping, kept silence on the intercom, hung on to their seat-straps and prayed for an early break-out atop the clouds. But there was no early break-out, and suddenly twenty-year-old Billy Bimson, perched in his vantage point in the upper turret, let out a shout.

'Jesus, look at the propellers! They're on fire!'

Faces peered out in alarm. Sure enough, arcs of eerie blue light shimmered around the propellers, glowing through the blizzard like fiery blue haloes. Billy Bimson saw them, Kiwi

Garvey in the nose could see them, MacDowell saw them too and turned to Peter in incomprehension.

'Guttenberg in the tail couldn't see them. 'What did Billy say?' he called uneasily. 'Did he say fire?'

'It's all right!' Garvey called. 'It's that St Elmer's thing. Static electricity, from the thunderclouds. Nothing to worry about.'

'Well it looks like fire to me.'

'It's St *Elmo*, Kiwi,' Chalkie corrected. 'Not *Elmer*. They used to see it on the masts of sailing ships when . . .'

Just then, and with an ear-splitting crash, a lightning bolt exploded against the fuselage, instantly filling the interior with acrid smoke and dancing blue sparks that leapt around the airframe like sprites. Fuses blew, circuit-breakers popped, gyros toppled, in a stroke the smoke-filled aircraft was blinded and crippled. On the flight deck the panel-lights failed, plunging the instruments into darkness. Out on the wings the port outer engine, maimed by the lightning, faltered, belched smoke and sparks, and with a tortured whine began to seize on its mountings. Peter stamped right rudder as the Lancaster yawed towards the doomed engine, the whole airframe shuddering from its death-throes. 'I can't hold her, Uncle!' he shouted. MacDowell snatched up a flashlight, playing its beam over the instruments. 'It's blown a bearing or something! We'll have to kill it now before it tears the wing off.' Peter nodded, grimacing with effort as MacDowell swiftly shut off fuel to the wrecked engine, pulled back its throttle and mixture levers and pushed the propeller feather button. In seconds the engine wound down to silence, the propeller slowed to a stop and the dreadful juddering eased. A few seconds more and Peter had retrimmed the rudders and regained control of the stricken bomber.

MacDowell held the flashlight on the blind-flying panel. 'Okay?' he shouted.

'I . . . I think so!' Peter scanned the panel through the haze of smoke, retrimming as he went. The aeroplane felt stable enough in his hands, but heavy and sluggish. Under normal conditions he knew a fully loaded Lancaster should fly acceptably on only three engines. It might even be persuaded to climb a little. Under normal conditions. Which these weren't. 'She feels heavy, but all right, I think. But half the instruments are out, so God knows. What about the others? Try the intercom.' The smell of smoke in the cockpit was strong. Both men feared fire back in the fuselage. Still gingerly testing the controls, Peter waited for the reassuring clicks of his crew checking in, but though MacDowell's mouth was working, no voices filled his ears. MacDowell shook his head. 'Nothing!' Then Kiwi's face appeared in the nose-tunnel by their feet, tapping his ear and shaking his head. MacDowell gestured him up and gave him the flashlight. 'I'll go aft!' he shouted, unbuckling his harness.

Ten minutes went by. With lightning still flickering all around, and Kiwi at his side holding the torch, Peter flew the aeroplane and took stock. It was a grim audit. Apart from the dead engine and blown instrument lights, his gyrocompass repeater was dead, as was his direction indicator, which left only the small standby magnetic compass to give heading information. But the stand-by compass wandered in useless circles, confounded by the magnetic interference of the storm. So he had no means of telling direction. Furthermore the artificial horizon was out, its gyro toppled, so he had to revert to basics, using the turn-and-bank and vertical speed indicators to try and fly level. But it was an unnervingly inexact business, and what with all the buffeting and turbulence, just keeping the bomber right way up required

17

all his concentration and effort, particularly as with every passing minute the machine grew heavier and more unmanageable in his hands. And there was more. The altimeter was working, as was the airspeed indicator, but little rate of climb showed and the airspeed was inexorably falling, despite full power to the remaining three engines. And every few seconds a loud report rang through the aeroplane, as though someone was throwing rocks at them. Ice forming on the propellers was flying off in chunks to strike the fuselage. He risked another look out at the wings, where thick accretions of clear ice now covered the leading edges, spreading back in glassy waves over the slab-like upper surfaces. He could feel the weight of it overloading the bomber, and the shape of it degrading its lift. Much more and the Lancaster would simply fall from the sky like a brick. He lowered the nose more to preserve speed. Now the bomber was barely holding level.

'Flight Engineer to Pilot.' A welcome Scots voice broke over the headphones.

'Yes, Uncle, Pilot here! What's happening back there? Is everyone all right?'

'Everyone's fine. I'm with Chalkie. Couple of small electrical fires are out, smoke's dispersing and we've managed to get battery power to the intercom. Hydraulics are out, burst manifold somewhere, Herb and Billy are cleaning up and checking for other damage. Chalkie's working on the direction finder and trying to get some lighting back, Jamie's navigating by flashlight, everything else, radios, Gee set, nav equipment, instruments, bomb panel, is pretty well smoked.'

Bomb panel. The fourteen thousand pounds of high explosives nestling in the Lancaster's huge bomb-bay. Peter glanced across to the bomb jettison switch to his right. Without power to the

panel, he'd be unable to release them. Even in an emergency.
'Pilot to Navigator.'

'Navigator here.'

'Jamie, I've got no DF and no standby compass, so I'm probably going round in circles.'

'So I see. I'm using the button compass from my escape kit, which seems to be working. Can you hold present heading for a minute or two?'

Calm and organised, poring over his charts by the light of a torch, and using a compass the size of a collar-stud to steer by, Jamie the navigator was still at work.

'I'll do my best.'

'Good. There's a spare compass in the emergency bag, I'll get Billy to bring it up in a minute.'

'Thanks I, ah, stand by a moment . . .' The wheel had begun to shake in Peter's hands, it felt like the earlier cyclical fluttering, but much worse. Suddenly the stall warning shrieked. At once he pushed forward, but too late. There came a falling sensation, like a big dipper at the funfair, a mushing feeling in the wheel, then a wing began to drop sideways. He kicked full rudder to hold it, seconds of agonised waiting followed, then with a lurch the nose fell, the shaking stopped and the Lancaster was diving, losing height, but recovering speed and control. It had stalled, nearly fallen into a full-blown spin, lost five hundred feet in seconds and, Peter knew, might never have recovered. He held the nose down to gain more speed, before carefully raising it back to horizontal. His eyes checked the panel, Kiwi white-faced beside him with the torch. The bomber was flying again, but only just, and as he watched, breath held, he saw the vertical speed indicator sag. They were starting to descend. Like it or not. And something else. The engines.

Something was happening to them. They sounded strained, and their note was changing.

'Navigator to Pilot. Is everything all right up there, Peter?'

'Yes. No. The ice. We stalled, and the engines don't sound . . . Can you get Uncle up here?'

'Will do. What height are we at?'

'We're at thirteen and a half thousand.'

'Thirteen and a half? That's not enough, we're barely halfway across.'

'That's all we're getting. In fact we're starting to lose it. And we're also losing power, get MacDowell up here!'

But MacDowell was already there, torch beam searching the dials and gauges.

'What's happening?' he said, plugging in his intercom.

'I . . . I don't know, it's the engines. The throttles are wide but they're losing power.'

'Christ!' MacDowell shone the beam over the wings. 'Christ, it's the air intakes. Look, they're all iced up. The engines are starving, they're starving of air!'

Thirty seconds later the Lancaster's remaining three engines, their air intakes completely blocked by ice, spluttered one by one to silence.

It was to be their final mission. Ever. Yet of his crew, only Peter knew. He had found out that morning. Squadron Leader Walker had called him in for a chat, then begun scattering bombshells like confetti. Barely was Peter through the door before the first one exploded.

'Come in Peter, and do sit down!' Walker beamed. 'Or should I say *Flying Officer* Lightfoot.'

Peter was astonished. And shocked. Commissioned as an

officer, after so long in the ranks with his friends, where he belonged. Flying Officer. They'd have to call him 'Sir'. It was unimaginable. And that was only the beginning.

'You'll make a splendid officer, I'm sure.' Walker went on, 'And by Jove, you've earned it. You've also earned this . . .' He handed Peter a memo. 'It's the Distinguished Flying Cross. I put in the paperwork a few weeks ago, and Harris himself has approved it, look: *In over fifty missions with Bomber Command, F/Sgt Lightfoot has demonstrated unflinching determination and dependability. This award could not be better deserved.* Harris's own words, Peter, what do you say to that?'

Peter still didn't know what to say. And before he could think of anything, the squadron leader dropped his third bombshell.

'Splendid. Now then, here's the thing. 61 Squadron is being detached to Aldermaston for a few weeks. Our turn for a spell with Coastal Command, evidently. You know, anti-submarine work, convoy protection, mine-laying, that sort of thing.'

Aldermaston, in Northern Ireland, daylight operations over the sea. No Germany, no flak, no fighters, a completely different job, practically a holiday. 'Aldermaston?' Peter found his voice at last. 'I see, sir. And when do we leave?'

'You don't. You're done. You and your crew. I'm finishing your tour after tonight. You chaps have done enough. More than enough.'

'But . . . But sir, we've still got two or three missions to . . .'

'I'm aware of that, Peter, but a second tour's a movable feast, as well you know. Twenty missions plus or minus a couple, what's the difference? You've done nearly sixty in all, and Group agrees that's more than enough. Anyway there's no point sending you to Aldermaston only to replace you in a week. We've new crews arriving and this detachment will be ideal training for them. What's the matter? I should think you'd be delighted.'

'Well, yes, sir, I am, of course . . .'

'That's the spirit. So tonight is your last op of the war, and, you'll be happy to hear, an easy one to finish with . . .'

And he'd gone on to explain about Turin, and the need to go back there, to bottle up enemy forces as a diversion to Allied landings in North Africa, to demoralise the Italians who seemed ready to throw in the towel, and to knock out the Fiat factory which was a key strategic target. But Peter wasn't listening, he was in shock. For he had foibles too, just like the rest of his crew. His was a terror of rejection, of being imprisoned, and so prevented from doing what he must. Like a bird forgotten in a cage. It was over, he kept thinking, everything he'd worked for, trained for and fought for. The excitement and the danger, the thrill and the fear, the stress and the relief, the sense of being truly alive, while so desperately close to death. Thirty missions flying Wellingtons during his first tour, ten more on secondment to a Beaufighter unit, now a second tour of twenty in Lancasters with 61 Squadron here at Syerston, with Uncle and the others. No not twenty, eighteen. Ending tonight. The moment he'd yearned for, and yet somehow dreaded, for more than three years. He didn't know whether to laugh or cry.

Walker was still talking, and impossibly, still dropping bomb-shells: '. . . There'll be about fifty aircraft taking part, from 1 and 5 Groups, plus a Pathfinder flight to mark the target. The weather looks a bit iffy, but nothing you chaps can't handle, and of course you'll be over France and Italy, so not much flak, little fighter activity, and only the usual half-hearted defences over Turin. Should be a breeze. Oh, but there is one more thing . . .'

Peter could barely take it in. 'There is?'

'You can't use your usual aeroplane, Q-Queenie. A super-charger needs changing apparently, so you'll have to take the squadron spare. B-Baker, bit of a hack, but it should get you there all right.'

B-Baker? Peter was aghast. B-Baker wasn't a hack, it was a joke, a total wreck, everyone in the squadron knew. Crews avoided it like the plague. They thought it was jinxed. B-Bastard it was known as. Peter wanted to protest, but Walker was already on his feet, pumping his hand and thanking him profoundly, and wishing him well and ushering him outside to the adjutant's office, where the final bombshell awaited.

'Sergeant Lightfoot?' the adjutant called, as Peter staggered for the door. 'I've your mail here.' Peter took the two letters, and stepped outside into the freezing February morning. I'll keep it as a surprise, he decided then. About this being our last op. I won't tell the others until we get safely back, then I'll tell them, and by God we'll have a party. Then he'd opened his letters. One, he read with sinking heart, contained his orders to go on leave after the mission, then report three weeks thence to 19 OTU, in Lossiemouth, Scotland, where he was to become a flying instructor. The other, impossibly, after six years of silence, was a letter from the girl who had got him into all this. Tess Derby.

Strangely Peter felt no panic when the Lancaster's remaining engines failed, and even the sudden silence, though shocking, was almost welcome after the unremitting howl of the Merlins. Choices were gone, he realised, further struggle useless, now it was just a matter of procedure, and time. Quickly and calmly he lowered the nose and retrimmed, until the Lancaster was gliding down the freezing air at a steady 130 mph. Out on the wings three propellers were now stopped and feathered, offering least aerodynamic drag. Only one continued to turn, the recalcitrant number four, windmilling in the slipstream like a child's toy, despite repeated attempts by MacDowell to feather it. Its drag made little difference. Settled in the glide, Peter noted the Lancaster's descent rate was 900 feet per minute, which by his calculations meant they would reach sea level in about fourteen minutes. But of course sea-level was of only hypothetical interest, for they were among mountains, some of which were as high as they were. So they might have a few minutes before they smashed into one, or they might have a few seconds, and that was all. He glanced at MacDowell, whose face for once was expressionless, then flicked on his intercom.

'Pilot to crew. Sorry everyone, she's had it. Bale out and let's be quick about it.'

No sound came, only the wind whistling through the airframe.

'Did you hear me? I said bale out. Right now. We'll go through the nose hatch, it's safer. Kiwi, you go open it, everyone else check in.'

One by one they checked in, then a minute or so later began squeezing onto the flight deck and down the narrow access-way to the bomb aimer's position. Billy Bimson and Herb Guttenberg came first. As they passed, MacDowell checked each had his chest parachute correctly attached, before helping them into the tunnel.

Next came the radio operator, Chalkie White. 'What about you two sods?' he asked with a wan grin.

'Uncle goes after everyone else.' Peter replied. 'Then I secure the wheel and follow.'

He met MacDowell's glance. Both knew that without an

autopilot the chances of Peter making it out were slim. Chalkie waited his turn to enter the tunnel, feet braced against the downward-sloping deck. Behind him a white-faced Jamie Johnson hovered near his navigator's cubicle, stuffing pencils and maps into his pockets as he clipped on his parachute. A moment later a blast of freezing air signalled that Kiwi had successfully jettisoned the nose-hatch. Below it icy black clouds raced by, beyond that lay the unknown.

Kiwi stared through the yawning hatch. 'Christ, I don't fancy that much!' he shouted above the wind. Gingerly he lowered his legs into the slipstream, shuffling forward until he was sitting in the narrow hatchway.

'Remember to keep your head straight and arms tucked!' Bimson cautioned.

'And give it a few seconds before you pull the handle, Kiwi,' Guttenberg added. 'To make sure you clear the tail.'

'Told you I should've joined the Navy!' Kiwi grimaced. 'Right then boys, here goes nothing!' He unplugged his intercom, and squirmed to the very edge of the hatch, one hand tightly clutching his parachute D-ring.

Just then they heard it. A cough, far out on the starboard wing, followed by a loud report, like a gunshot.

Bimson and Guttenberg looked at each other. 'What was that?'

'Hold on!' Peter's voice rang over the intercom. 'Hold on for Christ's sake, I think we're getting one back!' An engine. One of the engines was firing. They could hear it, banging and spluttering like a backfiring lorry. All except Kiwi Garvey, who was half out of the hatch.

Up on the flight deck, MacDowell was juggling throttle and mixture levers to the starboard outer engine. 'Come on you big bastard,' he muttered furiously. 'You can do it, come ON!'

Chalkie looked on. 'What the hell's happening?'

'Lower altitude.' Peter stared at the engine's rev counter. 'Ice must be melting a bit. Number four was windmilling, then it just began firing.'

Still MacDowell nursed the controls, cursing and coaxing, while the giant bomber slipped steadily down through the air. Then with a sudden tattoo of explosive backfiring, the Merlin roared to life. 'Got you!'

Peter felt the exhilarating surge through the controls as the engine powered up, but at the same instant knew it wasn't enough, for at best one engine would only delay disaster a few minutes. 'Well done Uncle!' he encouraged. 'Try the port inner. If we can get another going we've a chance.' MacDowell quickly throttled the number four to full power, then began his lever-juggling act with the number two. Meanwhile Peter, watching the airspeed increase, gingerly wound off nose trim, reducing the Lancaster's rate of descent. At the same time Jamie Johnson dived back into his cubicle, and in the nose, Bimson and Guttenberg, spreadeagled beside the gaping hatch, struggled to hold on to Garvey, dangling in space by his straps.

'What the hell!' he bellowed, as they dragged him back aboard.

'Come back! Uncle's got an engine running!'

In a short while Uncle had a second engine running, the port inner, but that was all, for the port outer was wrecked and the starboard inner refused to unfeather, and without electrical power there was no means to start it. Using maximum throttle on both good engines, Peter was gradually able to raise the air-craft's nose, steadily reducing its rate of descent until he had it stabilised at eight thousand feet. But it would go no higher, and he feared for the strain on the engines just to hold it there. A few minutes later, with everyone still in the forward part of the aeroplane, and the gaping nose-hatch still beckoning, intercoms were plugged in and an impromptu conference convened.

'This is Navigator. I can't be sure, but the fact we're still here suggests we've cleared the highest peaks. Or it could be we got lucky and transited through the Col Madeleine or something. Anyway we'll know for sure in the next ten minutes or so.'

'You mean, if we don't fly into a mountain we might be okay.'

'Something like that.'

'Well boys, I'm for staying,' Kiwi said firmly. 'I've been out there and I can tell you it ain't hospitable.'

'A mighty long walk to anywhere too,' Uncle added.

'Too right, I vote we stick with the crate and try to make it home.'

'Yeah, but the crate's a total wreck.'

'Herb's right,' Peter interjected. 'We're flying in a ruined machine on only two engines, one of them badly overheated. If either loses power again we've had it. Even if they do keep running there's a good chance something else will go wrong. We've already lost electrical power, hydraulics are out, hardly any instruments work, we've no radio and we're navigating on a pocket compass. If we can stay airborne for fifteen minutes or so, we'll be clear of the mountains and over Italy, it'll be safe to jump then.'

'Good point,' Chalkie said. 'Macaroni for breakfast anyone?'

'Not likely, I can't stand that Italian muck.'

'I'm with Herb and the pilot on this,' Billy Bimson said. 'I think we should jump.'

'So jump then, you crazy Canadian, I'm staying.'

'Say Kiwi, there's no need for . . .'

'Well, would you look at that,' MacDowell's Glaswegian tones broke in. He was staring upwards through the greenhouse roof. 'Up there lads, aye, look.' Seven heads peered skyward. And saw stars, sparkling against the firmament like jewels on velvet. Just for a few seconds, through a ragged break in the overcast, then they were gone. Somehow the sighting changed everything.

'The cloud's breaking.' MacDowell went on quietly. 'Just like they said at the briefing. I think it's a good sign. I think we should all return to our positions, and do what we can to get this aeroplane home.'

So they did. They held their original southerly course, stayed away from Turin, cleared the mountains past Vinadio, then turned southwest, skirting the Mediterranean coast at Monaco and Montpellier. With dawn soon to break, all agreed that turning north to fly home through occupied France – an unescorted British bomber flying low and slow in broad daylight – was to invite certain disaster from the enemy, so Jamie plotted a westerly route, bypassing Toulouse and then Bordeaux to the Bay of Biscay, then a curving sweep out over the Atlantic before turning northeast for a landfall off Cornwall. It was as ambitious a plan as it was long, but all agreed the safest option, and set eagerly to the task. In the nose Kiwi Garvey sat in his gun turret passing terrain and landscape information to Jamie, who sat behind his curtain drawing out his lines and feeding heading changes to Peter, who flew them using a spare compass taped to the instrument panel. Meanwhile the two gunners took charge of the Lancaster's defences, seated at their turrets ceaselessly quartering the sky for flak or fighters. Chalkie set to work trying to restore power to the radio, MacDowell nursed the two remaining engines and did what he could to husband fuel, and Peter flew, manhandling the lumbering giant through the dying night for the sixth consecutive hour.

Apart from the exchange of navigational information, the intercom was mostly silent, each man immersed in the job at hand. Somehow they slipped across France unseen. By the time they coasted out over the Atlantic near Arcachon, the sky was completely clear of cloud, the sun rising at their backs and daylight flooding the flight deck. Peter and MacDowell exchanged hopeful glances. The land was behind them, together with its threat of detection. Below them now lay a different foe, the cobalt-blue waters of the ocean, and a long sea flight home. Two engines still ran, one albeit hotter than it should, fuel was going to be tight, but their luck had held thus far, so maybe, their eyes said wordlessly, just maybe . . .

It was not to be. They were working on a means of jettisoning the bombs. Fuel was getting critical, and unburdening the Lancaster of fourteen thousand pounds would greatly reduce consumption. Plus no one wanted to make an emergency landing with bombs still aboard. But with no hydraulics and no electrical power, opening the bomb-bay doors and safely releasing the bombs was problematic. A back-up compressed-air system was available to blow open the doors, and an emergency release lever on the flight panel should in theory allow the bombs to be jettisoned. But no one knew of both systems being used for real, nor crucially whether enough compressed air would remain to close the doors again *and* lower the wheels for landing. In the end the fuel situation won the day and they elected to try the doors. Uncle pressurised the system, down in the nose Kiwi removed the safety pin and pressed the lever. With a resounding hiss the doors blew down and seconds later Peter felt the Lancaster surge upwards as the bombs fell to the ocean.

Without warning the starboard outer engine then blew up. It had been running hot all night, on the red-line since the Alps. It had saved them when it restarted after the ice, and it had served them right across France and out over the Atlantic. It might have continued to run, Peter and MacDowell both knew, or it might have failed any time. In the end it failed. Just as the bomb doors were hissing shut, they all heard a bang on the wing, gouts of black smoke and sparks flew, slicks of boiling oil poured forth, and the engine wound swiftly down to silence.

Little was said, for little needed saying. With just one engine remaining the Lancaster was finished and everyone knew it. Once again Peter found himself lowering the nose and trimming for descent, while around the aircraft everyone else prepared, resignedly and without fuss. Parachutes were discarded, spare clothing donned, Mae West life-vests inflated. Water bottles, uneaten sandwiches, soup flasks, chocolate bars, were gathered in a bag together with First Aid kit, flashlights, a flare gun and cartridges. Chalkie White used the last of the battery power to send out an SOS, before screwing down the Morse key in permanent transmit. Jamie gathered charts and pencils and hurried to fix a final position. MacDowell went aft to release the roof exit panel.

'What about the pigeons?' Billy Bimson asked at one point. In the event of forced landing or ditching at sea, two homing pigeons were carried in a canister on every British bomber on every mission. But opinion varied as to the correct procedure to use them.

'God knows. Hang on to them until after we ditch, do you think?'

'I heard you were supposed to chuck one out before ditching and one after. You know, in case of a problem during the ditching.'

'Chuck one out at 130 mph and it'll be blown to bits.'

'Well wrap it in something then, and hurry up about it.'

While Billy held the birds, Jamie wrote details on slips of paper and rolled them into tiny cylinders attached to each pigeon's leg. Then Kiwi wrapped one bird in a cloth and threw it through the gaping nose hatch.

'Lot of feathers,' Herb reported gloomily from the tail. 'No sign of the bird.'

'We've about a minute everyone,' Peter called. 'Come up from the nose now, Kiwi, everyone take up crash positions aft the main spar. Get the dinghy released as soon as possible after we ditch, and leave using the nearest exit. Use the break-out panels in the roof if necessary. Good luck, see you in the water.'

Alone now in the cockpit, he made ready. Bright shards of sunlight ricocheted off the sea, which raced by below like burnished steel. Flaps up or down, he wondered, trying to remember ancient ditching drills. He decided on flaps up, and knowing he should land parallel to the waves, banked a little to line up. Then at sixty feet he throttled the remaining engine back to idle and levelled off to lose speed, noting how quietly the aeroplane now flew, and how breathtakingly near the sea looked at that height. And how unnervingly solid. The left wing was hanging slightly low, he noted, so lifted it level one final time. Then he settled the Lancaster onto the water.

It was worse than expected, and it was better. The bomber hit, skipped once like a stone on a pond, then hit again, this time for good. The nose dug deep, everyone was hurled forward, the tail rose almost to vertical, then slowly sank back level. In the cockpit Peter watched in awe as the view outside turned green, then darker green, while a solid shaft of freezing ocean jetted up at him from the open nose hatch. She's diving for the bottom, he thought, fumbling for his straps, she's going down and not coming back. In seconds the water was swirling waist-deep around him. Gasping in the sudden cold he freed his straps, clambered onto his seat and began hammering at the Perspex escape hatch in the roof. At first it wouldn't budge, sealed by the weight of water pressing on it, then suddenly he saw sunlight as the bomber resurfaced, the catches freed, the hatch sprang clear and he was hauling himself up into daylight.

The others were already out, swimming gamely for the life-raft which had popped automatically from its housing in the wing. The Lancaster was sitting level but settling fast, Peter ran back along the fuselage roof to join them, one by one they flopped into the dinghy, gasping like landed fish. A moment of panic ensued when Billy remembered their surviving pigeon and swam back to retrieve it. Then another panic as the Lancaster began to sink and Kiwi had difficulty severing it from the dinghy. Finally Uncle took an axe to the cord, they paddled quickly clear, and watched in silence as B-Baker slipped quietly beneath the waves and vanished.

'Bugger me, it's gone,' Kiwi shivered, after an interval.

'Thank Christ for that,' replied Chalkie.

Their enemy now was the cold. And the clock. The North Atlantic in midwinter, in a tiny open boat, was no place to linger. Their Type 'J' inflatable liferaft, as carried on all Lancasters, was little bigger than a tractor tyre, and with seven men sitting in a tight circle around it, offered barely an inch of freeboard, no space to stretch cramped limbs, and no protection from the elements whatever. Though the sky was clear and the sea slight, waves constantly slopped aboard, requiring them to bail frequently and ensuring that their legs and lower bodies were permanently soaked. In no time they were stiff with cold. They had food and water enough, but long before they ran out of either, exposure would sap the life from them. Probably within two days.

For a long while nothing was said. Apart from the effects of shock and cold, after a nerve-stretching night without sleep, all were mentally drained and physically exhausted. And as the initial relief at their survival wore off, and the scale of their predicament sank in, gloom settled like a pall. The motion of the raft too was discomfiting, and some began to vomit. Then late morning Uncle broke up a bar of chocolate, poured the remainder of Chalkie's soup into a mug and passed them round.

'All right lads, let's see you tuck in. And no lollygagging.'

Bimson immediately turned and retched over the side. 'No thanks, Uncle.'

'Me neither,' Herb added. 'Couldn't keep it down.'

'I'm no joking, laddie. If you don't eat you'll die.'

'Uncle's right,' Chalkie added. 'Come on Herb, try a little. My Vicky made it.'

'Oh, well, okay . . .' Herb sipped soup, then passed the mug.

'Say, Kiwi, it looks like you got your wish to join the Navy.'

'Ha bloody ha.'

'Chalkie, do you think anyone heard your SOS?'

'God knows. Maybe. If they did, and managed to get a bearing on it, the air-sea rescue boys should be on their way.'

'Well I bloody hope so, because it's bloody cold!' Kiwi shuddered. 'And what's lollygagging anyway?'

'The pigeon.' Jamie Johnson straightened from reverie. 'The second pigeon. We should release it.'

The canister was duly retrieved and a dishevelled bird withdrawn. Having checked that his note was still attached, Jamie held the pigeon carefully aloft, then to a cheer from the others tossed it skywards. Wings clapping, the pigeon circled the liferaft twice, then settled back onto it. The operation was repeated several times more, with increasing vigour and much shouting and waving, but each time the bird merely flew round in a circle then landed back on the dinghy. Once it settled on Chalkie's head, from where it eyed them balefully. Eventually they gave up and left it in peace.

'Stupid fucking bird!' Chalkie cursed, swatting it feebly.

'We could always eat it, I suppose.' Billy mused. 'If things got desperate.'

'In case you hadn't noticed, you daft Canuck, things *are* desperate!'

'Kiwi, I told you before about using that word, now take it back!'

'Take it back? I'd like to see you make me!'

A half-hearted kicking match followed, enough to unsettle the pigeon and slop more water into the dinghy.

'Right, you twos can just stop that!' Uncle ordered.

'Oh, yes?' Kiwi countered. 'Says who?'

'Me.' Peter said quietly. 'I order you to stop.'

'What?'

'They've made me an F/O.'

They looked at each other in bafflement. 'Why, for God's sake?'

'I don't know,' Peter shrugged shyly. 'I never applied.'

'Blimey. Flying Officer la-di-da Lightfoot. Who'd have thought it?'

'There's something else. This was our last op. Group's finishing our tour early. We're all done.'

Another stunned silence. 'Why?' Chalkie asked again.

'Squadron's being detached to Aldermaston, they want the aircraft to train new crews. They say we've done enough.'

'They got that bloody right!'

'Jesus, I don't believe it. We're done. Finished.'

Further silence followed as they digested this, then slowly, and rather solemnly, the seven men leaned across the dinghy and shook hands with one another.

'Well done, Jamie, old mate.'

'Congratulations to you too, Chalkie.'

'Drink-up tonight eh, boys?'

'Well done Herb, well done Billy. No hard feelings, eh?'

'Thanks Kiwi. And thanks, Uncle. For everything.'

'You're welcome. Well done everyone.'

The morning dragged on. Around noon cloud began to amass from the west, robbing them of the sun's meagre warmth and bringing a bitter wind that cut through their wet clothing and splashed more water into the dinghy. With their discomfort complete, and now dangerously chilled and fatigued, they began to bail less, talk less, and care less. Knee-deep in the freezing water, one by one they lapsed into torpor.

Peter too. He found himself thinking of Tess, the girl he hadn't seen or spoken to in six years, yet whose memory remained forever fresh. Why now, he wondered, after all this time, had she decided to get in touch? Her letter, still carefully tucked in his breast pocket, said so much, yet so frustratingly little. *I'm all right, Peter*, it said, at the end. *Really I am.*

Someone was nudging him.

'Peter! Come on, wake up.'

Reluctantly he opened salt-stung eyes to find that dusk had fallen. White-topped waves hissed rather more menacingly about them. The others lolled against each other like drunken puppets. His legs had no feeling. Uncle was talking in his ear.

'Peter, lad. We nearly lost Billy over the side just now. Chalkie grabbed him, thank God.'

'Oh dear,' Peter mumbled blearily.

'So we've got to keep everyone awake and moving about.'

'Good idea.'

'If we can do that and make it through the night, we've a chance of getting picked up tomorrow. But if we nod off, we're dead. Peter are you listening?'

Peter felt a harder nudge. 'Yes! I'm listening. But what do you want me to do?'

Uncle's voice filled his head. 'It's time to take charge, son. You're an officer now. So act like one.'

Act like one. The words dropped unbidden into his subconscious, like rocks into a well. Where they lay, blocking the gently flowing waters of his mind.

'Are you listening, lad?'

No, not like stones in a well. More like leaves on the breeze.

'Come on Peter, think!'

I am thinking. *I found myself thinking about you, Peter*, she'd written. *Truthfully I suppose I never stopped*. Like leaves on a breeze? Or litter drifting on a stream.

'Peter!'

'Yes.' He sat up. 'Right. The drift.'

'The drift, right, do something!'

'Yes, yes I will. Ah . . . Jamie.'

No reply, only the ceaseless slap of sea against neoprene.

'Jamie, it's me, wake up.'

Still nothing.

'Pilot to Navigator!'

'What the hell is it?' Johnson's head rose reluctantly from his chest.

'Where are we?'

'What? Bay of Biscay, of course, where d'you think?'

'No, but I mean, where *exactly*.'

'Christ.' Jamie struggled more upright. 'Well, best estimate, Western Approaches, I'd say, about eighty miles off Ushant.'

'And how far is that from home, from England? In which direction, I mean.'

'Cornish coast will be about 150 miles to the northeast, give or take. Why?'

Others, Peter saw, were also beginning to stir. 'Listen,' he went on. 'The wind's southwesterly, right? So it's blowing us in the right direction, at maybe a couple of knots. And there's that warm current thing, what's it called . . .'

'Gulf Stream,' Kiwi interjected groggily.

'Gulf Stream, that's right, also flowing northeast at two or three knots, right?'

'So . . .?'

'So we row it! And sail it! We rig a little sail using a paddle for a mast, we use the other paddles to take turns rowing, we should easily be able to add three knots to our speed. That plus the five knots the wind and current gives us, means, what, nearly ten miles an hour! Don't you see? Fifteen, twenty hours or so and we've cracked it.'

'Hold on.' Chalkie croaked. 'Are you telling us that if we start paddling for it, by opening-time tomorrow night, we could be downing pints in a pub in Blighty?'

'Yes, exactly! We could!'

They couldn't, and he knew it, not in a million years. His reasoning was flawed. But it didn't matter, they believed him and were prepared to give it a try. And the effort of it sustained them through the freezing hours of darkness until the coming dawn brought renewed hope, and they could safely collapse, spent, back into stupor. There they lay, throughout that second day, huddled wordlessly around the dinghy. Then, less than an hour before sunset, a Coastal Command Sunderland flying boat out of Plymouth found them, picked them up and flew them back to land.

And that night they were downing pints in a pub in Blighty.

. . .*And the irony was, Credo jotted, before closing the file, the irony was that it was Tess Derby's husband who saved them.*

Chapter 2

The call had come at eleven in the evening, by which time Squadron Leader Walker, the forty-year-old officer commanding 61 Squadron, had been without sleep for forty-eight hours. Apart from snatched cat-naps at his desk, he rarely slept on operations nights, preferring to busy himself through the long hours of waiting with the mountains of paperwork squadron COs were burdened with. By around three or four in the morning his ears should detect the distant drone of Merlin engines and he could push his papers aside and drive out to the control tower to count his charges home. If by a miracle they all made it, he generally joined them for breakfast at the NAAFI before finally retiring to his quarters to sleep. But inevitably, and all too often, aircraft failed to return, whereupon he remained on hand until their status could be verified. Usually it didn't take long. 'He went down a flamer,' a crew would report with feigned casualness, or: 'He got bounced by a 110, didn't stand a chance.' Or simply: 'He blew up.' Then came reports to file, forms to fill, effects to collect and letters of condolence to write, before finally he might allow himself rest. Which then often eluded him.

B-Baker had been the only one of the fifteen Lancasters he'd dispatched to Turin not to return, in fact the only one of a combined force of fifty. A cruel irony, he felt, because although he couldn't tell Peter and his crew, he'd known all along the operation would be abandoned due to weather. Which was why he'd rostered them in the first place – so they would have an easy final mission. But his gesture had backfired and they had vanished, and whether it was because of enemy action, or problems with the weather, or technical issues, or simply because they didn't hear the recall, was largely irrelevant. Fifteen of his aircraft had taken off that night, one had failed to come back, and Walker, as always, felt personally responsible.

So he'd stayed up to wait, drinking cocoa, smoking his pipe, toiling through his papers, and endlessly rehearsing scenarios he knew so well. Almost without realising it, options began sprouting on his blotter like branches on a tree. B-Baker had enough fuel for nine hours' flying, he calculated, so might simply be crawling home in slow time, with an engine out perhaps, or by a longer route than everyone else. But as an icy dawn broke, he was forced to accept that Peter's crew could no longer be airborne. More branches sprouted. They could have diverted to another base, because of fuel shortage perhaps, or technical problems, in which case he should allow them another hour to sort themselves out before telephoning him. 'Sorry sir,' Peter would say. 'Had an engine problem and ran low on fuel, so we put down at Manston. Back in a couple of hours.' Many a time had Walker received that call from an overdue crew, masking his relief with a mild telling-off. 'Silly clots!' he'd chide. 'Get that aeroplane back here at the double. And no stopping off for a quick one.'

But when nine o'clock passed without word, Walker knew the situation was much worse. Only four viable options now grew on his tree. The first – that they were down on friendly ground but unable to contact him – was the most optimistic, yet least probable. But he couldn't bring himself to cross it out, and there was that story of the crew who crash-landed on Dartmoor and took all day to walk to a phone. So he left that branch ending in an aptly gnarled question-mark. The other three branches, starkly unadorned, acknowledged they were in hostile territory: down but all safe, down with dead or injured, or down and all dead.

Then followed the long middle watches of the day. It was a Sunday, so Walker attended chapel, leaving strict orders he was to be summoned at the slightest news. There, hunched in his pew, he prayed for the safety of Peter, Uncle and the others. After chapel he donned greatcoat and cap and took his spaniel Rosy for a walk round the perimeter, his breath misting the still February air, his feet denting the airfield's frozen sod. Then he returned to his office and telephoned his wife, on a visit to her parents in Gloucestershire. How was your night? she asked lightly, knowing there'd been an op on. One astray, he confided sadly.

Halfway through their conversation a tap came on the door and his adjutant appeared bearing a slip of paper. Walker read it, hurriedly ended the call and read it again. A Morse message had been picked up by Portishead radio on 600 metres, the standard distress frequency. The message had been faint and of indeterminate bearing, but the operator thought he heard 'QR', which were 61 Squadron's code letters.

Chalkie White's final transmission from B-Baker.

'When!' Walker demanded. 'What time?'

'Doesn't say, sir,' shrugged his adjutant.

'Get them on the bloody phone!'

Five minutes later he was through to Portishead.

'Let me see, sir. Ah yes, here it is,' the operator replied unhurriedly. 'Message received at oh-seven-forty-eight hours this morning.'

Walker checked his watch. 'Seven forty-eight? But that's over four hours ago!'

'If you say so, sir.'

'Why didn't you call me earlier?'

'Operator wasn't sure what he heard, sir. Then he went off duty at eight. Then there was lots of routine traffic to sort through when I came on, and what with it being Sunday and Sergeant Grayson off sick and all, it was a while before I got to it.'

'Corporal . . .' Walker struggled for calm. 'This is very important. Please tell me everything you can about this message.'

'I'll try sir, but like I say, I didn't take it. The slip just says an unconfirmed SOS was picked up via Dorchester receiving station at oh-seven-forty-eight, strength one and broken, possibly with code letters QR or YR attached. A minute's carrier-wave followed then transmission stopped.'

'Was there a bearing, a QDM, a range, anything?'

'No sir, no range and no bearing.'

Walker's fingers drummed his desk. 'So it could have come from anywhere.'

'Yes, sir. Although it would have been green sector.'

'What's green sector?'

'West, sir. Roughly. From Dorchester.'

'Over the sea, you mean.'

'Oh yes, sir. Over the sea, definitely.'

They were down. Ditched in the ocean. Four hours or more. Walker hung up then telephoned 5 Group HQ, who channelled his news to 19 Group Coastal Command in Plymouth. Within an hour, two Lockheed Hudsons and a Shorts Sunderland were fanning out across the Western Approaches in search. But without firm bearings their search area was vast, and by now the afternoon's winter light was waning, so after two hours they were recalled with instructions to resume at daybreak. Walker spent a second sleepless night tossing and turning on a cot-bed in his office, anxiously pacing the floor and counting the hours until dawn. Outside the sky was ink-black, and an icy wind dusted the parked Lancasters with sleet. Time was utterly critical, he knew. Very few downed airmen survived winter ditchings for more than a day or so.

At six the next morning Coastal Command telephoned to say the search aircraft were aloft and concentrating their hunt in an area southwest of the Devon coast. With nothing more to be done except wait and hope, Walker returned to his quarters, bathed, shaved and changed into fresh uniform, returning to his desk at eight-thirty to begin the week's work. 61 Squadron was due to fly again on Wednesday night, his job was to attend to the myriad details required to make that happen. Aircraft to be repaired or replaced, bombs and ammunition delivered and stored, fuel ordered, spare parts requisitioned, all of it with accompanying paperwork in triplicate. Then the bottomless rounds of meetings: meetings with his superiors at Group, meetings with planners, armourers, loaders, engineers, meteorologists, mappers, master navigators, master bomb aimers, flight commanders, the list was endless, yet forcing his exhausted mind onto the minutiae of the task at least helped him think rationally, and the time to pass. But with each hour hopes of a happy outcome for Peter and his crew dwindled. Twice during the morning he broke off from his duties to telephone his opposite number at Coastal Command, an ebullient Australian commanding 204 Squadron. 'Nothing yet, old chum,' the man encouraged, sensing his despair. 'But don't give up.'

Then at noon the breakthrough finally came in an extraordinary telephone call.

'Squadron Leader Walker?' a cultured voice enquired. 'Flight Lieutenant Quentin Credo here, sir. SIO, 57 Squadron.'

'Oh, yes?' Walker frowned. 57 Squadron, another Lancaster unit over at Scampton, in Lincolnshire. Credo, he'd said, Squadron Intelligence Officer. Walker had never heard of him. 'How can I help you, Lieutenant?'

'Well, I'm rather hoping I can help you, sir. I've got one of your pigeons, you see.'

'I'm sorry, did you say pigeon?'

'Yes, sir. Pigeon.' And then he'd gone on to explain, rather proudly, that Scampton's pigeon loft, run by a certain Sergeant Murray, who was an expert on the subject, was the regional centre for the rearing of 5 Group's homing pigeons.

'. . . Murray breeds and trains them, you see sir, then they're delivered to the various bases to adapt to their new homes before being sent out on ops. Trouble is, occasionally, rather than flying back to their bases, they forget themselves and fly back here . . .' Credo broke off '. . . Yes, sorry sir, Murray here says that apparently the Racing Homer is a breed particularly prone to this aberration. Anyway in short, a rather bedraggled bird landed back here this morning with note attached, Murray brought it straight to me, and I think it could be one of yours. May I ask, sir, are you missing any aircraft?'

'Yes, for Christ's sake! What does the note say?'

'Lancaster QR-B-Baker ditching 0800 Feb 25 position 48°19' north, 6°44' west.'

The first pigeon. The one Kiwi Garvey wrapped in a cloth and threw through the nose hatch. It had survived. And then flown four hundred and fifty miles in twenty-four hours back to Lincolnshire.

And saved its crew. Within minutes Walker had telephoned the coordinates to 204 Squadron's CO, who immediately redirected his aircraft to the area. A nail-biting two hours followed, then shortly before dusk Walker received the call he'd been praying for. B-Baker's crew had been found and picked up. Frozen, exhausted, but alive, they were that minute on their way back to Plymouth in a Sunderland.

After the call Walker turned his gaze to the window, and allowed himself a minute to ponder the miracle, and the lottery of circumstances that dictated a bomber crew's fate. Outside the Nottinghamshire skyline was fading to black once more. In a few hours crews all over England would be boarding their machines and launching into the unknown. Some would not be coming back. Peter's crew, he knew, had been very lucky.

And now their war was over, while his went on. He turned back to his desk and reached for his pen. Some hours later, just as he was finally preparing to leave his office, he received one last call. It was Peter, he was in a pub in Plymouth, and he was drunk.

'Jus' wanted check in, sir. Let you know we're ol' right.'

'Splendid news, Peter. Can't tell you how relieved we all are.' In the background voices sang 'I'm Forever Blowing Bubbles' to the banging of a piano. 'And now you're all done, eh?'

'Yessir. All done . . .'

An odd pause followed. 'So, Peter . . . Got any plans for your leave?'

'Well, sir, thought I'd pop up 'n say a few thank-yous and goodbyes and that . . .'

'Good idea. There's an SIO called Credo over at Scampton you should thank. And a pigeon fancier name of Murray.'

'Scampton sir? A what?'

'Never mind. All will become clear.'

'Oh. Right, sir . . .'

Another awkward silence. 'Everything okay, Peter?'

'Yessir. Only . . .'

'Yes?'

'Well . . .' Suddenly the dam broke. 'I don't want to come off ops, sir! I mean I *do*, and that, but I don't know what I'll do, I mean I only know ops flying.'

'Peter, what are you saying?'

'That I'll make a terrible instructor, sir, I'm just not cut out. Let me stay on ops!'

'I can't, Peter, you've finished. Done your bit. Superbly, too. And you will make a fine instructor, you've just got to give it time.'

'No sir, please, I just want to keep flying. And fighting. There's nothing else for me, don't you see?'

Nothing else? Walker rubbed tiredly at his temples. What on earth did that mean? Then he made a reasoned guess.

'Peter.' He sighed. 'Does this have anything to do with a girl?'

Dear Peter

I hope this letter finds you well. And after six years, doesn't come too much as a shock! Why am I writing it? Because I found myself thinking about you, that's all. Truthfully I suppose I never stopped. I learned through a contact that you were in the RAF, and on bombers too, which is a coincidence as I'm married to an RAF man on a bomber base. The contact kindly found where you were stationed, so I decided to write. I hope you don't mind.

How has your life gone since our childhood back in Bexley? I wonder all the time about that. I miss our friendship greatly and feel particularly bad about how it ended. I should have written years ago and tried to explain, but couldn't find the words. After the business at home it was decided I should leave Bexley, begin a new life elsewhere and not contact you. There was no choice in the matter. I came up here to Lincoln and moved in with my father's sister, who was good to take me in after what happened. Since then I have had no contact with my mother, although my father writes occasionally. I tried to continue my school studies here but it didn't work out, so I left school and got a job in the local library. Then in '38 I met Brendan and we decided to get married. He was ten years older, and worked on the RAF base up the road at Scampton. He's a sergeant mechanic in charge of grounds maintenance, which means he's responsible for keeping the airfield in flying condition. He's from Ireland originally and rather fond of the good life, he used to take me to sing-songs in the pub and was always telling jokes and so on, although lately there's been rather less of that. Since the war, I suppose. We live in sergeants' married quarters which are very small, but at least they're ours. We've been married four years now.

I won't pretend it's easy Peter because it isn't. My life hasn't turned out as I'd hoped. (Remember our great plans!) I didn't go to university and will never have a career. But you reap what you sow, as they say, and I'm all right, really I am.

And what about you? How has your life turned out? Have you found someone to share it with? I'd love to hear your news, should you ever feel like sharing it. If not then I understand.

Take care of yourself, I know well the risks you bomber crews face. With sincere best wishes

Tess.

According to Credo's file, the 'business' Theresa Derby referred to in her letter happened in 1936. She and Peter were sixteen, childhood best friends and near neighbours in the London suburb of Bexley where they lived – the Derbys in modern detached splendour, the Lightfoots across the road in terraced modesty. Though the children were close and the adults cordial, the two families led very different lives. Tess's father managed a bank in the City, while Peter's was a clerk at a factory. Mrs Derby held coffee mornings for good causes, Mrs Lightfoot cleaned Mrs Derby's house. Tess had a brother at Harrow, while Peter, an only child, wore his cast-off shoes. The Derbys were strict Roman Catholics, the Lightfoots lapsed C of E. Tess was going to an expensive college to finish her education, Peter would be finishing his at Bexley Secondary. The Derbys expected their daughter to go to university and marry well, while the Lightfoots expected Peter to get a job to help pay the rent.

As young children these differences were invisible. At five they attended primary school together. On their first day, seated side-by-side at the same table, Peter expressed admiration at Tess's leather pencil-case, while Tess marvelled at Peter's dark eyes and dexterity with Plasticine. Later that day a boy called Martin snatched the pencil-case from Tess, whereupon Peter rammed his Plasticine into Martin's ear and snatched the pencil-case back. Repercussions followed, but a lasting and powerful friendship had been forged, one based on mutual respect and attraction, Tess's quick intellect and Peter's fearless constancy. In no time they were inseparable, in school they moved in quiet unison like siblings, outside they ran with the crowd, or they ran alone, arms spread like wings across the playing fields, sprinting from the throng in hide-and-seek (at which Peter excelled), or chasing each other home at day's end.

At eleven they moved on to secondary school, where Peter, dark, compact, strong, performed best on the sports field, or in classroom tasks involving practical problems. Tess, taller, fair, willowy, outshone all with her logical mind, quick grasp and immaculate homework. They remained close, and mutually supportive, she cheering his goal-scoring from the touchline, he rapturously applauding her Titania on the school stage. At weekends they ventured further than the playing fields, catching a bus into Eltham for a swim in the lido, or taking a picnic to the river at Foots Cray, or lounging by the Thames at Erith reading the tabloids. One Christmas, out carol-singing when they were thirteen, Tess leaned across and stole a kiss during 'Silent Night'. Peter felt his heart falter at the touch of her lips, and knew he was hers for ever.

But it couldn't last. With the onset of puberty and shifting world events, trouble brewed on the horizon like a storm. For the first time an awareness of their differing status arose between them. Peter began to resent his indigence, that his father was perpetually cashless, that his mother cleaned for the Derbys, and that Tess and her brother lacked for nothing, yet the shoes he wore were borrowed. At the same time arousal smouldered within him, he felt tense and giddy when Tess drew near, and his nights were troubled by guilt and lust. Tess too felt unfamiliar stirrings at his touch, and sometimes ached physically for embrace, or more, yet at the same time she couldn't understand his moods, sensing they were her fault somehow but not knowing why. Meanwhile friends teased her about Peter's lowliness, dubbing him Light-pocket, and as her hair grew long and her body bloomed, other, richer boys began paying court.

Two incidents of note occurred at this time, one defining the strength of the bond between them, the other, ironically, sealing its fate. In the spring of 1936 Tess was invited to a friend's six-teenth-birthday party, a supposedly modest affair of chaste dancing and fruit cup. Peter was not invited, ostensibly on the grounds of numbers, but in reality because he wasn't consid-ered grand enough. Consumed by humiliation and a nagging uneasiness, on the night of the party he stole to the house and looked through the window. Waltz music played on a gramo-phone, coloured streamers adorned the walls, young people's voices chatted excitedly. In the centre of the room, couples danced in inexpert three-time. One pair, Peter instantly saw, was embracing more closely than was proper, and with a lurch he recognised Tess and one of her suitors. As they moved he saw the boy's cheek was pressing against hers, and his hand so low on her back that Tess had to reach behind and pull it back up, repeatedly. And then they turned and he saw Tess's face, which was tight-lipped and frowning and blushing all at the same time. And he wanted to shout out and leap to her defence, but suddenly vice-like arms were round his neck, and his hands were twisted up behind him, and he was being forced to the ground, while triumphant voices laughed about catching a burglar.

Within a minute the party had emptied onto the front garden where Peter lay pinned to the ground by three jeering sixth-formers. Only two thoughts were in his head: one to escape his captors, and two to get to Tess, who was by now gaping wide-eyed upon the scene.

'Peter!' she exclaimed, hurrying to him. 'For God's sake you bullies, get off him!'

The sixth-formers hesitated and Peter seized his chance, punching one in the face, another in the thigh and throwing the third aside. Then he struggled to his feet, the pair linked hands and without ado ran for the street. Minutes later, still running, they began to laugh, and went on laughing all the way home.

But though happily concluded, the incident served only to heighten the tension between them, as did Tess's approaching departure to college. Weeks passed in uneasy calm, then one sultry afternoon in July of that year, everything came to a head. Tess and Peter were sixteen, the school term had just ended, both families were preparing to depart for their summer holidays – the Derbys to Scotland for a month, the Lightfoots for a week in Margate. Bored with packing, Tess and Peter escaped to the greenhouse at the bottom of her garden. Behind it, hidden from view, lay one of their many hideaways, a huge mound of leaves and grass-mowings from the lawn.

'I got you this,' Peter said, producing tissue-paper. 'For when you go away.'

Tess unwrapped a tiny silver medallion. 'A St Christopher. Peter, it's beautiful!'

'It's to keep you safe. On your journey. Wherever you go.'

He helped her put it on, then they stretched out on the pungent softness of the leaf-pile, Tess reading her newspapers while Peter watched clouds wander through the sky, like sheep across a meadow.

'I'm signing up for the RAF,' he murmured after a while. 'Soon as war comes.'

Tess turned pages. 'Father says war won't come. Chamberlain will make sure.'

'It's coming, no doubt about it. And I aim to be ready.'

'Fine. But why the RAF?'

'For the flying. It must be the most wonderful thing in the world.'

'Sounds daft to me. Brother's down for the Hussars.'

'Hmm.'

Silence fell. Then Tess jerked upright. 'Goodness, how awful!'

'What is it?'

'Listen to this: "*Charlotte Bryant, thirty-two, convicted last month for the murder of her late husband, Frederick Bryant, was hanged at eight a.m. yesterday at Exeter prison. In accordance with her wishes, she was attended by a priest, Father Michael Barney, who reported that Bryant went quietly to the gallows, and met her end with Christian fortitude. Death was pronounced forty minutes after the execution, her body was then interred within the grounds of the prison. Bryant left five shillings and eightpence halfpenny to her five children.*" My God, Peter, I didn't know they still hanged women! Can you imagine anything more dreadful!'

'Serves her right. She killed her husband.'

'Yes, but she must have had a reason! And hanging, like that, from a rope round your neck, how absolutely terrifying, it makes me shiver just to think. It's so . . . brutal.'

Peter turned to study her. Twin spots of pink coloured her cheeks as she read, and her eyes were creased in a frown. One strap of her summer dress had slipped from her shoulder. 'I wouldn't be able to do it,' she murmured fearfully. 'I wouldn't be able to cope. Not in a million years.'

'Better than being banged up in prison for ever. That's what I couldn't cope with.' He reached out to brush moss from her hair. 'Anyway, you won't have to cope, silly. Not unless you knock off your husband. And I'm not going to let you do that, am I?'

'You?' She brightened. 'You, my husband? That'll be the day, Peter Lightfoot!'

'Cheek!' Peter threw leaves at her, Tess replied in kind, a spirited wrestling match ensued, then suddenly he was on top of her, pinning her arms above her head.

'Kiss me, Peter,' she whispered hungrily. 'Really kiss me, and hold me tight.'

Her breathing was heavy, her lips full, the hem of her dress was rucked to the thigh, the medallion pulsed at her throat. He hesitated. 'Jesus, Tess, I love you.' Then his mouth was on hers, and their tongues were pushing, and their hands were writhing like snakes across their bodies. Her breast was round and firm beneath his palm, her fingers found the buttons of his fly, her back arched as his hand pressed between her thighs, they kissed again, more urgently, seconds of frantic fumbling followed, his hips lunging as though in spasm, then her hand was holding him, pulling him towards her. 'Come on!' He thrust desperately, felt the enclosing warmth, and exploded.

Then Mrs Derby appeared behind the greenhouse and let out a horrified scream.

The act was as unpremeditated as it was predictable, but the repercussions would change their lives for ever. Nothing was said in the immediate aftermath. The next day the Derbys left for Scotland and the Lightfoots for Margate. Upon his return Peter searched the mail for news but found none. And though three weeks later Mr Derby came home with his son, Tess and Mrs Derby remained absent – visiting relatives, Mr Derby explained stiffly. Peter waited again, anxiously haunting the hallway of his house for word – a letter, a postcard, even a secret telephone call. But his wait was in vain and soon the days were turning to weeks. The holidays ended and he returned to school, alone and bereft, trying to ignore the whispers of school friends.

Then one evening in October a taxi appeared outside the Derby house. Suitcases were disgorged onto the pavement, but only Mrs Derby appeared among them. And that night an envelope was dropped through the Lightfoots' door. Inside it were two notes, one addressed to Peter's mother explained that Theresa was continuing her education at a boarding school in Cheshire, and since both Derby children were now effectively gone, Mrs Lightfoot's domestic services were no longer required. Peter's father flew into a rage when he read it, calling Mrs Derby a conceited cow and tearing the note to shreds. Meanwhile the second note was from Tess and addressed to Peter:

Dear Peter, I'm going to be studying away for the foreseeable future therefore it would be best if we were not to see each other again, nor you to attempt to contact me. I wish you well for the future, yours sincerely T. Derby.

The hand was hers, but not the words, Peter sensed instantly. As if they had been dictated by someone watching over her shoulder. Why, he wondered, was this happening to them? Was their offence so shameful? He pinned his hopes on the school holidays, fretfully counting off the long autumn days on his calendar. His studies suffered, he avoided his friends, his relationship with his parents, who banned all mention of the Derbys, grew strained. Only one thing mattered, that Tess still loved him, and would find a way to come back, or at least make contact. Late one night he heard the telephone ringing in the hall and leapt from his bed, certain it was her. But the ringing stopped before he could reach it. And at Christmas she did not come back, nor make any contact, and as the months passed he was forced to accept she had rejected him for what happened that day behind the greenhouse. That somehow he had committed a sin so gross that his punishment was to be banished from her life for ever.

It was like being imprisoned, then forgotten. Two years went by without a single word. He buried his hurt deep within him, re-applied himself to his studies, and got on with life without Tess. In 1938 he turned eighteen and left school, accepting the first job he was offered – a filing clerk at an insurance office. He hated the work but kept his head down and his eyes on the news-papers, channelling his frustration into the approaching cataclysm. Sure enough 1939 came, and with it Europe's descent into conflict. The day after Chamberlain broke the news to the nation Peter packed a bag, headed for the nearest RAF recruiting office, and went to war.

And became a warrior, and a man, focused, dependable, flying and fighting for three years straight, until the day he ditched B-Baker into the ocean, thus concluding a remarkable fifty-eight operational flights against the enemy. But with that he was through, no longer wanted, rejected in effect, once again, by that which he held most dear. Trapped by his inability to act. Like the years of waiting for Tess. The forgotten bird in its cage.

Two days after being plucked from the sea, Peter and his crew returned to Syerston to collect their baggage and say their farewells. By now they'd had their fill of riotous celebration, so their final parting was a muted affair. A glass of sherry with Squadron Leader Walker, a few back-slaps in the mess, a final shake of hands with each other, and it was over. All were due two weeks' leave, so Chalkie White and Jamie Johnson returned to their respective homes, Kiwi Garvey went to relatives in Sussex, and the Canadian gunners Guttenberg and Bimson to an RCAF recreation camp in Wales. Peter and Uncle MacDowell mean-while went to RAF Scampton in Lincolnshire.

The purpose of this visit, as far as Uncle was aware, was to thank two key people involved in their rescue – Scampton's intelligence officer, Lieutenant Credo, and the pigeon-loft man, Murray. After all, as Squadron Leader Walker reminded them over the sherry, had it not been for the quick thinking of these two, the chances of B-Baker's crew being found were minuscule, and everyone knew another night in the raft would have finished them. Uncle wholeheartedly agreed, but had another reason for going to Lincoln. He had nothing better to do. A widower with no children, he had lost his wife in an air-raid a year previously, which was why he'd signed up early for a second tour. Apart from elderly parents he rarely saw, the people he counted now as family were his crew. So, unaware that Peter's motives were equally ambiguous, he asked to tag along. Besides, he said, as they waited for their train, I want to see that wee pigeon again.

They arrived at Lincoln mid-afternoon, taking a taxi for the short ride up Ermine Street to the base. First, and in accordance with protocol, they reported to Scampton's station commander, a Group Captain called Whitworth, who received them warmly, then didn't know what to do with them, so sent them along to Credo's office. There they introduced themselves, said their piece, and tried not to look shocked at the appallingly burned face and gloved claw of the intelligence officer.

'Tea, gentlemen?' Credo enquired, rising to his feet. Then he quickly dismissed his injuries, as he always did, because aircrew fretted about these things. 'Excuse the appearance, Wellington hit by flak over Heligoland last year. Bloody careless. I got scorched somewhat putting out the fire. Milk and sugar?'

Politely they sat, listening to the cups rattling like castanets as he fumbled to serve them one-handed. As he poured, he chatted, his voice soft and refined, at odds somehow with his shattered visage and clumsy manner. 'Have you met Murray yet?' he asked, glancing at Peter, who shook his head. 'He'll be along in a minute. Quite a character. Charming wife too.'

While they waited they drank their tea, and at his bidding recounted the story of B-Baker's last flight. 'You did well.' Credo commented when they finished. 'Kept your heads, did everything right, and in the end it paid off.'

'It didn't feel like it at the time.'

'Believe me, less experienced crews would have panicked. And paid the price for it.' He picked up a pen and began jotting notes, awkwardly, with the wrong hand. Peter and Uncle exchanged glances. His uniform bore the maroon and blue ribbon of the DSO, the Distinguished Service Order, awarded for individual acts of outstanding bravery. It wasn't hard to guess what. Beneath fair hair, the flesh of his forehead, mouth and cheeks – the exposed parts around a flying helmet – were cruelly burned, red-raw, blistered and mottled with ugly yellow grafts like leather patches. His nose was a purple stump, his mouth an angled gash, grotesque like a clown's. Only his eyes seemed untouched, piercing blue amid the ravaged red. He looked up, catching their stares. 'Wore my goggles,' he said quietly. 'Useful tip.'

'Did your crew make it?' Uncle asked.

'Two did, four didn't.'

'Tough.'

'Indeed.' He sat back, surveying the pair. MacDowell was tall and high-browed with ginger hair and bristly moustache, Lightfoot shorter, more compact, dark and watchful, earnest and edgy. 'Anyway, gents, enough of me, I hear you're all done and dusted, and heading off to teach others how to do everything right, no?'

57

Peter cleared his throat. 'Yes, sir. Although actually I wanted to ask about that.'

'Really? Fire away.'

'Yes, well, I heard that some aircrew manage to get themselves signed up for a third tour of operations.'

Uncle stiffened beside him. Across the desk Credo blinked.

'Did you now? And where would you hear a thing like that?'

But before Peter could reply, a loud knock came on the door and Murray burst in.

'Is this them?' he roared.

'It is.'

'God's sakes, they don't look like much! And after all the bloody trouble I went to!'

'Quite. Ah, Flying Officer Lightfoot, Sergeant MacDowell, may I introduce Sergeant Brendan Murray.'

'The Irish pigeon fancier.' Uncle grinned, pumping Murray's hand.

'That I am! And you're a Scotchman, but nobody's perfect!'

He was big, big-shouldered, big-chested, with a big red face, wavy hair and forearms like hams. He turned to Peter, nearly a foot shorter. 'And this little fellow's English, God help him, but never mind!' And before Peter knew it he was swept into a bear-hug that drove the breath from his body and left his toes dangling above the floorboards. 'Lightfoot, you say? Bless me, are you a Red Indian or something!'

Formalities over, Murray took them on a tour of the airfield, which was much like Syerston only bigger and more modern, followed by another tea in the sergeants' mess, followed by a hair-raising drive in a battered van to a far corner of the field to inspect the pigeon loft, housed above a barn filled with agricultural machinery. 'My private little empire!' he explained, conjuring whisky from a cupboard. Then he showed them around the barn, and a well-tooled workshop, then up ladders to the loft, which was a large caged-in area next to a scruffy office. And he showed them the pigeons, cooing tenderly at them as he explained how they were reared and trained. Then he reached in and gently lifted one out, and Peter and Uncle looked on in wordless awe at the delicate creature of feather and flesh that had saved their lives.

'Incredible,' Uncle murmured. 'That this wee bird could fly so far. And so fast.'

'It's what God made him for,' Murray replied. 'Lucky for you.'

RAF Scampton came under the jurisdiction of 5 Group, Bomber Command, and was currently home to just one unit, 57 Squadron, although it was big enough to house two. 5 Group itself consisted of ten Lancaster squadrons, located at eight airfields in the Lincolnshire area, with a headquarters in Grantham. That was just one Group. In all, Bomber Command comprised six different Groups, amounting to some sixty squadrons spread over fifty stations across middle England. Managing this force to best possible effect demanded exceptional qualities of dexterity, resilience and determination in a commander.

While Peter and Uncle were admiring pigeons at Scampton, Bomber Command's leader, fifty-year-old Air Chief Marshal Arthur Harris, a pugnacious, no-nonsense bulldog of a man, was sitting in a darkened room in Teddington, Middlesex, watching a middle-aged scientist with white hair fiddle with a film projector. And rapidly losing patience.

'For God's sake man!' he scowled. 'I've got to be at the Ministry by six!'

'Any moment now,' the scientist replied nervously. 'It's the drive sprocket, it seems to be loose.'

'Well, tighten it, for the love of heaven, there's a war on you know!'

'Yes, sir. Nearly there. It is important, as you'll see.'

'It'd better be.'

A minute later he flicked the switch, and the projector clattered to life. On the screen appeared a grainy black-and-white image of a beach with seascape beyond.

'Where are we this time?' Harris demanded.

'Chesil Beach, sir. The Wellington appears in a moment. It was quite amusing really, the naval gunners at Portland must have thought we were a Dornier or something, because of our odd profile, and started taking potshots at us. Missed, thankfully.'

'More's the pity,' Harris muttered.

A twin-engined Wellington bomber appeared on screen, flying fast and low over the sea. Hanging beneath it, clearly visible, were two spheres, each about two feet in diameter. As the bomber drew level with the camera, one of the spheres detached itself, and fell to the sea, whereupon it began bouncing gamely over the waves, like a football kicked across a pitch.

'So it bounces, Wallis, we know all this!' Harris growled. 'And I've read your blasted paper. But it's too small for the dams, you said so yourself!'

'Yes, but I can make the full-size one now.'

'Which won't fit under a Lancaster, because the diameter's too big!'

'Not since I changed the shape.'

'You what?'

'It's not spheroid any more, you see. It's an *oblate* spheroid. A flattened sphere, more like a fat barrel.'

'Which means?'

'That the diameter's reduced because it's longer. So now it will fit under a Lanc.'

'And does it work?'

The man gestured at the screen. 'You've just seen it working. At least the scaled-down version.'

'Really? That was a barrel, not a ball?'

The man smiled modestly. 'Come next door, sir, to the tank. Everything's prepared, it won't take a minute.'

Harris followed him along a corridor and through swing-doors to a vast low-ceilinged shed. Dominating the shed was a shallow tank, twenty feet wide and barely three deep, but stretching over six hundred feet long. 'National Physical Laboratory let me use it a while longer,' he said. 'Jolly decent of them. Here, sir, this way, we'll watch at the receiving end.'

They set off along the tank's length, eventually arriving at a scaffolding supporting a curved barrier in the water. Like a dam. Several white-coated assistants hovered nearby with clipboards and slide-rules, two young women among them.

'Ready everyone? Good-oh. Right you are, ladies, in you pop.'

To Harris's surprise the women mounted stepladders on either side of the tank, before climbing as modestly as possible into narrow metal cylinders sitting in the water.

'They're glass-sided,' the scientist explained. 'So we can film what happens underwater. Bit of a tight fit though, what with the cameras and everything. Hence the young ladies.'

'Fascinating.' Harris glanced at his watch. 'Will this take long?'

'Less than three seconds.' The scientist picked up a micro-phone. 'Are you ready Walter?' he asked, peering towards the far end of the tank. A loudspeaker squawked an affirmative. 'Very well then, on my count. Three, two, one, shoot.'

Harris heard a distant crack, like a rifle-shot, then a series of hissing sounds as something approached rapidly up the tank. Like kissing, he thought, kiss, kiss, kiss, the noise went. Then he glimpsed the projectile itself, bouncing towards them at enormous speed before it slammed into the wall with a resonant thud, bouncing off it to splash a foot or so back.

'Watch!' the scientist said, leaning over the tank.

Harris watched. The projectile, metallic, and about the size of a cricket ball, sank from sight, still spinning, but as it did so it drifted back into the wall until, with a barely audible clunk, it made contact and stopped.

'Good grief,' Harris said, genuinely surprised. 'Does it do that every time?'

'Usually. As long as the water's reasonably flat.'

An assistant retrieved the projectile and handed it to Harris. It was solid metal, much heavier than a cricket ball, and indeed more barrel-shaped than spherical, yet it had skipped the entire length of the tank as effortlessly as a pebble across a pond.

The two men adjourned outside, where a staff car awaited Harris.

'What range, and speed are we talking about? For the real thing?' he asked.

'It would need to be dropped four hundred yards from the dam, at about 220 mph.'

'Height?'

'One hundred and fifty feet.'

'I don't know, Wallis,' he said, shaking his head. 'Deep down I still believe it's all poppycock.'

'It's not, sir. It's proven science. You've just witnessed it.'

'Hmm. And you really think you can develop a full-sized version, from scratch, get it built, and tested, and working reliably, all in three months?'

'Yes. Given the resources. And the commitment.'

'Well, we'll have to see.' They shook hands. 'I'll speak to Portal again. But I make no promises. It's the diversion of resources I can't stomach. That and putting men's lives at risk for something so utterly crackpot. No offence, that is.'

'None taken sir. Thank you for coming.'

'You're welcome. Ultimately it's not my decision, thank God. But for what it's worth, I still bet my shirt it'll never work!'

Several whiskies later, and with a wintry moon rising over the airfield, Peter and Uncle re-boarded Murray's battered van for a second hair-raising drive, out through the airfield gates, down into Lincoln, and a succession of rowdy, smoke-filled pubs. Everywhere they went, the reception was warm and the hospitality generous. And everyone in the city knew Murray, it seemed, and wanted to buy him drinks. Soon Peter was struggling to keep up, the pubs merging into each other with each passing pint, like a repeating dream.

All except one. Superficially it was the same as the others, crowded and raucous, but with two differences. Firstly the uniforms inside were khaki not blue, belonging to soldiers from anti-aircraft batteries around the city, and secondly, as they walked in, the jollity seemed to falter, then fade, until by the time they reached the bar it had dwindled to a murmur.

Murray smacked the bar. 'T'ree pints of your finest, please landlord!'

The barman glanced uneasily at Peter. 'Would you and your friends not be more comfortable next door, Sergeant?'

'T'anks, but we're fine right here.'

'No you ain't!' A voice called from behind. 'Not with 'im. This bar's for NCOs only. Officers go in the snug.'

Murray glanced at the new stripe on Peter's arm, then

winked, and turned to face the speaker, a red-faced artilleryman lounging in a corner.

'What's that you're saying, my friend?'

'You heard. He can't stay in 'ere.'

'Can he not? Well now, here's the t'ing. This young lad travelled here just to thank us for helping him. He's risked his neck more times than you can imagine, just so's our families can sleep soundly at night. So, if he wants to stand with us and share a pint, I say that's fine with me, and I hope it's fine with you.' He paused, still smiling. '. . . If not, then you and I can discuss it outside.'

The sergeant licked his lips, weighing up loss of face against Murray's deadly smile. And huge fists.

'One drink, mind,' he muttered, eventually. 'Then he goes.'

'Good decision! And have one for yourself!'

He was from County Louth in Northern Ireland, it transpired later, in yet another pub. He'd been telling Uncle his life story while Peter, in reflective mood, half listened. Born within sight of Dundalk racetrack where his father was groundsman, the young Brendan was raised on a seasonal diet of horseracing, hare-coursing, bare-knuckle boxing, hurling, cock-fighting and of course pigeon-racing. By sixteen he was six feet four, and knew most there was to know about sports, and gambling, and how to look after turf. This last became his stock-in-trade. In his twenties he crossed to England, where he worked as a navvy until joining the RAF 'in a fit of drunken insanity'. Yet his timing was propitious, for with hostilities looming the RAF was embarked on a massive airfield expansion programme. Murray's ground-management skills were quickly recognised, he advanced through the ranks, and was soon overseeing maintenance at a succession of airfields, before settling at Scampton.

'What t'at means, Uncle,' he explained, 'is that I supervise the subcontractors who take care of the grounds, see. I check they've got the right materials, and the right machinery, and the right know-how. And I make sure they're doing a proper job. If not, it's my neck on the line.'

'Important work at a base like Scampton,' Uncle agreed groggily.

'Exactly! Bad groundsmen, and nobody flies, it's as simple as that. Now, Scampton's turf is laid on sandstone, see, which is tricky to grow on, but excellent for drainage, so once the grass has taken, the upkeep's easy. Not like some of those clay airfields down south, which are a bloody nightmare let me tell you!'

'Aye, I can imagine.'

Peter watched Uncle. He drank so rarely when they were operational, he'd observed, hardly a drop, and was always so fastidious about his appearance too, always trimming his moustache and polishing his shoes. But since their tour had ended, he'd barely been sober, and stubble grew on his chin, and his tie was askew and his uniform soiled. As if he'd given up. As if with no war to fight, and no wife to go home to, there was no point. Mary, her name was, he'd learned, although Uncle never discussed her. She went to visit her sister in Liverpool one day, and got killed in an air-raid. Uncle had never got over it.

'Y'know, Brendan,' Uncle was prodding Murray's arm. 'I was wondering. About that wee pigeon. Y'know the one that saved us?'

'You mean old Bluie?'

'That's him. I was just wondering. Might you no' consider selling him?'

'Selling him? To you? What for?'

Uncle leaned closer. 'So's I can have him stuffed for my mantelpiece.'

Murray looked appalled, then saw Uncle's face, and in a moment the two were doubling over with guffaws. And at that instant, Peter, smiling politely, looked away, and saw Tess coming through the door.

She was wearing a belted overcoat and blue beret. Her hair was cropped. She was older, the innocence had gone, but not the beauty. The shock of seeing her was like a physical jolt. Peter's body went rigid, he felt his heart lurch, and the colour drain from his face. Her eyes, too, widened when she saw him, looked startled, yet also relieved somehow, as though a die had been cast.

'There she is at last!' Murray bellowed. 'Tess, quick! Over here, girl, come and meet two lovely lads from Syerston.'

For nearly an hour she stood at the bar and pretended she didn't know him. Even as Brendan introduced them, unspoken signals conspired to keep their association secret, as though by prior agreement. She wasn't ready, Tess knew. Even after six years, and knowing her letter would bring him to her, and knowing instantly her feelings for him were undimmed, she wasn't yet ready to confront all that implied, no matter how much she yearned to. So she stood close beside Brendan, sipping her drink and smiling as best she could, while the two older men joked and joshed with one another, and she stole sidelong looks at Peter, who was dark and guarded and even more handsome as a man than a youth. Then, just as they were preparing to leave, Brendan said he had to relieve himself, and the one called Uncle said he had to go too, so they went together, leaving her alone with Peter, who hesitated only a second before coming to the point.

'Why didn't you contact me?' he pleaded. 'At the beginning. Why didn't you try?'

'I did try,' she replied. 'But I couldn't.'

'Why not?'

'They said they'd have you arrested if I did. For rape.'

'What! But why, for God's sake?'

She licked her lips. 'Because of the baby.'

Chapter 3

Some days later, Quentin Credo closed the door of his Scampton rooms, turned the key, dropped his messages onto a side-table and headed for the drinks cabinet. After extracting Scotch, he wedged the bottle under his armpit, pulled the cork with his good hand, slopped liquor into a glass, and drank.

He slumped into an armchair, waiting for the alcohol to begin its work. Pain was coming at him in waves, like a tidal bore, beginning at its source among the ravaged tissue of his right hand, gathering momentum up his arm and shoulder, crashing across his body like surf onto a beach. It had been building all afternoon, ever since the pethidine wore off, simmering and stewing on the horizon like a storm. As each wave broke, viciously assaulting his nerves and senses, he held his breath to ride it, grunting with effort until it passed. In the intervals between, an undertow of fatigue sucked him towards black depths.

Only slowly did it ease, as the whisky spread its balm, blunting the pain to its customary throb. There was more to come, he knew, but first he must rest, and gather himself. His eyes fluttered shut, he felt sleep tugging, and utter exhaustion, like an old man. Like after the ten-mile cross-countries he used to run at Oxford. Used up. Which was ironic, because he wasn't an old man, he was twenty-six. And the only running he'd done that day was along a railway platform to catch a train to Sussex.

When he awoke an hour had passed and the room grown cold. His blurred gaze fell on his messages, Tess Murray had telephoned again, he saw, the Irish pigeon-fancier's wife. Telephoned as she had telephoned most days in the fortnight since her pilot friend had reappeared. Peter Lightfoot, his name was, the quiet young DFC from 61 Squadron. He'd phoned today too, the messages said. Twice. Quentin was impressed by their persistence, and their commitment, but what they wanted was as preposterous as it was impossible. They wanted him to get Lightfoot's orders magically changed, so he could transfer to 57 Squadron, there at Scampton, and fly a third tour of operations, instead of going to Scotland as an instructor. Something so far beyond Quentin's authority or influence it was laughable. Beyond anyone's, practically, short of Harris himself.

Briefly scanning his other messages, he hauled himself to his feet. Bar-chits, laundry-bills, memos about improperly censored mail and inadequately padlocked bicycles, the usual drivel. All except one – a terse note from his superior, Group Captain Whitworth, Scampton's station commander:

Quentin, who is this character Lightfoot who keeps pestering me for a transfer here? The answer is NO, can you deal with it please? Also Cochrane wants to see me tonight – some panic with Harris apparently. So I'll be down at Grantham until morning. Regards Whitworth. PS. Hope all went well at E. Grinstead.

He should eat but had no appetite. He should excuse himself further pain but that would be weak. He should have another whisky, then a warm bath, then go to bed and sleep. But sleep meant only dreams of Helen or fire-filled nightmares. So he crossed the floor to the hand-basin near his bed, filled it with scalding water, and poured in a measure of salt crystals. Then he rolled up the right sleeve of his shirt and plucked carefully at the black leather glove covering his hand, at the same time checking all was ready at his bedside. The glove came off, revealing the claw-like fingers and raw flesh between, where tissue had been cut away that afternoon. A renewed wave of pain washed over him like a warning, and he braced himself against the basin, feet spread, left hand on the wall, his eye carefully avoiding the shaving-mirror before him. Then with a gasp he plunged the hand in. Dizziness and nausea overcame him, he fought back from the faint, screwed shut his eyes, and let the salty water begin its work.

For ten excruciating minutes he stood at the basin flexing his fingers. Staring down at them, they seemed scarcely to move, just float there in useless agony, stiff and brown like burnt sticks. Finally, therapy over, he lifted the hand from the basin and moved unsteadily to his bed, wiping a single rogue tear from the scarred skin of his cheek. He lay down, opened a stoppered bottle, and dribbled clear liquid onto the surgical mask beside it. Then, checking the elastic attaching the mask to his bed was secure, he pulled it over his mouth and sucked at the astringent vapour.

Until he fell into sublime unconsciousness.

*

He'd been on a routine check-up to the pig-sty, the fond if unflattering nickname for the Queen Victoria Hospital in East Grinstead. Nestling amid wooded grounds, the hospital was home to a unique military institution, one which under the leadership of its charismatic director, Doctor Archie McIndoe, had evolved into the most advanced burns unit in the country, possibly the world. Its patients originated almost exclusively from the RAF, where fire was an ever-present danger, and their treatment was cutting-edge, experimental even, which is why they referred to themselves as guinea pigs, and the hospital as the sty. But always with respect, for the Queen Victoria was not a sty, it was a place of compassion, and hope, and courage beyond measure. Humour too, even occasional hilarity. Encouraged by McIndoe, patients discarded hospital garb and wore casual attire or their uniforms. They smoked and drank and swore and played cricket on the wards. They flirted with the nurses, and ventured into East Grinstead, where locals grew accustomed to the sight of mutilated airmen in the cinemas and tea rooms. They formed an exclusive drinking club called the Guinea Pig Club, appointing a pilot with no hands as secretary, so there'd be no paperwork, and another with no legs as treasurer, so he couldn't run off with the takings. McIndoe, forty, combative, fiercely protective, was honorary president.

'Well now, Credo,' he'd begun, at Quentin's check-up that afternoon. 'And how are we getting along?'

'Not too bad, sir,' Quentin replied, self-consciously turning his head for McIndoe to examine.

'Not bad? Looks pretty bloody brilliant, I'd say!'

'Yes, sir. Only, the hand . . .'

'We'll get to the hand in a minute. Now, about this face of yours. I'd say we're about ready to build you a new nose, yes? You know the WTP drill, of course.'

'Yes, sir, but . . .'

'Good-oh. So, the waltzing tube pedicle. First step is to separate a ten-inch-long strip of skin tissue along the top of your
shoulder, turning it under to form a tube, yet keeping it attached
at both ends, so it looks like a suitcase handle. Then, when we're
sure it's healthy and growing, usually three weeks or so, we
detach one end of the tube from your shoulder and sew it onto
your face, right here where your nose was.'

'Yes, sir. Three weeks, you say . . .'

'That's right. Then we leave it like that for another three
weeks, so the pedicle can take while still receiving a blood supply
from your shoulder. You can go home, carry on as normal,
etcetera.'

'. . . With a tube of skin joining my face to my shoulder.'

'Don't be facetious, Credo, it's worth the inconvenience.
Now, the next step, once we're sure the pedicle has taken, is to
cut the shoulder-end free, but leave it untrimmed. You'll look
like a proboscis monkey for a while.'

'Another three weeks . . .'

'Something like that. Then the final step is to trim the proboscis back into a proper nose-shape, including septum and
nostrils. Leave it for a couple of months to heal and the swelling
to go down, and Bob's your uncle! Bloody marvellous – here,
look at these photos . . .'

Quentin took the photos, although he didn't need them. He
knew all about the waltzing tube pedicle, so named for the way
it waltzed from your shoulder to your nose, or your eyelid, or
your lip. He'd seen countless during the four indescribable
months he'd spent as an in-patient at the sty. Once he'd come to
his senses. Borne in unconscious after crash-landing in his
Wellington, McIndoe and his team had first to stop him dying,

72

from shock, from catastrophic dehydration, and from bacterial infection, the three main killers of burns victims. Much of this early period Quentin spent adrift on a sea of pain and morphine. Days passed, weeks, while they worked on him.

McIndoe was a maverick, often discarding established techniques in favour of the unconventional. Severe burns were traditionally treated with tannic acid, which turned flesh to leather, then hardened to a crust, cutting off circulation and restricting movement. Removal of the dressings was destructive and agonising, and the tissue beneath often useless, so McIndoe abandoned tannic acid in favour of loose-weave dressings of toile and cotton, lightly applied and regularly changed. Fluid was replaced intravenously, wounds openly irrigated to promote healing, dead or dying tissue ruthlessly excised. Halibut oil and vaseline jelly were applied, and disinfectant powder dusted on using a straw. Then came another innovation. Early in his research McIndoe noticed that burned airmen rescued from the sea often fared better than others. Salt water seemed to restrict burn damage, flush out debris, keep joints flexible, encourage circulation. So he introduced saline baths, and steeped his patients daily until their injuries stabilised, and cured, and formed settled grafting surfaces. Guinea pigs called it the pickling jar. Duly pickled, only then did McIndoe begin the painstaking business of reconstructive surgery. Lightning-quick with a scalpel, this could involve him in as many as thirty separate operations on one patient, to remove what couldn't be used, repair what could, then laboriously rebuild and renew, using grafts of skin, cartilage and bone, and pedicles like the WTP.

And the results were often remarkable, Quentin conceded, glancing through the photographs. Indeed one man's finished nose looked no worse than an average rugby player's, and infinitely better than the charred stump it replaced. But the process was complex, and painful, and sometimes unsuccessful. And above all lengthy, and it was this protractedness that concerned him most. The weeks and weeks out of circulation. Yes, he'd be able to maintain a life of a sort, but not at Scampton, not working, and certainly not getting back on ops as he yearned. Nor could he venture out in public, except around East Grinstead, where strolling pedicle patients were the norm. His appearance was shocking enough. The notion of wandering London with a ten-inch proboscis dangling from his ruined face didn't bear thinking about, no matter how much McIndoe encouraged such integration. In reality he'd be imprisoned at home in Chiswick with his parents, or there at the hospital. For three months or more.

McIndoe was waiting. 'So what do you say, old chap, shall we book you in?'

'Well . . .' Quentin began cautiously, McIndoe was famously intolerant of procrastination. 'It certainly sounds marvellous, sir, as you say. But I wonder, could we put it off a while?'

'Put it off? I suppose so. But why?'

'You see, I'm to be re-evaluated for operational flying, sir. And I don't want to harm my chances, by disappearing from the scene as it were, for a long period.'

'Even for the sake of your appearance?'

'Even for that, sir. Also, much as I'd like one, a new nose won't help the evaluation. It's the hand I really need for that . . .'

'For God's sake!' McIndoe fumed. 'You bloody pilots, haven't you had enough?'

Quentin forced a misshapen smile. 'We just want to hit back at them, sir.'

74

'Really.' McIndoe eyed him witheringly, then began at last to examine Quentin's talon-like fingers. 'Hmm. Seen better. Still bathing them daily in hot saline?'

'Absolutely, sir. Twice daily. But there's still very little movement, as you can see. And unless I can get them working . . .'

'No chance of flying, yes I know. All right, listen, Quentin, I suppose I could try cutting away some of this adjoining tissue between the fingers, so they're less webbed. That might free up movement a bit.'

'Thank you, sir, I'd greatly appreciate it.'

'We can do it now.'

Quentin swallowed. 'Now?'

'Yes, now, under pethidine, if you're up to it. It'll hurt like hell, but you'll be home in time for supper. Or, we can admit you for a few days and do it under general anaesthetic, if you prefer.'

Quentin felt a familiar lassitude, as his body's pain-defence mechanism prepared for the coming onslaught. As it had learned to do so often over the months. Disassociation, he called it. The pain was real enough, but you had to distance yourself from it, otherwise you'd never cope. By stepping outside yourself, and going somewhere else. Somewhere less unpleasant. 'Yes, sir,' he found himself saying, as though in a trance. 'Now would be fine.'

At nine that evening, Scampton's station commander, Group Captain John 'Charles' Whitworth, a short, energetic, habitually worried-looking man of thirty, arrived by car at the Lincolnshire town of Grantham, crunching up the drive of St Vincent's, the former Victorian mansion serving as 5 Group headquarters. At the door he was asked, unusually, to present his credentials, which were carefully checked, before he was admitted to a panelled study with heavily draped windows and a fire crackling in the hearth. A few minutes later a lean, hawk-faced man wearing the uniform of Air Vice Marshal entered, and locked the door behind him.

'Charles.' He gripped Whitworth's hand. 'Good of you to come at such short notice. Your trip was uneventful, I trust. Please sit, let me pour you a brandy and soda.'

The Honourable Ralph Cochrane, aristocratic, slightly haughty, impressively effective, had been commanding 5 Group for just three weeks. Before that he'd commanded 3 Group, where he'd managed ten squadrons of Wellingtons, Stirlings and Halifaxes from headquarters in Exning, Suffolk. An advocate of low-level marking and precision bombing, he'd been in post there barely six months before the call had come from Bomber Command's leader, the legendary Arthur Harris, to move to Grantham and take over the crown jewels, the ten Lancaster squadrons of 5 Group.

Glasses filled, Cochrane got straight down to business.

'Everything we're about to discuss, Charles, it goes without saying, is absolutely top secret, understood?'

'Of course, sir.'

'Good. Ever heard of a boffin called Barnes Wallis?'

Whitworth considered. 'The Vickers chap? Co-designed the Wellington?'

'That's him. Looks like a country parson and talks utter gobbledegook, persistent as hell too, but a sound enough fellow, and a mind like a razor.'

'Yes, sir.' Whitworth watched Cochrane shift on his chair, as though reassessing his position.

'So. As you know, for some time Portal has been keen to

focus bombing efforts on German heavy industry, particularly the Ruhr valley area where all the major foundries, power stations and factories are.'

'Yes, sir.' Air Chief Marshal Portal was Harris's boss, head of the RAF, reporting directly to Churchill.

'Well, to cut a long story short, Wallis has been working on ways to inflict serious damage on targets in the Ruhr. But most of his ideas involve dropping very heavy bombs from very high altitude, which is a non-starter because we haven't aircraft capable of doing it.'

'I see.' Whitworth wondered where this was leading. So far he had heard little that wasn't common knowledge.

'However, he's now come up with something Portal believes might do the trick.'

'Really? What's that, sir?'

'I can't tell you. But Portal's very gung-ho about it. As is the Prime Minister.'

'Good heavens.'

'Indeed. Harris is less keen, in fact he says it's dangerous twaddle. But he's under pressure from Portal. So much so that he's ordered 5 Group to take it on.'

'That's excellent news, sir. But, ah, take what on?'

'I can't tell you that either. I can only tell you he showed me some film footage yesterday, and it's, well, astonishing really, if somewhat far-fetched. But more to the point, it's going to require a dedicated squadron, some heavily modified Lancasters, and a lot of training to pull it off. Now, tell me, how are things at Scampton?'

He's giving it to me, Whitworth realised with a thrill. Whatever it is, he's giving it to me, and Scampton, and 57 Squadron. 'They're absolutely fine, sir. Quieter obviously, since 49 Squadron moved out in preparation for laying concrete runways. 57 Squadron is due to follow when . . .'

'How's the grass?'

'Firm, sir, no problems, despite the wet winter. We've an excellent chief groundsman.'

'Good, make sure it stays that way, these modified Lancs will be heavy. What about security? Who's your SIO?'

'A young chap called Credo, sir. A flight lieutenant from 57 Squadron.'

'Is he sound?'

'Well, yes, sir. I believe so. Although he's only acting SIO, strictly speaking. What with 49 Squadron gone, the intelligence job has been somewhat low-key of late. He's a pilot normally, off flying ops following a bad fire in a Wimpy. But very bright, went to Oxford, trained as a barrister, all that sort of thing. And keen as mustard to get back in the fray.'

'I see.' Cochrane seemed hesitant, then came to a decision. 'He'll have to do, at least until RAF Intelligence can draft in bigger guns. But be sure he stays on his toes, Charles, secrecy is absolutely paramount. Secrecy and speed, that is.'

'Yes, sir. I'm sure he's up to it. And equally sure 57 Squadron is up to it too.'

'57?' Cochrane looked surprised. '57 Squadron isn't doing it, Charles. Harris wants to form an entirely new squadron. Especially for this one job. One drawn from the best 5 Group has to offer. That's why we picked Scampton, because with 49 gone, you've got the space to house them.'

'A whole new squadron? From scratch? Seven hundred men? It'll take months.'

'We don't have months. They've got to be flying in a fortnight.'

'Jesus.'

'Indeed. So they're going to need a lot of support, Charles, and guidance, and practical assistance. That's where you come in. Think you can do it?'

'Well, yes, of course I'll do everything I can. What's the new squadron's number?'

'It doesn't have a number yet.'

'I see. And who's going to command it?'

'Harris wants the CO of 106 Squadron. Some chap called Gibson.'

Mid-morning next day, a knock came on Quentin's office door.

'Young lady to see you, sir.' The adjutant winked. 'A Mrs Murray. Works part-time in the NAAFI, her husband is stationed here, she says it's urgent.'

'Thank you, Corporal, would you ask her to wait a few minutes please.'

Quentin withdrew a slender file from a drawer, opened and read. He'd been expecting this visit. And not just since Tess Murray and Peter Lightfoot began badgering everyone for a transfer to Scampton. He'd been expecting it for four months.

He'd first met Tess the previous October. He'd just started his job as intelligence officer, following release from the pig-sty and a spell of leave at home. Returning to Scampton he'd presented himself before his CO, only to be turned down for flying because of his injuries. Get that hand working, his CO suggested, in the meantime perhaps the station can use you. So he'd gone to Whitworth, who offered him the vacant intelligence job, on a temporary basis. A week later and with his feet barely under the desk, Tess had come to see him. She'd sat there, chewing her lip, looking embarrassed and avoiding his eye, a reaction he was learning to live with, but it turned out her discomfiture wasn't because of him. 'I need to get in touch with someone,' she'd explained, in an educated but hesitant voice. 'A man I used to know a long time ago. I believe he's in the RAF, possibly as a pilot, but that's all I know.' Then she'd looked straight at him, and held his gaze, and there was no repulsion, or ghoulish fascination like the people on the street, only worried determination. And in that instant he recognised something in her. Something they recognised in each other. This woman, so young yet so knowing, had experienced great pain and terrible loss. Like him. So he'd dispensed with questions, latched onto that one word 'need' and found himself offering to help. And in days he'd tracked down Peter Lightfoot at 61 Squadron over at Syerston, and duly passed on his address. Without ever questioning why.

Which was far from brilliant work, coming from an intelligence officer. But now she was back, and wanting more. And this time he would be more vigilant.

'Mrs Murray,' he began, when she was seated. 'Hello again. I trust you are well.'

'I'm fine, thank you. Um, have you received my messages?'

'Yes I have, and I apologise for not returning them, but I have been rather busy. Please, why don't you explain the situation, more fully, as it were.'

She eyed him, as if probing his sincerity, then explained, but not very fully, about getting Lightfoot transferred to Scampton. Then shrugged, knowing it sounded flimsy.

'Why is this is so important?' Quentin said.

'Because we need to be near one another.'

Need. That word again. 'Can you be more specific?'

Her eyes focused on a point midway across his desk. Her hair was longer than he remembered, she was tall and slender with

80

delicate features, fair complexion and troubled eyes. Too troubled for her twenty-three years. She still wore her overcoat and a woollen beret, with her handbag clasped to her lap. As if she couldn't stay long.

'No,' she murmured. 'I can't.'

'Then I don't see how I can help you.'

'But you must!'

'Mrs Murray, Flying Officer Lightfoot has received *orders*. They can't be ignored or changed simply because he doesn't like them.'

'But he wants to fly. On operations. Not be some instructor in Scotland.'

It was like children, Quentin felt. Two children wanting to be together. To them it was all absurdly simple. 'I see, so if we managed to get him posted to North Africa, for instance, flying on ops there, would that be all right?'

Her lips moved as she digested his words. Then her gaze fell. 'No.'

'I didn't think so. Look, I'm sorry, but it's clear to me your reasons for wanting this transfer are personal. This is a domestic matter, in other words, not an operational one. Therefore it would be quite inappropriate for me to get involved.'

'Are you married, Lieutenant Credo?'

'What?' That threw him. A sudden glimpse of Helen, and the scent of her honey-blonde hair as it caressed his face. Then she was gone. 'I don't see what . . .'

'Are you?'

'I . . . Well . . . Since you ask, I was engaged once, but not any more.'

'What happened?'

He gestured at his face. 'This.'

Still she held his gaze. 'I'm sorry. Things rarely turn out as we imagine.'

'Indeed.'

'It's not what you think, you see. Peter and me.'

'And what do I think?'

'That we're having some sort of affair, or something.'

'Are you?'

'No.'

'Then . . . What?'

'He beats me! All right? My husband beats me. One day he'll probably kill me. Only Peter knows this, and only Peter can help. Now are you satisfied?'

And there it was. Confirmation. Murray, the genial Irish giant, was not the man he seemed – something Quentin had already begun to suspect. In October, a week after Tess had asked him to find Lightfoot, Quentin had dropped by the Murrays' quarters to pass her the details, which he'd tactfully sealed in an envelope. But as he leaned to the door to knock, he heard a man's raised voice inside, followed by placatory entreaties from a woman. Menace seeped through the door like toxic gas. He could sense her fear, and feel his fury. He hesitated, then everything went deathly quiet. Unsure what to do, he retreated guiltily to his office. Next day he found her in the NAAFI and gave her the envelope. She thanked him, clutching it to her breast with relief. But there was no hiding the dread in her eyes, nor the purple bruising on her neck.

Then followed her letter to Lightfoot, his arrival at Scampton, and their plea for his transfer there. It was all starting to fit together. Yet incredibly there was more.

'Well, that is . . . Appalling,' Quentin blustered. 'Truly appalling. But surely, if it's a matter of marital problems, as it were, you should talk to the RAF welfare people? Or perhaps the chaplain?'

But she wasn't listening. 'It began months ago. Shortly before the station moved here from Feltwell. He started behaving oddly, he became secretive and moody, and drank more. Then one night he came in late, I asked where he'd been, he flew into a rage and hit me. He apologised and begged pardon and swore it would never happen again, but a few weeks later it did. He put his hands around my neck, until I thought I'd suffocate. I didn't know what to do, so I came to you, the station intelligence officer, and asked help finding the one person I could turn to. Now you're sending him away.'

Quentin sighed. 'It's not me sending him away, Mrs Murray, it's his job. People get moved all the time, that's the nature of it. And we don't write the orders, they come from Bomber Command, in High Wycombe. I can give you an address if you want, perhaps a letter . . .'

But she had given up. Stiff-backed and determined still, yet resigned to inevitable defeat. Quentin waited. Behind him, March sunlight glowed at his window, dissolving the mist that blanketed the airfield. From a nearby hangar drifted the busy sounds of machine-tools and whistling engineers. Farther away a Lancaster was running up engines.

'I had a daughter, you see,' she went on, more calmly. 'We did. Peter and I. A baby daughter. Long before I was married to Brendan. She was taken from me. Peter never knew about her until now. She's nearly six, and we, the two of us that is, we wanted to try and look for her. But if Brendan found out . . .'

'I see. I'm sorry. I don't know what to say.'

'Don't say anything. You might as well know, that's all.'

'I do wish I could help. Really.'

She forced a resigned smile. 'I'd like to believe that.'

'It's true. But operational orders . . . Well, they're practically set in stone.'

'So I gather.' She rose to leave.

'Although, perhaps, your daughter . . .' he found himself saying. 'I mean, I can't do anything about Lightfoot's orders, but I could make a few inquiries about her. See what the procedures are, your options, that sort of thing . . .'

'I wouldn't want to cause any more trouble.'

'You wouldn't.'

'Then, thank you.'

'You're welcome.'

She hesitated, studying him again.

'Your fiancée.'

'Ah.'

'Did it ever occur to you that perhaps she was wrong for you?'

'I beg your pardon?'

'Sometimes we're forced to make bad choices, out of necessity. Often we later regret them. But perhaps not being married to her, in the end, was the right thing, for you.' The small smile again, as a consolation prize, then she turned and left the room.

Quentin watched her go, then opened his file and began jotting notes. Then broke off, fingering his face, to ponder the question. And ponder Helen. And ponder the events that led to them not being married.

Properly. For the first time since they happened.

It was a gardening mission. Minelaying, in other words. In Heligoland Bight. Simple, straightforward, low-risk. That's why they called it gardening. You took off after dark, nipped across the North Sea, turned right before Denmark, and arrived in the sea area outside the Elbe, the river leading to Germany's biggest port, Hamburg. Then you sowed your mines and came home again. It was a regular run, almost a chore, performed in the hope of sinking the odd ship entering or leaving the Elbe. Meeting seriously organised opposition was practically unheard of.

57 Squadron was then still at Feltwell in Norfolk, and still operating the two-engined Wellington. But excitement was in the air, rumours abounding of a move to Scampton in Lincolnshire and conversion onto the wonderful new Lancaster with its vast bomb-bay and quartet of Merlins. Feltwell was busy with fresh crews arriving for final training: gunnery practice, bombing practice, night-flying practice, cross-country navigation, wireless procedures. Once all was satisfactorily completed, crews flew a supervised 'warm-up' mission, something safe and simple such as dropping pamphlets over France, or escorting a convoy up the coast, or minelaying in Heligoland Bight. Then they were deemed fully operational, and thrown unto the breach.

Quentin was by then an experienced pilot, with half a tour under his belt and a reputation for dependability. He was also newly promoted to Flight Lieutenant, popular with his cohorts and to everyone's envy, the proud fiancé of Helen, a local landowner's daughter. One afternoon he was detailed to take a new crew on a gardening mission. He'd be flying as supervisor, an extra pair of hands as needed. The other six – pilot, navigator, bomb aimer, radio operator and two gunners – were unknown to him, but all young and all green. He briefed them thoroughly, helped them kit up, then drove them to the aircraft to prepare. At dusk they took off, flying in loose formation with three other

Wellingtons, and made their way across the watery flatlands of Norfolk towards the coast at Cromer. The weather was good, with a slight sea, clear skies and three-quarter moon to navigate by. The crew settled to the task, turning points came and went, radio messages were received and sent, everything went as planned, before long they were nearing the target area and preparing to drop their mines.

Then they were coned by searchlights. Flak-ships were old warships, converted trawlers or barges, heavily armed with anti-aircraft guns, and manoeuvred into position to catch the unwary. The briefing hadn't mentioned them, nobody expected any that day, but there they were, and two of their searchlights found Quentin's Wellington and latched on, holding it securely like a hooked fish, while the gunners took aim. On board, panic, as blinding white light blasted the cockpit. Shouts of alarm came over the intercom, erratic gunfire burst from the tail, and at the controls the pilot froze, terrorised into immobility. Standard procedure was to throw the aircraft into a corkscrew and try to wriggle free, but you had to be quick, and you had to be decisive. Standing helplessly behind the pilot, Quentin grabbed his shoulders, shouting commands above the roaring engines. But the pilot could only sit, head shaking in rigid disbelief, and in a second came the flash and crump of explosions and the whole aircraft shuddered to the first salvo.

Quentin could wait no longer. He hauled the pilot bodily from his seat and quickly took control, slamming the throttles wide and kicking into the corkscrew. At the same time he reached to the bomb panel and hit the emergency release, freeing the Wellington of its load. At that instant a second explosion slammed into it, throwing it on its side, and riddling it with white-hot shrapnel. Control wires snapped, Perspex shattered, instruments smashed, and from out on the wing came violent shuddering as the starboard engine took hits. Quentin could hear the engine dying, and sense other damage through the controls. Crewmen had probably been hit, but the searchlights still held them and flak was exploding all around, so he tightened the corkscrew and shoved the nose to vertical. The Wellington dived, the slipstream rose to a shriek, the controls stiffened and shook in his hands, while the altimeter tumbled, five thousand feet, four, three, yet still the searchlights held them. He saw dark ocean spiralling towards them, glimpsed his pilot hunched on the floor as though praying, felt the airframe creaking in protest, held on for three more turns, then as the altimeter hit a thousand, wrenched the controls over and kicked opposite rudder. With a sickening lurch the corkscrew reversed, and a second later the cockpit went black. He held his breath and hauled back, the darkness shocking but also glorious. Seconds ticked, the ocean raced by below, he wound off roll and flattened the dive, holding the engines wide for speed. Still the darkness held and no flak found them. They'd slipped the searchlights. He checked outside and could see them, scraping the clouds in the distance like ghostly fingers, far to port and falling behind, with the bursting flak too wandering aimlessly away. He waited another minute to be sure, then levelled off and turned for home.

They were at five hundred feet. Good enough for now, he decided. Smoke filled the cockpit, and the sharp tang of cordite, a shrieking gale tore through a smashed nose-panel, some instruments were broken, the rudders felt spongy beneath his feet, but the Wellington was famous for taking punishment, and flew stoically on. More seriously the starboard engine was dying, sparks flew from the nacelle, and a geyser of black oil, and thick plumes of petrol vapour from a holed tank. Any moment the whole wing could be ablaze, but he needed the engine a little longer to make good their escape. He throttled it back slightly, then leaned to his crouching pilot. 'Go check everyone forward!' he shouted, gesturing towards the nose. Then he tried the intercom for the others, but couldn't raise anyone. All he could hear was an alarmed garble from the rear gunner. Pouring in, the youth kept shouting, something was pouring in.

Then came an incandescent flash to his right and the starboard engine blew, setting the entire nacelle and inboard wing ablaze. Quentin snatched back the throttle, cut fuel to the engine and hit the fire-extinguisher button. The engine slowed, then stopped, but the fire burned on, fed by petrol from the holed tank. Damaged fuel tanks were supposed to self-seal, and once sealed the fire should go out. If not the wing would burn up and the aircraft crash. He watched in helpless fascination, recalling the man who won a VC crawling onto the wing of a Wellington to smother a fire with a tarpaulin. And he was wondering how such a feat might be attempted, when a blood-curdling scream came over the intercom.

From then on, from the moment the screaming started until the minute Quentin passed out from his injuries, everything seemed to take place in extreme slow motion. In individual scenes, like an old-time film show.

The pilot reappeared, his arm pointing forward, his young face anguished. Quentin guessed injury or worse had befallen the bomb aimer and nose gunner. 'It's okay,' he encouraged, somehow summoning a smile. 'Come back here now, and fly her for me. I have to go aft.'

Then he was clambering rearwards into the main fuselage, past the slumped figure of the navigator, whose head was half blown away, and the wireless operator, who was staring in shock at the bloody remains of his arm. Quentin nodded at him, and smiled again, and said he'd be back to help. Then went on his way, into the cramped tube of the fuselage.

Which was completely ablaze, fed by fuel hosing from a damaged manifold, and fanned by the gale from the nose. The effect was breathtaking, as of a giant blowtorch, a concentrated blue-yellow firestorm roaring through the cabin. More fuel poured along the floor to collect in a fiery pool round the rear turret, where the screaming came from. The sight was humbling, a vision of hell. Even at the threshold Quentin could feel the lethal heat prickling his skin and sense the folly of embracing it. But a boy was trapped screaming in the turret, and Quentin must get him out. Goggles, he decided, he'd better wear goggles, and quickly retrieved them. Then stepped into the maelstrom.

To stand the slightest chance he must shut off the fuel, if not they'd all be finished in minutes. The starboard shut-off was at the wing-root, a lever beside the spurting manifold. He ducked closer. The heat was wild and savage, so intense he couldn't breathe, he could feel it burning his clothes, and scorching his forehead and cheeks. With his arm crooked against the inferno, he punched at the lever with his gloved fist. Nothing happened. He struck again and it slid half-shut. And with that blow the damaged manifold burst, and pressurised fuel, the very eye of the blowtorch, blasted straight into his face. He staggered back in surprise, feeling the raw fury of the inferno, feeling his skin charring, and the flesh clenching beneath, but feeling no pain, and no fear, only fury, and determination to shut the valve. Recovering his feet, he drove forward once more, rammed it shut, then fell sideways to escape. The blowtorch withered in seconds, starving of fuel, then died altogether. Smoke still billowed, metal glowed red, starlight showed where the roof had burned through, but the fire in the mid-section was out. All that remained now was the tail, still ablaze from spilled fuel. He felt a blast of cool air from the gaping roof, gulped it hungrily, then grabbed a fire-extinguisher and set off.

The rest was as a dream. He used the extinguisher as a shield, dousing fire as he went. But it ran out as he reached the rear turret, leaving pockets still flickering on the floor and bulkhead. Crouching in the cramped tube, the heat was murderous, blistering metal and melting wire like solder. The turret doors were shut, he saw, and the turret itself rotated, as though shooting at an angle. The doors could not be opened in that position, so to reach the boy inside he must centralise the turret. And to centralise the turret he must use the external hydraulic supply, mounted on the burning bulkhead. And to use the hydraulic supply he must undo a wire-locked valve, rotate it to the ON position, then turn the turret using a lever.

And to do any of that, he'd have to take off his glove.

Calmness washed over him. He pulled the glove off, and watched with detached fascination as his hand reached through flames for the valve. As his fingers closed on red-hot steel he saw them sear and smoke. As he undid the wire-lock, his entire hand started to pucker and bubble, and its skin to flake off in shreds, to be consumed in the flames just like paper. And as he opened the valve, and activated the lever, and rotated the turret to the centre position, he felt his hand shrivel and die. But still he held it there, until the task was done. When he had finished, and begun wrenching at the jammed doors, he felt himself sliding at last into a faint. But he kept pulling, until the doors opened a crack, then an inch. And just as unconsciousness overcame him, he smelled roasted flesh, as with a final effort he forced the doors fully open, and fell onto the charred figure inside.

Quentin turned his chair to the window, and gazed out over the misty field. Replaying the events of that day, forcing himself to relive them, in sequence and unedited like that, was something he'd avoided since they happened, in case the remembrance was more than could be borne. Yet somehow, after all this time, he felt better for it. All of it, even the aftermath which he hadn't learned himself until weeks later. How the radio operator, arm dangling, had bravely extinguished the remaining fire. How the young pilot found his nerve and flew them home on one engine. How at Feltwell, willing hands lifted the three of them out, leaving the four dead alone in the burned-out bomber until day-light. How so little was left of the rear gunner that his whole turret had to be removed, and destroyed. And how that Wellington would never fly again.

But he would fly again, he had decided straight away. It was his one goal and obsession, much to everyone's dismay. To prove he could still do it, and prove he had the nerve, but more importantly to prove he still had worth. As a warrior. As a man. And because if he didn't fly again, then what was the point of it all? Yet no one seemed to understand this. Not Archie McIndoe who said he'd done enough, not his father who was always angry, nor his mother who wept, not even his fellow pilots who admired his guts but were nervous of him. In case the same should happen to them.

And not Helen. She was dismayed too. About everything. For the short while she stayed around. A few unhappy visits to East Grinstead, the two of them staring wordlessly at the gardens beyond the window. A dwindling trickle of sad letters, a final 'Dear John' and she was gone. Like a swallow in winter.

Someone was knocking. Starting from reverie, Quentin swivelled his chair.

'Yes?'

Whitworth was at the door, face quizzical. 'Everything all right, old boy?'

'Yes, er, yes, sir. Thank you.'

'You look a little peaky.'

'No, I'm fine.'

'Good. Got a second?'

'Of course. Please come in.'

Whitworth entered, and sat, and studied Quentin, then leaned across the desk, and beckoned him nearer with his finger.

'Lord, have I got something to tell you.'

Chapter 4

Peter tightened the drawstring of his duffel bag, buckled the straps and hoisted it to his shoulder. He should probably buy himself a suitcase, he reflected, hefting its weight, especially now he was an officer. One of those smart leather ones with straps. Then again, money was tight and suitcases expensive, so it could wait. And if officers carrying duffelbags was unseemly, too bad, they should have left him as a sergeant.

Darkness had fallen. He tugged the blackout curtains closed, checking round his bedroom one final time. A child's room still, he realised, surveying the *Flight* magazine posters and model aeroplanes dangling on their strings. A bedroom where time had stopped at adolescence, and moved on to some other present. He turned off the light and closed the door.

He clumped downstairs, dumped his bag in the hall and entered the kitchen, nose twitching at another souvenir of youth, fried spam and overcooked cabbage.

'Tea's ready, love,' his mother said. 'Goodness, don't you look smart in your new cap and everything.'

'Thanks Mum.'

His father lowered his newspaper. 'Got your pay-book and travel warrant?'

Peter patted pockets. 'Yes, I've got everything.'

'What time's your train?'

'Eleven-thirty. It's the sleeper.'

'Do you get a compartment?'

'I've no idea. I doubt it.'

'Bloody well ought to. Seeing as you're an off—'

The telephone rang. He escaped to the hall. 'Hello?'

'It's me.'

'Tess! Thank God. Where are you?'

'Outside the NAAFI. Not very private, but I had to phone before you left.'

'I'm so glad. I was worried I'd miss you.'

'When are you off?'

'Soon,' he sighed. 'Up to Euston, then catching the night train to Glasgow.'

'That's nice.'

'No, it's a disaster, I feel I'm abandoning you.'

'We both know you're not. Will you see Uncle?'

'He's going to show me the sights, then put me on the train to Inverness, which is good of him. Then there's a third train to Elgin which gets into Lossiemouth late tomorrow night.'

'My.' A pause. 'It is a long way.'

'Australia as far as I'm concerned. Tess, I'm so worried, you're all alone there. With everything.'

'Don't be. I'm fine.'

A longer pause. Murmured voices drifted to him from the

kitchen, crackles and clicks came over the line, blown leaves rustled outside in the street. Peter leaned his forehead to the wall. It was three weeks since he'd been reunited with Tess, three weeks of elation and despair, as he learned of her life over six lost years, of the awfulness of her situation with Brendan, and of the revelation of their daughter. Everything had changed in those three weeks, and now, so soon after they had found each other, they were being forced apart.

'It's only for a while Peter,' she said, reading his thoughts. 'Six months, a year maybe, then we'll work something out . . .'

'I'll never manage it. I'd rather desert.'

'Don't talk like that. You've got to manage it. I need you to.'

He hesitated. 'I love you, Tess. It's wrong, but I can't help it. I love you and always have.'

'It's not wrong. I love you too.'

'What are we going to do?'

'Nothing. We've tried, and there's nothing more we can do. Just . . .'

'What . . .'

'Keep in close touch, Peter. Please. Write to me. Write here, care of the NAAFI, it's safer. And let me know a number where I can reach you.'

'Yes, yes, I will of course.'

Silence yawned, there seemed so much to say, then nothing at all, so they murmured unhappy goodbyes and hung up. Peter stared at the receiver, listening to its forlorn hum and the fitful March wind outside, then with a bitter curse slammed it down.

'Who was that, love?' his mother said as he returned to the kitchen.

He couldn't tell them, couldn't say anything. The Derby slight against his mother, even after all this time, was still unmention-able. 'No one. Wrong number.'

His parents exchanged glances. 'Come along and have your tea then, before . . . Peter? Where are you going?'

He strode down the hall, hurt and frustration seething within him. It was their fault, those people across the road. Six years he'd lost her, six long years of sadness and yearning and not knowing why. Then to be reunited, so fleetingly, only to lose her again, it was more than anyone could bear. He threw open the door, marched down the path and across the darkened street. In seconds he was there, everything so fresh in memory, so unchanged, the tiled step, the brass letter-flap, the wrought-iron bell pull. All exactly as he remembered.

Except Mr Derby, who looked older, and smaller.

'Good heavens. It's young Lightfoot, isn't it?' he said, peeling off spectacles. 'Flying Officer Lightfoot, I see. And is that a DFC?' Interest flickered, then quickly waned as his guard came up. 'Well now, and what can we do for you?'

'Can I come in?'

'Ah . . . We're just about to listen to the news . . . Africa . . .'

'It won't take a minute.'

He pushed past into the plushly carpeted lobby, redolent of wood-polish and potted hyacinth, and something flavoursome cooking in the oven. A radiogram was playing band music. He followed it to the front room, Mr Derby trailing in his wake. 'Um, Peter, this is probably not a good . . .' The room was even grander than he recalled, chintz upholstery, gilt mirror, mahogany bookcase, a grand piano bearing framed photographs of their son David in uniform, David in cricket whites, David in top-hat and tails. Nothing of Tess. Not one.

'Mrs Derby.'

She glanced up from her needlework, looked momentarily startled, then quickly composed herself. As if she'd been expecting this.

'Oh.' She plucked loudly at a thread. 'It's you.'

'Yes, it is. Excuse me, Mrs Derby, and I'm sorry to disturb you, but have you spoken to Tess lately?'

'Theresa lives in Lancashire. She's married now. We don't hear from her.'

'It's Lincolnshire, as well you know, and with respect, that's not what I asked. I asked if you had spoken to her.'

'Why? What business is it of yours?'

'She's my friend, that's what. And she needs help, from you. From her family.'

'If she needs help, she'll ask for it. Anyway, she has family. She has a husband.'

'Who treats her badly.'

'That is her business. She chose him, we weren't consulted, nor were we invited. We've never even met him. Now, if there's nothing else . . .' She set aside her needles and began to rise.

'Why didn't you tell me about the baby?'

'What did you say?'

'My daughter. I had a right to know.'

'You? A right?' Long pent-up anger flared. 'You're damn lucky we didn't have you arrested for rape!'

'Um . . . Emily . . . surely there's no need . . .'

'Keep out of this, Bernard! This, this *monster* ruined our daughter, and brought shame upon this house. Now he has the gall to come here telling us what to do!'

'No, I'm not telling you, I'm begging you.' Peter snatched a photograph from the piano. 'Look, Mrs Derby, where is she, your other child? Your daughter. She still exists, you know, and she needs you.'

'Put that down this instant!'

'Contact her, Mrs Derby, and offer her help. Please, like a mother should.'

'How *dare* you! Put it down and get out of my house!'

'Say it, Mrs Derby. Say you still love her.'

A hand touched his arm. 'Leave it, Peter, you're only making it worse.'

'Say it, please . . .' Tears were pricking his eyes.

'For God's sake Bernard, get him OUT!'

With a resounding crash Peter threw the photograph to the floor. Stunned silence followed, the Derbys gaped in horror. Peter glared at them, then turned for the door.

'For religious people, you know, you're completely bloody heartless.'

At eleven the next morning, two doyens of the air warfare business were meeting in a locked side-office at the Vickers factory in Weybridge, Surrey. They weren't pilots, they weren't even servicemen, they were civilians. Both in their fifties, with rumpled suits and ink-stained fingers, they looked more like schoolteachers, or accountants, or clerks, than aircraft designers. Roy Chadwick began his career before the First World War as a young draughtsman on the Avro 504. Thirty years later he was Avro's chief designer, the architect of more than two hundred types, and legendary creator of the Lancaster. Sitting across the paper-strewn table from him was Vickers' Chief Designer, Barnes Wallis, the man who co-designed the R100 airship, who revolutionised thinking with his geodesic construction technique, and who put Bomber Command on the offensive with the Wellington. Gently-spoken, self-effacing, with horn-rimmed glasses and thick white hair, Wallis's mild-mannered demeanour belied a famous determination. Yet he was not without self-doubt.

'Here's the problem, Barnes.' Chadwick began, unrolling a drawing. 'Your bomb has a whopping seven-foot diameter, see, far too big to reverse in under the nose of a Lanc. So it'll have to be loaded from the rear. But to do that we must lift the tail.'

'How high?'

'Seventeen and a half feet. As measured from the fuselage roof.'

'Seventeen and a half feet? Roy, that's miles! The nose will practically be on the ground.'

'It's a lot, I know, but the only way to load the bomb. Here, see, we hook a standard ten-ton crane to the Lancaster's rear lifting-point at frame 38, hoist the tail, then drive the bomb underneath using a modified Type E trolley. Once in position between the callipers, we lower the tail, winch it on board and hey presto, job done.'

'Good heavens, yes, I see, but what a palaver. I mean, what if something goes wrong? Crane slipping, lateral gust of wind, anything.'

Chadwick shrugged. 'Your bomb, old chap. Make it smaller if you don't like it.'

'Hmm.' Wallis looked thoughtful. 'It may yet come to that.'

'Problems?'

'You could say . . .' He hesitated, then reached for his briefcase. 'I'm not supposed to show anyone these, Roy, but then you're not anyone. Here, see, this is a schematic of the bomb without its wooden casing . . .'

Chadwick inspected the drawing, which resembled a giant oil drum lying on its side. 'Good Lord, it looks like the front wheel of a steamroller.'

'Funny you should say that, it is almost exactly the same weight and size – about four tons and four feet or so in diameter. But the point is, it has to be made into a sphere. Or at least an oblate sphere. And that's what increases the diameter to seven feet.'

'Why a sphere?'

'So that it skips properly.'

'It what?'

'Skips. Look, Roy, Harris would have me shot for telling you this, but the idea is to turn this oil-drum shape into an oblate spheroid, a fat barrel in other words, which when dropped onto water, skips along the surface like a stone on a pond.'

'God above.' Chadwick looked aghast. 'A four-ton bomb that skips on water. Will it work?'

'It already does, at least the scaled-down versions do. But the full-sized one just breaks apart when it hits the sea. The wooden casing can't withstand the impact.'

'How are you constructing the casing?'

'Like a barrel. With a central ring-like annulus to support wooden staves. I've tried strengthening the annulus, and the pillars holding it, and thickening the staves, but nothing works.'

'What about a steel annulus, and steel staves?'

'Think of the weight, Roy. We're already at ten thousand pounds.'

'Yes, of course. Have you tried dropping the thing without a casing at all? Just as a drum?'

Wallis sat forward. 'Actually, we have. And it does work, sort of, but not as reliably as the spheroid shape. You see, as a drum, it *has* to hit the water absolutely level, otherwise it just veers off in any direction. That would mean dropping it from much lower than I originally calculated. And we're already jolly low.'

'How low?'

Wallis hesitated. 'Very.'

'One thousand feet? Five hundred? Come on, Barnes, it's me!'

'One hundred and fifty feet.'

'What!'

'Yes. And it has to be exactly 150 feet. And exactly 240 mph. And exactly 450 yards from the target.'

'Good grief. I'm beginning to see the problem.'

Wallis winced. 'The crews won't. It'll have to be dropped at night.'

Chadwick eyed him incredulously, then cracked a wry smile. 'Right, well, best of luck with it all, Barnes old chap, I think you're going to need it! Now, would you like to see the modifications to the Lancaster?'

'Very much.'

More drawings appeared. 'So, here we are. Armour-plating removed, upper gun-turret removed, bomb-doors removed, but with fairings added to reduce drag. Deeper bomb aimer's blister added, callipers added to hold the bomb, plus the winch and driving mechanism to rotate it.'

'What speed?'

'Five hundred rpm. Backwards. Just as you specified.'

'Good. What about weight? And performance?'

'Even with all that weight reduction, the unladen weight is still about 1200 pounds heavier than a standard Lanc. The mods to the bomb-bay will add drag, as will suspending the bomb in the slipstream, you'll lose a few miles per hour in speed, and gain some vibration, but nothing serious.'

Wallis studied the drawings. 'Marvellous Roy, it all looks marvellous, thank you.'

'My pleasure. What will you do about the bomb casing?'

Wallis sighed. 'I don't know. Keep trying, I suppose. But if I can't fix it I'll have to leave the thing as a drum and go for the lower drop. I've no time for anything else.'

'At least that would help with the loading problem.'

'Yes, that's true. Thanks again, Roy.'

'Not at all. Good luck. With everything.'

They began returning the drawings to their briefcases. 'How many modified Lancs are you building?' Wallis asked.

'Harris wants a full squadron plus a couple of spares, so we're building three prototypes plus twenty production-types. Twenty-three in all. They should start coming off the production line in a couple of weeks or so.'

'As soon as you can manage it, Roy. Timing is desperately tight.'

'So I gather.'

'What's it called, by the way, this version of the Lanc?'

Chadwick shrugged again. 'It's not called anything. Just the type modification number. Lancaster Type 464 Provisioning.'

At Scampton, organised chaos. It had begun two days earlier with the arrival of the mystery squadron's vanguard – a contingent of ground mechanics shipped in from 97 Squadron. Disgorged at dawn from a bus, they stood around at the main gate, stretching and yawning sleepily. Nobody knew what to do with them, nor why they were there, including themselves. Within minutes Quentin received his first taste of the task ahead.

'Is that the SIO?' an irritated voice demanded. 'Main gate here. Look, sorry to trouble you and that, sir, but we've got a busload of erks from 97 Squadron turned up. Filthy lot of slobs too, by the look of them, no papers, no baggage, barely a decent scrap of uniform between 'em. Nothing but some half-baked instruction to report here.'

'Thank you, Sergeant. Would you please direct them to Number 2 hangar?'

'Number 2? That's 49 Squadron's hangar. What about some authorisation?'

'Authorisation will follow, Sergeant, I assure you. Now please send them along, although on second thoughts, they must be tired, perhaps we should get them fed and watered first.'

'Toss 'em in the bath-house more like, they pong to high heaven!'

Two days later and the numbers were swelling fast, with every hour bringing more. Loaders, armourers, engineers, fuellers, drivers, meteorologists, mappers, plotters, cooks, clerks, typists, orderlies, the entire human fabric of an operational bomber squadron, descending on Scampton like pilgrims to Mecca. In the admin building, Station Commander Whitworth and his team struggled to keep up – assigning accommodation, allocating transport, organising catering, tracking down belongings and equipment, and the laborious task of processing the new squadron's personnel. As security officer, this last fell to Quentin, whose desk was soon bowing beneath mounds of lists, documents and files. Every single man and woman on the manifest had to be checked and cleared, by him. And not all, he soon learned, were entirely suitable.

'I'm not having *him* working on my Lancs!' a furious chief mechanic protested, jabbing an oily finger at the list. 'Nor him neither, and definitely not him!'

'Really, Chief?' Quentin enquired. 'Why not?'

'He's a drinker, he's a shirker, and he don't know a spanner from an arse-wipe!'

'Succinctly put, Chief. I'll see what I can do.'

An ancient military tradition was being played out, it transpired. Instead of sending their best people to Scampton, as ordered, some squadron commanders were seizing this God-given opportunity to dispose of their worst. Consequently many that Quentin found himself checking were renowned trouble-makers, several had long disciplinary records, and some had even been to prison. Swiftly he rooted them out and sent them back. Indignant complaints followed, so he tipped off Whitworth, Ralph Cochrane put a stop to the practice, and gradually the influx of miscreants dried up.

Then by contrast came the aircrew, and with them the first hint that X Squadron, as it was presently dubbed, was to be no ordinary outfit.

'Jesus, look at all the gongs!' an orderly murmured, reading over Quentin's shoulder. 'DFC and Bar, DFC and DSO, DFM, DSO and Bar, Christ, look, this bloke's got two DFCs *and* he's a ruddy squadron leader! What do you think it means, sir?'

'Haven't a clue, Corporal.' Quentin replied innocently. But he knew tongues were already wagging.

Early on the fourth day, he was at his desk, wading through the latest batch of files, when a round-faced officer burst through the door.

'Where's Whitworth! I need . . . Christ, what the hell happened to you?'

'Oh, er, bit of trouble, sir. Last year. Wellington. Fuel fire thing . . .'

'Bloody Wimpys, high time they sorted that fuel system out. What outfit?'

'57 Squadron.'

'I heard about you!' The man grinned. 'Credo, isn't it? You did a bloody fine job.'

'Thank you, sir, although . . .'

Whitworth entered. 'Ah, Guy, there you are. I see you've found our intelligence officer. Quentin, have you met Wing Commander Gibson? He's X Squadron's CO.'

'Good to meet you, Credo.' Gibson held out a hand, then quickly offered the other. Just twenty-four, short and portly, he had a youthful face and dark wavy hair. 'Intelligence, you say? Good luck with that, we've got rumours coming out of our ears. In fact we must put a stop to them before they get out of hand.'

'Yes, sir, I've been giving it thought. Some sort of cover-story perhaps . . .'

'Good idea, let me know.' He turned to Whitworth. 'Sir, I came to see you about the crews. I'm still several pilots short.'

'Perhaps we can help.' Whitworth suggested. 'Quentin, you have the files?'

They gathered round Quentin's desk and began poring over names. Gibson, it seemed to him, as well as being lively and enthusiastic, appeared tightly wound, impatient with detail, and apt to make quick decisions. But some jumpiness was understandable, he conceded, for Gibson, one of the youngest wing commanders in the Service, had just completed his third tour of operations with Bomber Command. A staggering total of 172 missions.

'So, I've got Hopgood, Shannon and Burpee from my old unit, 106 Squadron,' he said after a few minutes. 'Then from 97 Squadron I've got Munro, Maltby and McCarthy, who are all good chaps. Who's on the list here from 57 Squadron?'

'Rice and Astell, sir,' Quentin offered. 'Both pilots I can vouch for.'

'Good. Anyone else from 57?'

'Young has come forward, he'd make a fine addition.'

'Dinghy Young, yes, I know him. Good. Who else?'

'We've a couple of possibles from 50 Squadron, two from 49, one each from 207 and 467, and one from 61 . . .'

'Only one? What's the matter with them?'

'Not sure, sir, Barlow, his name is, Australian I believe.' Quentin fingered the 61 Squadron file. One more possible contender was coming to mind.

'So how many's that in all?'

Whitworth totted names. 'Looks like sixteen definites, plus a handful of probables.'

'Sixteen? I need twenty-one *and* a couple of spares!'

'I'm sure more will come forward in due course, Guy.'

'That's not good enough, I need them now!'

To Quentin's surprise a fist hit the table. Gibson, he was learning, was not just impatient, but positively volatile. Whitworth was his superior, not some lackey to be shouted at, but Gibson seemed oblivious, and Whitworth unconcerned, as with a wink to Quentin he went on studying the lists. Silence fell, as the three men considered. The problem was that having padded X Squadron with pilots from his own coterie of favourites, Gibson had no more names to offer. And was beginning to get desperate. And impulsive.

'What about you, Credo?' he suggested suddenly. 'You're a good egg. Are you checked out on the Lanc?'

'Me? I, well, ah, unfortunately not, sir, although I'd like nothing better . . .'

'Quentin's off ops.' Whitworth patted his shoulder. 'Until this hand of his gets fixed. Anyway he's doing far too valuable a job here. Look, Guy, why don't you give us a couple of hours to ring round, I'm sure we can come up with more names.'

'All right.' Gibson looked dazed. 'All right, yes, sir, thank you, I've got to see the engineers anyway. Anything you can do. Greatly appreciated . . .'

And with that he departed.

'Christ.' Whitworth breathed, when he'd gone. 'Talk about a firebrand!'

'Yes, sir. Not quite what I expected.'

'That's why Harris picked him. He gets things done, no matter whose toes he treads on. And he is under monumental pressure, of course. Fancy trying to put a whole squadron together in a week. Madness, I say. Now, Quentin, what about this pilot shortfall. Any ideas?'

'What are his qualifying criteria, sir?'

'5 Group chaps of course. They must have flown at least one full tour, preferably more, have a sound record, be bang up to date on the Lancaster, and be gung-ho press-on types like him. Also . . .' Whitworth added uneasily, '. . . he prefers them to be officers.'

'Why?'

'He gets on with them better.'

'I see. Quite a tall order, then.'

'Indeed. Anyone spring to mind?'

Quentin fingered his files. 'One name, sir. Possibly.'

Tess searched her handbag for the slip of paper Quentin had given her. Something about a new service, he'd said, offering free advice to civilians. She found the note, written in his lopsided scrawl. Citizens Aid Bureaux, the service was called, set up like mobile clinics, in schools, church halls, even pubs. Lincoln's was in the Town Hall, the note said, every Wednesday afternoon.

The hall was packed. Women mostly, she observed, and their children, running noisily in and out of the waiting queues. At one end trestle tables had been set up, behind which sat the 'advisers' – local dignitaries and businesspeople usually, Quentin had said, Tess also saw a woman from the Red Cross among them. She took her place in line. Around her women gossiped animatedly, or nagged their children, or just stood in pensive silence. Most of their inquiries, it emerged, apart from worries about hire-purchase payments or an overdue gas bill, were to do with missing menfolk – servicemen posted abroad, airmen taken prisoner, or simply errant boyfriends. One girl, barely eighteen and heavily pregnant, told Tess she hadn't heard from her gunner husband in six months. 'Posted to Malta, then I never 'eard a thing,' she complained. 'He don't even know we're having a baby.'

An hour passed, the line crawled, Tess began to fret. She was due on shift at the NAAFI at six, before that, tea with Brendan, something he didn't like her to miss. Although he'd been unusually understanding of late, she reflected, solicitous even. Since Peter had come and gone. She wondered if he had any inkling of the phone calls that had passed between them.

Still the line inched too slowly forward. She checked her watch, and was about to admit defeat when three people ahead suddenly had the same thought, gave up and left. Ten minutes later she was seated before the woman from the Red Cross.

'Now then, and how can I help?' the woman began, after taking Tess's details.

'I'm trying to find a baby. Well, a little girl, now, she'd be six. Just six.'

'I see. What's her name?'

'I have no idea. She was taken for adoption. Shortly after birth.'

'By whom?'

'I don't know that either.'

'So, is this a missing-persons inquiry?'

'Well . . .' Tess shifted on her chair. 'I suppose not, not exactly.'

'But you want to find her. Even though she's not missing.'

'That's right.'

'Do you have some idea where she might be? An address perhaps?'

'No. Although somewhere in Cheshire, possibly.'

'Cheshire!'

'That's where she was born.'

'And lives now?'

'I don't know.'

The woman tucked loose hair under her cap. Her eyes were bloodshot, she looked tired and harassed. 'Look, I'm sorry, Mrs, er, Murray, but I'm not following this. You want to find a girl who was possibly adopted some six years ago. But you have absolutely no information about her, except that she was born in Cheshire. And isn't missing . . .'

'I am her mother,' Tess said quietly. 'Her natural mother, do you see? I was sixteen, and unmarried. She was taken from me without my consent. I'd like to find her. And make sure she's all right, and that she's healthy and happy. Do you understand now?'

The woman shuffled papers. 'I think I'm beginning to.'

More followed, but it was soon clear the Red Cross did not routinely involve itself in such unpalatable matters, and in any case had limited knowledge of adoption laws and procedures. In the end the woman's sole piece of advice to Tess was to write to the council in the borough where the baby was born, the address for which, she added coolly, could be found from telephone directories in the library. Tess thanked her and rose to leave.

'There is one thing I do know, however,' the woman added.

'Yes?'

'An unmarried mother of sixteen. They wouldn't need your consent. Not legally, that is. To take the baby. They'd get that from your parents.'

She wandered to the bus stop, cheeks hot from the woman's disdain – as though her misfortune was only what she deserved. By the time she arrived at Scampton, dusk was falling. She showed her pass and made for the married quarters. As she mounted the steps to their rooms, she saw light glowing under the door.

'Ah, Tess, love, there you are.' Murray closed his notebook and rose from the table. 'Been down in town, have you?'

'Just to the library. And a little shopping.'

She had neither books nor goods, but if he noticed he gave no sign. 'You look all fagged out, girl, let me fix you a cuppa. Kettle's just boiled.'

'I should get on with your tea. There's brisket left over.'

'Nonsense, I'll grab something later. You just sit yourself down now.'

'Are you going out?'

'Chief groundsman's work is never done, you know. Especially with this new mob arriving, it's like the whole place has gone mad. They want to get flying right away, apparently, so it's all hands to the pumps. Thank God the weather's been dry, I say. And I've got new pigeons to sort, too.'

She allowed him to steer her to a chair, then watched as he busied himself with teapot and milk. He'd tidied up a little. Their quarters, a lounge-kitchenette with bedroom, were looking almost presentable. His wire-bound notebook lay on the table. It contained his lists of jobs to be done, and notes about grass-seed and tractor-oil and pigeon-feed and inches of rainfall. And details of the bets he took from men on the station, which he thought she didn't know about. Along with the little black-market fiddles for whisky and cigarettes. His war diary, he called it, and carried it everywhere.

'Have you heard the latest crack,' he said, 'about their new CO?'

'No. What about him?'

'Utterly priceless.' He placed her teacup, and pocketed his notebook. 'The t'ing is, half the new boys arriving here don't have full uniforms, right, it all being such a rush and everything. So one of our busybody MPs starts writing them up for being improperly dressed. Then he takes the list to their CO, this fellow Gibson, and tells him seventy-five of his men are on a charge. Gibson goes raving spare, tears a strip off the MP, rips up the list, then throws the poor beggar out. Then he phones Stores and orders them to issue new uniforms for every man jack. Can't be done, Stores says, because we don't have 'em. It will be done, says Gibson, or you're for Iceland. Next morning, full parade, every single man's in proper uniform. Incredible no? I tell you, he's something special, that one.'

'Phyllis at the NAAFI says they're getting special Lancs too. Not ordinary ones.'

'That Phyllis talks too much. And where would she hear a t'ing like that?'

'Her husband's working in Hangar 2. He heard it from one of their fitters.'

'Then he should know to keep quiet about it. Careless talk costs lives. Even between husband and wife.'

He stood behind her, his big hands resting on her shoulders. 'I mean, take you and me, for instance. Now, I wouldn't go telling anyone your secrets, would I? And you wouldn't go telling anyone mine. Would you girl?'

'Secrets?' She felt his fingers on her neck, stroking, squeezing, encircling. 'No Bren, of course not.'

'That's right.' But still he stayed behind her, still his fingers squeezed. Tess felt her heart bumping, and terror rising in her throat. Seconds passed, the kitchen clock ticked, outside a distant Tannoy squawked.

At last the fingers left her. 'Good girl. Now, you take it easy and that's an order, I don't want you tiring yourself out. I'll pop in the NAAFI later, and make sure you're all right.' He kissed her head, and left the room.

She stayed at the table, listening to the metallic thud of his footfall receding down the steps and across the yard. Then she lowered her head into her hands. And held them there until the shaking stopped.

A little later she rose and retrieved her handbag, then went to the sideboard drawer where she kept her Post Office book and personal papers, and searching deep within, withdrew a ribbon-tied bundle. Loosening the ribbon she arranged the five birthday cards in a semicircle on the table, in order, cheerful celebrations designed with balloons and streamers and clowns and kittens and numbers with captions: '1 today!', 'Now you are 2!', 'Look I am 3!' Then she took out the new card she'd bought that afternoon and added it to the array. 'A girl of 6!' it proclaimed, picturing a little girl sitting on a pony.

Then she knelt on the floor before the cards, and gazed at

them in silence, until they began to melt and blur before her eyes.

'Happy birthday, my darling angel,' she wept.

'Why are we going back to the station, Uncle?' Peter asked, following MacDowell down Argyle Street.

'You'll see, laddie. Come along, keep up.'

'Yes, but it's hours until my train goes. Isn't it?'

'We're not going for your train. We're going to meet someone else's.'

'Really?' Peter hurried to catch up. 'Who?'

'I said, you'll see. Now get a move on, we're wasting valuable drinking time.'

'Indeed we are.' Although he'd had enough. Hours ago. Glasgow was wonderful, he decided, lively and friendly and full of terrific pubs, most of which they'd visited. As they had many other interesting places, such as the cathedral and the winter gardens and even the concert hall. But they'd been walking all day and drinking all day, and now Glasgow was rainy, and dark, and rather grimy, and he was exhausted, having slept barely a wink on the sleeper, which wasn't a sleeper at all but an overcrowded troop train full of shouting squaddies. And though catching his next train to Inverness was the last thing he wanted, he was beginning to yearn for a few hours' respite.

Respite was not on the agenda. Barely had they entered the station when a familiar Antipodean whoop echoed through the rafters. A moment later Kiwi Garvey's grinning face appeared above the throng, closely followed by Billy Bimson and Herb Guttenberg.

'Good God, it's the three musketeers!' Peter exclaimed, gripping their hands. 'What on earth are you doing here?'

113

'Come to see you two, of course! Think we'd miss out on a booze-up?'

'You're early, lads,' MacDowell grinned. 'But we forgive you. Right, first stop the station buffet.'

Half an hour and two pints later, the five were deeply ensconced. Herb and Billy, it emerged, having survived the rest-camp in Wales, were now kicking their heels at a tran-shipment centre in Liverpool, awaiting a troopship back to Canada.

'Weeks, they said, it might be.' Billy explained. 'So when we heard from Uncle that you were coming to Glasgow, we thought what the hell, and wangled a two-day pass!'

And also contacted Garvey, Herb added, who was similarly in limbo, pending repatriation to New Zealand, and a new life as a gunnery instructor.

'You must be excited, Kiwi,' Peter said, a little later. 'To be going home at last.'

'Too right.' Kiwi stared into his glass. 'Can't wait.'

'You could apply for that transfer to the Navy.' Despite the fog of alcohol, Peter couldn't shake the impression his crewmates seemed subdued.

'I might just do that.'

'What about you, Herb? Home to Canada? I bet you can't wait.'

'No,' Herb agreed. 'I can't. Although . . .'

'Although what?'

The men eyed each other, unable to say the unsayable. So Uncle said it for them.

'They think it doesn't feel right.'

'Well, it doesn't!' Billy said vehemently. 'We came here to do a job. Now they're sending us home before it's done.'

'Yes, it feels like . . . unfinished business.'

'Unfinished business, that's it!'

Peter nodded. It was exactly as he felt. And earlier, sitting on a bench in the winter gardens, Uncle had voiced similar thoughts. There's nothing for me now, laddie, he'd said sadly. With the flying over and Mary gone, there's nothing left for me now.

Peter glanced at his friends. 'I have a daughter. I only just found out.'

Incredulous stares were exchanged. 'What?'

'Years ago. With a girl. My best friend. Someone I grew up with. We lost touch . . .'

'The one you kept muttering about!' Kiwi sat forward. 'In the liferaft that night! Bess, isn't it?'

'Tess, yes, that's her. We met up again. Finally, after all this time. Now they're sending me to Lossiemouth.'

'Typical.' Silence fell as they considered. 'Bloody war.'

'I met a girl.' Billy added thoughtfully. 'Last week in Liverpool.'

'And?'

'Very nice. Name of Daisy. Unfortunately she's a prostitute.'

More incredulous stares. 'Is that it?'

'Well. Yes.'

'Christ.' Kiwi shook his head. 'Another pearl of wisdom from the mad Canuck!'

'Kiwi, I've warned you before about . . .'

'I vote . . .' Uncle raised his glass. 'Instead of all this carping and moping, I vote we count our lucky stars.'

'What?'

'We came through, didn't we? We're alive, all seven of us, while hundreds, thousands, never made it. That's a miracle, and we should thank the good Lord for it, count our blessings, and drink to absent loved ones!'

'Good idea.'

'Hear hear.'

'Lucky stars!'

'Absent loved ones!'

'Unfinished business!'

As their mood lifted and the beer flowed, a full-blown party ensued, the five carousing their way through a succession of pubs and bars. Soon Peter was blissfully intoxicated once more, cocooned by his friends, safely anaesthetised from the realities of his predicament, if only for a while.

Then he remembered his train. 'Jesus, what's the time?'

Uncle squinted at his watch. 'Time to go!'

They ran through rain-splashed streets, arriving breathlessly at the station with scant minutes to spare. Peter immediately set off in search of his platform, but strong arms stopped him. 'Not yet, laddie.'

'What?'

'One more mission!'

Telephone booths lined the concourse. Hurrying noisily towards them, Billy and Herb requisitioned one, while Peter was squashed into the next with Uncle and Kiwi. Loose change was fumbled from pockets, scraps of paper produced, and numbers dialled. Then cheers were echoing across the station, as for a miraculous few moments Peter's entire crew was reunited. And though he could barely hear Chalkie and Jamie above the excited shouts of his comrades, he heard them well enough to sense their kinship, and feel their warmth, and to return it, and to join with them all in singing 'I'm Forever Blowing Bubbles'. Then the Tannoy was announcing his train, and the phone calls hurriedly ending, and Uncle and the others were carrying him, shoulder-high, like a goal-scorer at a football match, across the concourse to his platform.

Where two military policemen waited.

'Oops,' said Billy.

'Crikey, it's the red-caps.'

'Well now,' one MP said dourly. 'And what have we got here?'

'Disorderly airmen, looks like,' said the other. 'Horrible to behold.'

Uncle stepped unsteadily forward. 'Sorry gents, just letting off a little steam.'

'Um, my train . . .' Peter mumbled, pointing at the gate.

'Not so fast, *sir*.' The first MP produced a notebook.

'But I must . . . It's leaving . . .'

'And I said, wait!' He thumbed pages. 'So, which one of you reprobates is Lightfoot?'

Peter froze. 'Pardon?'

'Are you deaf as well as English? I said *Light-foot*. Flying Officer Peter Lightfoot.'

'Well, that's me, yes. But my train . . .'

'You won't be needing it. Here, sign this, then clear off the lot of you.'

Peter signed, the MP handed him an envelope, he sliced it open, the others crowding round.

'Bugger me.'

'I don't believe it.'

'Wow! Count me in!'

'Me too.'

'Yes, but it just says Lightfoot. What does that mean, Peter?'

But Peter was beyond speech. Slowly his knees sank, until he was sitting cross-legged on the ground, staring in amazed disbelief at the telegram in his hand.

IMMEDIATE TO F/O PJ LIGHTFOOT STOP REPORT RAF SCAMPTON LINCS W/CDR GP GIBSON OC 617 SQUADRON IMMEDIATE STOP SIGNED AVM RA COCHRANE OC 5 GROUP RAF BOMBER COMMAND ENDS.

'Blimey, sent by Cochrane himself no less.'
'Must be important, then.'
'And who's 617 Squadron? I've never heard of 'em.'
'You have now.'

Two hundred miles away to the south, Charles Whitworth mounted the steel steps above Scampton's deserted Number 2 hangar, and traversed the long corridor of offices, feet echoing, until he reached the only one with a light showing.

'Hello Guy,' he said. 'Burning the midnight oil, I see.'

Gibson looked up. 'Hello, sir. Yes, I'm afraid so. Trying to keep on top of things.'

'Succeeding?'

'I'll let you know!'

Whitworth nodded. 'I've brought you the finished aircrew lists. Quentin did well, don't you think, drumming up the extra pilots?'

'Yes he did, thanks. Looks as if we're almost there.'

'Not all are as experienced as we'd like, but still some excellent names.'

'We'll manage.' Gibson forced a tired smile. 'We have to.'

'I know. And I'm sure you will.' Whitworth, face serious, produced a second sheet. 'Now, Guy, I know you're overloaded, and I hate to add to your burden, but this came through from the Ministry an hour ago.'

'What is it?'

'Well, it seems they're giving you 617 Squadron now.'

'What!' Gibson looked aghast. 'Who the bloody hell are *they*? And where, for Christ's sake?'

Whitworth grinned. '*They* are X Squadron, and they are right here in this hangar. Congratulations, Guy, it's your new number. You're official.'

It was the third week of March.

Chapter 5

Quentin straightened from the Elsan toilet, eyes smarting from the chemical disinfectant sloshing about within. Never, he cursed furiously to himself, never in more than two hundred flying hours had he been sick in an aeroplane before, no matter how rough the conditions, nor how stomach-turning the action. Until now. His humiliation was complete, or so he believed, glancing guiltily about. Yet he saw no one. The Lancaster was almost surreally empty, thundering through the afternoon air like a ghost-ship. The dustbin-shaped Elsan was at the back of the fuselage, just forward of the rear gunner's turret, in full view of anyone who happened to be about. But nobody was, fortuitously, or perhaps they were just being polite. Normally the upper gunner would be there, suspended from his turret in the roof, but the turret was unmanned, with Bimson, its gunner, moved to the nose, so the bomb aimer, the big New Zealander everyone called Kiwi, could concentrate on other matters. So too the rear turret, whose doors were tactfully closed. Quentin gazed nauseously at the turret, a Frazer-Nash FN20, identical to the one carried in the Wellington. With four Browning machine-guns, and two sliding doors. And an external hydraulic supply mounted on the bulkhead. Complete with wire-locked override valve. The Lancaster lurched in turbulence, bile rose suddenly in his throat, a second later he was doubling over the Elsan once more. And in that moment he knew it wasn't air-sickness he was suffering from. It was terror.

And the flight had seemed such a good idea. 'I'd like to come on one of your practice sorties,' he'd said to Peter Lightfoot, who owed him a sackful of favours for getting him and his crew assigned to 617 Squadron. 'See what you chaps get up to all day.' Whitworth liked the idea too, a golden opportunity to assess Gibson's training regime, he said. But what Quentin hadn't told either man was his main reason for going on the flight. Which was to see if his nerves could stand it.

Now he had his answer. He raised his head wearily from the bowl, only to find the rear turret doors had opened.

'You don't look so good, Lieutenant!' a grinning face shouted. 'Everything okay?'

'Fine thanks. Just something I ate.'

'Sure.' Herb Guttenberg held out a bag. 'Barley sugar. I find it helps.'

'Thanks.' Quentin accepted the sweet. 'Do you get sick, Sergeant?'

'Used to. First tour. The Whitley was terrible for that. Not any more.'

Quentin rose unsteadily to his feet. First tour, he pondered. This baby-faced Canadian, Guttenberg his name was, had flown two full tours. Voluntarily. And was now signed up for this latest madcap venture, voluntarily again, without even knowing what it was. As though it didn't matter, as long as he was with his friends. Amazing. Quentin waved a grateful parting and set off up the fuselage.

In fact they were all amazing, these 617 crews, he'd decided over the last two weeks. On the ground, just disparate gaggles of boozing, bickering, fool-about rascals of all shapes, sizes and backgrounds – ordinary, unremarkable, rather immature sometimes. But put them together in their aeroplanes, and they were magically transformed into something extraordinary, something polished and exact and smooth-running, like a bejewelled watch, or some fantastic seven-faceted machine, efficient and dependable, and precision-engineered with just one function in mind. To wreak havoc on the enemy. Then they landed, tumbled out of their aeroplanes and went back to being rascals again.

He ducked round the vacant upper turret, continuing forward to the first obstacle in his path, the three-foot step up onto the roof of the Lancaster's thirty-foot bomb-bay. Once up, it was forward again, stooping now, past the rest-area which consisted of a fold-down cot where a man might lie, until he reached an even greater barrier. This was the main spar, the boxed-in girder supporting the Lancaster's vast wings. The noise and vibration here were indescribable, mind-numbingly loud, far worse than the Wellington – the whole airframe shuddered from four roaring Merlins, each with the power of 1500 galloping horses. Quentin shut his mind to the din and struggled on. Beyond the spar lay the forward fuselage, the rest of the crew, and relative normalcy, but to reach them he had to bend almost double, squeeze through a gap between spar and roof, and drop down the other side. Awkward enough for an unencumbered man in light clothing, but for a fully-suited crewman bundled in flying clothes, parachute harness, oxygen mask and life-vest, and with only one good arm, practically impossible. Halfway through he lost balance and slipped. As he did so a hand shot out and grabbed him.

'Whoops there, Lieutenant!' Chalkie White leaned over from his wireless station. 'Mind the step!'

Quentin quickly recovered. 'Oh, er, missed my footing, damn clumsy, thanks . . .'

'My pleasure. Feeling any better?'

'I'm feeling fine, thank you, Sergeant! I just went aft to check on the rear gunner. Who is also fine. Ah, so, how's it going up here now?'

Chalkie turned to his console, wedged into the left side of the fuselage. 'Still a cock-up, if you ask me. We can't talk to Barlow's Lanc except by flashing messages with an Aldis lamp, and we can't send or receive command broadcasts from base because we're at 150 feet, which is far too low to receive anything.'

'I see. What about Carter. Any sign?'

'Nope. He was supposed to rendezvous with us and Barlow south of Bridlington, then fly to Derwent together. Barlow made it all right, but Carter never showed up. Got lost again, I expect. Hardly surprising, what with all these technical problems.'

'They are working on them, you know. The boffins. Everything will get fixed, in good time, I'm sure of it.'

'I bloody hope so, or this little caper could turn into a right balls-up.'

'Indeed.'

'Whatever it is.'

'Yes.'

'Such as sinking the *Tirpitz*?'

Quentin smiled. 'I wouldn't know, Sergeant. I'm only an intelligence officer.'

A few paces forward of the radio-operator's station was the navigator's cubicle, which for some reason was completely enclosed by a curtain, even though it was broad daylight. Quentin lifted a corner and saw that the navigator, Johnson, was deeply engrossed, hunched over what appeared to be an unravelling roll of toilet paper with lines and symbols drawn on it. Navigating at low level was proving almost as problematic as radio communications, he'd learned: with aeroplanes covering a mile every fifteen seconds, landmarks and turning-points were flashing by too fast to be identified. So 617's navigators were having to evolve new methods of finding their way, including using hand-drawn paper-roll maps, and the bomb aimer in the nose to act as their eyes. And all with only varying success, Quentin knew, with more than one crew getting lost, to the fury of 617's squadron commander.

He lowered the curtain, and stepped onto the flight deck itself. Peter and his flight engineer had their backs to him, Peter in the big pilot's seat to the left, the engineer MacDowell on the fold-down seat beside him. Both, like the navigator, were oblivious to his presence, deeply immersed in the job at hand, and thankfully so, Quentin thought, because the job at hand involved flying the Lancaster at 250 mph, at barely treetop height, over hilly Yorkshire countryside, in close formation with a second Lancaster. Whilst wearing blacked-out goggles. Spellbound by the speed, the contour-hugging motion, the hurtling green blur around him, Quentin edged behind Peter's seat and plugged in his intercom. Instantly his head filled with the calm but insistent tones of the New Zealand bomb aimer, lying in his Perspex blister in the nose.

'Small river coming in left to right. Copse of trees three o'clock. Village with church two miles eleven o'clock. Hill with ruin coming up beyond it. Line of pylons just below peak. That's the next turning-point, right Jamie?'

'Yes, it is. Okay, Pilot, turn left heading two-two-oh degrees, Derwent reservoir should then be straight ahead, about eight miles, watch out for town of Dunford, and caution Margery Hill to left, which rises to eight hundred . . .'

'Pylons! Jesus pull up, Pilot, pull up NOW!'

Reflexively Peter hauled back on the controls, MacDowell rammed the throttles wide, and Quentin stared in breathless awe as the Lancaster soared skyward, engines screaming. Seconds ticked, the aeroplane strained, clouds beckoned, then came Guttenberg's voice from the tail. 'Pylons cleared!'

Immediately Peter bore downward once more, eyes fixed to the windscreen as he forced the Lancaster back to ground level. 'Height, Uncle,' he called.

'Down, laddie.' MacDowell throttled back the engines, one eye on the altimeter. 'Down more. Three hundred feet. Now two fifty, down a little more, that's it, two hundred, down a little more, good, here it comes, hold it there, that's it one fifty feet spot-on.'

The Lancaster gradually settled once more into its terrain-hugging roller-coaster ride. Silence fell on the intercom. Then Peter spoke.

'Steady on two-two-oh degrees, Navigator, Derwent reservoir in sight. Sorry everyone, that was a bit close.'

'You're telling me!'

'Say, well spotted those pylons, Billy.'

'Couldn't miss the durn things. Even with these God-awful goggles.'

'Aye, they'll need to come up with something better for night-vision training.'

'And something better for navigating.'

'And radio communications.'

'And keeping the nose gunner's bloody feet out of the bomb aimer's ears!'

'Sorry, Kiwi, but there's nowhere to put them . . .'

'Say, where did Barlow go?'

Eyes peered outboard for the second Lancaster. 'I think he veered off, no wait, there he is! Christ, look, he's lost his trailing aerial, must have snagged it on something.'

They all watched as Barlow's machine, minus aerial, edged back into formation.

'Say, fellas . . .' Guttenberg commented from the tail. 'Would you say this operation is getting just a tad dangerous?'

'I think you could safely say that, Herb.'

A pause. 'Whatever it is!'

They flew back to base without further incident, completing a four-hour training sortie that began with an eighty-mile leg over the North Sea, then a rendezvous with two Lancasters which became a rendezvous with one, followed by a formation cross-country to Derwent reservoir, several low-level runs over the reservoir, a third navigational leg to the bombing range at Wainfleet, and low-level attacks there using dummy bombs, before finally flying back to Scampton. On that last leg, to Quentin's surprise, Peter offered him the pilot's seat. And to Quentin's further surprise, when he settled into that seat, and his left hand gripped the control column, and his feet found the rudders, and the huge bomber began responding to his touch and movement, he found that all fear left him, his nausea was forgotten and calmness enveloped him like a blanket, as though waking from a nightmare. And even if he was sweat-soaked and trembling with effort within minutes, and even if his useless right hand refused to grip the controls, so Uncle MacDowell had to operate the trim-wheels, and the throttles, and the flap selector, and pretty much everything, and even though this meant he might never fly again operationally, those few minutes were magically cathartic, bringing him acceptance, and healing, and clarity, and even a form of hope.

Afterwards, walking back to dispersal, the entire crew pronounced the mission a success, despite the technical difficulties.

Guy Gibson pronounced it something else.

'Useless!' he roared. 'Completely bloody useless, the whole lot of you!'

They were assembled in the briefing room, all twenty-two crews, a total of 154 men, to receive their leader's ire. The general thrust of which, Quentin gathered, was that because 617 Squadron had only ten borrowed Lancasters to train with, they had to be nursed, and used wisely, and taken care of. That afternoon all ten had been dispatched on training flights. But two had come back on three engines, two more gave up after getting lost, one had intercom failure and called it a day, one returned with engine-intakes stuffed with foliage, Barlow's came back minus an aerial, and one didn't come back at all.

'That was Carter,' Gibson growled angrily. 'He phoned a while ago. From Manchester. His navigator made another error, they ended up flying in circles, then ran low on fuel.' He broke off, pacing the floor. Around the room everyone waited in wary silence. Quentin did a quick head-count. Not twenty-two crews present, he realised. In fact, not even twenty-one.

'Carter said he'd be home in a couple of hours,' Gibson was saying. 'I told him to leave his navigator behind, because he was sacked. Carter said if his navigator was sacked, then his whole crew was sacked. I told him to make his choice. So he made it, and they're gone. Off the squadron.'

Shocked murmurs circled the room, airmen glanced around uneasily, yet astonishingly there was more. A second crew had failed to fly, Gibson added, for three days in succession because of various mystery illnesses. 617 had no time for illnesses, he said, real or imagined, so they too were off the squadron. Which left just twenty crews. To fix all the problems, finish training, adapt to new aircraft, and fly the mission.

Whatever it was.

'Can't you tell us anything, Guy?' one of his inner circle, Maltby, asked a few minutes later. Oddly, following news of the sackings, the mood in the room had lifted.

'Sorry, chaps, I can't. But I can tell you this. We've been brought together to do a special job. If we get it right, the result could be spectacular. I'm told it might even shorten the war. But to get it right we must practise low flying, day and night, until we can do it blindfold. Over land, and water.'

'So it is a ship then!' another stalwart, Hopgood, quipped.

'Maybe, Hoppy.' Gibson grinned, glancing at Quentin. 'You won't get it from me.' Then he became serious again, studying the floor, hands on hips. 'What you will get is this. Two things will decide the success or failure of this operation. Training and secrecy. We've already talked about training, but that's only half the battle. If we train well *and* surprise the enemy, then everything will be fine. But if they're ready for us, it'll be a bloody disaster, no matter how well trained we are. That's why you must all shut up about the mission. Stop asking, stop speculating, stop the rumour-mongering. Right now. Don't discuss it with anyone, not colleagues, not wives, not girlfriends, not even your crewmates. And for God's sake stop everyone else in the squadron talking about it, too.'

'That's all very well, boss, but how?' someone else asked. 'We're already getting stick from the 57 Squadron boys, calling us lazy bastards because we never fly ops. All we do is train. They know something's up. Everyone does!'

Whitworth had entered the back of the hall, Quentin saw. Together with two men in suits. Somehow he sensed trouble. Sure enough, while Gibson was repeating his tirade about secrecy, Whitworth signalled him. A minute later he was outside.

'Quentin, these gentlemen are squadron leaders Arnott and Campbell.' Whitworth introduced, a little stiffly. 'From Intelligence Section, the Air Ministry, you know.' Greetings were murmured, left hands shaken, Arnott was short and stocky, Campbell taller and leaner with a high forehead and swept-back hair. Neither seemed like an airman, Quentin felt, despite their apparent ranks. And why no uniforms? he wondered.

'You're the SIO?' Arnott eyed him dubiously.

'That's right, sir. Although, only acting SIO, strictly speaking.'

'Do you know the target for this operation?'

'I'm sorry?'

'You heard. The target, do you know it?'

'No, sir. Of course not. Hardly anybody does.'

'Correct. Let's walk.' Leaving Whitworth outside the briefing room, they set off across the field, the two men flanking Quentin, as though frogmarching him. Dusk was falling, the April evening cool, the dew-laden grass whispering rhythmically beneath their shoes. They kept on marching, nobody spoke, and soon they were hundreds of yards into the open. Only then, having triple-checked they were out of all earshot, did they stop.

Campbell lit a cigarette. 'You've done all right, Lieutenant. Up to now.'

'Thank you, sir.'

'It can't have been easy, with that hand, and everything.'

'The hand's not a problem, sir.' Why was he speaking in the past tense? Quentin wondered.

Arnott glanced around again, just to be sure. 'So. Using *Tirpitz* as a cover story. That was your idea?'

'Well, yes, sir, I suppose it was.'

'How did you know it wasn't the real target?'

'I checked the idea with Group Captain Whitworth and Wing Commander Gibson. If *Tirpitz* was the real target, I knew they'd never approve it.'

'A reasonable deduction. But they did approve it.'

'Yes. They approved it, and I went from there.'

'How?'

'I beg your pardon?'

'How did you promulgate the story. How did you put it about, in other words, that the target was the battleship *Tirpitz*?'

'Well actually, I didn't. People just began to assume it. I merely didn't contradict them. Too strongly, that is.'

'Very ingenious.'

'Thank you, sir. I call it rumour management.'

'How droll. When did it start?'

'What? Oh, almost immediately. Within a few days of the squadron forming, *Tirpitz* had become the buzz-word. Why, is something wrong?'

They didn't reply, but stepped aside to confer. Quentin waited, still clutching his flying helmet and gloves. The German battleship *Tirpitz*, currently hiding in a Norwegian fjord, had been a thorn in the Allies' side for years. One of Germany's biggest capital ships, its firepower, speed and location were a deadly threat to vital northern shipping routes. Several attempts had been made to attack it, or flush it into the open, but well hidden, ringed with mines and torpedo nets, and massively defended by anti-aircraft guns, no one had yet got near it. Effectively imprisoned in its fjord, it was nevertheless a potent and ever-present danger. Most at 617 Squadron, not unreasonably, assumed it to be the target of their mission.

Arnott and Campbell finished conferring. 'Thank you, Lieutenant, that will be all.'

'All?'

'You're being relieved of your responsibilities as station intelligence officer.'

'Have I done something wrong?'

'Not at all. It's just that the job is too big for one rather junior, part-time officer.'

'Yes, but . . .'

'With disabilities.' Arnott added.

'Sir! I really must protest . . .'

'. . . And a liking for ether.'

Quentin gaped, speechless with shock.

'It's all right, Lieutenant.' Campbell went on. 'We know what you've been through. And you're still on the team. It's just a much bigger team now, and much more specialised. We're going to tap phone calls, mail will be opened and checked, everyone issued with security passes, fingerprints taken, perimeter guards deployed and so on. It's a major operation. So we're taking over.'

'I see.' Easing him out, in other words. Casting him aside. 'But why? I mean why all the extra security, suddenly?'

'Because, Lieutenant, 617's mission is too important to fail. Mainly.'

'Well, of course, but . . .'

'So we want you to carry on with your duties. In the interests of continuity, you understand. But more as an observer, if you like.'

'An observer.'

'That's right. In fact we're sending you to Kent tomorrow, with Group Captain Whitworth. It'll be interesting, I can assure you.'

'I see. What's the other reason?'

'What other reason?'

'You said the extra security was because 617's mission was too important to fail, *mainly*. What's the other reason?'

The men glanced at each other.

'I have a right to know.'

'No, you don't. But since you ask, *Tirpitz* is being moved.'

Quentin felt a chill. 'What?'

'Resistance operatives in Norway have confirmed it. The Germans are moving *Tirpitz*. From its base in Narvik to a new base in Altafjord, hundreds of miles north.'

'But why? I mean after all this time, why now suddenly?'

Then he realised why.

The Germans had learned of a plan to attack it.

Quentin's car was a 1938 MGTA, a neat sports two-seater, glossy black with red leather trim, spoked wheels and fold-down roof.

Since his injuries, driving it had been difficult, so the car saw little use. Lending it to Peter for the evening therefore, as a thank-you for his ride in the Lancaster, was of no inconvenience.

It was Tess and Peter's third meeting since his posting to Scampton. The first two, emotionally charged daytime trysts on a bench in the park, served mainly to reconfirm the strength of feeling between them, which was more profound than either had realised. 'I never stopped thinking about you!' Tess wept bitterly during their second meeting. 'I thought I'd lost you for ever.' Peter held her tightly. 'I know. I know.'

By the third assignation, outside the church in Scampton village, they were more organised, and their emotions more controlled. Slightly. As Peter pulled up in the MG, down-shifting inexpertly through the gears, Tess emerged from the shadows.

'All right?' he asked, as she climbed in.

'Yes, I think so.'

'How long have you got?'

'I must be home by ten. Did anyone see you leave?'

'I don't know. Let's hope not.'

'Come on, let's get away from here.'

He reached for the gear-stick, but his hand brushed her arm and suddenly they were embracing, tightly, yearning rising in them again like a tide. 'God, I'm missing you!' she gasped, kissing his neck, his forehead, his eyes. He cupped her cheeks, and buried his face in her hair. Before they could stop, their lips were pressing, and parting, their careful resolutions crumbling to dust as desire overwhelmed them.

Then they pulled apart.

'No,' she panted. 'No, this isn't right.'

'We agreed.'

'That's right.'

'We'll wait.' They stared breathlessly at each other in the darkness. Peter touched her cheek and held her gaze, and saw the hunger in her eyes, the fullness of her lips, and the flush at her throat, and nearly wavered. Then she nodded.

'We can wait. We must.'

They drove out of Scampton, following blacked-out streets until they were clear of Lincoln, and heading east. She straightened her coat, forcing herself to relax. 'What did Quentin say? About using the car.'

'Nothing. I mean, he didn't ask why I wanted it, but I expect he knows.'

'Yes. He's been very good to us.'

'What did you tell Brendan?'

'I'm going to the pictures with Phyllis. I don't know if he believed me, he's terribly suspicious at the moment, about everything.'

'God, I hate this. You're taking so much risk.'

She forced a wan smile. 'It's worth it.'

After five miles they left the main road, following country lanes until they found a village with a quiet-looking pub. Soon they were settled in a corner, drinking half-pints of watery bitter.

'You look tired, Peter. Is everything all right?'

'Yes, I think so. Hard work, pretty flat-out, plenty of problems, and the CO's never satisfied, always tearing someone off a strip. But that's the job, I suppose.'

'How about Uncle and the others?'

'They're fine, doing really well. I'm so lucky.'

'Lucky?'

'Hardly any pilots had their whole crew join with them.'

'That's not luck. It's trust. And friendship.'

'Maybe. I know I couldn't do this without them.' He sipped beer. 'Oh, I nearly forgot, Credo gave me this.'

He handed her an envelope. She slit it, withdrew some sheets of paper and quickly read. 'It's a list of addresses. Regional offices of the Children's Adoption Agency. Pages of them, look! He says they keep records of all adoptions going back to 1924.'

'Even unknown ones?'

'He doesn't say. He says to write with any information about the baby's name, date and place of birth, parents, guardians and so on. Then they might be able to trace her. Assuming she was adopted.' She broke off. 'What does that mean?'

'I don't know. What if she wasn't adopted, I suppose. What if she's still in an orphanage or something?'

They looked at each other. 'Waiting to be adopted!'

'It's possible, isn't it?'

'Yes! God, I must get onto the letters first thing. I'll have to be careful writing them, but Peter, what if we find her?'

'Yes . . .' He hesitated.

'I can't imagine it.'

'Me neither.'

'Peter? What is it?'

'Nothing.' He gazed into his glass. 'Nothing. I was just thinking. About the baby. And Brendan. What he'd do if he found out.'

'Yes,' Tess sighed. 'God knows. He's so unpredictable at the moment. Laughing and joking one minute, angry and morose the next. In and out all hours too, working on the grounds. I never know when to expect him. Or what mood he'll be in.'

'He's feeling the pressure, like everyone. Is he, you know, treating you properly?'

'He gets terribly angry, but mostly at himself. Then he smashes things, crockery and so on. That scares me.'

'Do you think he suspects us?'

'I don't know. He says such strange things. The other night he came in, furious about something. I asked him the matter and he flew off the handle, shouting about how everything was fine until some garden job in Feltwell.'

'What garden job?'

'No idea, a grounds-keeping thing, I suppose. But it wasn't what he said, it was how he said it. White with rage, he was, and staring wildly, as if he didn't know me.'

Peter nodded. At the bar the landlady polished glasses, watching them suspiciously. As if she knew. 'Tess,' he went on quietly, 'I have to ask. Why did you marry him?'

She took his hand. 'Because he was kind, I suppose, at first. And attentive, and made me laugh for the first time in years. And he seemed to offer security, and hope for a future, things I'd long given up on. But it was a mistake, a sham, and I've regretted it ever since. Then the violence started, and it was like . . .'

'What?'

'The final punishment. Only I couldn't take it. And didn't know what to do. Except try to find you.'

He squeezed her hand. 'Thank God you did.'

They talked a while longer, finished their beer then drove home, wrapped in private thought. At the church he switched off and they held one another again, more calmly this time.

'I wish I could get you away from here,' he said at length. 'Right now, that is.'

She patted his hand. 'I'll be careful. Anyway it's you we should be worrying about. Do you still have no idea what it's about?'

'Everyone thinks, you know, the same old rumour. But nobody actually knows, except the CO, and he's told us to stop asking and concentrate on the training. So we're all agreed, Uncle and the boys and me, that's what we're going to do.'

Tess snuggled close. 'Good idea. I'll stop asking too.'

Peter checked his watch. 'Nearly ten, Tess.'

'I know. Just five more minutes.'

'Of course.' He hesitated. 'Can I ask you something?'

'Anything.'

'It's just, I can't imagine . . . I mean, I never saw you, never knew about . . .'

'About what?'

'The baby. Having it. And losing it. What actually happened. What it was like.'

Like dying. Over and again. Or like a nightmare that never fades. One that despite happening years in the past, remains ever-fresh in the present, and will revisit in the future, haunting like a ghost for ever, no matter how hard she blots it from memory.

She leaves for Scotland the morning after the 'incident', all four Derbys crammed in the car together with the holiday baggage. But apart from her brother David, who chats excitedly, there is no holiday spirit, only tight-lipped silence, all the way to the border. The next day they arrive at the manse and still the matter goes unspoken, and as the days pass Tess realises it will remain unspoken, raked over and left to rot like last year's leaves. Two weeks pass. She spends them mostly alone, exploring rock pools on the beach, or walking the scrubby heather, or lying on her bed in her room. Then one evening her mother comes in. Has our friend arrived? she asks, knitting her fingers. But Tess doesn't understand. What friend? At which her mother snaps. You know damn well what friend!

And Tess realises she means her monthly period, which hasn't arrived, and as more days pass and no friend comes, her mother grows angrier, and more tearful, and more religious, going to Mass every day, and carrying a rosary, and praying fervently for their deliverance at mealtimes. One day she takes Tess to the Catholic church and thrusts her into the confessional, saying the Holy Father needs to hear her sin. And Tess tells him, but no salvation comes, and no forgiveness, and no help, and with every passing day she is growing more isolated and afraid. Time slows to a crawl. At night she lies in bed listening to the arguments rising through the floor, in the mornings David keeps asking what the matter is with everyone, all day her mother frets and fumes, while her father shakes his head and steals sad looks at her.

At last the holiday ends, but Tess and her mother don't return to Bexley, they go to stay with her mother's relatives in the northwest, near Anglesey, then others in Prestatyn, then still more in St Helens, moving from one to the next like a grand tour. At each house, her mother arrives full of smiles and bluster, but within a week or two she's wringing her hands and weeping inconsolably, and it's time to move on before suspicions are aroused. Then Tess becomes too pregnant for staying with relatives, so they move into a guest house overlooking the sea at Southport, where they stay a month. By this time her mother hardly speaks at all except to give instructions. Go to your room, get your coat, eat your food, go to your room. Nor does she give Tess money, nor allow her to talk to the other guests, except to say good morning and good night. During the day they have to vacate the guest-house, so spend the endless autumn days walking Southport's blustery prom, or sitting in the rose gardens, or staring vacantly at end-of-season shop windows. Lonely and desperate, Tess makes two attempts to contact Peter at this time, once by postcard, which her mother discovers before she can post it, and once when she creeps downstairs at night to use the guest-house telephone. But the landlady hears it click in her bedroom and comes storming down in slippers and curlers, saying the telephone is not for public use. Then she summons Tess's mother, and tells her they must leave, saying the guest house is highly respectable and no place for good-for-nothing girls in trouble. So next morning her mother pays the bill, and pushes Tess into a taxi, and says that's it, young lady, it's the confinement home for you. Then she makes Tess write to Peter, saying she's gone away and not to try and contact her.

The confinement home is a special wing of a convent outside Chester called St Matilda's. It's where good-for-nothing Catholic girls in trouble go to have their babies. The rooms are freezing, the beds hard, the food foul and the nuns severe. Every day the pregnant girls are roused at dawn and marched to chapel to pray for their souls. Then they sweep out their rooms, which are tiny and damp and featureless like prison cells. Only then are they allowed breakfast, which is runny porridge followed by bread and margarine. All day is spent doing chores, cleaning or laundry or peeling potatoes. Three times a day they go to chapel. Between chapel and chores they attend scripture classes, or lessons about the error of their ways, or tramp round the vegetable garden like convicts. In the evenings they're sent back to their rooms, where Tess lies on her bed listening to the heartfelt sobs of other girls, many poor and uneducated, and some as young as thirteen, or worse still the terrified screams of those going into labour. Winter comes, then Christmas. She receives one card, from her father, expressing his sadness at her predicament, and the hope she is learning a lesson from it. Then comes 1937 and the temperatures plummet. Pipes freeze, breath fogs the air, ice laces the windows, the girls huddle together for warmth and comfort. Unexpected kindness comes from a young novitiate called Doreen, who takes pity on them and smuggles treats of fruit and chocolate. And books for Tess: *Black Beauty*, *Jane Eyre*, *Little Women*. Soon she finds herself reading aloud to the others, to keep their spirits up. Keeping her own spirits up is harder. What's going to happen to me, she asks Doreen one evening. At her neck she still wears the St Christopher Peter gave her, to protect her on her journey. Doreen shrugs. You'll have your baby, go home to your family, and everything will be forgotten. What family? Tess wonders.

Her pains start one night in late March. A midwife comes, but says it's too soon, so Tess is left in agony until the next evening, when the midwife comes again and tells the nuns to telephone Tess's mother. I don't want my mother, Tess screams, but they telephone anyway. Then they take her to a larger cell with white-painted walls, boxes of medical equipment and a rubber sheet over the bed. The midwife attaches Tess's legs to metal stands, then forces freezing fingers into her, bursting her waters with a needle. Then she goes away, and a while later the pains start in earnest. And though she fights hard, after endless hours more Tess can't help crying out. Towards dawn, feverish with exhaustion, she feels a hand touch her brow, opens her eyes and sees her mother. Compassion shows in her, just for a second. And the tears flow from Tess like a river.

The baby is born, a little girl. Tess struggles to see but her mother restrains her, and it is quickly bundled up and taken away. Her only memory of it is hearing its tiny cries receding down the corridor. Then Tess is given a pill and a hot water bottle and told to sleep. Later her mother rouses her with tea. She looks calm and relieved and in control, for the first time since the incident behind the greenhouse. Everything's fine, she explains. All taken care of. What is? Tess asks. The baby, her mother replies. She's in good hands, in foster care with a wet nurse. Daddy and I have signed the necessary papers, and in time she'll go to an orphanage, then be adopted into a nice family where she'll be happy and loved. But can't I see her? Tess pleads. No, her mother says, because that would be *wrong*. You will leave here and stay with Aunt Rosa in Lincoln, then in a few weeks when you're feeling better, you'll go to your finishing school in London. But what about Peter? Tess asks, and her mother's face hardens. You will never mention that person's name again. If you do, or if you try to contact him, we'll press charges and he'll go to prison.

So Tess goes to Lincoln and stays with Aunt Rosa, who is her father's sister, and scatty and mischievous and a bit radical, but also kind-hearted and full of humour. And in a few weeks, when Tess feels better, she decides not to go to finishing school in London, but writes a letter to her parents explaining how sorry she is for the trouble she's put them to, and how she feels it will be better for everyone if she stays in Lincoln and finishes her education there. And to no one's surprise they agree, and apart from an annual Christmas card from her father, never contact her again.

The small resort town of Reculver lies on the north Kent coast, about three miles east of Herne Bay. With its Roman ruins and distinctive two-towered abbey, it boasts commanding views over the wide and muddy waters of the Thames estuary, and a long stretch of quiet, easily cordoned beach with open farmland behind. At noon the next day, Charles Whitworth and Quentin Credo reported to the wooden hut serving as gatehouse to the beach. Beyond the gatehouse an armed military policeman stood guard by a barbed-wire barrier. In the distance beyond the barrier, milling around in hats and coats like reluctant guests at a winter picnic, stood a gaggle of onlookers.

'Is that them?' Quentin murmured, as his papers were checked.

'That's them,' Whitworth replied. 'The white-haired man standing with Gibson is Barnes Wallis. I can also see AVM Cochrane, he's talking to one of Portal's aides. The others are all Air Ministry bods. Nay-sayers, mostly.'

'Nay-sayers?'

'They don't believe in it. They want it cancelled.'

Their clearances finally accepted, they stepped outside, and passed through the barbed wire onto the beach itself.

'We'll stay back a little,' Whitworth said. 'Watch from here.'

Watch what? Quentin wondered, turning up the collar of his greatcoat. A cold wind blew. Overhead the sky lay dull and leaden. Away from Wallis's group, a naval rating lounged by a dinghy, while another man set a film-camera on a tripod, focusing it on the sea, where a hundred yards out two white marker buoys bobbed.

Twenty minutes passed, nothing happened.

'Sir.' Quentin began uncertainly. 'About those two men yesterday . . .'

'Abbott and Costello? I wouldn't worry about them.'

'No, sir. Only, the *Tirpitz* thing . . .'

'They don't blame you for it. Although the Admiralty is hopping mad, apparently. No, they think it was just loose talk. Nothing more sinister.'

'I'm not sure I agree.'

'You think there's more to it?'

'I think we should at least investigate that possibility, sir.'

Whitworth grunted. Another ten minutes went by.

'So, how's it all going at East Grinstead?' he said. 'If I may ask.'

'McIndoe wants me to have a new nose.'

'Really? Well, that's good, isn't it?'

'I don't know, sir. The hand's my main worry.'

'Not getting any better?'

'Worse if anything.'

'I'm sorry to hear that.' Whitworth raised binoculars, scanning the empty sea. 'Quentin. About Abbott and Costello . . .'

'Yes, sir.'

'There's no personal antipathy, you know. They're just doing their job.'

'They want me off the case.'

'Yes. But I want you on it. A real pilot, I told them, someone who actually knows the score. And someone intimately familiar with Scampton, and our set-up there.'

'I see, sir. And what do they say?'

'They don't like it!' Whitworth snorted. 'But I outrank them, so that's that.'

'Thank you, sir. I think.'

'Don't thank me. They'd be fools to lose you. You're a natural at this intelligence business. Must be all that legal training.'

'If you say so, sir.'

'*Praemonitus praemunitus*. Their motto, you know. Air Intelligence Branch.'

'Yes sir, forewarned is forearmed. Although, personally I prefer 57 Squadron's.'

Whitworth turned to him, studying the ravaged cheeks, stunted nose, fleshless lips. 'Remind me, Quentin.'

'*Corpus non animum muto*, sir. It's my body that changes. Not my spirit.'

'Indeed. Are you in much pain?'

'Quite a bit, sir.'

'The hand?'

'Yes, sir. I'm not sure it's worth keeping.'

'What about the new nose?'

Quentin shrugged. 'What's the point?'

A low drone came to them from across the water. The figures on the beach stopped milling and turned as one, binoculars raised, to face the sea. A moment later two specks appeared out of the grey, racing towards shore. The drone rose to a rumble, then a roar, the specks solidified and grew, until two bombers could be seen, side-by-side and low over the water. Lancasters. 'The one on the right is the first Type 464.' Whitworth said. 'It's carrying a full-size mock-up of the weapon. The other is a standard Lanc, carrying cameras. Watch closely, this is crucial.'

The two Lancasters approached, level at about 150 feet and at high power, Quentin saw, noting the throaty roar of the engines. Then the right one checked slightly, as though making a final adjustment, and a huge barrel-shaped object detached itself from its underside, dropping as though in slow motion towards the sea. An instant later it hit the surface, throwing an explosion of white foam and spray hundreds of feet into the air.

Then vanished beneath the waves.

The spray fell slowly back, like a falling veil, leaving a widening ring of white water. And nothing else. Binoculars were lowered, coats buttoned up, the gaggle of observers began returning up the beach.

'I'm guessing that didn't go according to plan, sir,' Quentin said.

'No,' Whitworth replied. 'No, it certainly did not. And unless it starts to very soon, it never will.'

PART 2

CHASTISE

Chapter 6

Later that day, following a second failed demonstration of the weapon, a crisis meeting was convened in a back office at nearby RAF Manston, where the Lancaster had been prepared for the tests. Present at the meeting were Air Vice Marshal Cochrane representing Bomber Command, Charles Whitworth and Guy Gibson representing Scampton and 617 Squadron, an unsmiling official called Ashwell representing the Air Ministry, and a sub-dued-looking Barnes Wallis. Also present, somewhat to his surprise, was Quentin.

'Who's he?' demanded Ashwell, straight away.

'My ADC,' Whitworth replied smoothly. 'Flight Lieutenant Credo. He's synchronising the security effort at Scampton.'

'Then I take it he's properly cleared.' Ashwell muttered testily.

'Of course.'

'Very well. Let's get on with it. I've a train to catch.'

Ashwell opened proceedings by summarising the day's

events – two test drops, two failures – then began to argue the case for cancelling the project. Quentin half-followed, hampered partly by his limited knowledge, but also because his head was reeling. Had Whitworth really said ADC? His aide-de-camp? Quentin had assumed his day in Reculver was merely a consolation prize for being sacked. He'd been preparing to return to Scampton that evening, pack his bags and steel himself for a long stay at Archie McIndoe's. Then Whitworth had asked him to remain on the case. Now apparently he was his personal aide. Synchronising the security effort, whatever that meant.

Ashwell was still speaking. '. . . Believe me, Wallis, nobody is more respectful of your skill and ingenuity, and I have nothing but admiration for your persistence, but today is the third occasion I've stood on a beach and watched this contraption fail. Now it's time to call a halt. After all, the latest date this mission can be carried out, as I understand it, is less than four weeks away.'

'Yes,' Wallis admitted quietly. 'Full moon, the middle of May. Water levels at the dams will be at their highest. After that they start going down.'

'Well, there you have it. A splendid idea, but too ambitious given the timeframe. Maybe next year. Now, I propose to return to London, draft the necessary paperwork cancelling the *Upkeep* programme and . . .'

'No!' Wallis interrupted fervently. 'It will work! It just needs more testing.'

'But there's no time for more testing. You said as much yourself.'

'There is time. And it *will* work, I'm sure of it!'

'So am I.' To everyone's surprise Guy Gibson stepped forward. 'If Mr Wallis says it'll work, that's good enough for me, and my crews. After all, we're the ones flying it.'

Glances were exchanged. Everyone knew Gibson's view was pivotal. If he remained supportive then Wallis had a chance, if he didn't the project was dead. Over the weeks of testing the two men had grown close, and standing there at Wallis's side, Quentin saw a completely different Gibson from the firebrand scourge of Scampton, more like a doting nephew with a favourite uncle. Earlier that afternoon, when the second bomb failed, disintegrating spectacularly as it hit the water, onlookers had witnessed the forlorn sight of Wallis peeling off shoes and socks and wading into the freezing water to search for wreckage. Most turned away in embarrassment, but not Gibson, who stayed at the water's edge to help.

'Gentlemen.' Ashwell was saying. 'Let's be honest. This is not just about the bomb. This whole programme is costing us hugely in other ways – manpower, technical support, production facilities, not to mention cash. Resources which are badly needed elsewhere. And what about all the other snags? The radios don't work, navigation's a problem, so is keeping height, finding the range, modifying the Lancasters, delivering them in time, loading the bomb, maintaining secrecy, the list is endless . . .'

'Nobody said it would be easy,' Wallis murmured.

'We're not asking for easy! We're asking for feasible.'

'It is feasible! I've already proved it.'

'With a scaled-down version dropped from a Mosquito. The full-sized one just breaks apart!'

'Yes, but I can fix it! And fix all the other problems too. I'm sure of it.'

'How can you be?'

'Because young men's lives are at stake.' Wallis pointed at Gibson. 'And if I wasn't sure, I would never allow it to continue.'

Ashwell surveyed the room, head shaking. Then picked up his briefcase. 'A week, gentlemen. Get it working by then, or the whole crackpot scheme is cancelled.'

The door slammed behind him. An awkward silence followed. Then Cochrane spoke for the first time.

'Barnes. I'm briefing Harris in the morning, so give it to me straight. Is it really feasible? Given all the problems, the timing issues, technical hitches and so on?'

'Yes. Probably. Oh, I don't know.' Wallis sighed. 'Only if our luck changes.'

Over the next hour Quentin learned all there was to know. The bomb was code-named *Upkeep*, the mission was *Chastise*. Its aim was to fly the twenty Lancasters of 617 Squadron into the dragon's den, the heavily defended Ruhr valley area of Germany's industrial heartland, there to attack three key dams using Wallis's bomb. These dams held back huge lakes, millions of tons of water vital to the many foundries, power stations and factories situated along the valley. Smashing the dams would not only unleash a monstrous tidal wave of destruction, but also render any surviving installations useless, by denying them water for months to come. Germany's war machine, it was hoped, would grind to a halt.

That was the theory. The devil, as always, was in the detail. Firstly, to have any chance of reaching their objectives, and getting home again, the Lancasters must fly the entire mission at ground level, and at night, hedge-hopping by moonlight across the Low Countries to the Rhine, then on to the Ruhr, using special routes planned for stealth and surprise. Secondly, assuming they made it, they must then attack the dams in the exact manner prescribed by Wallis, who believed just one bomb was enough to destroy a dam, providing it was precisely delivered.

Which was just as well, Quentin reflected, for each Lancaster would only carry one bomb, and the manner of delivery was very precise indeed. To begin with, the bomb itself, all four tons of it, before it was dropped, had to be spun up to an alarming 500 revolutions per minute, backwards, using a belt-driven winch in the bomb-bay. Only then could the attack commence. This must be made head-on, over the water, at right-angles to the dam. The aircraft's wings must be held precisely level, height above the water kept at exactly 150 feet and the airspeed fixed at 232 mph. The backwards-spinning bomb must then be released precisely 450 yards from the centre of the dam. Too soon and it would sink short, too late and it would smash against the parapet, or skip harmlessly over. Correctly dropped, however, it should bounce across the lake, gamely vaulting torpedo nets and any other obstructions on its way, until it arrived at the dam wall. There, using the last of its back-spin to hug the wall, it would quietly sink to the required depth of thirty feet, whereupon it would detonate by hydrostatic fuse. 6600 lb of Torpex, Wallis had calculated, exploding hard up against the wall like that, would cause fatal damage to its structural integrity. The monstrous weight of water behind would do the rest.

Quentin absorbed the information in breathless silence. It was as inspired a plan as it was audacious. Brilliant, original, creative, the perfect marriage of daring and ingenuity. And quite beyond his wildest imaginings. Privately, along with others at Scampton, he'd assumed the device was some huge torpedo, to be fired into the U-boat pens at La Rochelle or a battleship at Brest. But this invention was in a different league altogether, a four-ton bomb that skipped across water, then destroyed a nation's ability to wage war. Inspired. Bold. Magnificent.

Although not quite fully formed, he reminded himself. Not proven. Like a parcel at Christmas, pregnant with possibility, but as yet unknown. And listening to the debate around the table, understandable festive excitement, he noted, was more than tempered with wintry doubt. For despite all the proven hydrodynamics, and the weeks of tank-tests at Teddington, and the successful dummy trials using a Wellington, and a fully developed mini-version called *Highball* which skipped beautifully for thousands of yards, despite all these, the full-sized monster *Upkeep* had yet to bounce. Even once.

The evening wore on, discussion became heated, cooled, reheated again, with suggestions ranging from the impractical to the improbable to the downright impossible. Finally Wallis tossed aside his pencil.

'There is only one way,' he sighed wearily. 'In the available time, that is.'

'Well spit it out, man.' Cochrane's patience was wearing thin.

'Get rid of the bomb-casing altogether. Drop it in its cylindrical form.'

'Will that work?'

'Yes. But only if we reduce the impact. By dropping it lower.'

'Lower than 150 feet? How much bloody lower?'

'Too low. About sixty feet should do it.'

Stunned silence followed. Then Gibson cleared his throat.

'Um, sixty feet is less than the wingspan of a Lancaster, you know. Bank the aircraft a little, or sneeze or something, and you'd hit the water. And that would be that.'

'I do know, Guy,' Wallis said gently. 'That's why I couldn't ask you to do it.'

'By day it's easy,' Gibson went on, gazing at the table. 'You've lots of cues to judge height. But at night you've none. That's the problem. We need a way of judging height, accurately, at night, over water. If we can solve that, we could do it at sixty feet.'

Cochrane looked round the table. 'Yes, but how?'

Next morning Quentin began his new job as Whitworth's ADC. The title was unofficial, he knew, and largely honorary, an ancient military throwback to an era when an aide-de-camp was a leader's trusted adviser and confidant. His new position carried no extra rank, nor pay, and at first seemed little different to the old one. His in-tray was loaded with the usual paperwork, his phone calls sounded depressingly familiar, and as for 'synchronising the security effort', Whitworth was away on 5 Group business, so Quentin was none the wiser. Pulling in his chair, he reached for a pen and got on with it.

As the morning wore on, however, strange things began to happen. First a tray of tea and biscuits arrived, brought to him by a steward from the officer's mess. With it came a vase of freesias for his desk. Then came a black box with knobs, which turned out to be an intercom connecting him to Whitworth's office. Then an adjutant started dropping by, asking if Quentin needed any typing. Then a workman screwed a nameplate to his door. *F/L Q. Credo DSO* it said. Still no clue as to his title or role, but it looked impressively official.

Then there was Chloe Hickson.

He became aware of her mid-morning, a WAAF corporal, fluttering about the corridor like a trapped moth. When he left his office she sprang up and saluted, when he returned she saluted and sat down. Eventually, bemused, he confronted her.

'Bad form saluting indoors, Corporal. I'm not wearing a cap, so can't return it.'

'Oh. I see. Sorry, sir,' she replied, saluting once more.

'That's quite all right. Except you did it again. Um, who are you exactly?'

'Corporal Hickson, sir. Your driver.'

'My driver!' Suddenly Quentin found himself laughing, for the first time in months, an odd nasal guffaw reminiscent of a braying donkey. It sounded awful, but felt refreshingly good. 'A driver, ha! How marvellous, Corporal, you've quite made my day! And have we got a car?'

'Of course, sir. Would you like to see it? It runs you know.'

'A driver, a car, and it runs! My cup overfloweth.' He glanced up the corridor. Arnott was approaching, one of the newly installed intelligence officers, and not smiling. 'Thank you, Corporal, I'd love to, perhaps later?'

He returned to his desk. Arnott followed and locked the door behind him.

'I hear Reculver was another fiasco,' he began, sitting opposite Quentin.

'Not entirely successful, no. But lots of constructive discussion.' He lifted his phone. 'Tea, sir? I merely have to ask, these days . . .'

Arnott shook his head, and withdrew a sheet from his briefcase. 'This is a list of infringements.'

'Infringements.'

'Yes, infringements. Breaches of security rules. Mostly routine, as you'll see, but we'd like you to follow them up.' He smiled sardonically. 'Seeing as you're intimately familiar with the set-up at Scampton.'

Quentin glanced through the list: times, dates, misdemeanours, names. At once one jumped out. *Sgt B. Murray*. 'Of course sir, I'll look into it.'

'Right away, please.'

'Yes, um, have you unearthed anything, may I ask? Anything serious that is?'

Arnott leaned over. 'Lieutenant, there are no serious security breaches at Scampton. If there were we'd know about them. So may I suggest you concentrate——' He broke off as with an ear-splitting roar two Lancasters thundered overhead, seemingly inches above the ceiling. Windows shook, teacups rattled, Quentin's new freesias shuddered in protest. Arnott looked alarmed. 'What the bloody hell are they playing at!'

'Training, sir. So I believe.'

'Reckless lunatics.' The thunder receded, Arnott rose to leave. 'Oh, and one more thing . . .'

'Sir?'

'One of 617's pilots is carrying on with a married woman on the station. Lightfoot, his name is. That kind of behaviour leads to carelessness. So put a stop to it.'

After he'd gone Quentin turned to his window and read the list. The 'infringements' were indeed routine, he soon saw, a security pass mislaid, a harmless comment dropped, an innocent question posed. Almost as if Abbott and Costello were testing him, he felt. Or deliberately humiliating him. Or distracting him from the real business of security. Or all three. Yet what of Peter and Tess? he wondered. How had they been discovered? And why ask him to deal with it? Something was amiss. He pocketed the list, gathered up his new driver and descended to the pavement.

Where a decidedly careworn Austin 8 awaited. Which his driver couldn't drive. Quentin took the front passenger seat, which clearly unnerved Chloe, who expected him in the back. Then the engine wouldn't start, she turned it over and over until it flooded. When finally it did explode into life, she was unable to engage gear, peering anxiously over the wheel, one hand stirring the stick while onlookers smirked and the gearbox snarled in protest. Eventually Quentin rammed it into gear with his good hand, whereupon Chloe let the clutch out with a bang and the car promptly stalled.

At that he ordered her out. 'Swap seats, for heaven's sake. You change gears, I'll steer with my left hand and call them out. Got it?'

'Yes sir.' Chloe was close to tears. 'Sorry sir.'

'Don't apologise, Corporal, worse things happen at sea. So I'm told. First gear!'

They set off around the perimeter, erratically to begin with but soon settling to a rhythm, Quentin operating the pedals, Chloe changing gear and occasionally steering as required. First stop was Hangar 2, to caution a fitter heard grumbling about 'all this bleedin' low flying'. Next to the kitchens to tick off the cook who dropped her pass, thence to the telephony room where an inconsequential message had gone astray. At each venue the miscreant, cowed by the sight of the battle-scarred officer striding towards them, WAAF in tow, expressed immediate remorse for their lapse followed by heartfelt assurances no repetition would occur. Within an hour Quentin had crossed most names off the list and heard nothing to arouse further suspicion.

Then he went in search of Brendan Murray.

Whose offence, he read, as Chloe steered them round the field, had little to do with security, but related to his black-market activities. Apparently he'd short-changed an engineering sergeant over a carton of cigarettes. Quentin, unsure how much Murray knew about Tess and Peter, sensed he must tread carefully. Apart from occasional sightings, he hadn't seen or spoken to the unpredictable Irishman since the rescue of Peter's crew back in February.

They found him in the equipment barn, eating lunch with his civilian contractors.

'Well, and what have we here!' Murray grinned, as though expecting him. 'Come on in, sir, and how the devil are you?'

'Well enough, thank you, Sergeant.' Quentin stepped into the gloom. Seven or eight men sat at a table strewn with sandwiches and illicit bottles of beer. Murray was at their head, a black notebook open before him.

'Gents, this is Flight Lieutenant Credo.' Murray explained. 'A wonderful fellow and first-class hero. Got caught out on a mine-laying trip, flew his burning machine clear of Jerry's deadly clutches, then put the flames out with his bare hands, so saving the lives of half his crew.'

Murmured platitudes and discomfited glances, Quentin noted dully. Always the same, never accustomed to. Then a cough came from behind. Chloe, petite, steadfast, strikingly pretty suddenly, was framed in the doorway.

'Hello, and who's this beautiful young thing?'

'Oh, this is my driver, Corporal Hickson.'

'And welcome to you, young lady.' Murray rose, pocketing his notebook. 'Come and have a sandwich with the fellows here, so's Mr Credo and I can talk outside.'

'No, thanks,' Chloe replied lightly. 'I've already eaten.'

'Suit yourself.' They walked into the sunlight where Quentin outlined the complaint against Murray. As he did so the Irishman seemed to relax, he noted. As though he'd been anticipating something worse.

'That bastard engineer is a liar!' he countered immediately. 'And a thief. He owes me five guineas for betting.'

'That's as may be, Sergeant, but you do know that trading in cigarettes and spirits and other contraband is completely illegal?'

'Of course! So's the gambling, but everyone does it and where's the harm?'

'The harm, I suppose, is where you draw the line. This is a bomber station at war.'

'And my private dealings have never interfered with that. Ever.'

'So you'll carry on with them. Despite this warning.'

'I tell you what.' Murray smiled warily. 'I'll scale them back a bit, if you like. Put the lid on things. Just till this present nonsense is all finished.'

'What present nonsense?'

'The new squadron! The hush-hush training, the fellows in dark suits, everything.'

'You don't miss much, do you?'

'Best not to, in my experience.'

'Indeed. How did you know what happened on my last mission?'

'Common knowledge. I was at Feltwell that day too, you know. Bad business.'

'Of course. I forgot.'

'Will there be anything else?'

'Not for now. Thank you for your cooperation.'

'A pleasure. My regards to Charlie Whitworth.'

'Yes.' Quentin hesitated. 'And mine to your wife. I trust she's well?'

The eyes darted sideways. 'She's fine, sir. Quite fine.'

They parted at the barn. Back in the car Chloe was incredulous. 'Cheeky so and so!' she exclaimed as they drove off. 'He doesn't care, sir, does he? About anything!'

'So it would seem. Second gear, please. And have you really already eaten?'

'No, but I didn't want to miss anything. Like the question about his wife, sir. What was that about, if I may ask?'

'Nothing. Just a pleasantry. Third gear, Corporal.'

'Well he didn't like it. Not one bit.'

'Really? How could you tell?'

'Woman's intuition. Like I could tell he was lying. About the other thing.'

'Cutting back his business activities? I don't doubt it. Fourth gear, please.'

'No sir. Not lying about that. I mean about knowing what happened on your mission.'

In Flight Ops, a breakthrough at last. At three that afternoon, all twenty of 617's pilots were invited to assemble in Number 2 hangar beside one of their borrowed Lancs. In groups of four Gibson then called them onto the flight deck. As usual his inner circle went first: Hopgood, Martin, Maltby and Young, replaced ten minutes later by Shannon, Maudslay, Astell and Knight. Peter and the others waited their turn, feigning nonchalance, avoiding speculative chatter, yet sensing a development. His group would be next to learn of it, he knew, in accordance with established protocol. Gibson's eight favourites always took precedence, then Peter's group of six, then the final back-up group of five. Peter's group, an affable Commonwealth assortment, had been increasingly rostered to fly together, sometimes as a single unit of six, sometimes as two flights of three. They were led by Flight Lieutenant 'Big Joe' McCarthy of 97 Squadron, a twenty-four-year-old from Brooklyn, New York, who had enlisted via the Canadian Air Force. Also from 97 Squadron was Les Munro, a farmer from Gisborne, New Zealand. From Saskatchewan, Canada, was Vernon Byers who at thirty-two was the oldest of

617's pilots. Then came Peter's 61 Squadron cohort Norm Barlow, an Australian, who'd lost his aerial training over Yorkshire. Finally the only other Englishman, Geoff Rice, from Portsmouth, who was recruited to 617 simply by crossing Scampton's tarmac from 57 Squadron.

It was night-training equipment, the development Gibson wanted to show them. A new system called Two Stage Blue, whereby all the cockpit windows were covered with blue filters, while the pilot, navigator and bomb aimer's goggles were tinted with amber. The result was an uncannily accurate simulation of night, and meant that all training, regardless when it took place, could now be undertaken under real or simulated night conditions. There was more. New wireless equipment had been installed to improve communications, specially prepared navigational routes were being drawn up for the navigators, and down in the bomber aimer's compartment, the padded chest-rest had been lowered, stirrups had been rigged to keep the front gunner's feet clear of his head, and on his seat lay a curious wooden triangle.

'It's just a sighting aid.' Gibson explained vaguely. 'A chap called Dann knocked it up. Surprisingly simple, yet highly accurate.' He handed it to Peter. An adjustable V-shaped triangle with a peep-hole at the apex and two nails in either corner, it certainly looked and felt rudimentary. 'You hold it up to your eye,' Gibson went on. 'Then, when the two nails line up with the aiming points on the target, you know you're at the right range, press the bomb-release tit and Bob's your uncle. Workshops are knocking them up for every crew, we'll start trying them out today.'

'Where?' Big Joe asked innocently.

'Derwent reservoir. The two towers on the dam there. It's

as good as anywhere. I also want you to try getting as low as possible to the water. Say sixty feet or so. Your altimeter will be useless at that height so you'll have to judge it by eye. Be careful.'

Owing to the ongoing shortage of aircraft, Peter's formation of three didn't get airborne until evening. In the meantime they were kept at readiness in the ops room. Out of contact, that meant. These waiting hours were the worst for everyone, Peter knew. Once airborne the job took over, pushing earthly concerns aside. Until then there was only nerves and worry. After a while, and almost unconsciously, Peter's crew pulled their chairs together into a protective circle, shutting out the world like wagons on the prairie. Then, as on so many other occasions, they passed the time chatting, dozing, or simply sitting in companionable silence. Kiwi, Billy and Herb resumed the world's longest game of poker. They kept a record of the score, promising to settle up the day war ended. Chalkie and Jamie carried a pocket chess set, pulling it out whenever opportunity arose, even for just a few minutes. Sometimes a single game might last days. Uncle busied himself with personal grooming, polishing his shoes, or trimming his moustache, or buffing his greatcoat buttons till they gleamed like gold. Peter, his mind on the task ahead, idly watched his friends, or stared at a paperback, or feigned sleep. Mostly he fretted about Tess. They hadn't met in over a week, not since the night he'd borrowed Credo's car. Meanwhile she was alone and in peril, coping with an unstable husband, the search for a lost daughter, a hostile family, and an overworked pilot training for a deadly mission no one could talk about. They couldn't even telephone each other safely. Only that morning Gibson had publicly reprimanded an airman for being indiscreet on the phone. I can't come out tonight, the man had told his girlfriend, I've a low-flying exercise. Gibson had gone berserk, screaming at him in front of everyone until the poor man was on the verge of tears. Peter had watched in uneasy silence. Security people were everywhere, telephone calls were obviously being tapped. He wondered how long it would be before they were discovered. And Murray found out.

Finally and to everyone's relief they got airborne, racing low over the Lincolnshire countryside just as full darkness was falling. Broken cloud obscured a waning half-moon, otherwise the sky was clear and visibility good. Peter led a loose formation of three, Geoff Rice to his left, Vernon Byers to his right. The route to Derwent was a prepared one, tried and tested over many sorties, Jamie Johnson followed on his rolled-up map, adjusting for ground-speed and drift, while Kiwi called the now familiar landmarks and turning-points from the nose. Halfway across Nottinghamshire, however, Peter became aware of a presence behind him. A moment later a click came over the headphones.

'Navigator here. I'm on the flight deck.'

'Blimey!'

'What did he say?'

'He's come out from his cubby hole!'

'Jamie?' Peter queried. 'Everything all right?'

'We had a meeting,' Jamie went on. 'All the navigators. We agreed that staying at our desks on a low-level mission like this is pointless. Far better we come up and navigate from the flight deck. More pairs of eyes to help, and so on.'

'Well, good, it definitely will help, but are you okay with it?'

'Fine. I think. Actually it's quite exciting, isn't it, belting along above the treetops like this.' He laughed nervously. 'Makes me wonder what I've been missing.'

'Not much,' Chalkie quipped. 'Except by a few inches.'

'Good for you, Jamie lad,' Uncle added.

'Wow, Jamie on the flight deck. Who'd have bet on that?'

'Kiwi would.'

'No, I wouldn't.'

'Rear gunner to Pilot.'

'Yes, hello Herb, what is it?'

'Nothing. Just an intercom check.'

The three Lancasters reached Derwent without incident, and climbed to take up a circling pattern a mile to the north. Below them the reservoir lay like a shard of black glass. Studying it closely Peter signalled the others to wait, then wheeled over for the first run, the Merlins popping and crackling as Uncle throttled back to lose height. The lake, nestling amid tree-covered peaks, was nearly two miles long, narrow and sinuous like a dagger. He tightened the turn to lose height then rolled quickly level, jabbing rudder to line up. The altimeter read 100 feet, the water looked much nearer. He disregarded his instruments, fixed his eyes on the gleaming black, and let the bomber settle lower. Then lower still, until the shadowy landscape was rising up all around as though he was about to land. Beside him Uncle held the throttles, adjusting power to maintain speed; behind him, breath held, Jamie watched the tree-lined banks flash by in a dizzying blur. And lying down in the nose Kiwi tried to ignore the hurtling blackness beneath him, picked up his wooden triangle and held it to his eye.

'Can't see a bloody thing,' he reported. 'No, wait, hang on . . .' Far in the distance emerged the faint dark line of the dam, a square sluice-tower at either end. 'Okay, there it is, I see it. Come right a bit, Pilot, that's it, right a little more, okay that's good, hold it there . . .'

The lake curved left, then right again, Peter eased the bomber into a shallow S-turn to line up with the dam. As he did so, the aircraft slid under the shadow of the right-hand bank, and instantly he lost all visual reference.

'I . . . I can't see, can't see the height . . .'

'Pull up! Pull up now!' A cry from Guttenberg. Peter wrenched back, Uncle slammed the throttles wide and the Lancaster soared skywards, run aborted. Seconds passed, the engines strained, dark hills loomed, Peter hauled harder, stamping a foot on the panel for leverage, the hills filled the windscreen, then at last the starlit sky appeared and the danger slid by beneath.

In a minute normal order was restored, the climb angle eased, power throttled back, flight controls trimmed, until the Lancaster was settled in level flight once more. Then came the analysis.

'Christ that was close.'

'All right lads, well done, good effort.' Uncle encouraged.

'Good effort? It was a bloody disaster!' Kiwi countered. 'The towers weren't in line or anything.'

'Not to mention nearly getting killed.'

'This is crazy,' Billy added from the nose turret. 'Like riding a motorcycle blindfold. What the hell happened?'

'Propeller wash.' Herb replied. 'In the water suddenly, trailing out behind, you know, like a speedboat. Only four speedboats, one from each prop.'

'Jesus, how low do you have to be for that?'

'Too bloody low, the props could only have been inches off.'

'I knew I should've joined the bloody Navy.'

'I'd say you have.'

'Pilot to crew, well spotted there Herb, that was my fault, I lost vision in the shadows, must have dipped a bit. We'll try again in a minute . . .'

'Maybe I could keep a lookout for height,' Jamie suggested, 'Then, you know, tap on your shoulder or something to signal up or down. That way you could keep your eyes on the view ahead.'

'Good idea, Jamie, we'll give it a try.'

'Look, Geoff Rice is having a go!'

They watched as Rice's Lancaster made its descending turn to the head of the lake, then began its run, a small ghostly shadow racing silently across the water like a hunting nighthawk. All seemed to go well, Peter saw him correcting yaw with rudder, saw him make the S-turn for the final approach, saw him slide towards the starboard bank, and vanish briefly in the shadows. Then came an explosion of white.

'Jesus, he hit!'

'He's crashed, he's into the lake!'

'No, wait!' They watched in horror as the Lancaster, inundated, staggered back into the air, trailing a cloud of white spray. Then it was over ground, moving sluggishly, striving for height. Slowly it picked up speed, hauling itself laboriously from the landscape. A few seconds more and it was breaking free of the shadows, clawing height, and into safety.

'Christ alive, he made it!'

'Incredible. Flew smack into the water and survived.'

'Who'd have believed it? Look, he's got an engine stopped.'

Peter followed Rice's aircraft as it climbed slowly out of danger, one engine feathered, until at last it was circling in formation once more. He glanced across at Uncle, who caught his eye and shook his head. Then Chalkie appeared, flashing out a message with his Aldis lamp.

'What's he saying, Chalk?'

'He says the rear gunner got a soaking, his port inner engine's dead, some electrics shorted out but he's okay to make it home.'

'Thank Christ,' Peter said. 'Tell him to go ahead. We'll follow with Byers.'

'Will do. Hang on, he's saying something else . . .'

'What?'

'He says . . . Fucking madness.'

It was midnight by the time they landed back at Scampton. Predictably Gibson was still up and wanting an immediate update. Peter and Byers went to his office. Each had made two more runs, they reported, all with the same result: the new Dann sight worked well, but blind-flying the Lancaster down to sixty feet, and holding it there, in total darkness, was nigh on impossible. Not without risking disaster.

'I know,' Gibson replied, his voice unusually subdued. 'I tried it too and damn near hit. Rice was lucky they weren't all killed.'

'What about those new radio altimeters?' Byers suggested. 'They're supposed to be bloody accurate.'

'Bloody hard to get hold of too. Anyway they're still not accurate enough.' He pushed back his chair. 'Leave it for now. Apparently there's some new kit arriving tomorrow, something to do with spotlights, maybe it'll do the trick. In the meantime, Byers, go and get some rest. Lightfoot, the ADC wants to see you.'

'Now sir?'

'Yes.' Gibson shuffled papers. 'Lieutenant Credo. In his rooms. Right now.'

Peter hurried along the station's darkened paths to the accommodation blocks. Reaching Credo's door, he knocked and it opened at once.

'I tried to reach you earlier,' Quentin murmured.

'Sorry, I was locked in ops all afternoon. What is it?'

Quentin opened the door wider. The room was in shadow, lit by a single table lamp. One other person was present, a female, sitting on the edge of a chair, wearing a man's scarf at her neck.

'Tess!'

'Peter, thank God!' She rose and hugged him with relief.

'What is it? What's happened?'

'It's all right. I'm okay.'

Quentin handed him a drink. 'Here, have this, you're going to need it.'

'For God's sake tell me!'

'In short, I interviewed Murray this morning. Tonight he attacked Tess.'

'What!'

'It's true.' Tess cupped his face. 'But I'm all right, it's nothing . . .'

Her cheek was bruised, he saw then, and one eyebrow swollen. 'Nothing? Look at you! And what's this scarf? Tess, tell me!'

She touched the scarf, then pulled it aside. Angry red welts showed on her neck. As if from a rope, or tightly gripped hands.

'Jesus, what has he done?'

'I've bathed and covered them as best I can,' Quentin said. 'There's also bruising. Stomach and ribs mostly. She must get checked by a doctor first thing.'

'My God.' Peter searched her eyes, feeling fury rise inside him. 'I'll kill him. I'll get my service revolver and shoot him dead. Right now.'

'No, Peter, I beg you. Don't even think of it.'

'He's an animal! He deserves no better.'

'I know, but sit down, just for a moment. There's more. Let me explain.'

And she explained. While Quentin forced whisky down him, and eased him into a chair without even realising it. She explained how she'd got home that evening to find no Brendan. How he hadn't come home for tea, nor evening cocoa, as usual. How he hadn't appeared until very late, when he'd been drunk and abusive from the moment he came in. You shopped me, he shouted, you shopped me to that fucked-up bastard Credo. But she didn't understand, didn't know what he meant. No, Brendan, I haven't done anything. Don't lie, he yelled, you went to him and shopped me. And all the while he was following her round and round the table like a crazed dog. Suddenly he came at her, throwing the table aside and grabbing her round the throat with both hands. She saw the madness in his eyes, smelled the alcohol on his breath, felt herself being lifted bodily from the floor. She tried to fight free, but was powerless, unable to breathe, unable to struggle, and as unconsciousness beckoned he brought his face close to hers. And hissed the rest. 'I fixed him, and I'll fix you. And I'll fix your pilot boyfriend you think I don't know about. I'll fix the whole fucking lot of them.' Then he'd flung her to the floor, kicking and punching in a wild frenzy, on and on until she felt she would die right there. Then suddenly he stopped, and stood over her, panting breathlessly, before storming off into the night.

In Quentin's rooms, silence. A clock ticked on the mantelpiece, in the distance a lone owl hooted. Peter, aghast, struggled to find a voice.

'You must leave him,' he whispered. 'Now. Tonight. We'll get a room, a bed-and-breakfast or something. You stay there, I'll protect you. He'll never know.'

'I'm sorry, but you can't,' Quentin said.

'Why the hell not?'

'Various reasons. Gibson, for one. He knows about you two.'

'What? But how?'

'I'm not sure. Some tip-off to the intelligence people, possibly. Anyway the point is, he says you're to stop seeing each other, or you're off the squadron.'

'Fine. Then I resign.'

'No.' Tess knelt at his side. 'That's not what you want, Peter, and not what we agreed. Remember? We said you'd see this through, then we'll go away together.'

Peter shook his head. 'That was then, this is now.'

'Okay, but consider this,' Quentin went on. '617 is already down to twenty crews, instead of the twenty-one or two it really needs. If you pack it in, they'll be down to nineteen. And you'll be putting every one of them in even greater danger. Is that what you want?'

'I don't care. Tess is more important.'

'You do care. So does Gibson. He says you're one of the best. That's why he wants to keep you.'

'He said that?'

'Yes. He said if he didn't regard you so highly he'd have already sacked you. He needs you, Peter, he feels he can depend on you. And believe me, his confidence is low right now. You dropping out could jeopardise everything.'

'And think of your crew,' Tess coaxed. 'Uncle, Jamie and everyone. They've put everything into this too.'

'All right,' Peter sighed. 'All right, but Murray then. We'll get him arrested. For common assault or something.'

Tess and Quentin exchanged glances. 'We could try, yes . . .' Quentin agreed. 'But this is a military base on full alert, remember, so a complaint would be handled by the Provost Marshal's office, not the police. And what would we tell them? That a key staff member turned violent when he discovered his wife was seeing another man? They might not be too sympathetic.'

'God.' Peter was shaking his head. 'I don't believe this . . .'

'Please try.' Tess touched his arm. 'Quentin thinks there's more to it than we realise. He thinks it's better to keep Brendan here. Under watch.'

'Yes, but I'm not leaving you alone with him!'

'You don't have to.' Quentin checked his watch. 'There's a taxi waiting at the main gate. I've booked a room at the Royal. Tess can stay there tonight, then tomorrow find a room somewhere quiet. She'll write a note telling Murray she's gone home to her family for a while. He'll never know.'

'You seem to have thought of everything.'

'I'm sure we haven't, but it's all we can do for now. We'll try and arrange for you to see her when we can, but you should be aware this base is going to be locked down soon. No one from 617 will be allowed in or out, until the mission's over. In the meantime the best thing is for you keep your head down, and concentrate on doing the job.'

At Quentin's insistence Peter left first, returning by a round-about route to his quarters in the officers' block. Then Quentin followed with Tess wrapped in his greatcoat. At the main gate he helped her into the taxi and paid the driver.

'Are you sure you're up to this?' he asked her, leaning to the window.

'Yes. I want to stay close. And I want to help.'

'I'd dearly love to get hold of that notebook.'

'I know. But it won't be easy, it's always on him, except when he sleeps.'

'Leave it for now. Don't take any chances.'

'I won't. And thank you, Quentin. For everything. Here, your scarf.'

'Keep it. And don't forget the doctor, first thing tomorrow.'

'I won't. Thanks again.' She hesitated. 'What did he mean, do you think? Brendan. When he said he fixed you?'

Quentin straightened from the window. His right arm was throbbing again, a sure sign of strain. Overhead the starlit sky slowly turned, while the moon cast ghostly shadows and a vixen trotted along the road to Lincoln. *Tirpitz*, he'd thought immediately, when Tess told him what Murray had said. He'd tipped off Abbott and Costello about his *Tirpitz* cover story, and thus got him fired. For helping Tess. Either that, or something much worse, something so dreadful he could barely bring himself to consider it. The Germans. Might they have been forewarned of his gardening mission in the Wellington?

'God knows, Tess,' he sighed. 'God only knows.'

He turned from the taxi and went back to his rooms.

Chapter 7

And at that point, Quentin reflected, consulting his file, the stage was effectively set. Tess moved into a guest house in Lincoln, took sick leave from her NAAFI job and dropped from sight. Peter, increasingly preoccupied with training, stayed in contact as best he could, by note and occasional clandestine meeting, although as April turned to May, leaving the station became impracticable. Quentin put McIndoe off and stayed at work, consolidating his position as Whitworth's ADC, general security factotum, 617 Squadron bystander and roving busybody, thus fulfilling any number of briefs should anyone ask. Meanwhile Brendan Murray went to ground. Quentin, whose aim was 'supervised containment', kept tabs on him with spotvisits, and by befriending one of Murray's civilian contractors, who reported on his mood and whereabouts. The mood, he learned, was edgy, sullen and unforthcoming. As for the whereabouts, heavy rain and escalating aircraft movements kept him fully occupied tending Scampton's runways. Quentin kept his file up to date and watched from afar.

As for the dams mission itself, as is so often the way with grandiose British ventures, just when all seemed hopeless, everything suddenly began to go right.

'Quentin!' Whitworth hissed over the intercom a few days later. 'It works!'

Quentin glanced at Chloe, busy at his filing cabinet. 'Beg pardon, sir?'

'The *thing*. It works! Quick, get in here!'

Quentin hurried along the corridor, to be met by a beaming Whitworth, flanked by Arnott and Campbell looking attentive, if less joyful.

'Come in, Quentin, quickly and shut the door.' Whitworth handed him a photograph. 'This was taken yesterday down at Reculver. I was there, saw the whole thing. It works, look, it actually bloody works!'

Quentin studied the photo. It showed exactly the same stretch of shingle as before, and a similar gaggle of onlookers, including Ashwell, Gibson, Whitworth and a bare-headed Barnes Wallis. Who was waving his arms, triumphantly, like a conductor. At the massive drum-like bomb careering across the sea towards the beach.

'Good gracious.' Quentin stared at the picture. 'It's three feet in the air.'

'Yes! Oh, Quentin, if only you'd seen it. The Lanc came in exactly as before, only lower and faster and right between the markers. Then it released the bomb, which hit the water and vanished in the usual explosion of spray. I thought it was another failure to be honest, we all did, but a second later it reappeared, and threw itself back in the air.'

'Amazing. Good for Wallis. How many times did it bounce?'

'Four. Although I wouldn't say it *bounced* exactly, more sort of staggered. Nor did it travel terribly straight. But that doesn't matter Quentin, because the point is it *worked*. And you know what that means!'

'The operation is on?'

'Precisely!'

'Which also means, Lieutenant,' Campbell broke in, 'that Scampton's security status goes from yellow to orange.'

'Ah yes, of course.' Quentin wondered what that meant. And soon learned.

'Everything is far too lax.' Arnott handed him a file. 'There's rabbit damage to the perimeter fence, insufficient barbed wire at the main gate, too many people not displaying their passes correctly, plus the usual slack talk and general backsliding on important security matters.'

Quentin flicked through the file. The intelligence officers seemed wholly disinterested in Wallis's breakthrough. As though the mission was an unwanted distraction from the important work of security. As though things would be so much simpler *without* the mission. They also seemed uninterested in Brendan Murray, whom he'd repeatedly reported as someone they should keep an eye on, and uninterested in involving Quentin in anything remotely important. Which was starting to irritate him. 'Improperly padlocked cupboards, sir?' He read from the file. 'Pilfered light bulbs?'

'These things may seem trivial to you, Credo, but once you let complacency creep in, it's the thin end of the wedge. So see to them please.'

'As you wish, sir.' Quentin glanced at Whitworth, who winked, then nodded at more photographs on his desk.

'Want to see the target?'

Quentin picked up the photos, a sequence taken from high above a vast hook-shaped lake surrounded by fields and woodland. At one end lay the long bowed wall of a dam, topped by two sluice towers.

'That's the Möhne,' Whitworth said. 'Quite a monster, isn't it? A photo-reconnaissance Spitfire took the pictures from thirty thousand feet. Each picture is a week apart, the last one taken yesterday. What do you notice?'

Nothing, was Quentin's initial reaction, apart from differences in light and angle. Then he looked closer.

'The water level. On the dam. It's higher in each picture.'

'Well spotted. It's the same with the other two dams. These lakes are fed by snow-melt and winter rain. By May they reach their fullest, which is when Wallis says they must be attacked. After that levels start to fall, as do the chances of smashing the dams. So if we don't do it soon, we'll have to wait a whole year.'

Quentin checked Whitworth's wall calendar. 'And the crews need a full moon to fly the operation . . .'

'Which falls around the seventeenth of this month.'

'Good grief.'

'Precisely. We have very little time indeed.'

Campbell gathered his papers. 'So we'd better get on with it. Credo, get back to me on that file as soon as possible, would you?'

'Of course, sir.'

'Oh, and some schoolboys were seen hanging about outside the main gate yesterday. We certainly can't have that, so see to it too, would you?'

Quentin retreated to his office, where he found Chloe waiting with a tray of fresh tea. Since beginning work as his driver, her role had seemed to grow, he'd noticed, almost daily, such that she was now practically his secretary. ADC to the ADC, as it were.

'Blasted people,' he scowled, throwing down Campbell's file.

'Another list of chores from the intelligence chiefs, I presume, sir.'

'Those two are either damnably clever, Corporal, or damnably stupid!'

'Yes sir. I've a couple of messages for you. Your mother telephoned, wanting to know if you'd be home for her birthday this weekend.'

'Oh Lord. I completely forgot.'

'I thought so. So I said you were hoping to, but for operational reasons might not make it.'

'You did? Well done Chloe.'

'I also arranged a delivery of flowers.'

'Good thinking. Thank you. What else?'

'Some woman, a Mrs Barclay, from Staffordshire social services, returned your call of last week. She has some information for you. Shall I phone her back?'

'No thanks. I'll deal with it later. Anything else?'

'Doctor McIndoe called again. He wants to schedule you in. Urgently.'

'Oh.' Quentin sighed. Reflexively his hand went to his face, his fingers travelling the ravaged flesh of his cheek, the scarred lips, the raw stump of nose. All needed attending to. And his right hand was almost finished, so bad he'd started carrying it in a sling. He should have surgery on it, he knew, and everything else, and soon. Yet lately, what with all the activity and excitement at Scampton, he'd begun to forget about scalding hand-baths, and agonising skin grafts, and waltzing tube pedicles. He'd even given up using the ether. Almost. The prospect of a return to it all, even in the interests of an improved appearance, filled him with dread.

'Would you like me to put him off?' Chloe offered gently.

He looked up, studying her anew. Behind the diffident demeanour and frumpy WAAF uniform, she was slight of stature, with a round face, petite features, and chestnut hair in a neat bob. Tidy, he thought, and pretty, and wonderfully unblemished. 'What do you think I should do?' he asked.

'It has to be your decision.'

'I know, but . . . As a woman, Chloe, what do you think? Honestly.'

Steady brown eyes held his, without aversion or embarrassment. 'For me, for most women I'd say, it's not the appearance of a man that counts.'

'It isn't?'

'No. It's what he's made of.'

'I see. Thank you. Again.'

'Not at all. And there's one more message.'

'Which is?'

'The control tower called. The first batch of the new Lancs is due any minute.'

Quentin picked up his cap. 'Then I propose we drive out to meet them!'

They took the Austin, he at the wheel, she shifting gears. By now their actions were automatic, harmonised, no commentary needed, like pilot and co-pilot. Quentin merely had to depress the clutch for Chloe to select a gear – usually the correct one. Beneath a blustery overcast they sped across the rain-puddled concrete and round the perimeter to a far corner of the airfield. There a reception committee of 617 aircrew waited by a control caravan. Quentin recognised several, although Peter wasn't among them.

'Lightfoot's on a training sortie,' one said, ambling up as Quentin disembarked. It was John Hopgood, one of Gibson's inner circle, a twenty-two-year-old Londoner from 106 Squadron. 'Should be back in an hour or two.'

'That's all right, I came to watch the fun. Any sign?'

'Any time now.' Hopgood scanned the horizon, one hand cupped to his eye. 'I heard what you did, Credo. In that Wimpy. Dinghy Young told me. He was in 57 Squadron too, like Geoff Rice.'

'I know.'

'Bloody brave, it was. We all think so. Gibson too. Just wanted you to know.'

'Thanks. I appreciate it.' He glanced at Chloe, surrounded by fawning airmen. 'How's the night training? Are the new lights working?'

'Yes! I really think we've cracked it. And it's the simplest thing. Two spotlights, see, mounted on the underside of the Lanc, one aft of the bomb-bay, the other under the nose. Both angled downwards, forwards and to the right, so from the cockpit you can see them shining on the water, forward of the starboard wing. The boffins set the angles so the two beams converge at a height of sixty feet. Fly too high and the rear spot moves ahead of the forward one, too low and it drops behind. Line the two up, so they're exactly side-by-side and bingo – sixty feet!'

'And it really works?'

'Like a dream! Tried it myself last night. Navigator stands by the pilot, watching the spots and calling the height, you know, up a bit, down a bit, and so on. Meanwhile the bomb aimer sings out the range with his Dann sight thing, and the flight engineer fixes the speed with the throttles. That leaves the pilot free to concentrate on the flying. We made four runs at Derwent last night, and every one worked a treat.'

'That's very good news. What about the radios?'

'Latest plan is to fit VHF, you know, like the fighter boys use, so the Lancs can actually talk to one another, at least over short distances. Then we'll use standard W/T to send and receive Morse signals over long distances.'

Quentin cocked his head. From the west rose the drone of distant engines. 'It's beginning to sound as if it's all coming together, Hoppy.'

'And not a moment too soon. All we need now is a weapon . . .'

'Hmm. Can't comment there.'

'And a target?'

'Nor there. But how about some shiny new Lancs to play with? Here they come!'

The drone rose to a rumble and then to a roar as five of the specially modified Type 464 Provisioning Lancasters thundered overhead, settled into a wide left-hand circuit and descended, one by one, to land. A few minutes later they were taxiing across the grass towards the waiting airmen. Whose reaction was predictably scornful.

'Jesus, look at the bloody things!'

'That is ugly, what have they done to the bomb-bays?'

'They're all cut away, look, and the bomb-doors have gone.'

'Looks like a gutted fish. And what are those fork things sticking down?'

'And where's the upper gun turret?'

But there was no hiding their excitement. All those relentless weeks of training, and borrowed aircraft, whispered rumours, and jibes from other units, and suddenly the job they'd signed up for was becoming a reality. Quentin watched as the leading Lancaster shut down engines, to be immediately mobbed by the waiting airmen, swarming round it like excited children. Glancing over at an abandoned Chloe, who smiled and shrugged ruefully, he saw four schoolboys beyond, their faces pressed to the perimeter fence, fingers gripping the wire like prisoners in a camp, staring in awe at the aircraft. And he waved to them cheerily and went back to his car.

Over the next few days the remaining aircraft were delivered and assigned to their crews. 617 Squadron's identification letters, 'AJ', were painted in red on the side of each, together with a third call-sign letter. Allocating aircraft was a random matter, thus AJ-A for Apple went to Dinghy Young, AJ-B for Baker went to Bill Astell, Gibson got AJ-G for George, Hopgood AJ-M for Mother and so on. Peter's crew, to their delight, were allocated AJ-V for Victor, which they immediately rechristened Vicky in honour of Chalkie's wife. Barely had the engineers signed it off and towed it outside, when they were clambering aboard for a test flight.

'Smell that lads?' Uncle inhaled appreciatively. 'That's the scent of a brand-new aeroplane. Delicious, no? And mind you don't get your muddy feet all over it!'

'Only an engineer could call wet paint delicious. Say boys, what's the winch thing in the bomb-bay?'

'God knows.'

'And don't bother asking him, he'll only chew your head off!'

'Nose turret looks in order,' Billy Bimson reported. 'Clean as a whistle.'

'The new radios are in too,' Chalkie added, seating himself at his station. 'Latest Type 1143 VHFs and thanks very much.'

'New Gee set, too.' Jamie added.

'Same old Elsan,' Herb Guttenberg muttered, pushing past the toilet to the rear turret. With no upper gunner for company he was now alone in the main fuselage, completely cut off from his crewmates sixty feet away in the nose. Unperturbed, he closed his turret doors and squeezed into his seat, sniffing the oil on the four Browning .303 machine guns. Inside the turret felt unusually warm, as afternoon sunshine bathed the Perspex capsule with light. A clear-view panel lay in his line of sight, which he immediately made a note to have removed. Serious rear gunners always did, despite the cold and discomfort, the better to shoot more accurately. Then he checked his sights and worked the charging handles on the Brownings, which felt smooth and new. Each gun fired twelve bullets a second, four guns meant nearly fifty withering rounds every second, devastating firepower if properly used. Shooting at night required exceptional skill, especially at low level, and 617's gunners had been practising hard. Recently they'd come to a decision. Normally ammunition was loaded with every fourth bullet a tracer round, which glowed as it travelled so gunners could follow their shots. Herb and his cohorts, sensing they'd be flying into the teeth of a storm, planned to shoot with 100 per cent tracer, to create a visually shocking effect, maximise accuracy, and fool the Germans they were firing cannon. Wishful thinking, Herb knew, and the guns would run hotter and maybe jam more, but disconcerting the enemy, even for a few seconds, might mean the difference between life and death.

'Say fellas!' he called, sliding open his doors. Way in the distance he could hear the excited chatter of his crewmates. 'Say fellas! Can anyone hear me?'

'We hear you, Herb,' came Chalkie's faint reply.

'Oh, good. Any chance of an intercom check?'

Far away in the nose Kiwi stowed his kit, then stretched out to inspect the huge Perspex nose blister. In his pocket was a piece of string, of specially measured length and with a strategically placed knot in its centre. He and other bomb aimers had found that by tying the string to either side of the blister, then holding it to their nose to form a triangle, exactly the same geometric effect could be achieved as with the wooden Dann sight, only simpler and easier to hold steady. In theory, when the sluice-towers at Derwent lined up precisely with two grease-pencil marks made on the perspex, the bomber would be exactly 450 yards from the dam. In theory. Kiwi pulled out his pencil and unravelled the string. Tonight he'd try it for real.

Above his head Billy Bimson checked his two Brownings, his feet securely stirruped out of harm's way, his fireman teddy bear safe in his pocket. On normal ops the bomb aimer manned the nose gun, only dropping down to his bomb-sights for the run-in to the target. For 617's mission the nose turret would be manned throughout, hence the redundant upper gunner's move there. Clearly, though nobody actually said so, attacking the target head-on would need a full-time nose gunner.

'You all set up there, Billy boy?' Kiwi asked.

'All set, Kiwi,' Billy replied. 'Just wish we could get on with it.'

'Amen to that, mate.'

Up on the flight deck Peter was fastidiously adjusting his seat to match his height and reach. After much fine-tuning, he finally felt settled. 'Hello, Vicky,' he murmured, fingering the Lanc's flight controls. 'Pleased to meet you.'

'You talking to aeroplanes again, laddie?' Uncle nudged him. 'Haven't I warned you about that?'

'Sorry, Uncle. Force of habit,' Peter smiled. 'Remember that old B-Baker at Syerston?'

'Jesus, don't remind me! What a piece of junk.'

'Yes. But do you know, that day, when we boarded for take-off, I didn't speak to it. I never said anything, there wasn't time. And look what happened.'

Uncle's eyes narrowed, unsure whether Peter was being serious. Then he reached out and patted the panel. 'In that case, hello Vicky, Uncle MacDowell speaking, please be a good girl!'

They finished strapping in, powered up the master circuits, donned flying helmets and plugged in intercoms. Communication checks completed, they continued down the checklist towards engine start.

'Switches off.'

'Switches off.'

'Inner tanks on.'

'Inners on.'

'Pumps on.'

'On.'

Until they were ready. Then Uncle leaned to an open side-window. 'Contact starboard outer!' he shouted. Outside on the grass a mechanic raised a thumb. Peter pressed the starter and booster buttons and the number-four propeller clunked over, three times, four, coughed smoke, belched yellow flame from its exhaust, then erupted to life with a throaty roar. Five minutes later and with all four engines running, chocks were removed, brakes released and V-Vicky and her new crew went bumping across the grass towards the downwind corner of the airfield. There the control caravan waited, together with a short queue of

617 Lancasters. Peter joined the line and eased on the brakes, throttling the engines to idle.

'Looks like a bit of a wait, crew,' he reported. 'Shouldn't be long.'

'I hope not,' Uncle muttered. 'Merlins don't like waiting.'

'Say, look, there's Lewis Burpee and his boys in S-Sugar,' Billy said. 'Lew's from Ottawa, Herb, did you know?'

'I did know. His navigator's ex-50 Squadron. Damn fine navigator too.'

'I knew a 50 Squadron navigator once.' Jamie joined. 'Back when they were flying Hampdens. Worst navigator in Bomber Command. He got sacked eventually.'

'What for?'

'Destroying government property. One night he got lost coming home from Germany. Round and round they went, hour after hour, until the Hampden ran low on fuel and they had to land in a field. Somewhere in eastern France, the navigator said. Some locals came running up, but the crew couldn't understand them, and quickly set fire to the bomber before the Germans arrived. Then they ran away and hid. Next day the police found them hiding in a barn.'

'Where were they?'

'Wales.'

'Bloody idiots.'

'Their CO went mad. Perfectly good aeroplane burned for nothing.'

A green light flashed from the control caravan. Immediately a hiss of air as Peter released the brakes and eased up the starboard throttles, turning the bomber into wind. Then he ran each engine up to full power, checking the two-stage blower, the propeller pitch controls and the magnetos. Finally all was ready.

'Okay, Uncle, let's go.'

'Flaps thirty.'

'Thirty.'

'Radiators closed.'

'Closed.'

'Throttles locked.'

'Locked.'

'Rear gunner, all clear behind?'

'All clear behind.'

'That's it everyone, hold tight, here we go!'

'Say boys,' Kiwi called, as the engines rose to a roar. 'Did Jamie just tell a funny story?'

Tess woke with a jolt. The dream again. Massive hands clamped at her throat, wringing the breath from her like a noose. She sat up, shaking, fingering her neck, her heart banging in her chest. Overhead, a rumble of engines receded into the distance. It was these which had woken her, she realised. Lancs. They were non-stop now, training night and day, around the clock, so much so that even Lincoln's loyal residents were starting to complain. Bloody Brylcreem boys, a man grumbled at the butcher's yesterday, poncing about above the rooftops like that. Don't they know there's a war on? Everyone's nerves were stretching, she felt, including hers, including Peter's. Something would have to give, and soon. Before it snapped.

She swung her legs to the floor, wearily scrubbing fingers through her hair. It was early evening, she'd been dozing an hour, compensating for the sleepless hours of night. Her eyes travelled the room, drab and cheerless in the half-light. And untidy, her clothes spilling from a suitcase on the floor, scattered papers and discarded food lying everywhere, as though she was only staying hours, not days. Or weeks. She rose, and a crumpled page fell to her feet, stained with wet. She bent and recovered it, smoothed it, then pressed it to her heart. Quentin's note. The one delivered that afternoon. The one she'd waited six years for. It wasn't a dream. It was real.

He'd found her daughter. At least he'd found an address. In Croxton, in Staffordshire. Barely thirty miles from where she was born. All the research and the letter-writing and the telephone calls had finally borne fruit, albeit in an unexpected way. At first a tentative confirmation. Yes, Mrs Murray, a record does exist of your daughter. Then a follow-up letter. Yes, Mrs Murray, she was adopted, by a family living near Stafford: '. . . CT T. & Mrs G.', who also have an older son. She is healthy and doing well. Then a stone wall. No, Mrs Murray, we cannot give contact details or further information. It is against policy. But Quentin had done the rest, helped by a twist of fate. The letter contained an error, an unintended clue. CT was a military rank, he'd said immediately, reading the letter. Mr G., first initial T., was a Chief Technician, a senior NCO, in the Air Force too, the only service to use that rank. Which was the final irony. Her daughter lived in an RAF family. From then on it was relatively simple, at least for someone as resourceful and well connected as Quentin. There were no operational flying stations in the immediate Stafford area, he reported, but there was an RAF Maintenance Unit – MU16, based just outside the town, and not far from Croxton. A couple of quiet telephone calls later, and CT T. G. was identified as Chief Technician Thomas Groves, married with two children, all of 23 Poplar Lane, Croxton, Staffs.

And there it was, waiting on the hall table when she returned from the library that afternoon. She'd immediately spotted

Quentin's ragged handwriting on the envelope and known some-how, hurrying breathlessly upstairs, that his message was momentous. At the instant of reading it she'd felt herself falling, as though in a dream, and she'd sunk to her bed, turned to her pillow, and sobbed as though her heart would burst. And then finally she'd found sleep.

Now she must go there. Today, right away. First to the station to find out about trains to Stafford, then back to pack and pre-pare. She reached for her coat, but then hesitated. She should tell Peter first, she realised. The news was so important he must be notified. Somehow. And she should also thank Quentin, who had done so much, and not without risk. And she needed more clothes, and her post office savings book, and her best shoes. All of which meant going on base, and into her living quarters. A blood-chilling prospect, but unavoidable. She sat down again to think things through. And then a floorboard creaked, right outside her door. She froze, rigid with terror. And it creaked again, and she could see shadows moving beneath the door. Then came the knock, softly, almost apolo-getically. And a man's voice.

'Tess, dear. It's me.'

She crept to the door, one hand to her mouth, and opened. He'd aged, she saw at once, and shrunk, from the imposing man of her memory, his once dark hair now ash-grey, his posture stooped, his face drawn and lined.

'My God,' she said. 'Father, is it really you?'

'I'm so sorry, turning up unannounced like this.' Rheumy eyes took in the room. 'I wasn't sure . . . Is this where you live?'

'No. Well, yes . . .' she blurted. 'I suppose so, for the moment. But Father, what are you doing here? How did you find me?'

'With some difficulty!' he joked, then burst into coughing. He was wearing his smart City overcoat, which was too big for him now, and nervously fingering the brim of his trilby. 'Taxi dropped me at Scampton. Terrible palaver. Barbed wire, armed guards, dogs, endless questions, and they searched me, you know. What's going on?'

'It's . . . Oh, it's just some flap, Father, they're always having them.'

'Well they weren't letting me in, that's for sure, not without an appointment, and an escort. Nor were they going to contact you, or your husband. Brian, isn't it?'

'Brendan.' Tess felt a chill. 'Father. Please tell me they didn't send for him.'

'No. They fetched some security officer, a flight lieutenant, dreadfully disfigured, poor fellow. He asked me a lot of damn-fool questions too, until I managed to convince him I meant you no ill, whereupon he gave me this address. And got his driver girl to drop me here, which was decent of him.'

'Yes, he is. Very decent.'

'The landlady let me in, showed me upstairs, and, well, here I am.' He shrugged.

'Yes. Here you are. And do you, Father?'

'Do I what?'

'Mean me no ill?'

'None at all. I miss you, that's all. And came to tell you so. And see how you are.'

'After all this time. But why? I mean, why now?'

'Because it's long overdue. And life's too short . . .'

They walked up the hill to the cathedral, pausing frequently to rest. He was ill, she realised, breathless and weak. Soon she was slipping an arm round him for support. It felt strange, after all the years, embracing her father again, strange but not unnatural.

They arrived in time for choral evensong, where side by side in the vaulted transept they listened to Howell's haunting *Nunc Dimittis*, and watched brilliantly coloured evening sunlight pour through the great southern window.

'Exquisite,' her father murmured. 'I'd forgotten it was so big. Just look at the tracery.'

'You've been here before?'

'Once. On holiday with your mother. Before you were born.'

Tess looked up at the distant ceiling. 'When the weather's misty, which is quite often around here, the bomber crews say the cathedral seems to float in the air like a ship on an ocean. They can see it from miles away, guiding them to safety.'

'I can imagine,' he nodded, still gazing at the window. 'Peter's in bombers, I believe. He came to see us. He was worried about you. It didn't go well, I'm afraid.'

'He told me. We're . . . well, we're in touch.'

'I'm glad.'

Afterwards he bought her supper in a nearby pub, where they attempted to talk of happier times, or neutral topics like the war or the weather or news of old relatives. At first it felt stilted and false, but gradually she realised he wasn't there to scold or lecture, but just talk, and seek peace, and comfort, even reconciliation. David was in Africa, he said, and doing well, although she knew this from his occasional letters. As for her mother, he said she was in good health and left it at that. He ate little and his wine stayed untouched, and all too soon, clearly exhausted, he asked her to walk him to his hotel.

'It's the cancer, Tess,' he confessed, at the door. 'In my chest. And bones. Everywhere, really.'

'I'm so sorry.'

'Don't be. Anyway it's me who should apologise.' He gripped

her hand. 'I've an early train in the morning. Don't bother seeing me off.'

'Would you like me to visit you in Bexley?'

'Very much. But only if you feel up to it.'

'And Peter?'

His eyes searched hers. 'What happened, Tess, the way we treated you, was terribly wrong. I've always known, and always regretted it. I only pray you can find it in your heart to forgive us. Before it's too late.'

'What about Mother?'

'Her faith sustains her. It's all she has now. Don't expect too much.'

She walked back to her lodgings and up the darkened stairs to her room, which felt gloomy and claustrophobic suddenly. She picked up Quentin's note and reread it. Somehow its message too had shifted in perspective. And at the bottom, in his illegible hand, was something she'd earlier chosen to ignore.

PS. Tess old thing, I pass you this information because you asked me to. (Although I probably shouldn't — abuse of authority and so on!) But I beg you to use it cautiously, and not do anything rash. You should talk it over with Peter too, but not now, for obvious reasons. It is essential his mind be completely focused on the task at hand, for the short time remaining before he must carry it out. In the meantime, knowing your daughter is safe and well must be a great comfort. With best wishes Q.

The bombs arrived. Thirty-seven of them, on a convoy of low-loaders shrouded in tarpaulins, and driven straight to a guarded hangar away from view. With them came specially modified bomb trolleys, a ten-ton mobile crane and a wheeled gantry for loading. An additional nineteen practice bombs, identical in every detail except concrete-filled, were delivered to Manston for tests at Reculver. At last 617's crews got to see the weapon they'd trained so hard to use – and have a try at using it.

Results were encouraging, although not problem-free. Spinning the bombs up to speed took time and caused the aircraft to vibrate, sometimes alarmingly, which affected handling and performance, and if the drop was aborted for any reason it took forty minutes more for the bomb to stop spinning. Their rotation affected magnetic compasses too, and with accurate navigation vital, these had to be carefully re-swung. As for dropping the bombs, the relentless weeks of training had not been in vain, and the crews showed skill, determination and accuracy. But Les Munro in W-Whisky came in too low for his practice drop, and a huge column of water engulfed the aircraft, damaging the tail and nearly drowning the rear gunner. A day or two later Henry Maudslay in Z-Zebra made the same mistake and fared even worse, suffering elevator damage, losing the tailwheel and limping back to Scampton on only three engines. Most drops went smoothly however, and the bombs themselves behaved well, except for occasional waywardness, typically bouncing four or five times over distances of four to six hundred yards.

Which was good enough. Another week passed, the days grew longer, the weather turned mild and dry. Back at Scampton training continued, but with subtle differences. The priority now was on conserving both aircraft and crews in optimum condition, so emphasis was shifted away from the risky business of attack, and onto procedural matters, communications and navigation. The three groups that emerged in training were now formally consolidated: a primary flight of nine led by Gibson in G-George,

Peter's second flight of six led by big Joe McCarthy in Q-Queenie, and a back-up flight of five led by twenty-year-old Warner Ottley in C-Charlie. Training flights were increasingly flown in these formations and along prescribed routes, specially prepared to mimic the course to the targets. One night the whole squadron took off in battle formation, setting off in their sections to simulate the routes into and out of the targets. Like a dress rehearsal.

But if the flying programme slackened slightly, conditions on the ground were tighter than ever. Scampton was like a high-security prison, with leave stopped and personnel all but banned from moving in or out, even for a few hours. Guards roamed everywhere, patrolling fences, checking passes, accosting the unwary. Doors were barred, gates locked, barriers erected, while Number 2 hangar itself was practically a fortress. One civilian contractor, sent to make radio repairs on a Lanc, spent the night in the guardhouse after misplacing his papers. Another never made it through the main gate, despite the urgency of his visit. A virtual communications blackout was imposed, with news filtered, phone calls listened to and paperwork censored. Private correspondence too was opened and read, such that many people gave up writing to loved ones until the furore passed. Except the aircrew, who were told to continue writing home in order to avoid suspicion, keep subject-matter vague yet, perversely, enclose their wills if not already written. 'All quiet here,' Peter wrote in his letter to his father. 'Weather pleasant, reading quite a lot, not much else to report.'

And every day the water crept a little higher up the dams. Photographs arrived regularly, taken by reconnaissance pilots flying specially adapted high-altitude Spitfires.

'Look at these, Quentin,' Whitworth said one morning. 'Just arrived, hot off the press. I've called Gibson, he's on his way. Look, this is the Eder dam, and this the Sorpe. Or targets Y and Z as we should now be calling them. See the water? It's just feet from the top.'

'Yes sir, they look fit to burst. How about the Möhne?'

Gibson burst in. 'It's target X, Credo, for Christ's sake! Target X! Don't ever let me hear you calling it by its name!'

'No sir. Sorry sir.'

'Good. Now let's have a look.' He began studying the photos. Quentin and Whitworth stood back, exchanging glances. Gibson looked a wreck, his black hair dishevelled, his eyes bloodshot, chin unshaved, and a livid red sore showed on his nose where his oxygen mask chafed. He was short with everyone now, even his inner retinue, irritable and edgy from the endless weeks of organising, training, problem-solving, too little sleep and too much flying. Unless he rested, they both suspected, or flew the mission and got it over with, he would crack, and soon.

'We should get on with it,' he muttered, as though reading their thoughts. He gestured at the pictures. 'They're ready, we're ready, we should bloody get on with it!'

'I know, Guy,' Whitworth soothed. 'Cochrane's as eager as hell, believe me. So is Harris. But it's a political decision now. Churchill's fully briefed, and Portal too. He's in America, you know, seeing Roosevelt himself, it's all very delicate. But everyone's bang on the beam, and right behind you.'

'Then they should make the bloody decision!'

'What's that?' Quentin bent to one of the photos.

'What?'

'There. On the Möh . . . I mean, on target X'

Whitworth peered. 'Quentin, what are you talking about?'

Quentin picked up a magnifying glass, and focused it on the dam. 'That.' Then he leaned closer, and his neck prickled. 'Crates. There on the dam. Large wooden crates. And they weren't there yesterday.'

Chapter 8

Within an hour the RAF's photo-intelligence unit (PIU) at Medmenham in Buckinghamshire telephoned to confirm they too had observed anomalies in the latest dams photos. Enlargements were being processed, and would be couriered straight to 5 Group headquarters in Grantham. By lunchtime an emergency meeting was under way, and Quentin found himself sitting in Grantham's elegant boardroom, together with Guy Gibson, Charles Whitworth, Ralph Cochrane and an aide to Arthur Harris, who was waiting at the end of a phone in High Wycombe. Also present was Quentin's intelligence superior, Frank Arnott, and a senior technician from the PIU. Scattered across the table were blow-ups of the Möhne dam photograph.

'So there's no doubt,' Cochrane said, after a long period of inspection.

'None at all, sir,' the technician replied. 'Wooden crates,

twelve in all, about ten feet by four. Arrived last night under cover of darkness.'

'Bugger.' Cochrane shook his head. 'Not what we needed.'

'No, sir.'

'And the question is, what's in them?'

'That I can't say, sir.'

'Could it be anti-aircraft artillery?'

'Yes sir, easily. 20 millimetre flak or similar. Or extra lighting, or more torpedo defences or simply spare parts for the sluice towers, there's no way of knowing until the crates are opened.'

'When's the next photo flight?'

'Later this afternoon sir, but . . .'

'But what!'

'There's eight-eighths cloud cover in the Ruhr right now, and it's not forecast to clear until tomorrow at the earliest. We may not get any more photos for a while.'

'Christ. And Harris needs to know now. As do others . . .'

A lull followed as everyone digested the discovery. Much was at stake with this mission, including reputations, and a disaster was unthinkable. Quentin knew Cochrane's 'others' included Charles Portal, head of the RAF, currently in Washington and anxiously awaiting an update, also the Secretary of State for Air, the War Office, the Cabinet Office and, not least, the Prime Minister.

'Charles?' Cochrane turned to Whitworth. 'What do you make of it all?'

'A worrying development, and no question,' Whitworth replied. 'But serious enough to call off the operation? Impossible to say at this juncture.'

'Arnott?'

'I'm confident the operation has not been compromised, sir.

Not from within Scampton, that is. More photos, as soon as they can be obtained, will surely confirm this. I'm for pressing ahead.'

'Hmm. Credo?'

'Sir.' Quentin began doggedly. His head was aching and he felt hot and feverish, as though from the moment he'd first spotted the crates, he'd begun to feel ill with foreboding. 'My understanding was always that if there was the slightest chance the Germans were expecting us, then the mission could not go ahead. The risks to the crews would be unacceptable.'

'But there's no evidence they *are* expecting us!' Arnott waved a photo. 'These boxes could contain anything. Lavatory paper, for all we know!'

'But it is a terrible coincidence, isn't it?'

'What are you implying, Credo?'

'Only that we should consider the possibility the Germans know. After all, the *Tirpitz* got moved.'

'And whose fault was that!'

'Gentlemen!' Cochrane held up a hand. 'We're desperately short of time. And ultimately this is an operational decision.' He turned to Gibson, head down at the end of the table. 'Guy, old chap. What's your view?'

Gibson lifted his face from his hands. It seemed to have aged ten years in three months. 'Well, sir, the way I see it, every day that passes increases the risk. So I think we should go, immediately. Or call it off.'

'Very well.' Cochrane pushed back his chair. 'Thank you for your attendance, gentlemen, please wait here. I'm going to speak to Harris.'

They waited, half an hour went by, a steward brought glasses and a decanter, then a tray of sandwiches that nobody touched.

Finally, nearly an hour after he'd left the room, Cochrane returned, bearing a slip of paper.

'Sorry everyone, no easy matter conducting a three-way conference across the Atlantic. But we have a consensus.'

Gibson was rising to his feet. 'Sir?'

Cochrane held up the paper. 'This was issued ten minutes ago. It's from Portal to Harris: *Operation Chastise. Immediate attack of targets X,Y and Z approved. Execute at first suitable opportunity*.'

It was Friday 14 May 1943.

Quentin rode in the car back to Scampton with Gibson and Whitworth. At first nobody spoke, each wrapped in thought. Quentin sat in front, nursing a giddy head, and his arm which throbbed like the devil. But despite his own reservations, he could sense that Gibson was relieved at Cochrane's announcement – as though casting the die had lifted a weight from his shoulders. Settled in the back while Whitworth drove, he looked more composed than he had in weeks. More at ease with himself. More sanguine.

'The moon is good for Sunday night,' he murmured after a while. 'I'd like to go then. Weather permitting.'

Whitworth glanced in the mirror. 'The day after tomorrow. Excellent. I'll put the wheels in motion.'

'Not too much fuss, please, sir. No battle orders pinned up, or anything like that. We'll just call it a full squadron exercise. Up until the last minute, that is.'

'Very good. When will you brief everyone?'

'As late as possible. I'll tell senior flight crew tomorrow, then we'll brief everyone on Sunday, and aim to take off around 2100 hours.'

'Understood.'

'Will Mr Wallis be available for the briefing?'

'I'm sure he wouldn't miss it for the world.'

'Good. I think the boys would like to hear it from him.'

'He does have a way with words.' Whitworth checked the mirror again. 'Are you all right, Guy?'

'Yes, sir. I'm fine, now.' He gazed out at the passing countryside. 'You know, there's this odd thing. When you're running in low over the water, in the moonlight. We noticed it up at Derwent a few times. When the wind is calm, and the water's absolutely without a ripple. Like glass.'

'Really? What sort of thing?'

'Well, you're down on the water, coming in flat-out towards the dam, and the moonlight's shining overhead. But also from below off the water. And there's this perfect reflection of the dam ahead of you. Only upside down. As though there are two dams.'

'Sounds a bit disconcerting.'

'It is, slightly, although you get used to it. You just have to remember to keep flying the Lanc absolutely straight and level. Between the dams and the moonlight.'

The next day, the Saturday, dawned misty and mild. As the morning wore on the sky began to clear and temperatures to rise – literally and figuratively. Unusually, except for a few air tests, all of 617's Lancasters remained on the ground, undergoing maintenance and servicing, as did the aircrews who passed the day lounging around the mess, or soaking up the sun on the grass, or lying on their beds reading the papers. And attempting to ignore the rising buzz of expectation. Everyone knew Gibson had called a select few to his rooms the previous night, and today the select few were striding about trying not to look purposeful. Then at lunchtime the head of 5 Group himself arrived,

Air Vice Marshal Cochrane, to be met by station commander Whitworth and whisked off for meetings. Then early in the afternoon a light aircraft landed, flown by Vickers' chief pilot and carrying a worried-looking civilian with white hair, who someone swiftly identified as the famous inventor Barnes Wallis, before he too was spirited away.

'What the bloody hell's going on?' Kiwi grumbled, chewing on a grass stem. They were all together, Peter's crew, sprawled on the grass, while bees toiled diligently around them and skylarks twittered above. Across the airfield, shimmering in unseasonal heat, a gang-mower spewed grass-clippings high in the air, like a green fountain.

'Balloon's going up.' Chalkie replied firmly. 'Can't be any doubt.'

'About time too. This waiting is driving me nuts.'

'Could be some other flap, though, couldn't it?' Billy asked. 'Nothing to do with us, I mean.'

'What kind of other flap, you daft Canuck! We are the flap!'

'Kiwi, I've told you before about that word. One more time and I'll . . .'

'You'll what?'

'Steady now, boys.' Peter spoke up. 'Let's save it for Jerry, okay?' He glanced over at Uncle, the crew's regular peace-keeper. But the Scotsman was sitting apart, deeply engrossed in a much dog-eared letter.

'All right, Uncle?' he murmured, squatting beside him. The letter, he knew, was the last Uncle had ever received from his wife, before she was killed in the air-raid. Reading it, something he rarely did, was not a good sign.

'She . . . She wrote it from her sister's,' Uncle whispered hoarsely. 'Mary did. I said Liverpool could be dangerous, what with the docks getting bombed and that. But Mary said her sister was poorly and needed help for a few days, and though I argued, she wouldn't hear of it. So off she went.'

'I know.' Peter encouraged. 'You always said she was strong-spirited.'

'Aye, that she was!' Uncle forced a grin, though his eyes were glistening. 'That's why I loved her so. For her spirit.' His gaze returned to the letter. A moment later a single tear fell on to the page.

'Uncle . . .' But the Scotsman could only shake his head. Peter rested a hand on his shoulder, and turned his eyes to the distant mower, still plying Scampton's verdant turf. Brendan Murray could well be manning it, he reflected. And Peter hadn't seen nor spoken to Tess in a week. Not knowing anything, about her situation, her wellbeing, her state of mind, was torture, worse than not knowing about the mission. Last night, in desperation, he'd asked Credo for help. A message, he'd pleaded, a brief meeting, anything, just for a few minutes. But Credo was unusually brusque. Jesus, Lightfoot! he'd snapped. Not now for God's sake! Before stamping away clutching his arm. Everyone, it seemed, was right on the ragged edge.

'Peter,' Uncle murmured. 'This job. This mission.'

'Yes?'

'It's my last. Whatever happens. You understand?'

'You mustn't talk like that. You'll feel differently when it's over.'

'No I won't. I won't feel anything. I'm finished with it all.'

'Listen, Uncle, afterwards, we'll all get a few days' leave, we can go off . . .'

'Look!' A shout came from Billy. 'Here comes Jamie, and in a hurry too! Maybe he's learned something.'

All gathered round as a red-cheeked Jamie pedalled up on a bicycle. 'God, it's getting hot out here!'

'And?'

'And I've just come from the hangar,' he puffed. 'They're loading bombs.'

'Practice ones?'

'Real ones. On a couple of Lancs. As if making sure they fit.'

Chalkie let out a whistle. 'Well that's it then, boys. Job's on. Can't be any doubt. Wouldn't you say, Peter?'

'It's certainly starting to look that way.' He glanced at Uncle, who was carefully folding his letter away. Beyond him a battered staff car was making its way slowly round the apron, stopping at each knot of airmen, before moving on to the next.

'Now what?' Herb asked.

'Isn't that the SIO's car? The one with the dishy WAAF driver?'

'Looks like it. And coming our way.'

'Good-oh, she's a popsie all right.'

A minute later the car pulled up and Quentin leaned from the window. 'Briefing in the ops room at 1800 hours,' he said. 'Pilots, navigators and bomb aimers only.'

'What about the rest of us?' Billy grumbled.

'Sorry. Can't help. Flying Officer Lightfoot, could I speak to you a moment?'

Peter approached the car. Quentin was perspiring, he saw, his face waxy and pale. Beside him his driver, Hickson, sat inscrutably at the wheel. 'Sir?'

'Lightfoot. About last night . . .'

'Don't worry, sir. I shouldn't have asked, you've done too much already.'

'No, but listen. The southwestern perimeter. By the village

road. Tonight at midnight. She'll be there. You'll have to talk through the fence, and for God's sake keep it short. Also . . .' He broke off, wiping his brow with his sleeve.

Peter waited. Outside Hangar 2, a Type 464 Lancaster was being towed onto the grass, G-George, Gibson's own. 'Sir, are you all right? You don't look well.'

'I'm fine. Slight fever that's all. Listen, Peter, this is important. Be really careful, do you understand?'

'Of course, sir, no one will know, I'll make sure . . .'

'I'm not talking about tonight.' He nodded towards the Lancaster. 'I'm talking about that. When it comes down to it, just be terribly careful.'

That evening 617's sixty pilots, navigators and bomb aimers gathered in the ops room above Number 2 hangar. All were experienced airmen, all had been briefed on important operations before, but the air this time was more highly charged than any could remember. On a raised dais stood three tables bearing boxes draped in cloths. Another curtain hid a huge map of Europe mounted on the wall behind. At six on the dot the rear doors opened, everyone stood up, and four men walked up the central aisle to the dais: Gibson, Wallis, Cochrane and Whitworth. Gibson took centre stage, bade everyone sit, seconds of scraping chairs followed, then the room fell to attentive silence.

'You are going to hit the enemy harder than a small force has ever done before,' he began. Short, squat, feet braced, hands on hips, he looked every inch the leader in control. 'Very soon we are going to attack the major dams of western Germany. Smashing them will bring enemy industry to its knees and help shorten the war.' At that he picked up a billiard cue and pulled back the curtain. 'Here they are, the Möhne, the Eder and the

Sorpe dams. We will attack them in three separate waves flying by different routes shown here in red. Opposition will be stiff, but if we follow these routes accurately and attack the dams as we practised, then everything will be fine. In a moment I'll go into the details, but first I'd like to introduce the inventor of our weapon, Mr Barnes Wallis, who will explain the importance of the dams, and how we are going to smash them.'

Wallis rose shyly to his feet. 'Did you know . . .' he began, as on so many previous occasions. 'It takes eight tons of water to make one ton of steel . . .'

The briefing went on. After Wallis finished, Cochrane made a call-to-arms speech of encouragement: '. . . If Bomber Command is a bludgeon to Hitler, you are the rapier-thrust to bring him down,' before handing back to Gibson for the mission briefing proper.

617 Squadron's twenty Lancasters, Gibson repeated, were to be dispatched in three waves. The first wave, comprising his select nine, would take off in three sections of three, at ten-minute intervals, and fly a southerly route, crossing the Suffolk coast at Southwold before dropping down to wave-top height for the sea crossing, and a landfall near Schouwen in the southern Netherlands. From there they would continue at low level across Holland and into Germany, avoiding known flak hotspots where possible, until they reached the Möhne, where they would press home their attack. Once the Möhne was breached they would move on to the Eder. Meanwhile a second wave of six led by Joe McCarthy would be arriving on the scene. This wave was to take off ten minutes earlier than Gibson's, and fly a longer north-ern route, crossing the enemy coast 100 miles north at Vlieland in the Ijsselmeer. Their job, apart from diverting attention from the main group, was to attack the Sorpe, assuming all went well

with the Möhne and Eder. A third wave of five aircraft led by Warner Ottley would take off two and a half hours later, fly the southern route and provide back-up as required. If as hoped all three main dams were successfully breached, they were to attack secondary reserve targets of the Lister, Ennepe and Diemel dams.

'And that's it,' Gibson declared eventually. 'In a nutshell.'

'What about getting home?' someone piped up from the back. A ripple of nervous laughter followed.

'Ah yes, almost forgot!' Gibson grinned. 'Apart from the flight leaders who will stay to coordinate things, as soon as each aircraft releases its weapon it will make its own way home via the safest route – still at low level. The leaders will follow, then we'll all meet back here for breakfast. And a drink.'

'Or ten!'

'Absolutely. The whole show from first take-off to last landing should take no more than eight hours. Now, come and look at these.' He moved to the three tables and withdrew their dust-covers. Upon each was an exact scale model of the dams and their environs. 'I want you to memorise these in every detail, the surrounding terrain, the position of the dams, any known defences, the way in, and the way out again. Then go and sketch them from memory, then come back and check your sketches, until they're completely fixed in your minds, and you can find and recognise them blindfold.'

'Thank Christ it isn't the *Tirpitz*,' someone from Peter's wave murmured, as they shuffled forward with the others. 'At least with these we've a chance.' Soon all were crowding round the Sorpe model.

'Doesn't look too bad, does it, boys?' McCarthy said, after an interval.

'No sluice towers to line up on,' Kiwi pointed out. 'We'll have to estimate the range from the banks. Shouldn't be too difficult.'

'No. It's a good straight run-in from the southwest, not too much high ground around, and a nice clear climb-out after the drop. Should be a breeze.'

'Not like that Eder one,' Barlow added. 'Have you seen it? Nasty tight approach, steep drop to the water, hills everywhere. That's going to be a tough nut.'

'What about defences?' Jamie was still peering at the Sorpe model. 'This town here, Langscheid, right by the dam, any flak emplacements, do you think?'

'That's an unknown,' McCarthy said. 'So I guess we'll find out on the night.'

Tess waited in the back of Quentin's car, anxiously watching the perimeter fence. The car was parked in a quiet lane close to the fence, and hidden from view by a copse. Sitting behind the wheel was Quentin's driver, Chloe Hickson. Who had said very little since collecting Tess from her lodgings in Lincoln.

'It's terribly kind of you to go to all this trouble,' Tess said for the third time. Overhead the full moon, haloed by a summer mist, cast eerie shadows over the scene.

'Not at all. I'm merely following Flight Lieutenant Credo's instructions.'

'So you said. Um, is he well?'

'He's resting. He's been a little poorly. Why do you ask?'

'I was hoping to see him, that's all. In person. To thank him. For everything he's done for me. For us.'

'Perhaps you can thank him some other way.'

'Yes.' Tess wondered what she meant, and for a moment thought of Brendan's notebook, but at that moment she detected movement beyond the fence. 'There's Peter!' she whispered. 'Thank you, again, don't bother waiting, I'll walk back.'

She slid from the car and hurried to him. A moment later they were pressed against the fence, fingers entwined, kissing awkwardly.

'Tess, thank God. Are you all right?'

'I'm fine, just missing you.' Behind them she heard Chloe's car drive off. 'What about you? You look tired.'

'No, I'm fine. Hating being separated like this. Just counting the days.'

'Me too. How's it going?'

'It's on, Tess! Soon, very soon.'

'Thank heavens. You must be relieved.'

'Yes, I am, we all are. Tess, it's huge, you can't imagine.'

She squeezed his fingers. 'Promise me you'll be careful.'

'You sound like Credo!' he grinned. 'But I will. And the moment it's over I'll come and find you, and we'll get away from here, from Brendan, from everything.'

'I can't wait.' She stretched up and they kissed again.

'What about your news?' Peter went on. 'Have you heard anything? From the adoption people or anything?'

'No. Nothing of interest.' She smiled. No important news, she'd decided earlier, nothing that might trouble him. Only the encouraging, or mundane. 'But guess what? My father came to see me!'

'Good grief! When?'

'Last week. Just turned up out of the blue. Thanks to you.'

'Really?'

'He said you visited them and spoke up for me, which apparently impressed him no end, because he decided enough was enough, and came to make his peace.'

'Well, that's wonderful. And how was it?'

'Strange. But, we talked, you know, and it was okay. I think we've reached an understanding.'

'What about your mother?'

'In time, perhaps.'

'Tess, that's fantastic, I'm so relieved for you.' He glanced behind him. Far in the distance echoed the sound of workshops in full swing. 'I have to go, they've got guards patrolling every fifteen minutes.'

'Wait!' She fumbled at her neck. 'Take this. I want you to have it.'

She passed the St Christopher through the fence. 'It's to keep you safe on your journey.'

He stared at the medallion, glinting in the moonlight. 'Thank you, Tess.'

'God speed, Peter.' She pressed herself to the wire one final time, straining through the links to touch her lips to his. 'I'll be there with you, every step of the way.'

They kissed once more, then he turned and vanished into the night.

Chloe meanwhile drove the short distance round to the main gate, showed her pass, parked, and hurried up to Quentin's quarters. Where there was no answer. She hesitated, unsure what to do. When she'd seen him two hours earlier he'd looked awful, pale, sweating, and almost incoherent with fever. 'Go collect Tess for me!' he'd begged. 'Take her southwest perimeter. To meet Lightfoot.' Then he'd slumped back in his chair in a daze.

She knocked again, still no answer, then tried the door, which was unlocked, and entered. The room was in darkness save for

210

his reading light. But his chair was empty. At first she couldn't see him, but there was an overpowering smell: ethyl alcohol, she recognised, and something else, something much worse. Something sweet and sickly.

He was on his bed, panting like an animal and unconscious with fever. His shirt was plastered to his chest, his gloved right hand hung limply in space, while his left clutched a surgical mask attached by elastic to the bedhead. 'Quentin?' she whispered fearfully. 'My God, Quentin, what's happening to you?'

Ten minutes later Whitworth arrived, together with the station medical officer.

'I'm so sorry, sir. I didn't know what else to do but call you.'

'You did the right thing, Corporal.'

'He's burning up,' the MO said, peeling back Quentin's eyelids.

'An infection of some kind?' Whitworth asked.

'No, sir.' Gently he raised Quentin's right hand. 'It's this. It's necrotic.'

'Gangrene?'

'Yes. It's dead. Should have come off ages ago. Now it's killing him.'

'Christ. What can we do?'

'Hospital. Right away. And pray it isn't too late.'

'I'll take him, sir,' Chloe said immediately. 'Please. It'll be quickest.'

'Yes. Yes, all right. And stay with him, and keep me fully posted.'

The MO stood back. 'He should go to East Grinstead. McIndoe's place. It's further, but they've got his records and McIndoe's his best chance. I'll set him up on a drip, and send an orderly with him.'

'Good. Quick as you can, I'll phone East Grinstead.' Whitworth gazed down at Quentin, pale and shaking in the half-light. 'The poor boy. I was just trying to help, you know, help him get over it. Not being able to fly. Keep him busy, make him feel useful. He should have been at McIndoe's all along. I just made matters worse.'

'No, you didn't, sir,' Chloe said. 'You really did help him, I saw it, he belongs now, he has a job, a role, everyone respects him. I even heard him laugh. This is not your fault.'

Sunday 16 May passed in a blur of feverish activity. Preparing a squadron of Lancasters for a mission was a massive undertaking, requiring the coordinated actions of hundreds. Fuellers, armourers, signallers, radio technicians, fitters, parachute packers, planners, cooks, drivers, not to mention the 140 aircrew the twenty aircraft would carry. Preparing 617 Squadron that day required many scores more, for the new radio equipment, the preparation of the navigation routes, the lists of special codes and signals and, not least, the weapon itself. The weather remained unseasonably hot, tempers frayed, mistakes were made. At one point Barnes Wallis himself flew into a frenzy when he learned the wrong oil was being used on his bombs. A panicked search ensued, but no correct oil could be found, until it was eventually located at another station. Then a fully-armed *Upkeep* fell to the concrete whilst being loaded into one Lancaster. Groundcrew scattered for cover, nobody dared go near, finally one brave armourer returned to the scene. 'If it was going to go off,' he said, prodding it with his foot, 'we'd have been blown sky-high by now.' A few minutes later the bomb was safely back in its callipers and the loading work went on. Eleven thousand pounds of high-octane fuel for every aircraft, plus 1300 pounds of oil,

30,000 rounds of ammunition, and 9000 pounds of *Upkeep*. 'You know what that is, son?' a rigger said to his mate, as they stood before a fully prepped Lanc. 'A thirty-ton firecracker waiting to go off.'

The hours ticked by. Soon any pretence at practice missions was forgotten. A meal was served for all aircrew, the traditional pre-mission feast of bacon, two eggs and as much tea and toast as anyone wanted. Conversation was stilted, the tension palpable, stewards exchanged glances, everyone knew the boys would be fighting for real that night. Then there were the continual briefings – another sure giveaway. Weather briefings, signals briefings, navigation briefings, bombing briefings and late in the afternoon, a second full briefing for all aircrew by Gibson and his team. At last, barely hours before they would take to the air, every crewman learned where they were going, and why. As before, Gibson went through the details of the mission, as before Barnes Wallis explained the science, as before Cochrane exhorted them to heroic action.

Then suddenly, as the early evening sun began to go down and the heat to abate at last, everything grew still and quiet. A meditative hush fell over Scampton. The work was finished, twenty Lancasters stood at their dispersal points, fuelled, armed and ready to go. Their crews donned flying clothes, collected their harnesses, parachutes and Mae Wests, and wandered out into the mild evening air to wait, smoking, talking in low voices, or just staring out over the wide Lincolnshire countryside in contemplative silence. At 8.30 p.m. Gibson received the final go-ahead. The weather was clear across Europe, no abnormal activity was reported on the dams, diversionary ops were being dispatched, the way was clear for Operation *Chastise* to proceed. Dressed coolly in tie and shirtsleeves for the mission, wearing his parachute harness and prized German life-vest, he wandered among his men, offering a joke, a word of encouragement, a shake of the hand. Then shortly before nine he casually turned his wrist.

'Well, chaps. My watch says it's time to go.'

Chapter 9

It was to be an inauspicious beginning. All crews except those in Wave 3 boarded their aircraft and prepared for flight. Then at 2115 hours Gibson fired a red Very light, signalling engine-start. Fifteen Lancasters cranked sixty Merlins to life, but one, on McCarthy's Q-Queenie, immediately sprang a coolant leak and had to be shut down. In the cockpit of V-Vicky Peter and Uncle watched anxiously. McCarthy's wave was to take off ten minutes before Gibson's. Big Joe was its leader, his was the honour of leading 617 Squadron into the air. There was one spare Type 464 Lancaster available, but it was across the field and would need time to prepare. Clearly Joe would be delayed at best, possibly scrubbed altogether.

And V-Vicky was second in line.

'You know what, laddie?' Uncle watched as maintenance trucks careered across the field towards Q-Queenie. 'I'd say it's up to us.'

'You're right.' Peter reached for the throttles, released the brakes and began the long taxi to the end of the airfield, V-Vicky wallowing heavily beneath his feet. Behind, the others formed up in line, leaving Q-Queenie stranded. Peter and Uncle exchanged glances. Down to nineteen aircraft already, and they weren't even airborne.

Beside the control caravan, and in true Bomber Command tradition, a crowd of well-wishers had gathered to see them off. Among them was an anxious Barnes Wallis, also Charles Whitworth, and Scampton's two intelligence chiefs, Arnott and Campbell.

'Quite a sight, no?' Whitworth shouted above the thunder of engines.

'Certainly bloody noisy!' Arnott replied, clamping hands over his ears. 'Where's that clot Credo? He's missing the fun!'

'Hospital, Arnott.' Whitworth replied witheringly. 'Having his arm taken off.'

Arnott looked shocked and opened his mouth to reply, but his words were whipped away by V-Vicky's slipstream as Peter gunned the throttles, turned the overladen bomber into wind, and at a flash of green from the caravan set off down the runway. Slowly, laboriously, the aeroplane began its run, the giant bomb bulging incongruously between its wheels. Whitworth held his breath. It was all taking too long, he thought. But then the Lancaster's tail rose, and the Merlins began to bite, settling to a brassy snarl as V-Vicky picked up pace. Now the great machine was charging the distant fence like a spreading swan, engines singing, the sunset brilliant on its wings, and at last the wheels were skittering off, then on, then off the ground one final time, and Whitworth breathed with relief as it rose triumphantly into the evening air, tucked away its undercarriage, and turned east for the sea. Operation *Chastise* was under way.

On board all was quiet as V-Vicky's crew settled to their tasks. Soon they were crossing the coast near Mablethorpe and heading out across the North Sea for Holland. Peter eased the bomber down towards the water. Dusk was falling around them, the air warm and smooth, the ocean calm, and after weeks of training, racing along above the waves felt almost effortless. Behind them, strung out at one-minute intervals, were the four remaining aircraft of Wave 2: Barlow in E-Easy, Munro in W-Willie, Byers in K-King and Rice in H-Harry. Maintaining radio silence was paramount, but Herb reported them all in visual contact, while Chalkie exchanged ribald Morse messages through the astrodome. Elsewhere, they hoped, Gibson's Wave 1 was getting airborne and heading south.

All went well for about an hour. They stayed low to elude radar, and as darkness gathered V-Vicky's twin belly-lights were switched on to fix height above the sea. Meanwhile Jamie dropped regular smoke floats to check for drift, passing small course adjustments to Peter. The minutes ticked, tension rose, then jumped as he called 'Enemy coast ahead'. To cross it safely, the Lancasters must pass over the tiny island of Vlieland in the Frisian archipelago, then drop down again for the run across the Waddensee to the mainland. But stray a fraction north and they'd cross the next island, Terschelling, south and it was Texel, both aggressively defended. The margin for error, after a sea crossing of two hundred miles, was less than ten. As the five Lancasters raced towards the pale line of the shore in scattered formation, Vernon Byers's K-King was seen to climb and bank slightly to clear the northern tip of Texel. Moments later flashes of light split the night as a flak battery opened up. K-King was hit

217

at once, flew out of control, and exploded into the Waddensee. It had taken barely seconds, and watching in shock all knew there could be no survivors. At the same time Les Munro's W-Willie was also hit, sustaining damage to its communication and navigation systems. Meanwhile Geoff Rice cleared Vlieland unscathed and was hastily dropping down to the safety of the Waddensee. But shaken by Byers's crash, he misjudged the height, rounded out too low and H-Harry struck the waves, tearing off his *Upkeep*, which punched the rear-wheel up through the fuselage and buckled the Lancaster's tail. Fighting for control and with two inner engines flooded by seawater, Rice just managed to force H-Harry back into the air. But the aircraft was severely damaged and his weapon gone. He had no choice but to abandon the mission and limp for home on two engines. Shortly after, Les Munro, his radios and intercom dead, his compasses spinning uselessly, and with no means to usefully continue, also gave in to the inevitable, and after a gloomy conference with his crew, hauled W-Willie about and turned for home. Wave 2 had lost three aircraft in as many minutes.

That left just two, Peter and crew in V-Vicky, and his 61 Squadron cohort Norm Barlow in E-Easy. Without hesitation the pair closed up, flattened out low over the moonlit landscape, and set course for Germany. Fifty minutes later, and nearing the frontier north of the Rhine, Kiwi called a caution to Peter on the intercom.

'Pylons ahead, Pilot. Eleven o'clock one mile.'

'Got them, thanks.' Peter eased back on the controls to rise over the cables, but to his right Barlow's aircraft flew steadfastly on. A second later and in a blinding flash, E-Easy ploughed into the wires, staggered on as though tripped, then dived to the ground in a ball of flame. Peter looked on in stunned disbelief.

Barlow hadn't seen the wires. Like the time he lost his aerial at Derwent. Now they were all dead.

What had started out as a wave of six aircraft was now reduced to just one.

'Pilot to Radio,' he called, after an interval of silence. 'Chalkie, you'd better let them know the situation back at base.'

'Will do, Pilot.'

'And tell them we're going on.'

The leading section of Gibson's Wave 1 was also approaching Germany. They too had encountered problems, with a landfall well south of that planned and resultant brushes with enemy searchlights and flak. As yet no night fighters had found them, but all three aircraft – Gibson's G-George, Martin's P-Popsie and Hopgood's M-Mother – had received hits from ground fire. So bad was the flak in one location that Gibson broke radio silence to transmit a warning back to 5 Group headquarters, who swiftly rebroadcast it to all aircraft. Earlier, Hopgood had also spotted high-tension cables too late, and was forced to dive *under* them, narrowly avoiding disaster. No sooner had his crew recovered from that shock when they were blinded by searchlights and M-Mother raked by flak. While his gunners fired back, knocking out one searchlight, Hopgood threw M-Mother into evasive manoeuvres, but two flak bursts struck the bomber, one setting an engine alight, another hitting the fuselage, immobilising the rear turret and injuring several crew, including the pilot. Anxious seconds passed as the flight engineer shut down the burning engine and Hopgood fought for control. Finally order of a sort was restored, the fire went out and the flak fell behind. Hopgood called up his crew. All but the navigator and flight engineer had received injuries, he learned, Hopgood himself was bleeding profusely from a head wound, and from the front turret came only ominous silence.

'What do you want to do, Hoppy?' his radio operator called painfully. His leg was so badly injured it was almost severed.

'Keep going.' Hopgood mopped his bloodied head. 'It's what we're here for.'

Ten minutes behind them, Gibson's second section of three – Shannon, Maltby and Young – were halfway across Holland and as yet undetected. And ten minutes behind them the third trio of Maudslay, Astell and Knight was nearing the Dutch coast. Their landfall was accurate and they met no opposition as they thundered in over the dunes and turned east for Germany. Soon the silvery glint of the Rosendaal canal came in from the right and they dropped down even lower to follow it. Away to their left lay the night-fighter station at Gilze-Rijen, further on was a second night-fighter station, near the heavily defended town of Eindhoven. Incredibly they slipped past both without detection. Navigation now required a course change to intersect the Rhine. Astell was a fraction late on the turn and dropped behind the others. Searching ahead through the darkness for the telltale blue glow of their exhausts, his became the second aircraft to succumb to high-tension wires. B-Baker smashed through the top of an unseen pylon, broke apart and cartwheeled into the ground. Flying ahead, Maudslay and Knight knew nothing of its loss until a few seconds later a massive detonation behind them signalled the explosion of Astell's *Upkeep*.

Twenty-one dead and not a single bomb dropped. The time was just after midnight, two and a half hours into the mission. Three hundred miles away back at Scampton, 617's reserves, the five aircraft of Wave 3, were firing up their engines and taxiing out for take-off. Meanwhile deep beneath 5 Group headquarters at Grantham, Cochrane, Whitworth and Wallis, now joined by Air Marshal Harris himself, were gathering anxiously in the ops room, unaware of the extent of the casualties, or that out of twenty aircraft dispatched to the Ruhr, only fourteen remained, several of them damaged. Of the others, one was unserviceable, two were coming home damaged, and three had crashed.

One, however, miraculously, was getting back in the fray, or at least its crew was. Having abandoned their beloved Q-Queenie as unserviceable, big Joe McCarthy and his crew had raced across the airfield to the squadron spare, T-Tommy. But hurrying through the start-up checks Joe noticed that the compass deviation card, vital for accurate navigation, was missing. With a disbelieving roar he disembarked and sprinted for the hangar, where after a frantic search the errant card was found. An engineer gave Joe a lift back to the aircraft, but as he scooped up his parachute-pack, Joe accidentally grabbed the D-handle, whereupon the parachute opened, spilling silk all over the grass. 'I'll go without the goddam thing!' he bellowed. 'No you won't!' the mechanic replied and sped back to the hangar. Five minutes later T-Tommy was taxiing hastily out for take-off – complete with deviation card and replacement parachute. Now it was well on its way, thundering across the Netherlands at full throttle to catch up.

At the same time Gibson's trio was arriving at the Möhne, having dodged flak-ships on the Rhine, then picked its way into the Ruhr itself, weaving past the probing searchlights of Duisburg, Essen and Dortmund, bending north to bypass Hamm's lethal flak, until finally turning south for the run to the lake. Ahead dark hills loomed. As the three aircraft crested them the lake came into view, huge and silver-grey in the moonlight, together with its vast dam: long, solid, seemingly unconquerable.

'God above,' Gibson's bomb aimer said. 'Are we really going to crack that?'

The Lancasters began a wide orbit of the scene. As they did so, tracer curled up from emplacements on both sluice towers and in the fields beside the lake. Keeping a wary distance Gibson sized up the approach. At that range, the flak looked inaccurate, but intense. Twelve guns he estimated, probably twenty millimetre, from four or five emplacements. Briefly his thoughts strayed to the wooden crates of two days earlier. Were the Germans expecting trouble? He'd be first to find out. The initial approach along the lake was shielded by a wooded promontory, he saw, but once the promontory was cleared, the sharp right turn and final straight mile to the dam would be in the open, completely exposed to the full force of the flak. Nearly fifteen long seconds, he estimated, at the speed they'd be travelling.

'Signal from HQ, Skipper,' his radio operator called.

'Go ahead, Radio.'

'Wave 3 is outbound. Wave 2 four aircraft lost or aborted. V-Vicky continuing alone and in your vicinity. T-Tommy following, position unknown.'

'Christ! What the hell happened to everyone?'

'They don't say. But B-Baker's gone too from Wave 1. HQ suggests V-Vicky join us to replace him.'

'Understood, stand by a moment.' Gibson broke off, shocked, to gather his thoughts. Wave 2 decimated, leaving only Lightfoot and perhaps McCarthy. Wave 1 intact save for random flak damage, injuries aboard M-Mother, and poor Bill Astell in B-Baker who was gone. Wave 3 on the way and hopefully intact. As he looked, he saw three Lancasters cresting the moonlit ridge

222

north of the lake. Shannon, Maltby and Young had arrived, and not a moment too soon, time was pressing. Barely four full hours of darkness remained, and enemy night fighters might appear any second. They must get on with the job, and quickly.

'Yes, okay, acknowledge, Radio. Call Lightfoot on the W/T and get him here.'

'Will do.'

'Hello all aircraft, Leader here. Prepare to attack in order, I'm going in now. M-Mother, stand by to take over if anything happens to me.'

'Understood Leader. Good luck.'

With that the attack on the dams finally began.

Gibson throttled back and entered a wide descending turn, down-moon to the eastern end of the lake, four miles or more from the dam. Suddenly he felt very alone, and his Lancaster very small. Ahead, two road bridges spanned the water, the second two miles short of the wooded promontory, after which came the right turn for the final one-mile dash to the dam itself.

All went well. Gibson cleared the second bridge, skimmed over the promontory, then dropped down to the water. Then came the right turn, and with it the flak, coloured balls of fire looping up and past from the sluice towers and bank. Forcing himself to ignore it, he settled G-George down lower. The spotlights came on, the bomb aimer squinted down his Dann sight, the flight engineer eased up the power.

As the flak grew more intense, Gibson was struck by the mesmerising brilliance of it, scores of brightly glowing shells flashing by from several directions, some even bouncing off the water. But inaccurate, he noted, the only advantage of going first – the gunners had no idea what he was doing, or why. Suddenly only seconds remained, snapshot images filled his head: the engineer's white-knuckled hands on the throttles, the navigator urging him lower towards the spotlights, G-George shuddering from machine-gun fire as the nose turret opened up, the dam growing huge in the windscreen while the bomb aimer called corrections over the headphones: '. . . Left a bit. Left a bit more, straighten up, steady, hold it there, that's good, hold it, that's good . . .'

'Bomb gone!'

G-George bobbed upwards at the bomb's release, then soared over the parapet, Gibson hauling on the controls for height. In the tail the rear gunner began shooting furiously at the sluice towers. 'It's bouncing!' he shouted excitedly. 'The bomb, it's bloody bouncing, look!'

Above the lake five circling crews looked on. G-George had made it unscathed. And its *Upkeep* seemed to drop on target, right between the towers and four hundred yards from the dam. As they watched, it bounced three times, leaving creamy white rips in the ink-black water, but then it began to veer, and slow, then stopped, finally sinking thirty yards short of the left sluice tower. A few seconds later it reached depth and detonated, sending out a ghostly shockwave followed an instant later by a massive column of white water thrown hundreds of feet in the air.

'Good show, Skipper!' someone called.

'I think you've done it!'

'No. Wait.' Gibson turned in his seat, staring at the scene as G-George climbed away. The entire surface of the lake seemed to be boiling, as though lashed by a squall, with giant waves spreading out in a widening ring, and breaking in sheets over the parapet. Above it all the towering column of spray, hanging in the air like smoke.

Then gradually the tumult subsided, and the water settled, and the spray drifted clear. And everyone could see the dam was still there.

At that moment V-Vicky crested the ridge and arrived on scene.

'Jesus, there it is!' Kiwi exclaimed.

'Wow. Big bastard. Look at the dam!'

'Well done everyone. We made it. Well done, Navigator, spot-on.'

'Aye, nice work, Jamie.'

'I count five other Lancs circling.' Herb reported. 'No wait, six, one's climbing up to join them.'

'Look at the water. He's just had a go by the look of it.'

'That'll be the skipper in G-George then.'

A crackle came over the headphones.

'Hello all aircraft, Leader here, stand by for next attack. Hello V-Vicky, good to see you, join left circuit and await instructions. Hello, M-Mother, can you hear me?'

'I hear you, Leader.'

'Your turn. Wait a few minutes for the water to settle, then go when ready. Good luck, and watch out for the flak.'

All waited as Hopgood prepared, breaking from the circuit towards the eastern end of the lake. As they did so the final two aircraft of Wave 1, Maudslay's and Knight's, arrived on scene, bringing the total circling the Möhne to nine. Hopgood began his run. At first it went like Gibson's, the circling descent to the end of the lake, the straight run over the first bridge, then the second, and the next two thousand yards to the promontory, followed by the sweeping right turn into the attack. They saw his spotlights come on, saw them gradually converge as he drew lower, saw the flak begin to spew out towards him, but much more accurately than on Gibson's run. They saw, unaccountably, that Hopgood's nose gunner was not firing back, they saw the flash as the left wing was hit, then the trail of yellow flame as a fuel-tank ignited. They saw him resolutely holding height and heading, and the moment of bomb release, which looked straight, but later than Gibson's. They saw M-Mother clear the parapet, trailing flame like a comet, and struggling desperately for height. And then they saw the left wing detach and the stricken bomber explode in mid-air, before it crashed in flames to the ground. A moment later they were dazzled by a blinding flash, as his *Upkeep* blew up. It had bounced straight over the parapet and smashed into a power station in the basin below. The force of the explosion demolished the station, which began to burn furiously.

Two failures, another crew lost. After a shocked pause, the dismal news was tapped out over the W/T for Harris and the others waiting at Grantham. There was no reply, for none was needed. In essence a turning point had been reached. *Chastise* had so far cost four crews and six aircraft, all without breaching a dam, despite two determined attacks. The Möhne's defences were clearly formidable, and now the Germans understood the direction and method of attack, they were also focused and accurate, as demonstrated by the devastating assault on M-Mother. Twenty-two-year-old John Hopgood was one of Gibson's closest friends, his crew well liked by everybody. Other leaders might have baulked at this point, justifiably weighing up mounting losses against a dwindling probability of success. Other leaders might have decided discretion was the better part of valour, called off the operation and brought their depleted force home, to fight another day.

But Guy Gibson wasn't other leaders. 'Hello P-Popsie, are you ready?'

'We're ready,' Martin replied.

'It's your turn next. But we've got to do something about the flak, so I'll come in with you to draw their fire. A-Apple, you stand by to take over if anything happens.'

'Understood, Leader.'

'Right, P-Popsie, attack when ready.'

All watched in awe as Mick Martin swung his Lancaster towards the head of the lake, with Gibson's G-George following.

'Jesus.' Kiwi said. 'Can't we do anything to help them?'

'Yes we can.' Peter reached for the throttles. 'We'll make a pass downstream of the dam to try and confuse the flak. Use the spotlights, navigation lights, anything to cause a distraction and throw off their aim. And if you get a shot, gunners, you take it.'

'Will do.'

Peter wheeled V-Vicky about, making for the valley beyond the dam, Henry Maudslay, he noted, following in Z-Zebra. Meanwhile Mick Martin was dropping P-Popsie down towards the water, with Gibson tight on his flank. Above them, the remaining Lancs circled like watchful hawks.

The tactic worked. From his vantage point beyond the dam, Peter watched as Martin and Gibson cleared the promontory and swung into view, two swift shadows flattening out for attack. Their spotlights came on, brightly pinpointing their position, and Gibson's navigation lights began flashing to further distract the flak gunners, who opened up en bloc, flinging furious strings of brightly lit tracer at the two aircraft, which responded in kind, nose turrets sparkling as they fired back. At the same moment Peter felt V-Vicky shudder as Herb and Billy both opened up on the sluice towers. Six machine-guns firing seventy tracer shells a second, with Maudslay following with more. He glimpsed flashes as bullets struck masonry, saw figures in grey sprinting along the parapet for cover, glimpsed Martin and Gibson charging towards the dam, guns blazing, and Martin's *Upkeep* at the instant of release. Then Vicky was past and clear, and he was hauling her round for another pass. But the attack was already over, Martin's bomb bouncing across the lake as he and Gibson climbed to safety. All watched hopefully, yet despite an accurate drop, this bomb too began veering off course, lurching drunkenly towards the bank where it erupted in a huge blast of mud and water.

Disbelieving silence followed, then came Martin's exasperated shout: 'For Christ's sake! The drop was good, what the hell happened?'

'Nothing happened,' Gibson replied. 'It didn't bounce straight that's all. We'll wait for the water to settle then try again. Hello A-Apple, stand by, you're next.'

At Grantham the tension was palpable. Having remained at Scampton until the last possible minute, first to watch Wave 2 depart, albeit without Joe McCarthy, then to see Gibson's Wave 1 safely into the air, Ralph Cochrane, Charles Whitworth and Barnes Wallis had piled into a staff car and driven at high speed thirty miles south to 5 Group headquarters, there to monitor proceedings. The ops room was located deep beneath the building, a long windowless cellar with a raised platform down one side, maps of Europe covering the walls, a desk for the radio operator, and the ops blackboard itself, for chalking progress of the raid and its twenty individual crews. Joined by Lancaster designer Roy Chadwick and Bomber Command leader Arthur Harris, they arrived in time to learn of the three lost aircraft of Wave 2, and the aborted missions of Munro and Rice. Since then they had also heard that Astell's crew was lost, as was John

Hopgood's. Then, as if that wasn't bad enough, Morse messages began arriving from Gibson's team at the Möhne, signalling that three bombs in succession had been correctly delivered, yet failed to breach the dam.

Wallis was beside himself with worry, pacing the floor and shaking his head. 'No, no, it's no good!' he moaned, as news of the third failure came over the Tannoy.

Roy Chadwick did his best to console him. Equally keyed up, he'd begged to fly on the raid in one of his Lancasters, but was overruled by Cochrane. 'Buck up, old boy,' he murmured, clapping Wallis on the shoulder. 'Plenty of time yet. Plenty of bombs too.'

But Wallis was close to despair. 'One bomb should do it!' he kept repeating. 'I don't understand, Roy, one bomb should do it!'

Chadwick glanced at Cochrane, whose expression was sombre. Meanwhile Charles Whitworth was standing at the ops board, his back to the room, looking at the erased names of four dead crews and two aborted. Behind him sat a stony-faced Harris. 'I knew this was madness,' Harris kept muttering angrily. 'I bloody knew it.'

Whitworth, unable to stop himself, turned from the board.

'Excuse me sir, but these boys have flown their guts out preparing for this mission. At least let's give them a proper chance to pull it off.'

And back at the Möhne, they were finally about to. Three bombs gone and the dam seemingly unscratched, but unknown to them, its flak defences were buckling under the onslaught from the Lancasters' machine-guns. Dinghy Young swung A-Apple to the head of the lake for his attack, this time flanked by both

Gibson and Martin, while the others made diversionary passes over the dam. As he ran in the flak was noticeably slacker, with only one sluice tower still firing. Shielded by Gibson and Martin, and undistracted by flak, Young was able to manoeuvre A-Apple into perfect alignment, and for the first time deliver a bomb precisely and accurately to the centre of the dam wall, where it impacted with a thud and sank from sight. And as Barnes Wallis had predicted, having been correctly delivered, that one bomb did its job.

But not immediately. At first, and to everyone's dismay, they saw only the same eerie shockwave, the same exploding waterspout flung hundreds of feet in the air, the same waves slopping over the parapet to the basin below, the same ring of white spreading out across the lake. And then everything settled down, and the water subsided, and the mist drifted clear. And the dam stood defiant and unbowed, like a vast unmoving battleship.

Yet unknown to everyone, one fatally damaged below the waterline. Meanwhile the Lancasters circled, and watched, and waited, and once again, Gibson didn't hesitate. 'Hello J-Johnnie,' he called, summoning David Maltby. 'Attack when ready. V-Vicky stand by, you're next.'

Maltby circled, descended, and ran in, covered by Young and Gibson, while the others looked on. Flak was sporadic now, confined to intermittent bursts from one tower and a single emplacement in the trees. Maltby's run looked good at first but water vapour and drifting smoke from the burning power station were obscuring the target. And something else was happening, the whole dam seemed to be moving, heaving, crumbling along its crown, as though trying to get under way.

'Christ, it's going!' someone shouted.

'Bomb gone! cried Maltby's bomb aimer.

'Don't drop!' Gibson yelled. 'Break off, it's going!'

Maltby veered off, but his bomb was on its way, bouncing towards the dam, to explode just as its base burst outwards, unsheathing a solid shaft of water that spurted out into the valley as though from a giant hose. Seconds later the crown collapsed and a hundred-yard breach appeared, releasing the full weight of the reservoir. A giant wave of water leapt from the breach, arced into the basin below, and set off down the valley, smashing all in its path.

For seconds they could only look on in awed silence. Then a chorus of wild cheers and shouting broke over the radio, to be echoed four hundred miles away in Grantham, as Gibson's radio-operator tapped out the code for success. Before their eyes, a thirty-foot tidal wave thrashed down the valley. The power station, roads, bridges and factories, all were swept before it as though by a giant broom. Trees were uprooted, buildings dashed to matchwood, railway lines twisted like wire. The destruction was instant, overpowering and merciless. Peter followed Uncle's gesture, and looked down to see a tiny car racing along a road to escape, its headlights turning from white to brown to black as the floods overwhelmed it. Three miles down the valley lay the town of Niederense, he knew, where people were hurrying from their beds, anxiously climbing the hillside to watch the destruction. He wondered how many would still have homes to return to when it was over. And how many had left it too late.

But there was no time for wondering. Gibson came on, quickly silencing the chatter. The clock was ticking, dawn drawing nearer, and if the enemy hadn't guessed their purpose before, they certainly knew it now. Time to get going, he said, directing Maltby and Martin home. Four unused bombs remained in Wave

1, with much work still to be done. Calling Shannon, Maudslay, Knight and Lightfoot into order, and taking Young with him as reserve leader, he hauled G-George onto an easterly heading, turned his back on the Möhne, and set course for the Eder.

Chapter 10

The time was now 0100 hours. Back at Scampton all was tensely quiet, as if the whole station was holding its breath. Though the hour was late, many stayed up, taking the mild night air, talking in low voices, anxiously scanning the moonlit horizon. Any pretence of a 'practice' mission was long forgotten, everyone knew that 617 was flying for real, braving the enemy's defences to deliver its oddly shaped weapon. Now, as with all bomber ops, it was just a matter of waiting.

Tess arrived at the main gate by bicycle, showed her NAAFI pass and was admitted on site. Security was still tight, she noted, with patrolling guards, dogs on leashes, barbed-wire barriers and the rest. But somehow the mood had changed, the obsessiveness and the paranoia gone. As though now that the die was cast, and the mission under way, the fanatical need for secrecy was over.

She slipped along the darkened pathways to the NCO married

quarters. Brendan would be in the barn with his pigeons, she knew. He always stayed near his loft when a squadron flew ops, from the moment of take-off until the last wheels touched down. Because, as he was fond of boasting, it could mean the difference between life and death. One wintry night in '41, so his story went, a 57 Squadron Wellington had ditched in the North Sea, just twenty miles from the Norfolk coast. The crew released their pigeons from the liferaft, the first of which arrived at Feltwell less than two hours later. And within three, thanks to Brendan, the frozen crewmen had been found, picked up, and ferried home: 'Safe and sound and their feet barely wet.'

And his intervention had saved Peter all those weeks ago, she reminded herself, for which, if nothing else, she would be for ever grateful. She mounted the steps and paused at their door. No light showed beneath, all seemed quiet within. Withdrawing her key she let herself in. Immediately his smell hit her – cigarettes, beer, fertiliser, grass clippings. Fearfully she paused, ears straining, but the flat was silent. Turning on a table light, she scanned the room. Discarded newspapers, empty beer bottles, a pile of washing-up at the sink. But nothing unusual or suspicious. Two minutes then out, she told herself. And never come back. She unfolded a holdall and began moving quickly through the room, collecting cash from the tea-caddy, her post office book from the sideboard, her daughter's birthday cards, a novel she'd left by the window, a stack of her letters – one in her father's hand and opened. Then came the trinkets, her pitiful collection of childhood souvenirs: a porcelain horse, a silver spoon, the wooden crucifix Doreen had given her at the convent. And her one family photo, of her grandparents, given by her aunt Rosa. Swiftly she gathered them into the bag. All she needed now were some clothes.

234

He was waiting in the bedroom, on the bed, hands propped behind his head, his face in half-shadow from the open doorway.

'There she is,' he said, as though expecting her.

She should have run. She should have dropped the bag and sprinted for the door. But she couldn't move, frozen like a rabbit in headlights.

'What are you doing here?' she gasped. 'I mean, I didn't hear . . . I thought you'd be in the barn . . .'

'With the pigeons? Not tonight, old girl.'

'But why not?' He shouldn't be here. It was all she could think.

'Well, you see, your fancy boy and his little friends. Where they've gone, no one can help them. Not even my darling birds.'

'What do you mean? How do you know where they've gone?'

'Well now, that's for me to know and you to guess, wouldn't you say?' He sat up, stretching lazily. 'Anyways, I had this little feeling you might pop by tonight. Just to see your old man, eh?'

At that Tess found her feet, and began backing through the door. But in a flash he was off the bed and shoving her roughly aside. A moment later her stomach lurched as she heard the key turn in the front door.

'Listen, Brendan,' she began, fighting for calm. 'I'm sorry. I should have got in touch sooner, to explain everything.'

'What's to explain? That you've run out on your husband, and are living in sin with your fancy boy?'

'No. You're wrong. I'm not. But there have been . . . Well, developments.'

'Oh, really? Would that be developments about your adulterous doings with your fancy boy, whose wort'less skin I saved? Or maybe developments about bleating to that piteous sod Credo about my private dealings? Or maybe it's developments about telling your family about your terrible life with your cruel husband.'

'Brendan, I have never told my family anything about you!' The circling had begun, she realised, the slow dance of death around the dining table. She leading, eyes searching in panic for escape, he following, stealthy, watchful, like a cat with a mouse.

'Is that so? Then why does your father write he's sorry to hear of your troubles?'

'Because, well, because he's ill, Brendan. He came to see me. He wants to try and make up.'

'Very touching. So that's the developments you're talking of?'

'Yes.' She hesitated. 'Yes, that's right.'

'You're a lying whore!'

'No, it's true!'

'What about your bastard child?' He lunged then, grabbing her arm. She yelped, wrenched free, and fled to the kitchenette, and its one window. Which was locked.

'Well, and here we are now,' he taunted. She was cornered, cut off, with no possible escape. 'Didn't think I knew about that, did you? Your bastard child.'

'No,' she whispered tearfully. 'Brendan, what do you want?'

'Want? Only to be left in peace.'

'All right. I will leave you in peace. We need never see each other again.'

'Ah yes, but it's not quite as simple as that. What with you and all your blabbing to people. And there's the matter of your fancy boy too, and poor old Credo, and now your bastard daughter, who I might like to visit one day, just for a little chat, like.' Sweat glistened on his forehead, his cheeks were deeply flushed, his breathing heavy. Just like the previous times. He took another pace forward. Tess stepped back, hands fumbling behind her as she collided with the sink. Now she had no place left to run. And at that, despite the frantic beating of her heart, she found she was able to think calmly. And to confront the inevitable.

'You . . . You're a spy, aren't you?'

'Is that what you've heard?'

'It's what I think. You pass information to people who pass it to the Germans. Information about this station.'

'Really. And how would I be doing that?'

'Something . . . The notebook. I don't know.'

'No, you don't. You don't know anything. For you're nothing but a deceiving adulteress, with a child out of wedlock and now carrying on with another man behind her husband's back.'

'I am not. I have never been unfaithful to you.'

'So you say. But who do you think they'll believe? The respected RAF sergeant, or the lying adulteress covering her deceit with fanciful stories of spies?'

'I . . . Brendan, wait . . .'

He'd taken another step nearer. Now he was so close she could smell his breath, and see flecks of spittle on his lips. 'This is a military base you see, Tess. These are my people, we understand one another, and look after our own. They like me, you know, and respect me. So this business will be handled with discretion, and without fuss, let me assure you.'

'What business? What are you talking about?'

'The MPs, Tess. The military police. They'll look into the matter and find the respected Sergeant Murray was attacked by his wife, who as everyone knew, was having an adulterous affair with a pilot. And the poor, provoked, humiliated, respected Sergeant Murray was only trying to defend himself, and his dignity, and his honour, when she accidentally fell down the stairs and got tragically killed.'

'Brendan, for God's sake, I promise . . .'

'No you don't! You lie!' He lunged at her, full force, arms outstretched for her throat. But as he lunged, her hand came from behind her back, and the kitchen knife she was holding plunged deep into his chest.

That was how it happened, Quentin would later record, Murray's death, in the kitchen of their quarters on the night of the dams raid. Not that Quentin was present, or even compos mentis at the time. He was 150 miles away, in a bed, in a darkened room, in a hospital, and that was all he knew. He'd been slowly coming round, slipping in and out of consciousness, his fevered mind tormented by dreams of fire, and an agonising car-ride through blacked-out streets. Finally he came to his senses. It was night, he realised, he was thirsty and nauseous, and his head hurt. As did his right arm, which felt numb and painful within its thick cocoon of bandages. Painful, but with a different pain. He tried to sit up, but his head spun and blackness threatened, so he gave up. The room was oppressively warm and airless, despite the open window where a curtain stirred listlessly. Beyond it bright moonlight suffused the grounds with spectral grey, while in the distance a lone nightingale sang wistfully. He turned his head to listen to it and saw a girl curled on a chair by the window. Asleep, her head resting on her chest like a bird. Her shoes were off, she wore the crumpled uniform of a WAAF. Quentin wanted to speak to her, but suddenly found his chest was heaving, and his throat constricting, and tears were welling in his eyes like a child, and before he knew it he was weeping inconsolably. Weeping for the crewmen he'd lost in the Wellington, and all the countless others who never came home. Weeping for the fair-haired boy of his youth, so smiling and carefree but now lost and afraid. Weeping for the tragedy of war, and what it did to people, weeping for the souls of its victims, and for the heartbroken host left behind.

'Chloe . . .' he sobbed. 'Chloe, please wake up.'

And she woke, and came to him, and fed him water through a straw, and bathed his burning brow, and shushed and calmed him, until at last the crying stopped and he fell quiet.

Later they talked.

'It's gone, isn't it,' he said. 'The hand.'

'Yes, Quentin. Dr McIndoe says it all went very well. We caught it just in time.'

'I'm at McIndoe's?'

'We got here yesterday. In the night. You were very poorly.'

'Oh.' He considered. 'We?'

'I came with you.'

'That was very kind.'

'Not at all. I've notified your parents. They'll be here tomorrow.'

'Thank you. You are a remarkable girl.'

'I hardly think so.'

'I do. You work for Abbott and Costello, don't you?'

'How did you guess?'

Quentin forced a pained smile. 'Mysteriously promoted to Whitworth's ADC. Right after the *Tirpitz* thing. Given a driver who doesn't drive, but who follows me everywhere, watching my every move. They assigned you to keep an eye on me, didn't they?'

'Something like that. Although I prefer to call it helping with your work. And I do drive by the way. Rather well, as it happens.'

'Thought so.'

'The car was Whitworth's idea. He felt you should get out more.'

'He's a good man.'

'Yes. And so are you.'

'Not a traitor then.'

She patted his hand. 'Not even close.'

He turned his head to stare at the ceiling, the curtain casting moon-shadows over it, like waves upon a sea. 'So it was all a pretence.'

'What was?'

'Being friends.'

'Is that what you think?'

'I don't know. I'm afraid . . . Afraid it was all a sham. And . . . I . . . Couldn't bear . . .'

'Quentin. It's all right. Don't upset yourself.'

'Sorry,' he whispered. 'Self-pity. Inexcusable.'

'Perfectly excusable, given what you've been through.'

'Doesn't do any good though.' He sniffed. 'Emotions. I learned that.'

'You think so? Why do you think I'm sitting here with you?'

'Because those are your orders.'

'No, silly!' She laughed suddenly, like the murmur of a summer stream. 'It's because I want to.'

They sat together quietly. After a while she reached out, and slipped her hand into his. Then in the distance came the tolling of a church clock.

'What time is it?' he asked.

She checked her watch. 'A quarter to two.'

Then his eyes widened. 'And what day?'

'It's Sunday. Well, Monday now.'

'So . . . They're up there! My God, they're doing it right now. Peter and the others!'

'Yes, Quentin. They're up there. Doing it right now.'

*

240

Big Joe McCarthy was doing it at the Sorpe. Alone, the only member of Wave 2 to make it to their designated target. Now he had a problem. Having started late, flown T-Tommy at full throttle to make up time, dodged flak, eluded prowling night fighters, got lost over Hamm, and stirred up trouble attacking a flak-train, McCarthy had at last arrived at the Sorpe, only to find it deserted.

'You sure we got the right lake, buddy?' he asked his navigator, as they circled.

'Quite sure. Look there's the town just to the north of it, with the church tower and everything.'

'Okay. Right. But it looks damn quiet. No smoke, no fires, nothing.'

'No flak either.'

'Amen to that.'

'Yes, but where the hell is everybody?'

The crew looked on in pensive silence. Below them lay a scene of almost surreal tranquillity. The sleepy village nestling in the hills, beside its mist-covered lake, its waters still, its earthen dam solid and strong and peaceful, like a dozing giant. An unblemished dozing giant. Yet six aircraft had been sent to attack it, each carrying enough explosive to demolish a battleship. T-Tommy must be the last to arrive, so where were the others?

'They couldn't have bought it, surely.' Someone voiced their thoughts. 'Not all of them. Could they?'

'Christ knows. I vote we get on with it, and clear off.'

'Me too. This place gives me the creeps.'

With that Joe banked T-Tommy over for the attack. Only to find the prescribed strike plan unworkable. This dam was differently constructed to the Möhne and Eder, straight not curved, comprised of a central concrete core supporting sloped earthen sides, and thus impervious to a head-on assault with a bouncing bomb. To crack the Sorpe, Wave 2 had been briefed to fly lengthways along the dam and drop their weapons in the middle, as low as possible and without spin, the hope being that they would roll into the water, explode and cause a breach. But as Joe sized up the situation, he realised the terrain was much steeper than anticipated, causing problems not only with the approach, which was at rooftop height over the village, but also the climb-out, which was up a suicidally steep hill.

Nine times they tried, nine times they failed, circling round and round, struggling without success to get T-Tommy into position. So low was the approach that the church-tower flashed by above them, so steep the climb-out, it felt like scrambling up a cliff. And at each attempt, no matter what Joe tried, the run would end in a 'No drop!' cry from the bomb aimer. Who soon became far from popular.

'Jesus! Just drop the bloody thing will you?'

'How can I? We're too high, we'd miss by a mile!'

'Any lower and we could plant it with a trowel!'

'Well I'm sorry. Maybe it can't be done. Maybe this is why nobody else dropped.'

'Listen, boys.' Big Joe broke in. 'If I cut power earlier and slow right down before the church, I reckon I can glide in for a straight shot, real low, and still have time for the pull-out. Let's give it one more try. If it don't work we'll go find something else.'

It did work. T-Tommy, slipstream whistling, dived down to the dam for the tenth time, levelling out barely thirty feet above the crest, and at a slow 170 mph.

'Go! Now! Do it!' Joe yelled.

'Bomb gone!'

With that throttles were slammed wide, the Merlins roared and the lumbering machine began its scrambling ascent to safety. As it did so, banked hard over to clear the hill, seven faces peered aft to see the results of their labours.

The bomb had been placed precisely in the centre of the dam. As they watched, it rolled down as planned, then exploded, a phenomenal blast that lit the scene like a flashbulb, churned water to foam and threw a column of earth and stone high in the air. Big Joe and his crew, despite a litany of woes and against all the odds, had fought their way to their target, and done precisely what they were supposed to.

But it wasn't enough. And as the smoke cleared and spray settled, they saw their determination had been for nothing. The Sorpe dam, apart from minor damage to the parapet, was completely intact. Scarcely believing their eyes, they circled round once more to be sure, then turned T-Tommy about and set course for the long flight home.

Meanwhile the five aircraft of Wave 3 were heading into Germany. Theirs was a roving brief, each Lancaster controlled individually from Grantham using Morse code. The first to take off was twenty-year-old Warner Ottley and his crew in C-Charlie. They flew into Holland via Gibson's southern route, pushing on undetected towards Germany and the Ruhr. Nearing the flak-ringed city of Hamm they received a Morse message directing them to the Lister dam, thirty miles south of the Möhne. Acknowledging the message, they adjusted course accordingly. Three minutes later Grantham sent a second message changing their target to the Sorpe. Again the course was altered, but possibly confused by the contradiction, C-Charlie strayed too close to Hamm, already on alert following McCarthy's incursion. Twenty miles away to the south and heading for the Ennepe dam, Bill Townsend and his crew in O-Orange saw a distant aeroplane coned by searchlights, followed by streams of tracer, then a monstrous flash as its bomb blew up. 'That's one of ours,' Townsend said without hesitation. He was right. C-Charlie was gone.

And a hundred miles back, Canadian Lewis Burpee was threading S-Sugar between the night-fighter stations west of Eindhoven. These bases too were on high alert following repeated fly-pasts of 617 Lancasters that night. Nearing Gilze-Rijen airfield, a single searchlight captured the low-flying bomber in its beam, dazzling Burpee, who instinctively pulled up for safety – straight into the sights of the flak gunners. S-Sugar received multiple hits, burst into flames, and cartwheeled into the ground. A few seconds later its *Upkeep* went off, bathing the scene in yellow, and destroying many airfield buildings. A sixth *Chastise* crew was dead.

At the Eder, problems for Guy Gibson and the remaining crews of Wave 1, who were running dangerously behind schedule. Late leaving the Möhne, having expended too much time destroying it, they then had problems finding the Eder, which lay amid forested hills and dark valleys interlaced with many lakes and rivers. All had trouble, with David Shannon in L-Leather actually squaring up to attack a completely different dam before realising his mistake. Eventually Gibson found the correct target, tucked in beneath steep hills on a bend in the lake, and began firing off Very lights to round up the others.

Who arrived on scene to find it unassailable. Time after time they ran in, only to abort because they were wrongly aligned, or too high, or too slow. And as each attempt came and went, an increasingly impatient Guy Gibson and his deputy

Dinghy Young fussed around overhead, nagging them like nervous sheepdogs.

'Try a bit of flap, Henry.' Young suggested, as Maudslay ran in yet again.

'I tried that last time and nearly stalled on the turn!'

'Well go a bit faster then.'

'Then I won't have time to line up!'

The problem was the topography. The lake lay among steep-sided hills like a lizard in a burrow, narrow and serpentine, with a sharp twist at its head where the dam stood. To approach it required a two-mile run-in, starting high on the northern shore and at ninety degrees to the dam. From there the bombers had to plunge a thousand feet to the lake, cross to the southern shore, pop up again over a wooded spit, make a sharp ninety-degree turn to port, then drop down to attack height for the last dash to the dam. And whereas at the Möhne they had fifteen seconds to perfect the final run-in, the Eder gave them barely seven in which to line up, fix height, set the speed, determine the range and release the bomb. And after the run, like the Sorpe, a dangerously steep pull-up was required to avoid a hill. Finally, to further complicate matters, early-morning mist now drifted over the scene, intermittently blurring landmarks and obscuring the dam. The only good news was a complete absence of flak.

But time was marching on and Gibson getting anxious. At Maudslay's next failed attempt, he called Shannon back into the fray.

'Hello L-Leather, Leader here. Look, Dave, we must get on with it. Give it another try and just do the best you can. Z-Zebra, you stand by to follow.'

Shannon circled L-Leather into position, the others watching closely as he dived for the water, crossed the lake, turned over the spit and ran in. The bomb fell free, they saw it bounce, then impact the dam, but well to the right of centre. A few seconds later came the familiar flash of the shockwave, followed by the upsurging tower of spray and spreading ring of water.

Shannon was exultant, certain he'd succeeded. Yet no breach appeared. Gibson waited to be sure, then called in Maudslay in Z-Zebra. But almost from the start his run appeared problematic, with Maudslay pulling away suddenly before resuming course, then wrestling the bomber down to the lake, overshooting the turn, and struggling to line up for the drop, which was dangerously late. A blinding flash illuminated the valley as his *Upkeep* exploded against the parapet, just as Z-Zebra was passing over it. All feared he'd blown himself up, flames, smoke and debris obscured everything, anxious seconds passed, then they glimpsed the bomber heading away down the valley, flying very low and trailing smoke.

'Hello Z-Zebra.' Gibson called. 'Are you okay?'

Maudslay's reply was eerily faint. 'I . . . I think so, leader. I don't . . .'

'Z-Zebra can you hear me?'

But after a ghostly hiss of static, Maudslay's radio was silent.

Only two armed aircraft remained, and still the Eder stood. Les Knight went next, the no-nonsense Australian driving his unwieldy beast over the ridge and down to the water like a rancher on horseback. His run looked better, crossing tidily to the southern shore, up over the spit for the steep turn to port, then quickly back down for the drop. His spotlights lined up, his heading was true and his bomb-release timely, his *Upkeep* making three straight bounces before impacting the dam, slightly right of centre, and sinking from sight.

Then it went off, the lightning flashed, the lake erupted, the veil of spray drifted. And nothing happened.

Knight looked on in disbelief. 'Christ, boys,' he lamented over the VHF. 'What do we have to do to crack this bastard?'

'Good try, N-Nan,' Gibson replied. 'Okay V-Vicky, you're last, so it's up to you. Attack when ready.'

Peter has been ready all his life. This is what it was for, his modest beginnings in Bexley, the denials and deprivations, the taunts of the moneyed and the second-hand shoes. His childhood with Tess, an alliance, then a friendship, then finally adolescent love. The desperation of their parting, and the lonely years of silence. Then war, the recruiting office, the anxious weeks of fitness tests and aptitude tests and marching on parade grounds before acceptance for flying. Tentative fumblings at the controls of an aeroplane, the tiny Miles Magister, then the Fairey Battle, then the twin-engined Oxford. Then conversion to bombers, onward to war, and sixty operations in Wellingtons, Beaufighters, Manchesters and finally 61 Squadron and the mighty Lancaster. All for this. A thirty-second dash across a lake to attack a dam.

'Pilot to crew. Call in please.'

They all call in. Jamie standing behind him, watching the spotlights, one hand ready on his shoulder. Kiwi prone in the nose, his string-sight in one hand, bomb-release in the other. The two gunners, hunched in their turrets, ever vigilant for trouble. Chalkie at the radios, monitoring the fast-spinning bomb and ready with his Morse key. Uncle at his knobs and dials, tending his quivering charge like a trainer with a thoroughbred.

Peter settles lower in his seat, tightens his harness, and throttles back, feeling the aeroplane vibrate in his hands from the revolving bomb. 'Ready Uncle?'

'Ready.'

'Good. Let's have twenty degrees flap.'

247

'Twenty degrees.' Uncle reaches for the lever.

A voice breaks suddenly over the radio. 'Say, Peter mate. You might want some flap.' It is Knight, circling overhead in N-Nan.

'What? Oh, yes, I know, Les, thanks.'

'I didn't bother with flap,' Shannon adds helpfully.

'Yes and look at your run!' Young quips.

'Go to hell, Dinghy, the run was spot-on!'

'Ignore him, Peter, use flap if you like . . .'

Uncle glances at Peter. 'You want this?' Peter shakes his head, and with a flick of the switch the radio goes dead. 'That's better. So what's the plan?'

'We do it like Knight. Only steeper down to the water, a faster run to the far side, and tighter turn onto finals. All right?'

'Aye,' Uncle grins. 'But we're not a bloody Stuka y'know!'

'We are now!'

With that he snatches back the throttles, shoves the controls forward and V-Vicky, engines popping, plunges over the edge like a gannet off a cliff. The sky vanishes, the hillside blurs, forest and lake fill the windscreen. Down he dives, slipstream shrieking, altimeter spinning, before hauling back against the protesting airframe, to level off a hundred feet from the surface.

'Flaps up, full power!'

The Merlins roar, the bomber surges forward, hurtling over the water towards the southern shore. Ahead dark hills rise steeply. They cross the lake in seconds, then thunder up the bank, and pull up and over into the turn, left wingtip brushing the trees. Peter looks up through the perspex, waiting, a whirl of black trees, the wildly canting horizon, the aircraft shuddering in his hands as he tightens the turn yet more, until suddenly the angled shadow of the dam swings into view. Quickly he rolls level again, throttles back the power and kicks V-Vicky into a harsh side-slip, the wings banked left, rudders forced right, skidding the aircraft down the hillside to the water.

And the last dash to the dam. Which lies dead ahead. Seven seconds away.

'Spotlights on!' He levels off, flat-turning to line up. Immediately a squeeze from Jamie — go lower — while beside him Uncle eases up the power.

'Two hundred mph, two-ten, two-twenty . . .'

'Target in sight.' Kiwi from the nose, his string-sight to his eye, pencil marks on the towers. 'That's good, but go left, left more, good, steady . . .' Five seconds.

Another squeeze from Jamie, go down, then another, down more, then a pat, hold it there.

'Two-thirty dead-on!' Uncle at the throttles.

Kiwi: 'Left a touch more, hold it there, yes, steady . . .' Three seconds.

A light squeeze at his shoulder, down a fraction. A pat, hold it there.

'Steady . . . Steady . . . Hold it . . . Bomb gone!'

V-Vicky bucking upward as though breaking from a leash, Uncle slamming the throttles wide, Peter hauling back for the stars, arms crooked round the controls for leverage, one foot pushing against the dash-panel.

Herb in the tail, watching their bomb. 'It's bouncing! It's bouncing! It's bouncing!'

Anxious seconds scaling the hilltop, still straining, then breaking clear at last, levelling off, throttling back and circling to see. Breathless silence on the intercom. Then the flash on the water, the ring of blue lightning, and the whole lake jumping, and blurring, and bursting apart, blasting a tower of white a thousand feet in the air. Then the misty curtain hanging, and drifting, while rubble and masonry fall back with a splash.

An unruffled report from Uncle.

'We've damaged her, lads,' he says quietly. 'There, look, halfway down.'

A furious circular jet is escaping the dam, like foam past a shaken bottle-top. Then as they stare the whole section blows out, and solid water spurts from the hole as though from a hose. Seconds more and the crown above begins to collapse, crumbling into the breach, which spreads and widens until a hundred-yard gap has opened in the wall like a punched-out tooth.

Releasing the mighty waters behind. They've done it, they realise, breached the Eder. In seconds a tidal wave thirty feet high is crashing to the ground, storming down the valley, flattening all in its path. It looks like lava, Peter thinks: thick, glutinous, unstoppable, deadly.

'Jesus Christ,' Chalkie intones. 'Would you look at that.'

'Well done everyone.' Uncle says. 'Well done Kiwi, spot-on with the drop.'

'Thanks boys. Nice work yourself, Pilot. And Jamie.'

'I'm real proud of us all,' Billy announces simply.

'Yes.' Peter wipes sweat from his eyes. 'Yes, we all did it. Everyone in the squadron.'

'Rear gunner here. Why's it so quiet on the radio?'

Peter and Uncle exchange guilty glances. The radios are still off. 'I suppose we'd better . . .' Peter says, reaching for the switch.

But Uncle stays his hand. 'In a minute laddie,' he grins. 'Let's just savour the moment.'

It was the second and last dam to be breached on Operation *Chastise*. But not the last attempt. Nor the last casualty.

Five minutes later Wave 1 split up and headed for home, at high speed and low level, using pre-planned exit routes. Meanwhile the three remaining aircraft of Wave 3 were approaching the area, still armed and still pressing on. Two full hours after Joe McCarthy had left the Sorpe in T-Tommy, Canadian Ken Brown arrived there in F-Freddie, only to encounter the same problems. He too found it near-impossible to manoeuvre in over the village for the drop and then climb safely out again. Worse still, the mist had thickened, frequently obscuring the dam in a blanket of grey. Precious minutes were expended making aborted runs and waiting for a clearance. At last the mists parted and having dropped flares to mark his path, Brown made his attack, successfully placing his *Upkeep* near the centre of the dam. But despite his diligence, the results were once again disappointing, with only superficial crumbling of the parapet caused by the blast. Signalling the failure to Grantham, he too then turned for home, leaving the terrified villagers in peace at last.

Cyril Anderson in Y-York had a similarly frustrating trip. Arriving in the Hamm area late, flak-chastened, and with an unserviceable rear turret, he like Ottley was first directed to one dam, the Diemel, before being quickly diverted to a second, the Sorpe. This too caused confusion on board, and with thick mist below further hampering navigation, Y-York was soon lost. A while later, still uncertain of his position and with the clock ticking remorselessly towards dawn, Anderson gave up and turned for home.

Meanwhile Bill Townsend and crew in O-Orange were running in to attack the Ennepe, twenty miles south of Dortmund. Earlier they'd watched in horror as Ottley's C-Charlie was shot down over Hamm, then they survived their own flak-storm near Dülmen, which they only escaped by flying along a forest firebreak, so low that the trees to either side were *above* them. After further navigational problems in the thickening mist, they finally reached the hook-shaped Ennepe and prepared to attack. But when the radio operator started the winch to spin the bomb, O-Orange began to shake alarmingly, either from an unbalanced bomb or a faulty winch. Nor did it reach the required spin rate, so when it was dropped, in line and on target, it bounced just twice before sinking fifty yards short of target and exploding harmlessly. All watched as the ring of white spread out and subsided. Then came the voice of Townsend's navigator.

'Um, navigator here. I'm beginning to think we attacked the wrong dam.'

'We what?'

'That lake. I've a feeling, looking at it now, that it's the Bever. Not the Ennepe.'

'What's the Bever?'

'A smaller lake, about five miles from the Ennepe.'

'Christ, the CO will murder us!'

'Well chaps,' Townsend said resignedly, 'the bomb's gone and there's not a thing we can do about it.'

'Except perhaps not tell anyone . . .'

'Hmm. Navigator, let's have a course for home. High time we got out of here.'

Townsend's mission now became a desperate race against time, and with the sky visibly brightening behind them they dropped down low, opened the throttles and set course for the long trip home.

Meanwhile elements of Wave 1 were nearing the coast and safety, Shannon exiting Holland near the Helder peninsula, Gibson through a known flak-gap near Egmond, and Knight hugging windmill-lined canals north of Haarlem. As each thundered down the beach and out to sea and safety, exultant cheers rang over their intercoms, together with relieved chatter and promises of wild celebrations to come. Henry Maudslay and his crew would not be joining them. Miraculously Z-Zebra had survived the explosion of its bomb at the Eder, and though badly damaged and with injuries on board, its crew had nursed the ailing aircraft back across Germany. But passing Emmerich on the Rhine, and almost within sight of the Dutch border, they strayed too close to flak batteries and were shot down, exploding into a field. *Chastise* had claimed its seventh crew.

The eighth was Young in A-Apple. Having flown a textbook mission to the Möhne, breached it, taken over from Hopgood as deputy leader, continued to the Eder, then flown all the way west again, Dinghy Young, so nicknamed for his habit of successfully ditching in the sea, drew near to the coast at Castricum, five miles north of Ijmuiden. There he made one fatal mistake. Seeing the beckoning sea ahead, and exhausted after many hours flying at ground level, he allowed A-Apple to rise a little. But too soon, and a flak battery spotted it, catching the Lancaster with one lucky burst. A-Apple went out of control and exploded into the sea. This time there were no dinghies.

Which just left V-Vicky. The ninth and final victim of Operation *Chastise*. Shot down by a night fighter over Borken in Germany.

PART 3

APRÈS LE DÉLUGE

Chapter 11

It is late afternoon. A young woman sits on a park bench in Stafford. Shower clouds gather, a breeze stirs leaves in the trees overhead, sparrows peck hopefully at her feet. Children play on swings nearby. One, a little girl, sits alone on a roundabout, singing to herself, and trailing a hand through the air as it turns. An older woman watches her, reminds her to play carefully, then comes to sit on the bench.

'Looks a bit like rain,' *she says, studying the sky.*

'I'm sorry?' *The younger woman stirs.* 'Oh, yes.'

'Come here often, do you?'

'No.'

'Just on a visit, then.'

'A visit. Yes.'

'Relatives?'

The younger woman looks at her, her face crumples and she bows her head. And after a pause, tears start falling onto her lap.

The older woman is concerned. 'Gracious me, dear, what on earth is it?'

But the younger woman only shakes her head.

'Are you feeling ill? Do you need a doctor?'

'No,' she whispers. 'Not ill. I'm sorry. It's . . . I lost someone. Someone close.'

'Oh, dear, you poor thing. Here take this.' She produces a handkerchief, and offers it to the younger woman, patting her lightly on the back, like a child.

'Thank you.'

'You keep it dear. This blooming war, breaks your heart.'

They sit in silence a while. At length the younger woman raises her head.

'All right?' The older woman studies her. 'Feeling a little better now?'

'Yes. Thank you. I'm so sorry.'

'Don't be silly. We all need a good cry sometimes.'

The younger woman nods. 'She's yours, then?'

'Beg pardon?'

'The little girl on the roundabout.'

'Peggy, you mean? Yes, she's mine all right.'

Peggy. Peggy Groves. A nice name. 'She's very pretty.'

'Pretty mischievous you mean!' The older woman laughs. 'No, but she's a good girl really. Apple of my eye.'

'I can see.' The young woman hesitates. 'Is she . . . A happy girl?'

'Oh yes, happy as they come. Always playing and laughing about. Bright too, spot-on with her reading and that. Bit of a dreamer, sometimes, but there's no harm in that, is there?'

'Dreaming? No, no harm at all.' She begins buttoning her coat.

'You off then?'

'Yes. I . . . It's time.'

'You sure you're well enough? Do you want us to walk with you?'

'No. Thank you, you've been too kind already. I have to . . . I wonder, is there a police station near here?'

'Police? Why, have you lost something?'

'Lost? No. Not lost . . .'

'Oh. Well, there's a police station off the High Street. Behind the town hall. About ten minutes' walk.'

'Thank you.' She holds out her hand. 'It was nice to meet you. Goodbye.'

The older woman, face quizzical, turns on the bench, and watches her walk away.

One evening ten days or so later I was sitting at home in my parents' house in Chiswick reading the papers when I received a telephone call. It was a recall to duty, and not a moment too soon, for what with my mother's doleful looks, my father's anger at the world, and endless sympathy visits from friends and relatives, I was more than ready for escape. And the call, unknown to me, was the precursor to a most extraordinary day, a day during which I would become defence council in a murder case, resign from the RAF, get drunk with a VC, throw furniture at a senior officer, meet the King, and decide upon a new face. Oh, and become engaged. Although not necessarily in that order.

The caller was Charles Whitworth.

'Quentin, dear boy, how are you?'

'Hello, sir. I'm well, thank you, all things considered.'

'That's good news. What about the hand?'

'The hand's fine, sir.' The hand was gone of course, but I knew what he meant. 'Much more comfortable without it.'

'Glad to hear it.'

'Yes, sir, and I must thank you for stepping in when you did. Doctor McIndoe said it was a close-run thing.'

'Nonsense, that Hickson girl of yours saved the day. How is she, by the way?'

So he knew about Chloe. 'She's well, sir, so I believe.' But I hadn't heard. Summoned by Abbott and Costello the day after the raid, I'd had no news in a week.

'Good. Good.' Whitworth sounded distracted.

'Sir.' I lowered my voice. 'No word, I suppose. Survivors . . .'

'No. No word. But it's much too soon, Quentin, you know that.'

'Yes, sir.'

'Now then. Feel up to a little work?'

'Of course. What did you have in mind?'

'Well, the thing is, someone you know is in a hell of a pickle. I can't talk about it over the phone, but if you can get to Lincoln city police station in the morning all will become clear.'

A 617 pilot on a drunk-and-disorderly charge was my first thought, or some mechanic arrested for brawling in a pub. Hardly urgent, I guessed, but any excuse would do. I glanced at my parents, busy pretending not to listen. 'Yes sir, that does sound serious. If I catch the early train I could be there mid-morning?' A sigh of dismay came from my mother, while my father scowled into his briefcase. I shrugged at them, as if to say, what can I do?

'Fine. And when you're done there, Quentin, come up to Scampton. And wear your best uniform, there's someone I want you to meet.'

Next morning I caught the train from St Pancras. It was my first proper outing since leaving hospital, and more of an ordeal than I'd expected. The usual stares followed me across the concourse, my ruined face crimson, my handless arm at my chest. It was trussed up in a black sling, and though it felt more comfortable without its useless appendage, unnervingly real pain issued from the absent hand, and the stump itched infernally. Nor was I fully fit, I realised, still breathless and light-headed from the fever. I hurried to the train and slumped into a seat, self-consciously inspecting myself in the window. Beyond it, grimy terraced tenements slowly gave way to fields of ripening corn. The brush with gangrene, the days of delirium, losing the hand, Chloe, these things had altered my perspective, I sensed. Across the compartment an elderly couple were staring at me in undisguised horror. 'Can I help you?' I asked after a while, my standard challenge to gawpers. They looked suitably chastened, then left the compartment a few minutes later, whereupon I felt ashamed. Enough is enough, I decided then. Time to book into Archie McIndoe's for a revamp.

I arrived at Lincoln at ten, walking beneath crisp summer cumulus up the hill to the police station. The air was mild and summery, overhead a 57 Squadron Lanc flew training circuits into Scampton. It felt good to be back, really like coming home. At the station I gave my name to the desk sergeant. A few minutes later he led me to a back room, guarded unusually by an armed military policeman. Keys were produced, and the door opened. 'All yours, guv,' the sergeant winked. 'And best of luck with it. Bang on the door when you're done.'

It wasn't a hungover mechanic sitting forlornly at the table, it was Tess Murray. The last time I'd seen her was some three weeks earlier, and for a second I barely recognised her. She'd changed beyond all recognition, thin and pale, lank hair tied severely back, her dress crumpled, her shoulders slumped. Nor did she look up when I entered, just stared at the table, hugging herself, and rocking slightly.

'Tess? Good God, Tess, it's me, Quentin.'

She gave no reply. Just rocked.

'Tess, what on earth happened?'

Still the eyes never left the table. But she did speak. 'He's dead. I killed him.'

I thought she meant Peter. I thought she was blaming herself for getting him into 617 Squadron and Operation *Chastise*. But why then was she under armed guard?

'Well now, Tess.' I encouraged lamely. 'We don't know that, do we? I mean, at the moment he's just missing. Officially. They all are.'

She shook her head. 'Brendan,' she murmured. 'I killed Brendan.'

'You what?'

'I killed him. And they're going to hang me for it.'

Gradually it all came out. How she'd slipped onto the base on the night of the raid, her plan being to recover a few essentials before leaving next morning with Peter. Then letting herself into their quarters, and Brendan discovering her there, the deadly circling round the table, the lunge and the kitchen knife. She spoke hesitantly but clearly, in clipped phrases between long silences, as though assembling events in order, so I had only to listen. She offered no mitigating circumstances, made no claims of self-defence nor diminished responsibility, she simply recounted the facts. And blamed herself. And expected full punishment for it, resignedly, fatalistically, as if her whole life had been leading up to this.

Shocked and incredulous, it was all I could manage to take it in. Then I realised this was a formal statement she was making, and a confession, so fumbling notepad and pen from a pocket I began to take notes. And question her more closely. After the killing, it transpired, she'd fled the flat in panic and gone back to her lodgings, her one last chance being that Peter would return at dawn as promised, and together they might present the true facts to the authorities, in the hope of a sympathetic hearing. But as the hours ticked, daylight dawned at her window, and no knock came at the door, she began to despair. Finally, around nine, she went to a phone-box and got through to her friend Phyllis in the NAAFI. Who was beside herself with anguish. Oh Tess, she could only sob, so many of those brave boys gone! But what of Peter? Tess asked fearfully. Gone, Phyllis kept repeating, they're all gone.

She'd wandered the streets in shock, then returned to her rooms and lain on her bed without moving. The next morning she'd taken the train to Stafford, found her daughter's address and followed her to the park with her adoptive mother. Having seen her little girl, and spoken to her mother, and satisfied herself the child was safe and well, she'd walked to the nearest police station and handed herself in.

Now she was back in Lincoln under arrest for murder. And if she did plead guilty, I soon realised, and insisted on offering no defence, as she seemed bent on doing, then she might well hang for it. Which was unthinkable given Murray's record of violence, drinking, and other nefarious activities. Everything was recorded in the file I'd passed to Abbott and Costello. With that dossier, and perhaps the doctor's report from Murray's earlier attack, the worst she should expect was a manslaughter conviction, more probably the lesser charge of death by misadventure, or even a full acquittal based on the French *crime passionnel* principle. All that was needed was time to assemble a case. And persuade the defendant to put up a fight.

Which was proving impossible. 'Tess, have you spoken to anyone?' I asked at one point. 'A lawyer, a solicitor, someone to represent you?' But she only shook her head. And mine was spinning. Barely hours earlier I had been tucked up at home like a contented octogenarian, sipping cocoa and flicking through *Horse and Hound*. Now I seemed to be chief defence counsel in a murder case. For someone who didn't want defending. The room was airless and claustrophobic, I could scarcely believe what I was hearing, let alone assimilate it. I needed time to get out and think.

'Tess, listen to me. You are not going to hang, that's a ridiculous notion. You shouldn't even go to prison in my view. You didn't mean to kill Brendan, you acted in self-defence and I know we can prove it. But you must have faith, and hope, and show some determination.'

'For what purpose, Quentin?' she replied then, gazing at me dully. 'I pushed my family away, my daughter has another mother, and I lost the only man I ever loved. Then I killed my husband. I have no friends, no future, absolutely nothing to live for.'

'Of course you do!' I racked my brains. 'What about Peter?'

'Peter's dead. They all are. Everyone says so.'

'But we don't know that! All we can be sure of is he's missing. He could be a prisoner, or injured in hospital, or even on the run, Tess, trying to get back to you!'

The eyes flickered briefly, with something resembling hope, like embers stirring in a fire. Then died again. 'No. I brought him here. And it killed him. I did it, just like I killed Brendan.'

'All right.' Exasperated, I tried one last tack. 'All right, maybe you're right. But don't you think you should at least give him one chance to prove you wrong?'

I left my contact details with the desk sergeant, and some money, and a list of basics to get for her, and told him to ring me any time, no matter the reason. Then I caught the bus for the short ride up to Scampton, arriving at the main gate only to find pandemonium. A monstrous flap was on, with long queues at the gate, armed MPs everywhere, mysterious-looking civilians peering in dustbins, sniffer dogs on leads, the works. Fortunately a gate guard spotted me and waved me forward.

'Welcome back, Lieutenant!' he grinned. 'Glad you could make it.'

'Make what, Corporal? What on earth's going on?'

'Royal visit, sir. Didn't you know? The King and Queen are coming today. To meet the dam busters.'

Dam busters. I'd seen the phrase in the papers, heard it on the wireless, even observed it splashed across a wall from the train window, but this was the first I'd come across it within the RAF itself. 617 Squadron, it seemed, were now officially the dam busters, complete with royal seal of approval – hence Whitworth's summons, best uniforms and all the rest. But royalty aside, I had business to attend to, so ignoring the holiday atmosphere, strings of fluttering bunting and cheery greetings from colleagues, I set out for Number 2 hangar, and the offices of Messrs Abbott and Costello Ltd, intelligence purveyors to the realm.

Only to find everything being packed into boxes and loaded onto a van.

Frank Arnott was there, standing amid the detritus, incongruously dressed in full squadron leader's uniform, complete with pilot's wings and medals. Which was enough to put my back up straight away.

'Ah, Credo, there you are,' he said, tossing a file in a box. 'I trust you're recovered. Wouldn't want to miss the fun, eh?'

'Group Captain Whitworth asked me to attend, sir. And I am quite well, thank you. Um, are you leaving?'

'We certainly are. Job's done and we've other fish to fry. Leaving for London straight after the party.'

'Really? So, Operation *Chastise*. All the security work here at Scampton. 617 Squadron. The files are closed?'

'Closed and on their way back to HQ. One or two loose ends to tidy up, of course, but nothing that need detain us here.'

I wondered which loose ends. 'I see. Only the thing is . . .'

'Yes?'

'Sergeant Murray. The groundsman I wrote to you about.'

'Ah, yes. The one murdered by his wife when he discovered her having an affair with a pilot. Nasty business. Stabbed clean through the heart, you know. Body lay there undiscovered for four days.'

'Yes sir. Only she didn't murder him. She was acting in self-defence. Murray had a history of violence towards her, and was also mixed up in petty crime, black-marketeering and so on. It's all in the material I sent through to you.'

'Is it.'

'Yes sir.' I held my breath. 'As are matters relating to his possible spying.'

'For which you have presented not one shred of evidence.'

'Well, no, sir, not as such, but taking the dossier as a whole . . .'

'It adds up to precisely nothing. Unsubstantiated tittle-tattle.'

And there it was. The nub. I suspected Murray of supplying information to the enemy, Abbott and Costello didn't believe a word of it.

'Sir.' I persevered. 'He has a record as long as your arm. He has ties with criminals here and back in Ireland. He's been badly in debt. His behaviour is secretive and suspicious. And some of the things he said to his wife . . .'

'. . . Who killed him for another man . . .'

'. . . Suggest the actions of someone engaged in subterfuge.'

'All right, Credo!' Arnott broke off from filing. 'Such as what, precisely?'

Such as saying careless talk costs lives, such as screaming I'll fix your boyfriend, such as threatening her to silence. Such as, though I could hardly bear to believe it, such as Feltwell. 'He talked about Feltwell,' I sighed.

'What?'

'He told his wife, when drunk one night, that everything started going wrong following a garden job when the squadron was at Feltwell. She thought he meant groundskeeping or something. But he meant gardening. As in mine-laying.'

'So.' Arnott nodded. 'That's what this is about. You think he tipped off the Germans about your mine-laying flight. The one you were injured on.'

'Possibly.'

'Is it not also possible, and perfectly understandable, that you're simply looking for someone to blame? Other than the enemy, that is.'

'Yes, it is. I freely acknowledge that. But taking everything as a whole . . .'

'. . . It amounts to nothing. I've read your file, Credo, you've no proof.'

And I'd argue otherwise, but as far as he was concerned, he'd done his job, the mission was over, and anyway Murray was dead. Arguing with him was pointless. Anyway, other matters were pressing.

'That file, sir,' I went on, after a pause. 'It is vital to his wife's defence.'

'I doubt it.'

'The court must have it. It can't be withheld.'

'It most certainly can! That file, everything to do with this entire operation in fact, is top-secret military intelligence. No civilian court in the world can subpoena it. Right now it's on a lorry back to HQ, where it will be duly processed, then stored. For at least fifty years.'

'But the case for her defence rests in that dossier!'

'I'm sorry, Credo, you can't have it and that's final. She'll have to take her chances. Anyway, has it not occurred to you she's lying? Our analysis is she probably did murder Murray. Had it all planned out months in advance, so she could be with her boyfriend. And if I were you, I'd watch your own back, you're not exactly un-implicated.'

Another file hit the box with a thud. 'What do you mean?'

'For God's sake man, you got her boyfriend posted here! You helped them find ways to see each other, you paid for a room in a hotel, organised her lodgings, you even lent them your bloody car for their little love trysts!'

Chloe. As thorough as ever. Bless her. He knew everything. Almost.

'Did you get his notebook?'

That slowed him. 'What notebook?'

'He kept a notebook. Of everything he did. I mentioned it in my report. No doubt you searched his rooms after his body was discovered. Did you find it?'

Arnott fussed with papers. 'I've no idea what you're talking about.'

An awkward pause followed, him sorting files while I stood by and fumed. In the hangar, freshly uniformed ground crew were gathering, smoking and chatting excitedly, while outside a brass band limbered up.

'Where's Corporal Hickson?' I asked.

'Away. On a training course. Out of contact. Look, Credo . . .' he went on reasonably '. . . Try to think of the bigger picture. This is a party. A rare chance amid all the grime and drudgery to celebrate a success. This whole operation was a massive undertaking, involving hundreds, no thousands of individuals, who all worked together and pulled off a great victory. You included. And you can rest assured your contribution hasn't gone unnoticed. So let's just enjoy the moment.'

But I wasn't having his platitudes. 'A great victory, sir? We sent twenty Lancasters over there. Only eleven made it back. Nine didn't, nine whole crews, that's sixty-three men lost, and probably dead. I'm afraid "great victory" doesn't do them justice.'

'What's justice got to do with it? This is war, Credo, not a court of law. Risks have to be taken, people get killed. If you want justice, sue the Nazis, they started it.'

'They were expected, sir. Gibson and the others. They must have been, to sustain losses like that.'

'Christ, you and your bloody conspiracy theories!' He strode to his desk, rifling through piles of photographs. 'Here, this was taken the day after the raid. Look at it Credo, it's the one they printed in the newspapers, of the Möhne. Kindly note the hundred-yard gap where the bomb smashed through the dam. And the empty lake behind. And no doubt you've read of the havoc wreaked by the floods.' He thrust the photo at me. 'Crushing the enemy, that's what this is about!'

Duly I studied it. 'Yes, sir. And they did a fantastic job. I never said otherwise.'

'Correct. Now look again. What else do you see? Trees, Credo, trees! Your famous wooden crates. Do you know what was in them? Ornamental conifer trees. In pots. To decorate the dam!'

I looked again. He was right. Trees had appeared, at either end of the dam, and at odd intervals along its length, as though to blend it into the surrounding forest. And it did work, kind of. 'Camouflage.'

269

'If you like.' He lit a cigarette and wandered to the window. I stared at the picture. 'But that's my whole point.'

'What is, for God's sake?'

'It could have been flak, or searchlights, or torpedo nets, or anything. It just happened to be camouflage.'

'So?'

'So, why? Why now? What made the Germans decide to camouflage the dam just before we were due to attack it?'

'Who the hell cares?' he bellowed. 'It's over, Credo, mission accomplished! You've seen the newspapers, you've heard the wireless, the whole country's cheering. Nothing else matters!'

'It does to me!'

Which is when I threw the furniture. Well, kicked a wastepaper basket, but then I was convalescing. And it was a metal one, and flew gratifyingly straight, and only narrowly missed him.

Twenty minutes later, bizarrely, I was standing beside him being introduced to the King. Everyone had assembled outside in the sunshine, uniforms straightened, buttons gleaming, polished shoes lined up on painted white lines on the grass, while Ralph Cochrane and Charles Whitworth shepherded the royal entourage along, occasionally pausing here and there for a chat. To my consternation, having passed me once with barely a startled nod, the King stopped and came back.

'J-jolly bravely done, old ch-chap,' he murmured, in his quiet stammer. 'Did anyone else in your crew get h-hurt?'

'I . . . Ah . . . Well, no . . . You see, sir, I wasn't actually . . .'

Whitworth stepped swiftly forward. 'Flight Lieutenant Credo wasn't flying that night, your majesty,' he explained. 'He was my aide-de-camp, sir, during the operation. In charge of synchronising the security effort.'

A derisive snort from Arnott beside me. And there was that insane phrase again: *synchronising the security effort*. Nor was Whitworth's use of the past tense lost on me. He *was* my aide-de-camp, he'd said. Clearly I was out of a job again. The King winced, and looked baffled, then mustered a kindly smile. 'J-jolly bravely done,' he muttered again and moved on.

Afterwards came a reception, at which I finally got to speak to aircrew on the raid. But not until the formalities were over. Champagne, sandwiches, and hours of queuing, like guests at a wedding, for more confused conversations with VIPs. 'You poor dear man,' the Queen said to me sadly. '. . . To lose your hand to those dams.' Followed by endless rounds of speeches from Cochrane, Whitworth, Gibson, and a royal equerry who thanked us on behalf of the King: 'For lifting every English heart in the land . . .' at which an aide whispered urgently in his ear, and the gaffe was hastily corrected to include Commonwealth hearts too. Then Barnes Wallis himself stepped up, and in his anxious self-deprecating way, made a rather melancholy speech about sacrifice and loss and the tragic futility of war.

'Poor bloke,' the Australian Les Knight murmured in my ear. 'Been inconsolable since he heard about the casualties. Says he'd have never gone ahead if he'd known.'

Finally the speeches ended and I was able to corner Les and a few other pilots. With their tongues loosened by champagne, hopefully they were ready to unburden themselves to one of their own.

'Rotten luck, Geoff,' I commiserated to Rice, who was a former 57 Squadron colleague. He'd lost his bomb and narrowly escaped disaster pancaking H-Harry into the Waddensee. He'd also received a grilling from Gibson for it, and still looked upset two weeks later.

'Thanks, Credo. But I cocked up, and everyone knows it.'

'Don't think like that. It could happen to anyone. You did damn well getting your crew safely home.'

'Too right he did!' Les clapped us both on the shoulder. 'God bless all you 57 Squadron boys.' Rice shot me a sad glance. Both the other crews from our squadron, Dinghy Young's and Bill Astell's, had been lost.

David Maltby sauntered over, glass in hand. It was his bomb, following Young's, that sealed the Möhne's fate. 'I say, did you hear about Anderson?' he murmured conspiratorially. Heads leaned forward to listen. Anderson had also been on the receiving end of Gibson's wrath, having abandoned his mission in Y-York because of a faulty rear turret and problems with fog. Now it seemed he was to be sacked altogether. 'Not just for giving up,' Maltby explained, 'but for bringing his bomb home, completely against orders!'

'Yes, but Munro brought his bomb home too.'

'Ah, but Munro's a chum of Gibson's.'

And an officer, I remembered. Whereas Anderson was not.

I left the thought unspoken. 'Congratulations on your DSO, Maltby. I hear your bomb pitched up a perfect yorker at the Möhne.'

'More of a googly, actually,' he smiled. 'And the dam was already going when I attacked. Dinghy got it really.'

'Why do you think it took four bombs? Wallis always swore one should do it.'

Maltby shrugged. 'The first three weren't on target. The CO's went left and short, Mick Martin's was a complete wide, and poor old Hoppy's went straight over the top.'

272

Glances were exchanged. One of the unwritten rules of aerial combat is you don't discuss death. Not in direct terms. Except, perversely, when you feel like it. And only then in euphemisms: he got the chop, he got the hammer, he bought the farm, he didn't make it.

'What happened?' I tried gently.

'Hoppy went in second, after the CO. By then the flak gunners had got themselves organised, and knew the direction of attack. M-Mother was riddled, a complete flamer before he'd gone halfway.'

Knight took up the story. 'He must have known he was finished, but kept right on with the attack, and even got his bomb away, but too late and we saw it bounce over the dam. M-Mother flew on down the valley, burning furiously and trying to gain height, then blew apart in the air.'

Rice shook his head. 'Poor bastards. Couldn't have stood a chance.'

'You know Hoppy told Shannon he wouldn't make it,' Maltby added quietly. 'Swear to God. He took Shannon aside just before we boarded, and said he knew he wasn't coming back.'

'What did Shannon say?'

'Told him to stop being a bloody fool. But he could tell Hoppy meant it.'

A pause while we stared at our shoes, and upended our glasses, and peered round for the steward. I glimpsed a laughing Joe McCarthy, stalwart of the Sorpe, standing head and shoulders above the throng. And the ever-boyish David Shannon, so sure he'd cracked the Eder, and celebrating his twenty-first birthday that very day. But so many faces I'd grown to know were missing. Barlow, Maudslay, Byers, Burpee, and fifty-nine others. Including Peter, Uncle, Chalkie and the rest.

'V-Vicky bought it on the way home,' Les Knight went on, reading my thoughts. 'I know you were friendly with Lightfoot and his boys. They pulled off the perfect run at the Eder, you know, really I never saw anyone fly a Lancaster like that, he threw that thing around like a Spitfire, finishing with a power-off sideslip with flap, down to the water for the final run-in. Bloody marvellous. The drop was spot-on too, the bomb hit smack in the middle of the dam, then punched a hole in it like a fist through wet cardboard.'

'Good for them. Did you see where they went down?'

'I'm not sure exactly. We all split up for the run home, it was quite misty and starting to get light, but I was aware someone was off to my left and about a mile behind, and I think it was V-Vicky. Then somewhere around the German–Dutch border we saw a glow, sort of climbing up from that direction like a firework, then it faded and we lost sight of it. Then there was a flash as it hit the ground.'

The afternoon wore on, the champagne flowed, the noise levels grew. At some point the royal party, wisely sensing the onset of disorder, departed for quieter pastures. With them went any pretence at decorum. Ties were loosened, buttons undone, gin and whisky bottles appeared, as did wives, girl-friends and WAAFs rounded up from the women's quarters and typing pool. A piano arrived, shunted in at breakneck speed by a posse of cheering airmen, and before long a sing-song was under way, together with dancing, games and general tomfoolery. The pilot's way, I reflected, watching them play like overexcited children. Fly hard, party hard and don't think. For tomorrow you fade and die, just like the bubbles of your dreams.

I stayed on the periphery, extracting all I usefully could from my group before they too abandoned me to join the mayhem. Then, with my head spinning somewhat, and feeling oddly forlorn, I left them to it and made for the door. Outside the evening air was soft and mild, filled with the musical murmur of voices, and the scent of dewy grass and rambling roses. I inhaled deeply, gazing out over the verdant airfield and the wide Lincolnshire sky tinged with violet, and thinking Scampton never looked more beautiful. And how I didn't belong there any more. That it was time to leave this island sanctuary, build a raft, paddle away, and rejoin the world. As someone else.

'Hello, Quentin. Lovely evening.'

Charles Whitworth strolled up, brandy glass and cigar in hand. His tie was loosened, his cap slightly askew.

'Hello, sir. Yes, it's been quite a day.'

'I'll say. How's the Murray woman?'

'In a pickle, sir, as you said.'

'Can you help?'

'I'm not sure. I hope so.'

'Let me know if you need anything.'

'Thank you, sir.'

He puffed on his cigar. 'So. I hear you attacked a senior officer with a waste-basket. That's quite a feat for a man with only one arm.'

'Ah. Yes. Sorry about that, sir.'

'Don't be. He had it coming, the pompous oaf.'

'I expect there'll be, you know, consequences. Repercussions.'

'I wouldn't worry. We'll put in a word. My hunch is you won't hear a thing.'

'Thank you, sir.'

'It's nothing.' He waved his cigar dismissively, turning to

survey his domain. 'Do you know, Quentin, I've loved being station commander here. Best posting I ever had. They're closing it soon, though. To lay the concrete runways.'

'So I hear. Where will everyone go?'

'57 Squadron's going to East Kirkby, 617 to Coningsby.'

'And you?'

'God knows. They haven't said. But it won't be the same here. Afterwards, I mean. One of the last of the all-grass bomber stations and that. Something of a throwback to the past. But then everything changes, doesn't it? Sooner or later, if you get my drift.'

I did. I wasn't a pilot any more, and never would be. I wasn't an SIO, or even an acting SIO, nor was I his aide-de-camp. I wasn't anything really, except an embarrassment to the Service. It was time to leave it, and I felt ready.

'You have nothing to reproach yourself for, Quentin,' he went on intuitively. 'And much to offer. Common sense for a start, operational experience, good judgement, a listening ear, a compassionate heart. The RAF needs these things. Say the word, and I'll have you on 5 Group staff in a trice.'

'It's kind of you, sir, but it's the front line for me, or nothing. And I feel ready for a change. A new start.'

'Thought so. And does Corporal Hickson figure anywhere in this new start?'

'I, well, gosh, that is, I don't, know, really . . .' I blustered. 'I'd like to hope so . . .'

'Good. She's in London, by the way. Cooped up at RAF intelligence headquarters, and none too happy about it by all accounts. It's in Highgate, you know, place called Athlone House, masquerading as a convalescent home for injured officers, so you should fit right in!' He grinned, then slipped a note in my hand. 'Telephone this number, tell them you're my ADC and ask for Signals. That should get you through.'

'I . . . Well, I don't know what to say, sir.'

'Don't say anything. Just get on with it. *Carpe diem* and all that. Oh, and for God's sake don't tell anyone!'

With that, cigar in mouth, he turned and ambled away across the grass.

So I called her. Not ten minutes later. And we had a curious conversation.

'Quentin! Thank God. I've been out of my mind! Where are you?'

'Scampton. Lunching with the King. As one does.'

'Bad boy. You're supposed to be on sick leave.'

'I got bored. And things came up. How are you?'

'Missing you. Hating this. It's odd . . .'

'What is?'

'I used to love this job. But since you and I began working together, you know, on the operation there, everything changed. And now I don't feel the same about it.'

'Hmm. Exactly my thoughts. Which is why I'm packing it in.'

'What?'

'Resigning my commission. Quitting the Service. Medical discharge or somesuch.'

'Crikey. What will you do?'

'Not sure. Take a long break. Get the face fixed. Become a one-armed barrister.'

'Goodness! Well, that's absolutely marvellous. How does it feel?'

'It feels good. Would you care to join me?'

A pause. But only a short one. 'As your driver, I suppose.'

'Very funny. As my wife, Chloe. Will you marry me?'

'I'd love to. More than anything. But I have one request.'

'Name it.'

'Your face. Tell me you're not getting it fixed for me?'

'No. It's for me. For a long time I couldn't see the point. Now I do.'

'Then fine. Wonderful. I'm yours. When?'

'Soon as we can arrange it. But Chloe, I have a request too.'

'Yes?'

'I can't tell you now. But I am going to need your help with something.'

We signed off. I stood for a moment, hefting the receiver, scarcely daring to believe it. I was engaged. To the most wonderful girl in the world. I felt a great weight lifting from my shoulders, and a sense of closure, as though a line had been drawn in the sand, I'd stepped over it, and need never look back. Then, overcome with relief and weariness suddenly, I plodded off to my rooms for what would turn out to be my last night at Scampton.

Letting myself in was like walking onto an abandoned stage set, eerie and artificial, part of some other person's fictitious existence. I poked about reluctantly, struck by a faint lingering odour: disinfectant, ether, and a tinge of something rank, like dead lilies. It was two weeks since Chloe, Whitworth and the station MO had rescued me from there. The orderlies had tidied up cursorily, but evidence still remained of those final feverish minutes. A discarded bandage, a length of rubber tubing, a dropped hypodermic, and my ether mask, complete with dropper-bottle and elastic band. Once, the time had been nearing when I'd untie that elastic, and leave the mask on until the end came and the struggle was over. It was Whitworth who saved me, taking me to Reculver that day, making me his ADC, giving me Chloe. Encouraging me to feel part of 617 Squadron, and what they were trying to achieve.

I swept everything into a bin, threw wide the window for air, then retrieved my Scotch bottle and poured myself a stiff one. Outside, the sounds of merrymaking continued, somewhere a gramophone was playing Glenn Miller, far away across the airfield a lone dog howled in protest. I raised my glass to the night, and drank.

Five minutes later Guy Gibson came barging through the door.

'*Après moi le déluge!*' he spluttered in awful French.

'I beg your pardon, sir?'

'*Après moi le déluge!* It's our new squadron motto. What do you think?'

'Well, I think it's very good, sir. Most appropriate. Madame de Pompadour, isn't it. Mistress to Louis XV?'

'Haven't a clue, Mick Martin thought of it. Ah, look! I heard you had whisky, thank God for that!'

'Oh, yes, I do. Would you like one?'

'No, I'd like three! And make them doubles. And have one yourself!'

'Well, yes, all right sir, if you insist . . .'

'I do. And stop calling me sir.' He winked. 'At least until tomorrow.'

He was drunk and dishevelled, his cheeks flushed, his thick black hair flopping over his brow. I poured him a glass, he took it and slumped into a chair, eyeing me curiously.

'You lost the hand, I see, Credo. Sorry about that.'

'Can't be helped. Actually I'm better off without it.'

'Bit tricky for the flying though. But then there's always that Bader chap, flying fighters with no legs, so anything's possible. Although I hear his rudder control's awful.'

They were very alike, I realised, Bader and Gibson. Both hot-tempered, pig-headed taskmasters. Both equally sure they were right, and convinced of their own immortality. Both awe-inspiring leaders. Fish out of water in peacetime, but at war, exactly the right men at the right place and time.

'They're giving me a bloody VC, you know, Quentin.'

'So I heard. Many congratulations. And may I say richly deserved.'

'You think so? I was terrified. Absolutely quaking, from start to finish.'

'Of course. You'd be inhuman not to be. But you trained these men, and inspired them, and gave them confidence. Then led them to the dams, from the front, and succeeded against all the odds. And brought them home again.'

'It was orders, I had no choice.'

'You're wrong, Guy. At the Möhne, after Hoppy bought it. When you went in alongside Martin like that to draw the flak. That wasn't orders. It was magnificent. And worth a Victoria Cross alone in my view.'

'Maybe.' He downed his glass. 'But we still lost far too many.'

A reflective silence followed. Outside in the corridor airmen were heading noisily for bed. Beyond the window the dog still barked. I leaned across and refilled his glass, sensing now might be my only chance. 'May I ask you something?'

He waved his hand. 'Fire away.'

'Do you think they were expecting you? At the Möhne, that is. Did you get the impression the Germans were ready for you, in any way?'

A nail-biting pause while he considered, his eyes focusing unsteadily on mine.

Then a knock came on the damn door. 'Sorry to disturb you, Lieutenant,' an orderly said. 'Telephone call. City police station.'

'Thank you, I'll be right there.'

Gibson was still thinking, still remembering, still staring glassily.

'Guy?'

He began levering himself to his feet. 'God knows, Quentin.' He said finally. 'But I will say this. It certainly bloody felt like it.'

Tess was on the telephone. She sounded tired and resigned still. But different somehow. More composed.

'Tess. Are you all right? Has something happened?'

'No. Nothing. I'm all right. They said I was allowed to call you. Once, that is.'

'That's right. Do you need something?'

'No, I'm fine. And thank you for the toiletries and things. It was very kind.'

'Not at all. I'll be down first thing in the morning to see you.'

'Thanks. And thanks for contacting my family. My father sent a telegram. About arranging representation and that.'

'Good. They have to know, Tess, you can't do this on your own.'

'I suppose not.' She paused. 'About the notebook . . .'

'Yes.'

'I tried.' She sighed at the memory. 'I searched him, afterwards . . . You know. And I did look round our rooms. But I couldn't find it. Sorry. I know how important it was to you.'

'No matter. Thanks for trying. It can't have been easy.'

'No.' Another pause. 'Quentin. Do you really think there's any chance?'

'Of course! Every chance. You'll beat this thing, Tess, even without the notebook, I'm certain of it!'

'No. I meant Peter. Do you really think there's any chance he's alive?'

Chapter 12

There was.

Peter awoke. He was lying on a straw palliasse, in a small room with concrete walls, steel door and tiny barred window, through which daylight poured, together with the now familiar sounds of boots on gravel and revving auto-engines. The window was set high in the wall, and had no glass, only bars. On his first day there he had discovered his cell was mostly below ground, and that by standing on tiptoe he could see through the window, out onto a vehicle compound. High stone walls with shuttered windows surrounded the compound, suggesting the courtyard of a grand town house. At one end wrought-iron gates opened onto a busy street, from where grey-painted staff cars and motorcycles drove in and out at intervals, carrying Germans clad in Luftwaffe uniforms.

He rose from his palliasse and went to the window. From the angle of the sun and light traffic noise, the hour must still be early. Soon would come breakfast, hard black bread and a mug of bitter coffee, passed through a slot in the door. After that more hours of waiting, until they came to get him for the day's first session with Major Kessell. He stood at the window, inhaling the June morning air. Beneath it he'd scratched fourteen marks on the concrete with a rusty nail. He picked up the nail and scratched another. Today was his fifteenth in captivity.

He was a prisoner of the Abwehr, he'd learned, Germany's military intelligence organisation, or a department of it connected to the Luftwaffe. You are safe now, Herr Lieutenant, they'd told him, 'loyt-nant' they pronounced it, even though he was only a Flying Officer. You are safe now with us, they said, among your fellow airmen. But he didn't feel safe, he felt vulnerable and disoriented, and consumed by loss and guilt about something he couldn't remember. And then the questioning had begun, which was when he felt least safe of all.

He'd first come to his senses on the night of the raid, lying on his back in a clump of bushes. It was cold, and dark, and quiet, and whispering white silk billowed around him like a cloud. He didn't know where he was, nor how he got there, nor how long he'd been lying there, he only knew the moonlit sky was turning grey, that some tiny creature was moving in the undergrowth nearby, and that blood leaked from a handkerchief tied over a painful gash to his head. He knew V-Vicky was gone too, but of her last moments, and those of his crew, he could remember nothing.

He stayed on his back for a while, summoning himself, and fighting an unbearable urge to weep. Grief seemed to wash over him like waves onto a deserted beach, yet he didn't know why. Eventually he rolled onto his knees and, fighting the pounding in his head, forced himself to his feet. Fumbling catches, he released his parachute, bundled the silk into a ball and hid it among the bushes, along with his Mae West. All he was wearing now were the clothes he had flown in: black shoes, uniform trousers, shirt-sleeves and tie. Turning his back on the brighter sky to the east, he set out for home.

This, his first bid for freedom, lasted an hour, three miles in the gathering dawn before he was spotted by a soldier on a bicycle returning from a night on fire-watch. The soldier blew loudly on his whistle, unslung his rifle and gestured for Peter to approach with hands held high. Having searched him for weapons and stolen his watch, the soldier then marched him at rifle-point into the nearest village, where children at the road-side shouted taunts, and an old woman spat at him as he passed. In the village he was locked into the back room of a hall while the authorities were notified. During the wait he was given a crust of bread and some bitter ersatz coffee, and the local doctor came and stitched the wound on his head.

'You are fortunate, young man,' the doctor murmured in heavily accented English. 'People don't like being bombed, you know.'

Peter said nothing, just gritted his teeth as the needle pierced him.

'Indeed, the last British airman to be shot down in these parts was found with a pitchfork through his chest.'

He asked the doctor where he was, and was told Westphalia, which meant nothing. Then he asked if any other airmen had been found the previous night.

'There was a crash,' the doctor replied. 'Several kilometres away. Bodies were recovered. That is all I know.'

He spent the night in the village hall, during which he was given turnip soup and more ersatz coffee. Either German people don't have much to eat, he decided, sipping the watery soup, or they don't waste it on prisoners. Time passed. Apart from the doctor, nobody visited, though he occasionally heard footsteps in the corridor outside. The room was small and windowless, little more than a store cupboard, and with no bed or mattress he passed a restless night shivering on a blanket on the floor. Soon his head began to throb and he felt weak and nauseous. He rose and tried the door, finding it to be solidly framed and securely locked. When he shoved at it with his shoulder, dizziness overcame him and he slid to the floor in a heap.

Next morning two plain-clothes policemen collected him in a car and drove him east, deeper into Germany, for about an hour. Soon they were entering the outskirts of a larger town which from the street signs and shop names Peter identified as Borken. Here he was ushered through the doors of a civilian police station and locked into a cell with barred door, cot-bed and washbasin. More soup arrived, together with a lump of rancid sausage that he forced himself to eat. In the afternoon he was taken into a room with desk and chair, a few minutes later one of the policemen entered, and Peter faced his first interrogation.

Which was barely an interrogation at all. 'You are in the custody of the Borken *Reichspolizei*,' the policeman said, in pretty good English. Peter had never heard of it. Then the man slid paper and pencil across the desk. 'Please write down your name, address, date and place of birth, full family details, military unit, specification of your aircraft, names of crewmen, and purpose of your mission. Please be as thorough as possible, as this will greatly help in your processing, and the notification of your next of kin. Thank you. I will return in thirty minutes.' With that the man rose and left the room, turning the key behind him. Not a single question had been asked.

Peter stared at the sheet for thirty minutes and wrote down nothing. When the man returned and saw the empty page he flew into a rage, smashing his fist on the table, cuffing Peter round the head and cursing him furiously in German. Peter sat motionless, his eyes fixed ahead, and waited for the end to come. But it didn't come, and after a few minutes the man calmed down, straightened his clothes and lit a cigarette. He even apologised for his loss of control.

'Please,' he pleaded, jabbing a finger at the page. 'You must tell me something. Otherwise I will look very bad. Anyway, it is a legal requirement, you know.'

Peter sensed the man was of low importance, and anxious only to improve his status. 'I can't tell you all these things,' he replied, speaking for the first time. 'I'm only supposed to give my name, military rank and service number.'

'That would be a start,' the man simpered, proffering the pencil.

'All right. But first I must use the lavatory. It's been many hours, you know. Then I'll tell you.'

Two minutes later Peter made his second bid for freedom, levering himself through a tiny hinged window above a lavatory cistern in the washroom. The window opened outward onto a narrow alley, he wriggled through and dropped heavily to the ground. Choosing a direction at random, he followed the alley which led to a lane, which in turn rounded a corner onto a busier thoroughfare. Suddenly he found himself hurrying along a crowded street, in broad daylight, in Germany, wearing his RAF trousers, shirt and tie. Incredibly, although heads turned curiously, no one challenged him, until just as he was crossing the road to enter a park, a shout rang out behind, followed by a pistol shot into the air. Peter stopped, placed his hands on his head and waited. Five minutes later he was back in the room with the desk and paper.

'That was stupid and irresponsible!' the policeman shouted furiously. 'What possibly could you hope to achieve?'

'Escape.' Peter shrugged. 'It's my duty.'

And something was achieved. Wheels began to turn. For as reports were filed, memos circulated and phone messages logged, word was spreading that a downed British airman, an officer at that, was in custody in Borken. Furthermore, the officer in question might be a survivor of the extraordinary raid on the Ruhr dams which had wreaked such havoc. A raid which, despite being played down by the propaganda ministry, had astounded the public with its audacity, and caused a furore in Berlin extending up to the Führer himself. Consequently Section 1L of the Abwehr, the department of Germany's military intelligence responsible for aviation-related matters, was most keen to interview the aforesaid officer. So much so that within twenty-four hours Peter had been collected from Borken and driven sixty kilometres to the converted mansion in Dortmund that served as the Abwehr's district headquarters. Where the questioning began in earnest.

Somehow, miraculously, a handful of those lost on Operation *Chastise* had survived.

But desperately few. Vernon Byers and his crew in K-King were the raid's first victims, downed at 2300 hours by a chance flak round as they coasted in over the Dutch island of Vlieland. Nobody survived that crash. Some days later K-King's *Upkeep* exploded, harmlessly if spectacularly, in the Waddensee. At about the same time as the only body, that of the rear gunner, was given up by the sea off Harlingen.

Fifty minutes after K-King's loss, Byers's Wave 2 associate Norm Barlow was racing E-Easy low across the Rhineland when it struck high-tension wires and pancaked into a field. Eyewitnesses said the bomber looked partially intact as it careered across the ground, but then exploded into flames before anyone could get out. E-Easy's crew were burned beyond recognition. Its *Upkeep* became detached on impact, and rolled away into trees, but didn't go off. The next day the local Bürgermeister had himself photographed standing next to it, thinking it was a fuel tank. Later, the military arrived and took it away for defusing and examination. Within a fortnight Luftwaffe engineers had produced detailed drawings of every aspect of Wallis's revolving bomb.

No one survived from Bill Astell's B-Baker, which was the third to be lost at 0015 hours. Bill had written home on 14 May — cheerfully making no reference to the raid then just two days away, and enclosing his will, which was witnessed by Norm Barlow and Henry Maudslay — both also fated to perish. B-Baker took off in the third formation of Gibson's Wave 1, in company with Maudslay and Knight. All went well until shortly after crossing into Germany, when Astell was late making a turn and fell behind. Minutes later he collided with a pylon and crashed into a field near Marbeck. Local farm residents, already woken by the passage of low-flying Lancasters, saw a flash as B-Baker struck the pylon, then the Lancaster exploded into the field. All watched as a huge drum-shaped object rolled away in flames. Seconds later the *Upkeep* went off in a monstrous explosion which created a crater 'big enough to swallow a house'. The fire was so intense, it was an hour before anyone could get near B-Baker's wreckage.

Fifteen minutes later the end came for John Hopgood's M-Mother. Having been hit by flak en route, with an engine damaged and crewmen injured, including a mortally-wounded nose gunner, a radio operator with a shattered leg, and Hopgood himself with a head wound, M-Mother lost the final battle on its run-in to the Möhne. Yet astonishingly, and against all odds, men would survive. Raked by flak as it sped over the water, M-Mother burst into flames, and having narrowly cleared the parapet, was seen heading north, trailing fire and fighting desperately for height. Aboard it Hopgood knew the aircraft was finished and gave the order to bale out. In the nose the bomb aimer, Fraser, jettisoned the nose-hatch, only to see trees rushing by below. Without hesitation he knelt down and tumbled out, simultaneously pulling his D-ring. The chute deployed at once, the tailwheel flashing by inches from his head. A few seconds more and he was already on the ground. Meanwhile the rear gunner, Burcher, was scrambling out of his turret to retrieve his parachute. Crouching by the Elsan to clip it on, he was met by the sight of the radio operator, Minchin, crawling down the fuselage towards him, injured leg trailing. With incredible courage Burcher released the main door, made sure his friend's parachute was attached, grabbed its D-ring and pushed him through. Then he plugged in his intercom and spoke to his captain.

'Rear gunner ready to bale out.'

Hopgood's reply was a scream. 'For Christ's sake go!'

So Burcher went. But struck the tail and landed heavily, badly injuring his back. Yet he survived, as did Fraser the bomb aimer. Minchin did not.

The Canadian Lewis Burpee and his crew died at 0200. They had taken off in S-Sugar as part of the Wave 3 mobile reserve, but were caught over Holland by flak batteries from the night-fighter station of Gilze-Rijen. S-Sugar's end was witnessed by Ken Brown and his crew following behind in F-Freddie: an aircraft in flames falling like a comet, then a colossal flash as it hit the ground and the bomb exploded. The airfield was extensively damaged, S-Sugar reduced to fragments.

Twenty-year-old Warner Ottley's C-Charlie was also part of Wave 3, taking off shortly after midnight, and making its way safely cross-Channel, through Holland and on into Germany. But following confusion over messages changing its target, the bomber strayed too close to Hamm's lethal defences and was brought down by flak. Crashing into a field beside a wood, C-Charlie's *Upkeep* went off, demolishing the aircraft. The rear turret was sent flying, yet incredibly, after finally coming to rest, its occupant, Sergeant Fred Tees, managed to extricate himself and crawl out. Shocked and burned, he walked from the scene and into captivity.

At around the same time, 0230 hours, Henry Maudslay's Z-Zebra was brought down near Emmerich. Having sustained damage and injuries when their *Upkeep* exploded against the parapet at the Eder, Maudslay and his crew nursed their ailing machine back across Germany, and almost to within sight of the Dutch border. There the oil town of Emmerich lay in their path, and Maudslay had to decide whether to fly over it or make a lengthy detour around. He chose the former, the flak found them, and this time nobody walked away.

Then came Dinghy Young, whose brilliantly placed bomb so fatally damaged the Möhne. He'd then followed the others to the Eder, ready to take over as leader should anything happen to Gibson. Then he scurried homeward, expertly weaving A-Apple past searchlights and flak, hedge-hopping all the way to the

Dutch coast and safety. There, with the dawn growing at his back and the welcoming sea beckoning, Dinghy allowed A-Apple to rise into the sky above Vlieland. A chance flak-burst caught him, and the Lancaster exploded into the sea. Nobody survived. The time was 0300 hours.

Which just left V-Vicky.

Peter finally learned of its fate in Dortmund, that fifteenth day of his captivity.

After his breakfast and a visit to the washroom – where he was allowed to wash and shave, but with only a cup of water, as supplies were 'disrupted' – he was escorted as usual to the first-floor office of his inquisitor, Major Leopold Kessell of the Abwehr's Luftwaffe section. The office was comfortable and well appointed, with shuttered French windows leading onto a balcony overlooking the compound. Panelled bookshelves lined the walls, a chandelier hung from the ceiling, plush carpets adorned the polished parquet floor. Peter was admitted by an adjutant and shown to his chair before a mahogany desk bearing a framed photograph of Frau Kessell together with silver inkpot and letter-opener. A few minutes later Kessell entered bearing a china coffee-cup. Forty, self-assured, immaculately uniformed, he seated himself across the desk, filled his pen from the inkpot and resumed his interrogation.

His principal technique for which, Peter had soon learned, was not to ask anything he didn't already know, but to inform Peter of what he did.

'Good morning, Flying Officer Lightfoot,' he began in his flawless English. 'And it is a fine one, quite warm, no? Now then, you'll relieved to hear that the injuries to Sergeant Tees are not life-threatening. He has flash-burns, but is receiving excellent hospital treatment. Pilot Officer Burcher's injuries are more serious, I regret, but he is in good hands.' He opened a file. It was buff-coloured, with an eagle on the front, and clearly labelled: 617 Squadron, 5 Group, RAF Bomber Command. It was always present during their interviews, and had been steadily growing in the fortnight since Peter had first seen it. Not from what he might have said, he hoped, or not said, but from the sheaves of documents that arrived on Kessell's desk each day.

'Well, now, this is interesting,' Kessell studied the latest sheets. 'It says here that a Sergeant Fraser has been found and identified as a possible member of your squadron. Apparently he was apprehended near Soest on the night of the seventeenth, which, if I'm not mistaken, is not far from where Sergeant Burcher was found. This suggests they were of the same crew . . .' He thumbed through the file. 'Ah yes, of Flight Lieutenant Hopgood in aircraft AJ-M. What do you think, Officer Lightfoot, does that sound right?'

Peter said nothing and kept his expression neutral, his by now well rehearsed response to probing. He also made a point of showing no interest in the file or its contents. He'd heard the Germans kept dossiers on every RAF squadron, right down to names of aircrew. 617's seemed amazingly detailed, yet he had no wish to add to it. Instead his attention ventured to the French windows, which today, unusually, were open for fresh air. Peter estimated he could cross the floor and be through the windows in three seconds. Then came a vault over the balcony, followed by a one-storey drop to the compound, which was far but achievable. After that it was a sprint for the street, which was unlikely to go unchallenged. Much depended upon surviving the fall uninjured, the compound being empty, and whether the gates were locked.

'. . . Some further bodies from other crews have been recovered and buried with appropriate military honours,' Kessell went on, flicking through the sheets. '. . . Though sadly many have yet to be identified owing to, well, fire damage, and the very severe nature of their injuries. And of course the bodies of Pilot Officer Byers and Squadron Leader Young and their brave crews may never be recovered, having fallen in the sea. Oh, but some better news just in, Peter, two Canadian sergeants, Bimson and Guttenberg, have turned up alive and well.'

The matter-of-fact delivery, the hypnotic turning of pages, the closely watching eyes, Peter fell for them completely. He was astonished and there was no hiding it.

'What?' he gasped. 'Where?'

'Bocholt, it seems. A military hospital for NCOs, fifty kilometres from where you were picked up. They're fit and well evidently, receiving attention for injuries sustained in the action against the dams.' Kessell smiled. 'So you do know them, Peter. You know them all. This confirms you are from 617 Squadron, and the crashed Lancaster AJ-V was yours.' He reached across and patted Peter's arm, as if to say, bad luck, game over. Then went back to his papers. 'But I'm afraid your second pilot, Sergeant MacDowell, did not survive. He was found at the controls. Nor too did the wireless operator and navigator, sadly, ah, what were their names?'

'White. And Johnson.' Peter replied dully. Kessell would find out soon enough. Or already knew. He'd been saving this information, Peter realised. Saving it until he had a clearer picture, the better to spring his trap. Which Peter had walked right into. He didn't care. Chalkie and Jamie. And Uncle. All gone. It was beyond bearing. A fragment of memory came to him: Uncle leaning across him, shouting something and hauling at Vicky's controls while someone, Jamie perhaps, or Chalkie, wiped blood from his eyes with a handkerchief.

'But of course, one is as yet unaccounted for . . .' Kessell was still talking. 'Which would be, what, the bombardier, yes? What was his name again, Peter?'

Kiwi. They hadn't got him. Which might mean he was dead, or might mean he was alive. And running for it. 'I'm not telling you,' he said angrily. 'I'm not telling you another damn thing!'

'But you have told me so much already.' Kessell looked affronted. 'And of such interest and value.'

'Well, no more!' His eyes went to the windows, the need to escape now almost overpowering. Uncle, Chalkie, Jamie. Dead. With Uncle at the controls. Second pilot, Kessell had said, yet Uncle was no pilot. And why didn't they get out? What could have happened?

'Peter,' Kessell reasoned, reading his mind. 'Consider these, your fallen comrades. Your mission, what the English newspapers are calling the Dam Busters, was an exceptional undertaking, you know, so brave and imaginative. But far too costly, and ultimately of trivial effect, and thus irresponsible. Air Marshal Harris recklessly sent you young men to die in vain. Nearly half were wiped out, you know, a criminal waste of courageous lives. So you assisting me in piecing together missing details is no act of betrayal, but an honour to their memory, and a kindness to their relatives.'

Peter leaned over. 'I watched two dams go, Major, one of them close to. I saw the effect, and there was nothing trivial about it. And we went there because we wanted to. We were volunteers. All of us. Nobody died in vain.'

'But . . .' Kessell gaped. 'Do you mean, it was you? The second dam? It was, wasn't it? You broke it!'

'I'm not saying that.'

'Yes! My God, it's true, ha! I'm sitting with the man who broke the Eder!' He rose from his chair, chuckling in disbelief, strolled to the windows, closed and locked them. As he did so, Peter slipped the letter-opener into his cuff.

'Well, well, well.' Kessell resumed his seat and picked up his pen. 'So, Flying Officer Lightfoot and his crew in AJ-V were at the Möhne *and* the Eder, where they successfully broke the dam. Admirable, truly admirable. But now, Peter, this must mean you were part of Wing Commander Gibson's main attack force. So tell me about that, please.'

'No. I want to go back to my cell.'

'But Peter. You must stay and help me.'

'No. I refuse.'

A wince, as of pain. 'That would be so foolish. Because, as I've said before, if you refuse, I must hand you to the Gestapo, who only want the same information as me. But their methods for obtaining it are so awful, quite barbaric. I couldn't bear that. So stay, Peter, and help me here. For the sake of the relatives. Perhaps you'd like some tea? Oh, and may I borrow that letter-opener . . .'

That night, the rest came back to him. For hours he lay on his mattress, staring at the fading square of light at his window, and thinking of Uncle and the others. More fragments of memory were surfacing now, wreckage from a sunken ship. Panicked shouts on the intercom, an engine in flames, the smell of cordite and the taste of blood. But still the full picture wouldn't emerge, and repeatedly his mind wandered to earlier times. Of their first training sorties together, seven far-flung strangers bound by rank and a common cause. Their eighteen missions with 61

Squadron: Hamburg, Cologne, Münster, Berlin and the rest. Their final disastrous flight in B-Baker, the ice and the lightning, the freezing hours in the liferaft, and their miraculous rescue. Singing 'I'm Forever Blowing Bubbles' over the intercom in Q-Queenie, in the sergeants' mess at Syerston, in the liferaft to keep warm, and even over the telephone at Glasgow station. Then joining 617 Squadron: 'I'm not sure this is a good idea,' Jamie had said, but joined anyway, just to be with his friends. And Chalkie's wife, Vicky: 'Hopping mad, she is,' Chalkie had grinned, yet signed on with the rest of them. And Uncle, like a father to him in the air, so wise and unflappable, yet so lost and alone on the ground. 'Leave it to me, now laddie,' he'd said, reaching for the controls. 'It's time you went.'

He awoke in pitch blackness to the wail of an air-raid siren. For a moment he lay, disoriented and confused by the unfamiliar sound. He'd been dreaming of Tess. She was behind the door of a strange room, calling his name over and over, while an eerie whine rose and fell in the background. He blinked in the darkness. The siren went on, soon joined by others, then a finger of blue light appeared beyond his window, stirring the sky like a wand. Blue light: master-searchlight that meant, radar-controlled to lock on to the target, so others could follow and join in. Then he heard the rumble of approaching engines, and leapt from his mattress. Dortmund was under attack, Europe's largest inland port, Kessell had told him proudly, sending steel and coal throughout the Reich. The engine noise grew louder, from a drone to a throb, Peter was sure he heard Merlins, scores of them, Lancasters that meant, or the Mark 2 Halifax. Then came the first bark of anti-aircraft guns, heavy flak, 88 millimetre, capable of firing shells thirty thousand feet or more. He strained at his window, but could see only the criss-cross beams of the searchlights, and flash of distant artillery. Then the first bombs fell, far to the north, and he felt the ground quake beneath his feet, and heard the rumbling crump of explosions. Soon the engine noise was deafening, the sky filled with scouring beams and bursting flak. High above he glimpsed a tiny cross, trapped in the lights and trailing orange, a moment later a brighter flash and it blew up. Bombs fell closer now, stamping across the city towards him, like the boots of an angry giant. With each explosion, flickering light lit the courtyard like flashbulbs. A fire engine raced past, bell trilling. He glimpsed running guards, heard guttural shouts and heavy footsteps beyond his door. They'd forgotten him, he realised, left him to die like a rat in a trap. Or a bird, forgotten in a cage. Then came a searing flash, a deafening explosion and a shockwave that punched him like a fist in the back. Glass shattered, dust and grit fell from the ceiling, the floor shuddered. He dropped to his knees and crawled to the door, smashing his fist against it in panic. 'Let me out!' he shouted. 'For God's sake please let me out!'

After the Eder, the race is on to get home before the breaking dawn. Gibson gives the order, nobody hesitates: Gibson, Shannon, Young, Knight, Lightfoot, five crews open the throttles, drop down to the trees, and set off into the dying night. Soon they become separated, but this is no longer a formation exercise, it's a mass scramble for safety. On board V-Vicky Peter fixes his gaze on the windscreen, Uncle holds the throttles wide and Jamie stands behind, unrolling his lavatory-roll maps, while Kiwi calls warnings from the nose: 'Searchlights to port, eight o'clock three miles, village with church-spire dead ahead, line of pylons coming from the right . . .' Thirty minutes pass, they track north round Hamm, jink south to clear Münster and Dülmen, then the hills fall behind and they flatten out low over crop fields, scurrying west for Borken and the border.

Which is where the night fighter finds them. A Messerschmitt Bf110, fast, twin-engined, well armed. Its pilot can't believe it, all night he's been chasing phantoms, repeatedly vectored onto intruders no one can find. But they've been searching in the wrong place, up, instead of down. For at last there is his enemy, far below, dashing through the shadows like a fleeing thief. What is the RAF thinking, he wonders, gesturing to his gunner, flying heavy bombers on the deck like that, have they gone mad? Flicking his guns to on, he banks steeply over, and dives in for attack.

The black-painted Messerschmitt carries four 20mm cannon, devastating firepower at close range. Its first burst rips into V-Vicky without warning, tearing open the port wing and destroying an engine. 'Night fighter six o'clock!' Herb yells and immediately shoots back. In the cockpit Peter wrenches at the controls, stamping rudder against yaw, and weaving as low as he dare, while Uncle hits the extinguisher and shuts down the flaming engine. Then the Messerschmitt fires again, this time pouring cannon into the fuselage and cabin. As it does so, Herb gets a bead on the twinkling guns and lets fly with two long bursts. 'I got him!' he shouts, watching the fighter pull up and away, smoke trailing. The attack is over in less than a minute.

But the damage is done, Vicky is dying, and crew are injured, Jamie Johnson mortally so, hit in the chest by a cannon shell. Chalkie too is hit, blood pumping from a shattered left arm. Tearing a cable from his console, he ties it on, tightens it with his teeth to stop the bleeding, then stoops to Jamie, who is slumped on the floor beside him. And in the cockpit Peter can feel himself fainting. Blood pours from a wound on his head, running in hot gouts into his eyes and mouth. He can't see, his arms are like lead, and unconsciousness beckons. But he can feel the rudders, slack and useless beneath his feet, and sense the intense fire raging on the wing, and knows it's over. 'She's had it, Uncle,' he murmurs feebly. 'She's had it, I'm sorry.'

He's teetering on the edge of oblivion. Then strong arms are around him, hauling him from his seat, and wiping blood from his face with a rag. 'Leave it to me, now laddie,' a comforting voice says. 'Everything's all right. Have you got him, Kiwi?'

'I got him.'

'Good. Time to go now. All of you.'

With that Peter falls into unconsciousness. And it's Uncle that takes over, and gives the order, sitting there, straight-backed in the pilot's seat, resolutely hauling the doomed bomber heavenward. 'Off you go then lads, and no lollygagging.'

They go. In the tail Herb centres his turret, slides open the doors and grabs his parachute from its hook by the Elsan. In an instant he's clipped it on his chest. 'Are you there, Billy boy?' he calls over the intercom.

'We're here, Herb,' Billy replies. 'Getting Peter out, be following right along.'

'Make sure you do.' Herb unplugs his intercom, swings his turret side-ways, slides open the doors and tumbles backwards into space.

Down in the nose, Kiwi and Billy are hooking on Peter's parachute, holding him, slumped unconscious in the gaping hatch.

'What do we do?' Billy shouts.

'This!' Kiwi pulls the D-ring on Peter's chute, gathers the silk and throws it into the slipstream. In an instant Peter is plucked from sight.

'Go, Billy!' he shouts, then quickly follows, diving head-first into the night.

On the flight deck, Uncle struggles with the doomed machine. The left wing is completely ablaze, and with both engines dead, dragging the bomber into a deadly spiral. He glances down, Chalkie is on the floor beside him, cradling Jamie in his arms.

'Are you no' going, Chalk?' he shouts. But Chalkie just smiles, and shakes his head. Seconds later the blazing left wing folds up in the heat, *and Vicky flicks into a spin. Uncle releases the controls, reaches down and clasps Chalkie's hand.*

On the morning after the air-raid, instead of being shown up to Major Kessell's office as normal, Peter was escorted outside to the rubble-strewn compound, and into the back of a Luftwaffe staff car. A few minutes later Kessell himself joined him.

'Good morning, Flying Officer Lightfoot,' he breezed as usual. 'I trust you passed a comfortable night.' He was freshly shaved, crisply dressed, and smelled of polished boots and expensive cologne. And was unshakeably cheerful, as if the air-raid never happened. As if to acknowledge it might show weakness. He even, as they drove through the gates, shook out a newspaper and began reading, thus shutting out the view beyond the window. But their progress soon slowed, as the car threaded its way around debris piles and craters, and eventually Kessell was forced to take notice. 'Many of the bombs fell in the residential quarter,' he said, peering at a shattered building. 'Thirty dead in all, so I'm told. Which is regrettable, I'm sure you agree.'

Peter was still thinking of Uncle, struggling at the controls of V-Vicky. And of Uncle's adored wife Mary, taken from him by a German air-raid. And how her death had erased his will to live. Now they were both gone. 'You bombed the people of London,' he replied. 'And Liverpool and Coventry, and the rest. You killed thousands, old and young, women and children. That's what I regret. I regret you ever started this war.'

Kessell seemed oblivious. 'The commercial sector suffered some damage,' he went on. 'As did the industrial quarter. But the canal is quite unharmed, you know, and the docks and mar-shalling yards only superficially. Rest assured, all will be restored to full serviceability in a few days.'

'Bully for you.'

'You're missing the point, Peter. I am speaking strategically, not morally. My point is, *the damage you cause may appear significant, but is ultimately of no consequence.*'

They drove on. Peter assumed that the city tour, with its medieval churches and spacious parks, was for his benefit, some kind of salutary lesson, and made up his mind to show no interest. But after a while he noticed they were heading out of town, and eastwards into the countryside. Soon the road grew narrow and winding, the terrain more hilly, the car plunging in and out of dark forests.

'Where are we going?' he asked uneasily. Apart from the driver, a guard was sitting in front. Holding a machine-pistol.

'Be patient, Peter.'

An hour passed. The landscape became more rugged, the hills angular, the forest primordial. Kessell, to Peter's surprise, stopped reading, folded his arms and went to sleep. Discreetly Peter tried his door handle, only to find it disconnected, and his guard winking with amusement. After another hour, and himself nodding with fatigue, they rounded a bend and arrived at a road-block. Explanations were exchanged, papers passed, Peter's face closely scrutinised, then they were waved through. They continued another half-mile, passed between entrance gates, ascended a twisting driveway, and broke suddenly into the clear.

Spread out before them was the vast expanse of the Eder reservoir. Or what was left of it, a shrivelled river twisting through three thousand acres of empty lake bed, and stretching away to distant tree-lined shores. Sailboats and ferries lay stranded, high and dry like beached fish, a pleasure steamer, frozen in mid-motion, cruised the drying mud, while piers and jetties jutted out to nowhere from the shores. Peter stared in awestruck fascination. Halfway across, the remains of an abandoned village had resurfaced after thirty years under water. Near it a long-submerged bridge still spanned the river. A mile away on the northern shore, a Gothic castle stood guard, high on its hill overlooking the scene. The starting point, he recognised, for V-Vicky's dive to the water, and the dash to the near side, and the sharp left turn for the final attack.

'So, Peter.' Kessell gestured expansively. 'Behold the fruits of your efforts.'

Minutes later he found himself standing on the curved wall of the dam itself, where the scene was one of urgent yet organised activity. A narrow-gauge railway had been installed, to carry materials in and rubble out. Scaffolding had been erected, cranes and hoists swung busily to and fro, while labourers hurried to the barked orders of engineers waving plans.

One such engineer, a bespectacled civilian in his fifties, approached them.

'Ah, Herr Doctor,' Kessell greeted him. 'Peter, this is Doctor Holzmann, the senior engineer supervising repairs. Herr Holzmann, may I present Flying Officer Lightfoot. The man who broke your dam.'

A stiff nod from Holzmann, who eyed Peter balefully, as though confronted with the hooligan caught vandalising his car. Behind him a younger assistant looked on curiously.

'Shall we visit the breach, Major?' Holzmann suggested.

They set off along the parapet, Kessell and Holzmann leading, Peter following with his guard. They passed beneath the right-hand sluice-tower, then on another hundred yards towards the centre of the dam. Which ended abruptly at the edge of a cliff.

'Good God!' Kessell peered into the abyss. 'Look what you have done, Peter.'

Peter looked. The drop was dizzying. Seventy feet straight down to where the river still trickled into the valley beneath. At its base the dam was over a hundred feet thick and built of solid reinforced concrete, yet it had been cleaved as though by a giant axe. Across the U-shaped void, eighty yards wide, the dam rose up again, before continuing in a sweeping curve to the far shore.

'The point of penetration was about ten metres down,' Holzmann explained to Kessell. He was speaking in English, for his benefit, Peter gathered. 'The explosion caused quite a small breach, which widened under the pressure of water. Thus weakened, the parapet above then collapsed and rolled over the edge.'

'Extraordinary. How bad is the damage?'

'Minor. We shall have the breach repaired and the lake refilled within ten weeks. Well in time for the autumn rains.'

'Really? That is remarkable.' Kessell glanced pointedly at Peter. 'And the collateral damage?'

'Insignificant also, Herr Major. Some loss of industrial production, damaged crops and livestock and so on, some power shortages and water restrictions. But everything will be restored to normal within three months. Herr Director Speer has visited and promised everything we need. Including forced labour.'

'Casualties?'

'Seventy. Mostly civilians.'

The message being, Peter assumed, as they started back along the parapet, that the mission was a complete failure, a waste of time and effort. And lives. He stooped to pick up a fragment of steel rod, snapped in two as though a toothpick.

'The hydrodynamic energy required to do that is phenomenal,' a voice murmured beside him. Peter looked up, and saw Holzmann's young assistant.

'Is that so.'

'Certainly.' He gestured at the rod. 'Thirty kilotons of reinforced masonry was blown out by the blast. That required very precise placement of a very specific charge.'

'If you say so.'

'I do. Your attack was a work of genius, Herr Lieutenant, as was the scientist behind it. I'd very much like to meet him.'

'Come to England. I'm sure it can be arranged.'

'It was my intention. To study engineering in London. But the war came.'

'Ah.'

'So much suffering. So much bloodshed. It is regrettable.'

'Indeed.'

The youth glanced cautiously about. 'Do not pay too much attention to Herr Holzmann's pronouncements, Herr Lieutenant.'

'Why?'

'Because yes, the dam will be repaired, and in the timescale he states. But the damage is greater than he admits. Lateral cracking from one of the other bombs, structural fragilities in the base, it will be years before we can operate at full capacity again. And the collateral damage is also worse. Four power stations destroyed, many factories rendered useless, rail and road bridges swept away, not to mention severe disruption to water supplies. And that's just from the Eder. The damage from the Möhne is even worse. Did you know, a twenty-ton electricity turbine was picked up by the deluge and deposited downstream like so much litter . . .'

Back in the car, Kessell appeared satisfied. 'Now, Peter. I hope you have found this instructive. Your mission failed, you see, failed to starve us of water, failed to deny us power, failed to hinder armament production. It even failed to damage the dams, except superficially. So now you will return to Dortmund with your guard, and tomorrow we will reconvene in my office and continue our discussions. And I am utterly confident you will be both cooperative and forthcoming, yes?'

'Are you going somewhere, Major?'

'I have meetings to attend in Hamm, so will drop you at the railway station there. You and your guard will return to Dortmund by train. Please try not to be a nuisance.'

But Peter was a nuisance. He escaped, hacking his way through the train floor using the shard of steel from the dam.

They had to wait two hours in Hamm, their Dortmund train delayed because of disruptions to services. Caused by him. Once under way at last, it crept along at a snail's pace because of flood-damaged tracks. Also caused by him. Soon dusk was falling over the mist-clad countryside, much of it wooded, that lay beyond the grimy windows.

'*Toiletten, bitte*,' Peter hissed to his guard, who ignored him. In the seat opposite a dozing mother sat with her daughter, a young girl of just six or seven, with dark eyes and pigtails, who stared at him in open fascination. '*Toiletten!*' he repeated, nudging the guard, then grimacing and holding his stomach. But the man only scowled and shook his head. At which the little girl reached over and jabbed the guard with her finger, gabbling at him in bossy tones, a single word of which Peter recognised as '*Diarrhöe*'.

Muttering irritably, the guard led him to the cubicle. '*Fünf Minuten!*' he warned, holding up five fingers.

Which was enough. The toilet floor was of wood and partly rotten. In no time, Peter had levered up the pedestal, a minute or two more and the hole beneath was wide enough to squeeze through. Below, the sleepers rolled slowly by, and the wheels clanked and creaked hypnotically. With no further ado, he lowered himself into the gap and dropped to the tracks.

Chapter 13

Not that we knew much about it back in Blighty, but it was to be the beginning of many months on the run for Peter. Months during which he would jump trains, ride buses and swim rivers, masquerade as a tramp, a businessman, a factory worker, even a wounded German soldier. Months during which he would change and grow, acquire new skills, discard old habits, learn stealth and cunning, patience and vigilance, how to forage, to scrimp and to survive, and how to kill with his bare hands. Months during which he would live in five countries, adopt a dozen different identities, and travel more than two thousand miles, many of them on foot, in his unending quest for freedom. Months in which he would endure hardship, pain and starvation on a scale unimagined, yet never once lose his urge to return home to the woman he loved.

From Dortmund he fled north, hiding out during the day, travelling by night, route-marching fifty miles in forty-eight hours to the Dutch border, which he crossed unchallenged near Burlo. In Holland he turned west, subconsciously following V-Vicky's planned track home, and stealing a bicycle, making better progress and living rough on raw potatoes and pilfered fruit. Pedalling twenty miles a night, by the fifth night he was nearing the coast at Leiden, almost within sight of the North Sea, and just a boat ride from safety. But there, exhausted, starving, and knowing he could go no further without help, he discarded the bicycle and banged on the door of a farmhouse.

His choice was providential, the farmer sympathetic to the Allies, and he was swiftly taken in, fed and rested, before being handed to a local resistance group who hid him in an attic. Days passed, gradually plans for his escape and repatriation began to emerge, but to his horror, these all involved him going south, via France, the Pyrenees, Spain, Gibraltar and a ship ride home. But why, he pleaded, when I am already so close, surely all I need is a boat? Because the ports are not safe, they explained. You would never make it, and would compromise us. You must travel by the accepted route.

Which would be slow, tortuous and two thousand miles long. He left Leiden at dawn next day, escorted by train across into Belgium for a week's stay in a church, where he was repeatedly interrogated by a man from the Belgian Resistance or 'White Army'. The questioning was thorough and aggressive and included demands he reveal 617 Squadron details, personal information and V-Vicky's serial number. Only reluctantly did he comply. Days later the man returned, all smiles, to say he'd been approved, which Peter guessed was via radio contact with England. From then things moved faster. Clothes were supplied, and false documents including identity papers complete with photographs. The travelling resumed, first by train across Belgium and into France near Lille, thence via train and tram to the southern outskirts of Paris itself, where he spent two weeks living in a succession of safe-houses. There on the streets he learned to walk with his head up, wear a preoccupied expression, and remain thirty paces behind his escorts, so as never to draw attention to them should anything happen. It rarely did, although he once rubbed shoulders with a German pilot in a café, and another time squeezed onto a tram to find himself amid a dozen armed infantrymen. And frequently he had his papers spot-checked, and his face minutely scrutinised, by officers of the Gestapo. Caution, vigilance and an undaunted bearing saw him through these tests.

After Paris, south again: Bourges, Clermont-Ferrand, Aurillac, sometimes by train, sometimes by bicycle, or truck or car, often on foot. A day in a haystack, two nights in a cellar, a week in a barn, then onward once more, alone, in pairs, occasionally in groups. One night, somewhere in the Limousin, he found himself camping with eight other runaways, including an elderly Jewish couple, two American airmen and an RAF fighter pilot. Or someone claiming to be. By now Peter was a professional fugitive: canny, suspicious, uncommunicative. The fighter pilot talked too much, so Peter kept his head down and said nothing to him. Weeks passed. Onward he travelled, handed from one group to the next like pass-the-parcel. Earnest youths, girls on bicycles, impoverished farmers, elderly aristocrats, the people who helped him were as diverse as they were efficient, nervous, impatient, or infuriatingly wordless. But all were united in their hatred of the Germans, and invariably kind to him. Especially the strangers. Once, standing alone on a crowded train, he saw a German officer pushing slowly through the throng towards him. Terrified, he could do nothing but stare at his shoes. Then a newspaper was pressed into his back, and the one word *Lisez*, read, whispered in his ear. Hurriedly he unfolded the newspaper, a minute later the German passed without a glance. A newspaper, an apple, a piece of chocolate, occasionally money, he never knew his benefactors, yet somehow they knew him, and their compassion always moved him.

Then one crisp autumn morning, many weeks after his escape from Dortmund, he awoke in a Gascon farmhouse to see snow-capped peaks far to the south. 'The Pyrenees,' his host told him over breakfast. 'Once across, you are in Spain.'

'How long will that take?' Peter asked.

'These are dangerous times for the *Maquis*,' the farmer replied, referring to the bands of freedom fighters hiding in the region. 'Recently the Boches annihilated an entire village and everyone in it, just for giving them food. You will need to be patient, and learn to live and work with them. Then, when the time is right, they will guide you across the Pyrenees to safety.'

So Peter finished his breakfast, took to the road, and became a mountain outlaw.

These things, as I say, we would not learn for months to come. All we knew was he was missing-feared-dead, a status detrimental both to Tess's predicament, which was becoming acute, and her state of mind, which was more and more defeatist. Peter was not just her best friend and ally, he was the vital third player in this triangular drama, and a key witness, and without him her defence was weak. More pointedly, as each week passed without news, Tess's motivation to fight on crumbled.

I saw her often in the early post-dams period. And met her father, whose deteriorating health was a further worry for her. He'd hired a respected criminal barrister to manage her case, and together we interviewed her several times. She responded factually enough, but we could see she was only going through the motions. 'What do you think?' I asked the barrister after one such session. 'She needs to buck up,' he replied grimly. 'It's almost as if she *wants* to hang, for God's sake. And unless she pulls herself together, she damn well will!'

All was looking increasingly desperate, but then, just when we needed it most, providence took a hand, and we had a small but significant breakthrough. It came in the form of a curious letter from Mrs Barclay of Staffordshire Social Services, who I'd liaised with during the search for Tess's daughter. She wrote saying the girl's adoptive mother, June Groves, had been to see her. Apparently June had met a distressed young woman at the park in Croxton one day, and something – intuition, empathy – led her to believe that the girl had come purposely to see her and her daughter Peggy. In fact she suspected she'd followed them to the park from their house. Anyway, June had been sufficiently troubled by the episode to report it to Mrs Barclay. Not as a complaint, it turned out, but out of concern for the girl. Who she sensed might be Peggy's birth mother.

To cut a long story and several phone calls short, June Groves, bless her, said she had no objection to Tess visiting again, under suitable conditions, so they might all get to know one another a little. A wonderful gesture and exactly the stimulus Tess needed. I came up to Lincoln to break the news. We're not out of the woods, Tess, I cautioned her, not by a very long chalk. But from her relieved demeanour and much grateful tear-shedding, I could see a will to live had been rekindled.

Meanwhile events were unfolding in the Credo camp. Firstly, and most importantly, Chloe and I were married one blustery Saturday in July, a gloriously celebratory event despite a sudden downpour and the privations of rationing. Apart from an excellent turnout from family and friends, Charles Whitworth also attended, together with a few 617 stalwarts, including Les Knight and my old 57 Squadron colleague Geoff Rice. And Archie McIndoe pitched up with a carload of guinea pigs from East Grinstead. Good God, he exclaimed, as we assembled noisily for photos. You look like escapees from a mannequin factory. Which is more or less what we were.

Chloe was wonderful, enchanting and radiant in a beautiful satin gown borrowed from a cousin. Standing next to her at the altar, with her arm resting on mine, was intensely moving. New life seemed to surge through my veins, while the old one drained away, and I felt the happiest I'd ever been. Thank you, I found myself saying to her afterwards, thank you for everything. Her family came from Suffolk, so we honeymooned in a borrowed cottage there, passing an idyllic fortnight lounging on deckchairs by the sea, sailing a day boat on a river, and wandering the local sights. One such venue became a favourite, a mystical thatched church overlooking a river, and we visited several times, including once on bicycles with a picnic. One evening we encountered an American bomber pilot, sitting trance-like in one of the pews. His war was then reaching a bloody climax, he looked dazed and pensive, we wished him well, and tactfully withdrew.

After the honeymoon I was due to check into East Grinstead for the facial reconstruction work. But it had to be be put off, yet again, by events outside my control. A date had been set for Tess Murray's arraignment, so it was all hands to the pumps to prepare her case. I spent many days at her barrister's chambers in London, working up the documentation with him. It was interesting and instructive work, and I learned much about criminal law, but soon we found ourselves at odds. In short, he felt her best defence was to plead diminished responsibility, whereas I wanted nothing less than complete acquittal. Disagreements arose, and some increasingly heated discussions. 'This isn't a bloody crusade, you know, Credo!' he yelled one day. 'You're taking it all far too personally.' Which was true, but then I had a vested interest. And knew a few things he didn't.

I began taking matters into my own hands. Crucial to Tess's defence was evidence that Murray was violent towards her, something we knew, but as yet couldn't prove. What we could prove was that he drank, was prone to fighting, and involved in petty crime, gambling, racketeering and the rest. Not enough to justify murder, but better than nothing. Essential to everything, however, was the dossier I'd compiled. The one Abbott and Costello buried in the vaults of RAF Intelligence HQ.

So I got Chloe to 'borrow' it. So I could make a copy. This was the favour I asked over the phone the day I proposed marriage, and would be one of her final acts before resigning from the job – just as well, as the intelligence community takes a dim view of employees snaffling files. Yet all went smoothly, with the deed done and the file replaced in just a couple of days. The copy was mostly hand-transcribed, of course, and far from complete, and we could never produce it in court. But that wasn't my plan.

While this file-copying was going on, Tess's lawyer had researched Murray's past, and turned up a number of interesting details, including convictions for theft and assault, plus a previous wife whom he'd forgotten to divorce. A young girl he'd married in Dundalk as a teenager, had a son by, then abandoned when he fled Ireland leaving a trail of debts in 1936. The girl in question was quickly traced and interviewed, and crucially, more than willing to testify that Murray attacked her, several times, once strangling her so severely that she had to go to hospital.

Her testimony combined with Tess's, together with the diminished responsibility plea, should be sufficient to convince a court his killing was in self-defence.

Thus good enough for the murder charge to be commuted to manslaughter, so saving her from the gallows. But not good enough for me, for I still had an axe to grind, and one rainy evening that July I arranged to meet Frank Arnott. To grind it.

The last time I'd seen him was six weeks earlier, at Scampton on the day of the King's visit. The day he'd fobbed me off so royally that I'd kicked the bucket. He hadn't lost any of his charm.

'Ah, Credo!' he called loudly as I entered the bar, which was busy. 'There you are, you frightful beggar. Filthy night, eh? Here, let me get you a drink.' From his truculent manner and collection of empty glasses, I gathered he was ahead of me on that score. So much the better. I let him buy me a beer, and suggested we adjourn to a table in the corner.

'What for?' he quipped. 'Going to throw something again?'

I was, in a manner of speaking, although it was a while before he realised it. Quietly I explained our meeting was in public, because the subject was in the public interest. Gradually he began to follow. As he did so, his mood soon sobered.

'What the bloody hell . . .' he spluttered, when I produced my copy of the dossier. 'Where did you get that?'

'From my head mostly. That and the carbon copies I made at the time.'

'Your head? What on earth are you talking about?'

'I sat down, went through it all in my mind, and reproduced it from memory.'

'Well, you can just unreproduce it. That material is top secret!'

'No it isn't, it's unsubstantiated tittle-tattle, you said so yourself. Black-marketeering, brawling, illegal drinking and so on. Nothing secret at all.'

'Nevertheless it's classified! You absolutely can't have it. Nor can you use it. Not in court, Credo, I've already warned you about that.'

'I don't intend using it in court. I'm selling it to the newspapers.'

Now he was aghast. 'You're what?'

Technically speaking I was still in the RAF, and he my superior officer. But we were both wearing suits, and sitting there on neutral ground with the gloves off so to speak. And he looked so shocked and shabby suddenly, I couldn't resist milking the moment.

'Frank,' I reasoned. 'You've seen the papers, this trial is big news. Just what the public needs, a nice murder scandal to take their minds off the war. With a woman to hang at the end of it too. Newspaper editors are desperate for the inside story. And since I wrote it, as it were, dutifully reporting my suspicions to my superiors, who ignored them, I don't see why they shouldn't have it.'

'You wouldn't dare.'

'Wouldn't I? Imagine the headlines: *Murder Victim Was Dam Busters Drunkard*, or *Bigamy at 617 Squadron*, or . . .' I lowered my voice, '*Was Slain Pigeon-Fancier a Spy?*'

'It's preposterous! You're an RAF officer. I order you not to . . .'

'I'm out of the Service, Frank. With nothing to lose. Believe me, I can. And will.'

Stunned silence settled over the table. Around us the hubbub swirled, while outside a bus swished through puddles. I sipped my beer, watching him. Time, I decided, for the *coup de grâce*.

'I've got this too.' Furtively I opened my jacket, lifting a notebook from the breast pocket. 'It's his, Frank. The notebook I told you about. The one you couldn't find.'

'Christ.' He eyed it glassily. 'Where did you get it?'

'Under the floorboards, in their quarters. Tess put it there in a panic after the killing. It's got everything, Frank. Names, dates, times, messages, the lot.'

Thus, the crux. For us both, really. Was Brendan Murray a spy? I suspected it, but hadn't proved it, and then ironically didn't want to. Frank and his chums never believed it, nor similarly did they want to. As far as they were concerned their security operation at Scampton had been watertight. Any suggestion now that it was not, such as me going public with the dossier, or producing Murray's war diary, could prove highly embarrassing to a lot of people. Heads might roll. Frank's included.

Another pause, followed by a resigned sigh. 'So what do you want?'

'Quash all charges. She's innocent and you know it. You also know how to fix it. You speak to your boss who speaks to his boss, who has a word with his opposite number in the Home Office, who tells the Home Secretary it's not in the country's interests to proceed with this case. State secrets, defence of the realm, wartime exigencies, damaging publicity, call it what you will, there's no hard evidence and the case should be thrown out. If it isn't, 617 Squadron will inevitably become embroiled, and every document in this file will come out, including my suspicions about Murray. And his notebook. My God, Frank, Gibson himself may have to take the stand. You too, probably. Is that what you want?'

'This is blackmail, Credo.'

'No. It's justice.'

'And if we do quash the charges?'

'That's the end of it. The whole thing goes away.'

'And we get the file, and notebook.'

'You don't want them, Frank. They're an embarrassment. According to you he wasn't involved in subterfuge, remember? You closed the file on him. So I'll destroy them for you, the dossier and the notebook, I'll destroy them both. The minute she's released. You have my word.'

And that, more or less, was the end of it. In due course the Crown Prosecution Service dismissed the charges, citing self-defence and new evidence from Murray's violent past. Tess went home to Bexley to be with her ailing father. Meanwhile her barrister, mildly piqued, bought me lunch, claiming he would have got her off anyway. Possibly, but I couldn't take the chance. Afterwards I kept my promise, took the file and notebook (which I'd bought at Woolworths and filled with scribble) to the bottom of the garden and burned them both to ashes. Arnott, I suspect, did exactly the same with the original file, thus erasing Brendan Murray from the intelligence archive altogether. A while later I sent him a postcard saying our business was concluded, and never heard from him again. Except once.

After that, it was finally off to East Grinstead for the refurbishment work on my face. It was long and tedious and painful and there's no need to go into details, except to say Archie did a WTP for a new nose, and several ops to improve my lips and cheeks. He also tidied up the stump on my arm, the better to accept a prosthesis, when the time came. All in all I was there nearly two months. Chloe was wonderful – if not for her I'd have certainly gone mad. We booked her into a B&B nearby, and daily she would appear, smiling and beautiful, dispensing magazines and good cheer like Florence Nightingale in heels. Only prettier.

Everyone on the ward got to know her. She became a symbol of hope and optimism, particularly to the newer boys, some of whom were in a dreadful state. To them she was like a sister, while I was her proudest of husbands.

During my stay I wrote up my notes on Operation *Chastise*, and caught up with news of 617 Squadron. Which, it transpired, was going through the doldrums. After the dams raid, and once the fuss had died down, the question had soon arisen as to what to do with 617, which had been formed with that one specific mission in mind. Now the mission was over, and at such desperate cost, the squadron was something of a spent force. It possessed about ten serviceable Type 464 Lancasters, which were useless for anything other than carrying an *Upkeep*, and its aircrew complement was down by nearly half. Some argued the sensible thing was to disband it, disperse the remaining crews to other squadrons, and get on with the war. But sensible was unthinkable, for in the public's eyes 617 was a colossus, permanent and indestructible, and War Ministry publicists, ever mindful of the power of propaganda, well understood its value. But if disbanding was unthinkable, so too was risking it in combat, thus sending it back into action was also a non-starter. Overnight it seemed, 617 Squadron had become like the crown jewels, a potent symbol of national unity, too precious ever to be used.

A temporary fudge was agreed while Bomber Command pondered the dilemma. First everyone was sent on leave, then upon their return a trickle of replacement crews began to arrive, who all required training, so a flying programme of sorts resumed. Low flying, night flying, zooming across reservoirs using the spotlights and Dann sights, the regimen was much as before. Further bombing trials also took place, involving forward-spinning

*Upkeep*s dropped at low level over land, so old hands like Shannon, Martin, Maltby and the others could enjoy showing the new boys how it was done. But without a mission, the training seemed pointless. Rumours abounded, as always, about possible attacks on dams in Italy, canals in the Netherlands, or U-boat pens in the Atlantic, but nothing materialised. Except grumbling and frustration.

Not helped by Guy Gibson, who drove everyone mad. On the theory idle hands do devil's work, and tiring of the endless late nights and drunken carousing, he decided to whip his charges into shape, working them flat-out, hauling up stragglers, dressing down defaulters, and generally running them ragged. Literally. To their horror he instituted compulsory early-morning PT. On the first day three hungover airmen failed to turn up, thinking he wasn't serious. He was. Once located and turfed out of bed, they were publicly rebuked, then ordered to run round the airfield perimeter, all four miles of it. Next day, rashly, two more didn't show up. They had to repeat the ordeal, only wearing gas masks this time. After that there were no further absentees.

Weeks passed, training continued, crew numbers rose, replacement aircraft arrived, but still no sign of a return to operations. Boredom set in, and bickering, and silly mistakes. One day the undercarriage collapsed on Les Munro's Lanc when he skidded on landing, and Mick Martin's beloved P-Popsie was rendered unflyable in a taxiing accident. 617 was stagnating. Worse still, it was becoming a joke within 5 Group, whose other squadrons were busier than ever bombing Germany. The one-op wonders, they became known as, to their chagrin. Or the arm-chair heroes. Or even the bed-busters.

Then in July, a mission at last. Relief and excitement spread through the squadron, only to turn to dismay when the details emerged. Leaflet dropping. Later that night the great 617 Squadron flew unmolested to Italy, and dropped leaflets urging demoralised Italians to throw in the towel. 'I know how they feel,' Big Joe McCarthy grumbled. 'We're nothing but newspaper boys.'

A few days later, a double hammer-blow. Wing Commander Guy Penrose Gibson, VC, DSO, DFC and Bar to both, was to be grounded. Not only that, but replaced as officer commanding 617 Squadron. Ralph Cochrane broke the news to him. You've done all anyone could ever ask of a man, he said. Now it's time to stop, and take a well-earned rest. That was the official line. Privately a high-level decision had been taken that Gibson was simply too valuable to risk losing. Winston Churchill was shortly to depart on a flag-waving tour of America, Gibson would go with him. After that, an extended period of leave, followed by lecture tours, morale-boosting events, publicity drives, perhaps even an autobiography. Gibson knew it was coming but was still distraught. Flying was his life, he knew nothing else, he wanted nothing else. He'd joined the RAF at eighteen from school, and given it his all. Now, after a staggering 173 operations against the enemy, it was clipping his wings.

His replacement, Wing Commander George Holden, was felt by some to be a curious choice. It would also prove a tragically brief one. A 4 Group man, with most of his experience in Halifaxes not Lancs, Holden had commanded 102 Squadron, notching up an impressive forty-five missions, including high-risk ones such as secretly flying commandos to Malta, and attacks on the cruisers *Scharnhorst* and *Gneisenau*. He arrived at 617 in mid-July, and set about getting to know everyone, and familiarising himself on the Lancaster. With the squadron almost at full strength again, operations soon followed – albeit still not to Germany. Milan, Bologna, Turin, Genoa, docks, railways, a viaduct, a power station. Routine high-level stuff, mostly unopposed, mostly inconclusive, some involving stopovers in North Africa, where crews lay about sunbathing in the heat before stocking up their Lancs with wine and dates for the return. These trips went on through August, during which 617 moved out of Scampton, and twenty miles down the road to Coningsby. Then one day Holden was briefed by Cochrane to stop all ops and resume low-level training at maximum intensity. Because another special mission was brewing. One only 617 Squadron could take on.

One afternoon I was sitting in the hospital in East Grinstead poring through my notes, when an extraordinary telephone call came through. By then my convalescence was well advanced, and in truth I was itching to get out of the place and on with married life with Chloe. As I walked up the corridor to reception, my new nose seemed to dominate the view ahead, although McIndoe swore it was his best work, and Chloe said I looked like Stewart Granger. At reception I picked up the phone.

'Credo?' a familiar voice enquired. 'Arnott here.'

'Hello, Frank,' I replied cautiously. 'What can I do for you?'

'You can forget we're having this conversation.'

More cloaks and daggers. 'Yes, all right, Frank,' I sighed. 'What is it?'

'Radio intel bods at RAF Chicksands picked up some Sigint. From Belgium.'

Sigint. Signals intelligence. A radio message, in other words. 'I see. What sort of Sigint?'

'Can't say. It's not my bailiwick. And weeks old by the look of it. I came across it by accident.'

'Came across what, Frank?'

'The transcript. Of a weekly transmission from a Belgian Resistance operative. Routine stuff, he's just checking in with a news update, weather report, shopping list, that sort of thing. But tagged on the end is an RTV.'

'RTV? For God's sake, Frank, can't you speak English!'

'Request to vouch. Could we vouch, in other words, for someone he was in touch with. Another operative, for instance, or a nosy neighbour, escaped POW or something.'

Hairs were prickling on my neck. 'Vouch for who?'

'A friend of yours. One Flying Officer Lightfoot.'

'My God, Peter! Really?'

'Which means he's alive. And on the run. Or was, when this message was sent. Just thought you'd like to know. For the Murray woman, and so on.'

'Well, yes, Frank, yes I'm delighted to know. And so will she be. Thank you. Thank you very much.'

'My pleasure. We're not all total bastards, you know. Goodbye, Quentin.'

I wandered back to my room in a daze. Later Chloe dropped in and we marvelled at the news, and its implications. One of which was the excuse I'd been waiting for to discharge myself. 'We'll tell Tess in person,' I decided. 'Bexley's not far from here, we can drive up tomorrow in the MG.'

Chloe nudged me. 'You mean you can drive while I shift gears.'

'Just like old times, eh? No, but Chloe, it'll be a marvellous surprise for her, don't you think?'

She agreed, and we began making arrangements, but incredibly, more was yet to come. The next afternoon, I packed my bags, said goodbye to Archie and the guinea pigs, and sat down on my bed, somewhat apprehensively, to wait for Chloe. I had mixed feelings leaving the hospital after so long. It was like severing a final apron string: exciting, terrifying, a blind leap into the unknown and so on.

'Flight Lieutenant Credo?' an Antipodean voice asked. I looked up to see a broad youth with wavy hair standing nervously before me. He was in RAF sergeant's uniform, the letter 'B' for bomb aimer on his wings. It took a moment – he'd lost weight, and aged a little – then I got it.

'Garvey! It's Kiwi Garvey, good heavens, how marvellous to see you!'

'You too, sir. I see you got your new nose!'

'And you made a home-run, you clever chap! How on earth did you do it?'

By sea, we learned, as we drove with him up to Bexley. The young New Zealand stevedore had returned to his roots and stolen home aboard a ship.

Or rather, several ships, and over several weeks. As the miles passed in the MG, his story emerged, along with more details about V-Vicky's fate and that of his crewmates. After baling out of the burning aircraft, Kiwi had managed to hook up with Billy Bimson and Herb Guttenberg, but they could find no sign of Peter, who they estimated could be anywhere within a three-mile radius. 'But I'm sure he was alive when we got him out,' Kiwi said anxiously. 'He was.' I was able to reassure him. As for Chalkie, Jamie and Uncle, they all feared the worst, having seen no further parachutes emerge from the stricken bomber, which crashed into a field several miles away. Suddenly they were all alone, in Germany, with the dawn coming. Billy had cuts and bruises, while Herb had injured an ankle on landing and was in great pain. Nor could he walk unaided. Billy and Kiwi helped him as best they could, one under each arm, but the going was slow and agonising, so with daylight growing around them, a short conference was called. 'You go on, Kiwi,' Billy urged. 'I'm staying with Herb, we'll take our chances.' The last Kiwi saw of them, they were sitting by the roadside, waving bravely. Later that day they were taken into captivity. Meanwhile Kiwi struck out in a westerly direction until after several days, eighty foot-slogging miles and many close calls, his seaman's instincts brought him to the Dutch port of Rotterdam. The port was heavily secured, ringed with barbed wire, checkpoints, flak and machine-gun emplacements, and crawling with Germans. But by waiting and watching, and using his inbuilt knowledge, Kiwi was eventually able to steal on site and hide away in a warehouse overlooking the docks. The warehouse held dried beef carcasses from South America, so Kiwi could feed himself while he watched the harbour comings and goings. Three nights later he saw what he was waiting for. A mixed cargo-carrying coaster with Scandinavian markings being loaded by conscript labourers, toiling up and down a gangplank bearing boxes. Timing his moment, he slipped from the shadows, picked up a crate and joined them. Beside their bent and emaciated bodies he felt huge and exposed, but no one gave him a second glance, and within minutes he was hidden beneath the canvas cover of the ship's lifeboat. The next night the ship undocked and headed north. He left it at Cuxhaven and jumped a second ship which dropped him at Trondheim in Norway. A third came back to the Polish port of Gdansk in the Baltic, where he boarded a fourth which docked at the neutral port of Helsingborg in Sweden. Recognising the blue and yellow Swedish flag flying over the harbourmaster's office, he walked off this ship and handed himself in. His final ship, two weeks later, having been checked and cleared, was to Newcastle-upon-Tyne.

'That was a month ago,' he recounted. 'Since then I've been

kicking my heels waiting for transfer papers and trying to track everyone down. I went to see Chalkie's wife, and Jamie's Mum and Dad. I hope it helped. Uncle didn't have anybody to visit. Then I heard 617 got moved to Coningsby, and someone there told me you left to get married and where to find you. Congratulations on your wedding by the way, sir. You too, Mrs Credo.'

'Why, thank you, Sergeant,' Mrs Credo replied warmly.

Kiwi grinned, then looked uneasy. 'About 617, sir . . .'

'Yes.'

'Well, the old guard's gone, and the CO too, and there's so many new faces. And what with it not being at Scampton any more. It's not the same, is it?'

'No. I suppose not.'

'What the hell happened?'

The Dortmund–Ems canal, as the name suggests, stretches from Germany's industrial centre in the Ruhr to the North Sea at Ems in Holland. With major roads and railways suffering constant Allied bombardment, this canal was fast becoming the Reich's main artery for the transportation of raw materials, fuel and armaments across Europe and beyond. U-boats built on the Ruhr were carried along it for launching in the sea, heavy guns, anti-aircraft artillery, shells, bombs, bullets, coal, oil, over thirty million tons of vital warmongery travelled its length every year. Unsurprisingly it was well defended. But not invulnerable. One section, near Ladbergen, fifteen miles north of Münster, ran above low-lying terrain on reinforced earthen embankments. One or two powerful bombs, it was calculated, accurately dropped from low level, would breach the embankments, draining the water from the canal and thus effectively closing it. 617's mission was to steal into Germany, at night and at low level, just as it had on *Chastise*, and drop single twelve-thousand-pound bombs to smash the embankment. If successful, it would be a spectacular return to glory.

But it was a disaster. Eight of the best crews were selected for the operation, to be carried out using conventional Lancasters. Astonishingly, even though 617 had been in existence six months, this was only its second mission to Germany. Most of the pilots were dams veterans, and included Knight, Shannon, Maltby and Rice. Two more, Wilson and Divall, had also trained for *Chastise* but missed out through non-selection or illness. The final two, Allsebrook and Holden himself, were newcomers. At midnight on 14 September the eight took off in two waves of four as planned, but halfway across the North Sea and flying at fifty feet to elude radar, they received a recall signal because of fog over the target. Disgruntled, they wheeled their aircraft for home. Except that David Maltby, perhaps underestimating his heavily laden Lancaster, misjudged the turn and tipped a wing in the waves, sending the bomber cartwheeling into the sea. A shocked Dave Shannon circled the area for two hours, anxiously scanning the wreckage for signs of his friend. Eventually air-sea rescue services arrived on scene, but could find no survivors. The crew whose bomb had finished the Möhne was gone.

On the next night eight crews tried again, with Mick Martin in Maltby's place. This time they were cleared to proceed all the way, but as they flew deeper into Germany the mist began gathering below. Holden led the first wave, with Knight, Martin and Wilson in his wake. On board his Lancaster were several members of Guy Gibson's triumphant crew from the dams raid. Just after crossing into Germany, Holden climbed to three hundred feet to clear a church tower, while the other three instinctively stayed low and swerved around it. A single flak gun on a factory roof saw Holden's bomber and fired. A shell hit a wing-tank, setting the bomber ablaze. Moments later it exploded into the ground, killing everybody.

Mick Martin now took over as first wave leader, while Allsebrook led the second formation of Rice, Shannon and Divall. By now thick fog was forming on the ground, making navigation difficult and low flying lethal. Aircraft became separated, rendezvous points were missed, the operation began to disintegrate. Nearing a canal junction called the Wet Triangle, Allsebrook's Lancaster took a flak hit, went out of control, clipped a crane and exploded into the dock, killing all on board. Some miles away, and at almost the same time, Les Knight and his crew were also in trouble. Flying at extreme low level to avoid flak, they all felt a violent jolt as the Lancaster hit trees. Les quickly pulled up, but the two port engines were wrecked and flying controls damaged. Les jettisoned the bomb and struggled upwards, but with a starboard engine also failing, he knew the Lancaster was doomed, and gave the order to bale out. All exited safely, leaving Les to attempt a forced landing in a field. The stricken machine hit trees, ploughed in nose-first, and burst into flames. Les Knight, hero of the Eder, died in his seat.

Harold Wilson held the distinction of being the first pilot posted to 617 Squadron, but missed the dams raid owing to illness. He and his crew managed to locate the correct section of canal, and began a series of runs through the fog to try and attack it. Flak gunners repeatedly heard the bomber circling, then suddenly saw it looming from the mist at close range. Several guns opened up, the machine was riddled, burst into flames and crashed. Witnesses approaching the wreck allegedly heard cries of help from within, but the flames were ferocious and with ammunition exploding all round they couldn't get near. Then the bomb went off, destroying everything.

George Divall joined 617 too late to complete training for the dams raid, and Dortmund–Ems was only his fourth mission with the squadron, the others being over Italy in July and August. Yet being one of the original intake earned him a shot at the canal. But he too became separated and lost in the poor visibility, strayed too far north and was brought down by flak near Recke. None in his crew survived.

That left only the three veterans Rice, Shannon and Martin. All were separated and having great difficulty locating the target. Rice spent over an hour searching, and received several flak hits for his efforts, all to no avail. In the end only Martin and Shannon found the right stretch of canal and attacked it, but the bad visibility and formidable defences thwarted them, and both bombs missed. Ordering Rice to jettison his bomb and abandon the hunt, Martin turned the three survivors for home.

Ralph Cochrane was waiting anxiously back at Coningsby. Upon landing and hearing the news of the others, a distressed Mick Martin begged to be allowed to try a third time the following night. Cochrane was greatly moved. 'What with, Mick?' he replied simply. 617 had lost six of its best crews in two nights, including its new leader. The next day, having received the report, Air Marshal Harris banned all low-level operations for heavy bombers until further notice. Dortmund–Ems marked 617 Squadron's lowest point, and would be the last-ever mission of its kind.

Chloe, Kiwi and I arrived in Bexley in time for tea, finding the address along a tree-lined avenue. On one side of the road the houses were closely packed terraces, on the other, the Derbys' side, stood rather grander detached residences. We parked and walked up their path. The door was opened by Mrs Derby, a small grey-haired woman with a steely gaze.

'You've come about the Lightfoot boy,' she said immediately. 'I'll get Tess.'

Tess appeared, looking terrified, and suddenly my surprise idea didn't seem so clever. Chloe saved the day.

'It's all right!' she beamed, squeezing Tess's hand. 'It's the best possible news!'

'I must tell the Lightfoots,' Tess fussed, once she'd recovered herself. 'Mother, I must run and tell them right away.'

'Why not ask them over for tea?' her mother replied. A momentous gesture, I was later to appreciate. And relations had clearly thawed a little between Tess and her mother, we saw, during the course of the tea. There was still a distance between them, an awkwardness and avoidance of eye-contact, but they conversed and cooperated and produced tea together, and made us feel welcome, and tended to Mr Derby, who sat in an armchair bundled in blankets. 'Thank you,' he whispered, when I bent to say hello. 'Thank you for what you did for Tess.'

Tess herself took me aside a little later. 'Look,' she whispered, producing a photograph. A little girl, with fair hair and apple cheeks, was sitting on the knee of an older woman. 'Peggy,' she said proudly. 'Peggy with her mother. They sent it to me.'

Then the Lightfoots arrived, in their fifties, unassuming, and managing to look both worried and relieved at the same time. 'Can it really be true?' Mrs Lightfoot asked anxiously.

It can, I assured her, although our optimism must be tempered with caution. 'The message was sent several weeks ago, you see, Mrs Lightfoot. But the fact that Peter was safely in the hands of the Resistance must be a good sign.'

'Too right!' Kiwi added, waving a biscuit. 'Mark my words, the lad'll come through and no worries.'

Tea went on, the conversation, a little stilted at first, gradually growing warmer and less awkward. Chloe and Kiwi saw to that, she with her infectious enthusiasm, and Kiwi with his air-force jokes and saucy badinage. Before long polite smiles were breaking out, even the occasional titter. A form of reconciliation was taking place, I realised, as I looked on, a moment of healing and release. Six years of pain, bitterness and enmity coming to an end. Because of a son's survival at war. Which seemed appropriate.

A week or so later, Chloe and I drove to Scampton to collect the last of my belongings from my rooms. And to take a last look at the place before finally leaving the Service. Out of respect, and to make it easier getting in, we both wore our RAF uniforms, for what would be the final time. The guard waved us through, we drove to the empty car park and disembarked into a sunlit autumn afternoon.

The place was deserted, just a few skeleton staff in evidence, and eerily quiet – no thundering Merlins, no hammering workshops, no whistling or singing or shouted commands. Just the busy chatter of birdsong, and the distant rumble of contractor's vehicles, busy laying swathes of concrete across the virgin turf.

'Shall we take a walk?' Chloe suggested, slipping her hand in mine.

We visited my old office, and Number 2 hangar, and the ops room and the mess, to find them all empty. Then we strolled across the grass to see the work on the runways. A temporary HQ had been set up in the equipment barn by the contractors, with bulldozers, steamrollers and tipper-trucks parked outside. A civilian engineer in a tweed jacket stood at a table, poring over drawings.

'How's it going?' we asked.

'It's going to plan. Just about,' the man grinned. 'Ground's firm, which helps. Turf's in good condition too. Makes it easier to plane off.'

Giant rolls of cut turf stood at intervals along the newly scraped runway. Crushed hardcore would come next, flattened by roller, before the final pouring of concrete. 'Can't you use the grass for anything?' Chloe asked. 'You know, a football pitch, school playing fields, that sort of thing?'

'No call for it.' The man shook his head. 'There's a war on, you know! Pity too. Whoever tended it knew his stuff.'

Chloe's eye caught mine, we chatted with him a while longer, then began to move off.

'Don't know anything about the birds do you?' he asked.

'What birds?'

'The pigeons. In the loft above the barn here. Hundreds of 'em. They make a terrible racket sometimes. We feed them on bread and old sandwiches and that. But no one lets them out or anything. They seem to have been abandoned.'

We went into the barn and climbed a rickety ladder to the caged-off area above the workshops. Inside it we found a desk, chair and cupboard, with a chicken-wire door into the bird-loft itself. Where the pigeons eyed us warily.

'Poor things,' Chloe said. 'They've been completely forgotten.'

'With Murray gone, I suppose nobody gave them a thought.'

'We must release them, Quentin. Open the shutters so they can get out and fly.'

Easier said than done. But we duly clambered among the roosts and perches, soiling our nice clean uniforms on dust and feathers and God knows what, until we reached the windows and pushed them wide. Sunlight flooded the loft suddenly, causing the birds to start and shiver in restless anticipation. But none dared move, so we began stamping and shooing noisily, at which they suddenly awoke from stupor, and in a great squall of flying feathers and clapping wings, took to the air, poured through the windows, and launched themselves into the heavens.

We descended the ladder and went outside, brushing filth from our uniforms. Overhead the pigeons wheeled in joyous celebration.

'Quite a sight!' the engineer said. 'That's the last we'll see of them.'

We peered upwards, watching as they danced and darted like a shoal of fish. Beyond them a light aeroplane was circling overhead, as though preparing to land. 'I doubt it,' Chloe said. 'They're homing pigeons, you know.'

We wandered back across the field, arm-in-arm into the sunset like Nelson Eddy and Jeanette MacDonald in *Sweethearts*. But halfway there, the light aeroplane, a Miles Magister, came in to land, taxied up and shut down. A tall, handsome-looking man stepped nimbly down, wearing the uniform of a Group Captain. Disconcerted somewhat, Chloe and I stepped apart, came untidily to attention and saluted.

'Hello, you two,' the man smiled. 'Sorry to drop in unannounced. But this is Scampton isn't it?'

'Yes, sir, it is. But I'm afraid nobody's here.'

The man peeled off flying gloves, and stared around. 'I know. I just wanted to look at the place, you know, get a feel. I'm Cheshire, by the way.' He reached over and shook hands. 'Leonard Cheshire. I'm the new CO of 617 Squadron. Or will be in a few weeks.'

I'd heard of him. Another 4 Group man. Brilliant in the air by all accounts, a matchless pilot with three full tours under his belt, and great plans to turn bombing into a precision art, yet modest and approachable on the ground. A born leader, and exactly what 617 needed. 'That's very good news, sir. They've been having a difficult time lately. Morale and so on.'

'Yes. We must do something about that.' He leaned across to pluck a pigeon feather from my lapel. 'And you are?'

'Oh, sorry sir. Quentin Credo. Flight Lieutenant, formerly of 57 Squadron. This is my wife, Corporal Chloe Hickson, er, Credo, that is.'

'Well, I'm delighted to meet you both.' He smiled again. 'Did you say formerly?'

'Yes, sir. Invalided out of ops. Then became SIO here at Scampton, then ADC to Group Captain Whitworth. For the dams raid, and so on.'

'Really? You were here for that. How wonderful. And what are you doing now?'

'Nothing, sir. Leaving the Service, actually. Taking up law.'

'Ah.' Cheshire nodded, and cupped his eyes to the setting sun.

'That seems a pity,' he murmured. 'I'll be needing a good ADC.'

Postscript

Operation *Chastise* – A Summary Analysis
by Quentin R. Credo

Leonard Cheshire took over the reins in November 1943 and indeed oversaw 617's rebirth and rise to new glory. Specialist precision bombing was his stock-in-trade and under his stewardship the squadron flourished in the role. By the war's end, 617 had carried out 1600 operational sorties against the enemy, including, appropriately, the successful breaching of the Dortmund–Ems canal in September 1944, followed two months later by the sinking of *Tirpitz* in its Norwegian hideaway. Both attacks were carried out using another Barnes Wallis invention – a five-ton bomb called *Tallboy*, dropped from high altitude using special sights. Cheshire finished the war a VC (617's second), left the RAF and went on to become a great humanitarian and philanthropist. Meanwhile 617 Squadron flew on, continuing in its precision strike role to this day. Its squadron badge features a breached dam with lightning bolts, its motto is *Après Moi le Déluge*. Operation *Chastise* remains its most famous exploit, with the mission passing into legend as one of the best-known feats of aerial daring in history.

Yet was it worth it?

Propaganda-wise the answer has to be yes. At home the reaction was euphoric. After four years of blackouts, shortages, bombings, rationing, not to mention lost menfolk, war-weary Brits at last had something spectacular to celebrate. Newspapers carried the story for days, endlessly reprinting pictures of the breached dams and floods, as well as the heroes themselves. The royal visit to Scampton of 27 May was also heavily covered, with hordes of press given free rein to record the day. Inevitably fact and fiction sometimes became confused in the excitement and some wild reporting took place, yet few cared, it was all so wonderfully 'British': the daring objective, the brilliant scientist, the secret weapon, the valiant crews, the brave sacrifices. Like Scott of the Antarctic, or the Charge of the Light Brigade, only more successful. Similarly *Chastise* raised hopes that the war might actually end one day, for it was not just a bold exploit, it was a blow straight to Germany's heart, and its success surely signified that an end was in sight. So the nation celebrated: excitement in the streets, back-slapping in Cabinet, congratulatory debates in parliament, and a jubilant Churchill declaring: 'Wherever Germany's centres of war industry exist, they will be destroyed.' Our Allies too were duly impressed, with both America and Russia sending hearty congratulations (the latter also demanding full details of the bomb).

Similarly there can be no denying that enemy morale was undermined by the raid. Despite Goebbels's Propaganda Ministry working overtime to play it down, the people of Germany, and especially the Ruhr, were genuinely shaken by the attack, partly by its effects – widespread flooding, dislocated water and electricity supplies, disrupted transportation – but also by its sheer audacity. Being bombed from altitude was nothing new to them, but that a small force of British aeroplanes could sneak up to their door, with impunity, and wreak such havoc *by attacking dams*, was deeply unsettling. This disquiet went right to the top, where Hitler, pre-occupied with his beleaguered eastern front, was reportedly badly shaken by the raid, which he referred to as 'This disaster in the west'. He was also furious with Goering and his Luftwaffe for failing to stop it.

But within days news was coming through that damage to armament production was slight and temporary. This partly because the Sorpe wasn't breached, and partly because newly installed alternate electricity and water supplies were unharmed. (Had the raid taken place twelve months earlier, one German report stated, the results would have been catastrophic.) But worried about follow-up attacks, and the dams' general vulnerability, Hitler himself ordered Albert Speer, his Minister of Armaments and Munitions, to take personal charge of repairs, and of protecting the Ruhr's water supplies from then on. Speer jumped to the task, and within three months both Möhne and Eder dams were repaired. Within six, armament production, which had never faltered significantly, was running at full capacity again.

Yet not without cost. Vast quantities of engineering and construction materials were needed to make the repairs, plus a labour force estimated at thirty thousand to carry them out. These had to be found from somewhere, and were mostly diverted from other projects, such as the Atlantic Wall defences being built against Allied invasion. And once repaired, every dam in the Ruhr had then to be defended by permanent forces manning the flak guns, searchlights, machine guns, smoke-launchers, torpedo-nets, barrage-balloons and the rest, a sizeable equipment inventory, and a manpower estimated at 1500 soldiers, the equivalent of a full battalion.

But in the final analysis, was Germany's war machine put out of action by the raid? And did the raid shorten the war? The answers must be not greatly, and probably not. Although it was close, with Speer himself admitting that the consequences could have been much worse. And the human cost was high: with about 1300 lives lost in the floods, mostly civilians, at least half of them foreign-conscript factory workers, including women. As for 617, apart from Peter Lightfoot and crew, fifty-three men lost their lives, a 40 per cent loss rate that Bomber Command deemed acceptable, but many, including Barnes Wallis, were never able to come to terms with.

And were they expected? Did the Germans have at least some advance warning that an attack on a dam was imminent that May? This is the question I have long wrestled with. It is true that most of 617's losses that night were caused by accidental crashes or flak hits whilst en route. Only John Hopgood's M-Mother was shot down over a dam, the Möhne, and indeed the Eder and Sorpe had no manned defences at all. But the Möhne was well defended, and had it not been for the bravery of Gibson and others in diverting fire, and attacking the flak positions, losses could have been higher.

And two overriding questions remain:

1. In the weeks following 617's formation early in March 1943, the popular assumption among its crews was that their target was the battleship *Tirpitz*. Apart from a trip to Trondheim for a refit, *Tirpitz* had been holed up in a Norwegian fjord in Bogen, Narvik, since July 1942, placing it just within reach of long-range bomber attack. Suddenly, in late March 1943 it

was moved to Altafjord, some 250 miles further north. Why?
2. Shortly before the dams raid itself, mysterious wooden crates began arriving at the Möhne dam. These, it transpired, contained conifer trees and were deployed along the dam wall, clearly in an attempt to camouflage the dam into the surrounding forests. Again, why?

As time passes, memories grow dim, so we may never know. Yet interest in Operation *Chastise* shows no sign of waning, and every year new facts emerge about the operation. One day, I believe, we will learn the complete truth.